TWO IRISH BR
SISTERS–DEST
DOOMED TO TRAGEDY

Marnie realised Gabe had one arm around her
waist, and that the other was touching her hair, let
loose from the habitual braid she still wore at
Larksby, and falling in gleaming waves to the small
of her back. She heard the sound of her own
breathing, shallow and ragged and waiting.

'Oh, Gabe, I never wanted the hurt between us to
go on so long,' she said, all in a rush. She looked up
into his face, her heart in her eyes, and the man in
him was stirred by the sight of her soft, trembling
mouth, so that it was more than he could do to
resist kissing it. He felt her arms tighten round his
neck and her body shape itself to his as if she
couldn't be close enough to him ... and why
should he resist what was offered, when he was so
in need of comfort?

The Savage Moon

ROWENA SUMMERS

SPHERE BOOKS

First published in Great Britain by
Sphere Books Ltd 1982
Copyright © 1982 by Rowena Summers
This edition first published by Sphere Books 1996

TRADE
MARK

Set in 10/11 English Times
Printed in England by Clays Ltd, St Ives plc

Sphere Books
A Division of
Macdonald & Co (Publishers)
Brettenham House
Lancaster Place
London WC2E 7EN

Dedicated to the one I love

PART ONE

CHAPTER ONE

She ran as fleet of foot as any small scuttling animal of the Fens, her grubby little bare feet sploshing in the muddy waters' edge. It seemed as if she had been lying at full stretch for hours at the rim of the dyke, watching the kingfishers skim and ripple the shimmering surface. Her face glowed, her brown eyes were wide and her mouth parted in a seven-year-old's wonder and concentration. It was only when she heard the navvies calling good-naturedly to one another at the end of their day's dyke digging that she realised how cold the afternoon had become, and that the pale, wintery sun was fast disappearing behind the horizon.

Then she scrambled to her feet, not heeding the muddy stains on the creased and crumpled apron that covered her hand-me-down skirt, pushing the wiry tangle of curls back from her face with grimy hands. And remembering to pat the pocket of the apron in which there were the carefully-tied pennies, and the deliciously rose-pink hair ribbon Mrs Kettle had given her for delivering the pie her Ma had made. She turned to race the last half mile home.

It was just possible to make out the curl of grey smoke from the chimney of the cottage in the deeper mottled blue-grey of the sky. The cottage that would be filled to overflowing by the time they all crowded in for their evening meal, her Ma and Da, the three tall brothers, her sister Marnie, her little brother Davey, whom she adored from the top of his head to his chubby little feet. All crowded in and jostling for room, with the talk of mole-catching and rabbiting and the price of flour and Farmer Pinnock's dairy maid who had run off with the butcher's boy from the town last week. And over and above all the buzz of talk would be the aroma from Da's clay pipe, from cooking and baking and Davey's steamy baby washing, the acrid smell of the candle lantern that swayed and creaked in the draughty cracks through old timbers in the cottage that had once been two tiny ones and been knocked together to house them all. And there was the mixture of warm bodily smells, sometimes sweet, sometimes rancid with the whiff of the river her brothers brought home with them, but all nonetheless familiar.

There was just one more plank to cross over the dyke before she started the last sprint across the field for home. She trod carefully, bare feet flat for balancè, small white teeth digging into her lower lip with concentration. And just as she reached the other side a burning pain shot up her small heel with such suddenness she screamed out and lurched the last few steps over the plank, to go sprawling on to the dew-damp grass in the field beyond.

The pain was so sharp she could think of nothing else for a few seconds. It blurred her senses and blinded her eyes with salty tears, causing the sharp little teeth to dig into the trembling lower lip until the taste of blood was in her mouth.

'Well, and what have we got here?' a rough voice with a lazy accent she didn't know said suddenly. It was very close to her, and she jerked her head with fright. 'Is it one of the little people already about even before the parish lantern's up?'

She blinked her eyes, her gaze irresistibly drawn up to the sky, but there was no moon to be seen yet, and it was well known, even at seven years of age, that the little people would stay well under cover during the daylight. The brief pause in her pain was over and the tears came brimming up again as her eyes levelled with a pair of coarse lace-up boots with the sackcloth around them caked in mud and clay. She knew he must be one of the navvies her Da had warned her against talking to. He was wearing a filthy smock they called a slop which was black with mud instead of white, and a soft-brimmed hat pulled well over

10

his eyes. As he peered down at her she felt a scream welling up inside her, for he looked like the very devil himself.

'Hey, hey, I'm not after hurting you, my lamb.' The rough voice was amused and not unkind, she decided. 'It's hurt you are already, by the looks of it. Let's take a gander at that foot. See here, Gabe, you'll be better at removing a splinter than me. Your fingers are less clumsy than mine.'

A second face appeared beneath a chummy hat as big as the other one, a younger face that smiled encouragingly at her from dancing blue eyes in his mud-grimed cheeks. As he knelt down beside her, Jenny could see he wasn't a man at all, even though he was very tall and gangling. With his face close to hers, she guessed he wasn't much older than her sister, Marnie, who was twelve years old, and to Jenny, a very superior being. The thought sent the first fear of these rough strangers scurrying out of her head, though she screamed sharply as the boy lifted her bare foot and pulled in his breath at the sight of the ugly greenish wooden splinter standing out proudly from the flesh.

'You're not touched yet, girl, but it's a big 'un all right,' he commented. His blue eyes considered the child, wishing she wouldn't look up at him with that mixture of fear and God-like trust in her face. Damn it, he was just a poor Irish labourer, grubbing a living as best he could and wishing his brother Mick hadn't insisted that the only way to earn a decent living was to come to England. Because he was tired and hungry, and he'd give anything right now to be going home at Drory and have some of his Mammy's home cooking . . .

Mick had said they might get to America one day, but that was the kind of goal that had somehow got smothered deep in the dykes and drains of the Fens, and only roused itself on rare occasions now when Mick set himself to dreaming again. It had only been a dream to Mick, and he'd be happy enough to settle here and one day buy a farm of his own, maybe . . . but when the idea of America had found its way through to Gabe's imagination, he had absorbed every word his brother had said about the land of opportunity and plenty across the water, and stored it away in his memory. After all, they had travelled half across England to reach the Fens . . . his thirteen-year-old mind could not encompass the vast difference between crossing the Irish Sea in a rotting hulk of a boat, and the enormous expanse of ocean that separated Britain from the wonderful unknown adventure . . .

'Will you pull the splinter out, Mister?' the child whimpered plaintively. Gabe glanced at his brother. It was going to hurt and hurt bad. He didn't like hurting anything, but it was true his fingers were more sensitive than Mick's for this kind of job.

'Come on, my lamb, Mick'll hold you tight and you'll be thinking of your supper instead of what Gabe's about,' the older youth said comfortingly. He squatted down on the damp grass and lifted the child on to his lap, his strong arms folding round her thin chest so that her back was pressed tightly against him. He was warm, and she could feel him breathing. She relaxed for a second, because it was warm and reassuring. Her Ma and Da didn't have too much time to spare for cuddles . . .

She gave a sudden almighty yell as Gabe's fingers pulled the offending piece of wood out of the ball of her heel. Blood spurted out after it, and the tears splashed down her cheeks. She was frightened by the sight of blood.

'Calm yourself now,' the one called Mick was saying soothingly, one hand against the tangle of curls that fell over her face. He smoothed it back from her dirt-streaked cheeks. 'The blood's a good sign, girlie. It'll clean the wound better'n all your spirits.' Not that they had any spirits, and Mick would have given his right arm for a swig of ale right now. He wasn't a heavy drinking man, but he was fair parched tonight, and he wouldn't be sorry to get to the 'Duck and Drake' and soak himself in the smoke-filled hazy warmth of the Inn, and later, the crushing embraces of Peggy, the amply-proportioned barmaid. He savoured the image of her for a minute, feeling himself rise just at the thought of her lush warm body . . .

12

'It needs proper cleaning,' Gabe was saying. 'I'll slosh a gob of water over it to check that all the wood came out, Mick.'

He pulled the stopper on the leather waterbag he carried around his middle and tipped it over the point where the splinter had speared the child's foot. The shock of the cold water stopped her crying for a moment and the mud on her heel spread away from the wound in a small circle of cleanliness before blood gushed out again.

'He'll be a doctor yet–a horse doctor, most likely, but he has the touch and the thought! How does that feel, girlie? What's your name, anyway?'

'Jenny Bray. It's Jennifer really,' she added as proudly as she could, having only recently discovered that her name was somewhat similar to one of the young ladies at Larksby, the big house where her Da sometimes had work.

'Jennifer! That's too grand for a little scrap like you. Jenny it shall be,' Mick declared, and if it hadn't been for the pain in her heel she'd have felt put out for all that he was a stranger, because she wanted so badly for someone to call her Jennifer and nobody did. Nobody thought she was grand enough, and how could she act grown-up and dignified right now, when she was just seven years old with a tear-stained face and a stinging pain in her heel?

'I think she's fit for home,' Gabe said in a satisfied voice. 'You'll do, Jennifer Bray.'

He gave her a sudden, brilliant smile and there were dimples in his cheeks and a twinkle in his eyes, and his hair was dark and springy with curls under the chummy hat. His hands were gentle and healing, and he had called her Jennifer . . . and though she didn't fully recognise the emotions that were almost bursting inside her chest, she looked at him with mute adoration shining on her face.

The older one–Mick–was laughing softly.

'It seems you've made a conquest, Gabe. Now then, Jenny, see if you can put your foot to the ground and stand on it. How far do you have to go?'

She didn't really want to drag her eyes from the beautiful

13

face of the young man gazing at her with that tummy-tingling look, but she put her small foot down carefully to the damp grass, wincing as the pain shot up the injured heel.

'I can't,' she wailed. 'It hurts bad. Ma will be looking out for me soon, and I'll get a rocking if I don't get back soon. It's over there–the cottage with the smoke puffing out like Da's pipe and the roof like a squashed chummy.'

Mick burst out laughing. He snatched the soft hat from his head and perched it on her own, pushing it flat over her tangled curls.

'Like this, you little minx! Can't your Daddy attend properly to his own thatch then? There's enough reeds handy to cover a cathedral, I'm thinking.'

Jenny twisted round and stared at him resentfully. Her Ma always said her Da was a Jack-of-all-trades, but Jenny was aware of the slight criticism in Mick's voice and not too sure whether she should protest about it or not in view of the fact that he and Gabe had come to her rescue. He wasn't so old as she had thought at first, not old like her Da, and without his chummy on his head he wasn't so dark and frightening. He was about as old as her brother Kenneth, and just as brash and knowing, in a way she didn't understand. He was a man, and she didn't think she liked him much, for all that he had held her so comfortingly.

'It looks as if I'll be carrying you then, and delivering you to your Daddy's doorstep.'

Mick still held her in his arms, and prepared to rise to his feet while Gabe took a quick drink from the waterbottle before he rammed the stopper on again. It was turning to dusk very quickly now and fingers of mist were beginning to crawl over the fields. Somebody would be out looking for this child very soon ... almost as soon as the thought entered Mick's mind he heard shouting away to the right of him and his head jerked up swiftly to see four large bodies looming up towards the dyke where he and Gabe still squatted with Jenny. Four large, angry-looking Fenmen, shouted out Jenny's name as they approached and suddenly caught sight of the crouching figures by the plank.

14

'By God, it's some of they Irish navvies,' the oldest of the four roared out. 'They've got our Jenny atween 'em. Come on, me bors.'

'Circle 'em, quick,' one of the others yelled. 'Don't let 'em get to the plank, Joey.'

'If they've touched her, I'll murder 'em,' the first one thundered out as he raced towards the dyke, his breath rasping and harsh. Mick could see murder in his eyes anyway as he approached, and the younger men fanned out to surround them.

'Let's get out of here, quick,' Gabe was on his feet and scrambling for the plank, but his brother stopped him.

'No point in it. They're in such a tear they'll jump the dyke and have us down before we're halfway across the field. Besides we've done nothing wrong.'

'Try telling them that. It's act first and think second with them!'

Gabe's voice was full of apprehension and he twisted away from his brother's restraining hand. He wasn't usually scared of anybody or anything, but four angry Fenmen with murder on their minds wasn't a confrontation he much desired. He flung himself towards the plank but it was too late. With one gigantic lunge the one called Joey threw himself on Gabe and flung him to the ground, winding him.

'God damn you,' Gabe gasped out. He kicked out with the heavy dyke digging boots and caught Joey in the leg. Immediately one of the others was there to back him up, hauling Gabe to his feet and throwing punches at his face, his head, his throat.

'He won't be so pretty once we've finished with him, Da,' Joey yelled out. 'This'll teach you to fumble little girls' skirts, you Irish pig! Perhaps this'll stop your leching for a while.'

He lashed out with his boot. Gabe dodged back, missing the full brunt of it, but still being caught in the groin with enough impetus for stars to dance in front of his eyes as an excruciating pain knifed through him. As he staggered back

15

after the brutal kick he suddenly found himself slithering on the muddy rim of the dyke, and the next second he went over the edge with an almighty splash.

The two men gave a cheer, and without stopping to see how Gabe fared in the six feet of dyke water, they turned their attention to Mick, still clutching the child to his chest as their two companions approached him menacingly.

'Are you all bloody maniacs?' Mick's accent became more pronounced as he yelled out in a red rage at·their attackers. 'The babby's not hurt–at least not by the two of us. She had a rotten splinter in her heel and we fetched it out for her. Look–if you don't believe me, look at the blood, and ask her for yourself!'

'The blood could be from elsewhere . . .'

'Shut your noise, Kenneth,' the child's father ordered. He peered at Jenny's heel, where the blood still trickled out and mingled with the dirt marks on the front of Mick's slop. 'Is that the way of it, Jenny? Did you have a splinter? I'll have the truth now.'

'It was a great big one, Da, and it hurt bad. It was as green as grass and as sharp as . . .'

'All right, all right,' he cut her short in an irritable voice that was nevertheless tinged with relief. 'This is no time for your fancy stories, and if there's been an injustice done here, we'll put it to rights. Get that boy out of the water before he freezes and I'll take the child.'

She was passed from Mick to her Da. He didn't often hold her, and somehow his arms were more awkward and less comforting than Mick's, for all that she didn't much like the Irishman. But he hadn't hurt her, and she was only dimly aware of the fact that Da and her brothers thought he had in some way she didn't understand. She snuggled up nearer to her Da's face in this unusual embrace, and the raw smell of baccy he exuded was sweeter than Ma's new-baked bread at that moment. She glanced to where her brothers were hauling a bedraggled Gabe out on to the muddy bank. He looked a sorry sight, his lovely dark springy curls plastered tightly to the contours of his head

16

like rats' tails. He was shivering and furious, and he wrung the water out of his slop with tight-balled hands.

'You'll come back to the cottage and get dried out,' Da commanded. 'I daresay some rabbit stew wouldn't come amiss either, and I reckon a supper will be fair recompense for your wetting.'

It was the only apology they'd get. Gabe glared, and the three brothers glared back. Their Da might think they owed these navvies a bite and a warm, but nothing could hide the fact that they were some of those Irish rogues and charmers, and the three lusty brothers had already had their fill of the local girls having their heads turned and scorning the attentions of the Fenmen for such as these gypsies. But it didn't do to argue with Da.

'Thank you. A meal will be very welcome,' Mick's voice was clipped. He didn't particularly want to stay any longer than necessary with these, but a good hot meal in a warm cottage would always be preferable to the two of them returning to the miserable makeshift hut accommodation they shared, where the rusty old oil-heater would hardly dry Gabe's clothes before morning. If they had to spend an hour at the Bray's cottage it would be an experience to laugh over in the Duck and Drake later, and he felt only a momentary pang at thinking his embraces with Peggy would have to wait. But all the better for waiting perhaps!

The two of them tramped across the field behind the older man who carried Jenny high on his shoulders now, and the stiff, silent backs of the brothers, and both Mick and Gabe knew they were only tolerated because of the way they'd come to the child's rescue. More than that, because she'd verified the truth of it.

If she'd been a few years older, with that imaginative mind her Da had hinted at, she could so easily have screamed out 'rape' in preference to getting a rocking for being home late, and neither would have given much for their chances of survival then.

Life was cheap when large families scratched for a living, as Mick knew only too well, even if Gabe was young enough

17

to forget quickly the effects of the famine that had stripped them of their meagre livelihood in Ireland, their reasonably-filled bellies and their dignity. And had put more than a smouldering resentment in many an Irishman's heart for the English and their blundering attempts to help. Small wonder then, that he chose his companions with care, and was still asking himself if he was making a foolish move to step over the doorstep of the Fenman's cottage.

But it was done now, and an anxious-faced woman, flushed and steamy from the kitchen and the clutches of the toddler at her skirts, came into the parlour to greet her family, and immediately railed into Jenny once she saw that she was safe.

'Leave off, Ma, she's all right.' Her husband dumped the child on a chair and peered at her puffed-up heel. 'She'll want this washed and bound though. These bors fetched a splinter out, and one of 'em took a ducking. We can manage a bit of drying out and some grub, can't we?'

'We can always stretch a stew if nobody minds it tasting more of flour than meat,' Ma said tartly, but her eyes flickered her thanks to the two Irishmen standing awkwardly by. 'Move yourself then, Ted, and find the bor some dry clobber. You'll be about his size, and show him where to take off that wet slop that's dripping all over my floor. And you, Marnie, see to your sister's foot for me while I get Davey settled with his drink.'

She issued her orders like a general instructing his troops, and they all moved. She extricated the clinging hands of the baby and dumped him in an ancient highchair, where he set up a howling and banging until she placed a cup of warm milk in front of him. Mick grinned, suddenly swept up in a rush of nostalgia as it reminded him of the way his own family had once been, before the potato famine had put them on the road to their separate destinations, and sent Gabe and himself to this corner of England. He rectified the thought . . . he and Gabe had chosen to come here, because Mick had fancied it was most like the part of Ireland where they'd lived. Most like Drory. The brief

18

nostalgia faded as he realised these people were still hostile to him and his brother. For all their hospitality, they were merely repaying a debt, and once it was paid they'd be back on equal terms again. Equal terms that made suspicious enemies of them.

He suddenly realised there was another member of the family he hadn't noticed before. A girl with a proud awareness in her face even though she was barely Gabe's age. With clear brown eyes, bolder than her sister's, and a direct unblinking stare that was older than her years, and a shiny curtain of gleaming brown hair that was in sharp contrast to Jenny's wiry tangle of curls, as if it had had hours of industrious brushing applied to it. It fascinated Mick, that hair. He could hardly take his eyes off it, though purely because of the unexpected bright sheen of it in such drab surroundings—and Marnie noticed.

Mick didn't know then that her one aim in life was to be admired, and that she bent her head to attend to her sister's injured foot with more gentleness and patience than she would normally have shown to her stupid little sister. She knew exactly the tender impression she was creating. Even though Mick—and the other one whom she had only glimpsed for a minute before Joey hustled him upstairs to change his clothes—were only navvies and wore navvies' shapeless slops and held their chummy hats awkwardly, they were outside the family.

'This is very kind of you, Missus,' Mick said in sudden embarrassment as he caught Da's keen eyes on him while he studied Marnie's hair.

He averted his eyes from the older girl and took stock of his surroundings. It was a fair-sized cottage, poorly furnished, but fairly clean, with the varying smells of baking and damp washing inclining to add to the impression of cleanliness. He guessed rightly that Mrs Bray probably took in washing and baking, and this was confirmed when she asked Jenny sharply if she'd brought back the pennies for the rabbit pie she'd delivered to Mrs Kettle. The child produced the pennies from the pocket of her apron, and a

19

strip of shiny pink ribbon as well.

'Mrs Kettle gave me this . . .'

Marnie snatched it at once, her forefinger smoothing over the satin surface in a curiously sensual way that startled Mick as he watched her. In an older girl, the movement would have stirred him.

'It's mine!' Jenny snatched it back. 'You wouldn't take the pie. Tell her it's mine, Ma! She always wants what's mine!'

'I'm only feeling it, baby,' Marnie hissed. 'Here, you're welcome to it. It's not long enough for my hair, anyway.'

She flipped the gleaming weight of her hair over her shoulders, her eyes glancing at Mick as she did so. Her Da laughed, not sensing the provocativeness of the glance or the action.

'Like a couple of cats they are at times. Well now, if your mate's ready, you'd best come to the table, bor.'

'He's my brother, Gabe, and I'm Mick. Mick O'Brien.'

Da grunted, his brief expansive mood leaving him as he introduced his family by name, grudgingly, as if he was giving out something of himself that he guarded closely: Kenneth, Joey, Ted, Davey, Jenny with the hurt foot. And Marnie with a swinging curtain of hair and a provocative gleam in her eyes. They'd have trouble with that one, Mick decided. He was glad when Gabe finally appeared from upstairs with Ted, dressed in a rough shirt and trousers, an old pair of thick socks and boots on his feet, his dark hair already springing back into bouncy curls round his head. And immediately Marnie's attention was switched from Mick to his young brother, he saw with amusement. A good job neither of them was any older, or he guessed that Gabe would be sniffing around here more often than was good for him. And with the little one–Jenny–looking up at him with that calf-like devotion in her tawny-coloured eyes . . . Mick hid a smile. Marnie wasn't the only one who was going to charm the birds off the trees in a few years' time. And his brother was going to break a few female hearts before he settled down, and with no more effort than a twinkling glance from his blue eyes and a deepening of the dimples in his cheeks. A real Irish charmer, was Gabe, without really knowing it yet. He got round the rather granite-faced Ma by a genuine acclamation of her rabbit stew.

'Best stew around these parts,' Da said proudly. 'If it weren't for Ma's nifty fingers we'd have starved long since when the babbies were small.'

The three elder babbies glowered across the table, clearly not caring for their family affairs to be bandied about with these navvies. Ted underlined the brooding feelings between them.

'If you want to keep the clobber tonight, you can collect your own things in the morning,' he said suddenly. 'They'll take hours to dry out.'

And they wouldn't want them staying here for hours, Mick thought. Anyway, he was getting restless for Peggy's arms and all the rest of her that was so accommodating, and he didn't fancy Gabe would take too kindly to the antagonism stretching out across the width of the scrubbed parlour table. He thanked them all quickly and said he and Gabe would be on their way, and they'd call back in the morning on their way to work, if that was all right with Missus. She nodded her agreement, already busy with getting Davey to go to bed.

'Right then,' Mick said again. It was difficult to say goodbye as if this was a normal kind of social visit, but at last they were out of the cottage and across the mist-blanketed fields, where the disused windmills loomed up eerily as if they floated on a grey sea in the moonlight–the parish lantern as Peggy called it–and were over the planked dykes towards the Duck and Drake.

They spent frequent evenings there, and Gabe had a running war game of soldiers and armies with the landlord's son in the cellar, where Mick suspected the two of them drank far more ale than they should. But he was usually too well lulled in the pleasantly friendly atmosphere of the Inn, where the customers were used to his face and his brogue by now, to bother too much about Gabe until it was time to drag him out and to make their unsteady way back to the rickety hut. By then it seemed like a palace . . .

And long before that time came, the Inn would have officially closed its doors, and the landlord would be busily entertaining his privileged cronies to his special brew in a back room, and all of them exchanging the lewdest jokes they could devise to the accompaniment of ribald laughter and ruder comments.

And Mick would be snug and warm in Peggy's bed for an hour or so, covering her luscious naked curves with his hard muscular body, his head cushioned on her ample breasts, and both of them soaring to a mutual delight.

CHAPTER TWO

Morning was Gabe's favourite time of day. Not the part that meant shivering out of warm blankets and sluicing his face with the shock of cold water before struggling into his working clothes ... but later, when he and Mick had breakfasted on hunks of bread and honey and swilled them down with a strong brew of tea, and then leaving the hut behind them in the sharpness of the Fen morning. To strike out across fields that were as soft and springy as a carpet before starting on another day's dyke digging and hauling the sticky clay from the ditches to be spread out between the dug trenches like rows of soldiers. Claying was boring and muscle-aching, and often by the end of the afternoon Gabe would be wondering why they did it, and where one ache ended and the next began. It was a relief to see the sun begin to sink low in the sky and redden the horizon, but by then he was usually immune to its beauties.

Only first thing in the morning, in the weird yellow-green dawn light and with feathery fronds of mist and ground-frost spangling the fields, was Gabe able to feel articulate about the Fens. At such times the cool, gleaming yellow ribbons of the dykes were so breathtakingly beautiful they could make the hairs on the back of his neck tingle just by looking at them. They made him think of purity and cleanliness and the remoteness of nuns, untouched and virginal before the clamour of the clay gangs ripped through them with spade and pick and shovel.

For some strange reason he couldn't explain, the dawn-fresh dykes sent a pleasurable shivery feeling into his loins, just because they were so unsullied. And on that particular morning when he tramped across the fields with his brother

Mick, earlier than usual because they had to call in at the Brays' cottage to collect his working clobber, they made him think of the girl with gleaming hair. The one they called Marnie, who'd smoothed her sister's satiny ribbon so lovingly.

Last night at the Duck and Drake, he and Fred Jackson, the landlord's son, had finished busily re-enacting the Battle of Waterloo in the cellar of the Inn, and their excitement had risen to a hot-cheeked hiatus with the fever of the battle and the jugs of ale they had illicitly tapped from the barrels and joyfully consumed. They had finally slumped, exhausted and bemused, against the rough potato sacks stored in the cellar, whose musty smell only added to the pleasure of their special place, rumpling their buttocks and backs to fit into the lumpy sacks for the best possible comfort in a companionable haze.

'I wouldn't even change places with your Mick right now,' Fred grinned knowingly as he waved his jug of ale about and spread his stocky legs out in front of him. Gabe grinned back, each of them knowing Fred referred to the buxom Peggy and pretending to be worldly-wise about the whole enterprise, when in reality each was as virginal as the unbroken dykes of the dawn morning.

'You ever met any of a family called Bray?' Gabe said suddenly.

'Yeah. The oldest one's been around here a bit lately when he's back from his lighter job on the river. He's got a hot for Peggy the same as your Mick has, but I don't think he's got anywheres yet, bor.'

Gabe sat up quickly, eyes bright with interest.

'How do you know that, Fred? I wish I lived at an Inn,' his voice was envious. 'You get to know everything.'

'I heard 'em, see? Well, not her and Kenneth. But I've heard things from her room before, when she had another chap from over Lynn way, and she ain't made the same sounds with Kenneth!'

'What sort of sounds?'

24

Fred grinned, his eyes gleaming darkly in the smutty candle-light.

'Like a couple of pigs grunting and heaving, and with the light out and all . . .'

'Hells-teeth! You ain't heard our Mick as well, have you?' Gabe didn't much like the idea of that. It was all right for Fred to screw an ear to Peggy's door to hear her and some unknown chap from King's Lynn together . . . or Kenneth Bray trying it on and getting nowhere . . . it was something else to think this little tick was eavesdropping on Mick. He didn't think his brother would go a moles-foot on it either.

He suddenly realised Fred was looking a bit sheepish.

'Well, I ain't really heard 'em. I got a cuff round the ear when me Da saw me hanging around her room, and told me I was too young for that game yet. But I know for a fact Kenneth Bray's been up there and I ain't seen him come creeping out in less than an hour.'

Gabe stared at him. An hour? That long? That wasn't just for kisses and cuddles, he bet himself. He wished he wasn't so damned ignorant of things he ought to know. By now, at thirteen, he ought to be fully aware of what a man's job in bed should be, but he wasn't at all, damn it. He and Mick hadn't got around to that kind of discussion yet, and Mick probably assumed he knew all about it anyways. The older he got, the more difficult it became for him to ask. Particularly as just lately he'd become aware of all sorts of uncomfortable and yet exquisitely sweet sensations that were sometimes sharp and almost explosive, at others more like a long slow lingering dream. He wondered if Fred knew all about them too. Fred seemed to know everything, and what he didn't know he guessed.

'These are Ted Bray's clothes,' he said quickly in the small silence. 'I had to borrow 'em, because mine got soaked when I took a ducking in the dyke.'

He knew he'd been wrong to admit to a ducking when he heard Fred's raucous laughter. He took a deep swig of ale, feeling his head swim in the deliciously alarming way he was beginning to enjoy.

'How'd you find your way in there, Gabe? I thought you was supposed to be diggin' them out, not diving in 'em. And how'd you get inside the Brays' cottage, bor? They don't take kindly to navvies. Kenneth and Joey both work on the river, and they think they're a cut above the rest of us. I'm getting a job with them as soon as my Da lets me. I'm sick of humping barrels for him.'

Gabe stared at him in consternation. He'd never thought of Fred leaving the Inn. It wouldn't be the same without him. Who would he play soldiers and armies with in the smoky gloom of the cellar? It was the best game in the world, with the added excitement of tapping the barrels whenever they felt like it, but Fred was still nudging him to tell how he'd got to the Brays' cottage. His pride wouldn't let him admit he'd been kicked and practically tipped over the rim of the dyke. He was still a bit tender in his private parts, but that didn't hurt so much as his pride.

'I got a splinter out of the girl's foot,' he said carelessly. 'Must have been standing too near the edge of the dyke and I fell in. Anyways, her Da took me and Mick back for supper and a change of clobber.'

'Marnie, was it?' Fred's eager face was a full red sun.

'No. The little 'un. Jennifer.'

'Oh, her.' Fred dismissed her with a toss of his head. 'Full of stories, that one. What about Marnie, though? All right, ain't she? Peggy reckons she'll have competition there when Marnie grows up a bit.'

Gabe fidgeted in the coarse, unfamiliar trousers that were somehow pressing in on him, thoughts of Marnie's teasing mouth and come-on eyes filling his mind. Fred guffawed.

"Daft as that Jenny Bray sometimes, is Peggy. You always know when she's been into town and fetched some of them soppy magazines she looks at. You can tell by the way she struts about the place sticking herself out in front and pulling down the top of her dress till me Da tells her to put 'em back in again before she knocks the customers' eyes out . . .'

He stopped talking, his leering grin frozen, his mouth hanging half open with the ale still wet on his lips as he stared at his companion, still fidgeting uncomfortably.

'You pig, Gabe. You've peed yourself!'

But he hadn't. The images Fred had conjured up in his mind of Peggy strutting about with her dumplings boiling over, and the new sensations stirring inside him whenever he thought about Marnie, and the tantalising roughness of the coarse trousers against his skin had resulted in a sudden warm surge in his loins that gushed as suddenly as blinking, and he crossed his legs in swift embarrassment. He told Fred not to be so daft and it was only the ale he'd spilled, but it wasn't the ale that made him tackily uncomfortable for the rest of the evening, and uncaring whether his troops won or lost their wooden battle.

He was glad to go with Mick when he came calling for him a long while later, but half-ashamed of the secret thing that had happened, as it had done with increasing frequency lately, and half-knowing what Mick had been up to with Peggy after closing-time in her stuffy little room at the Inn, made the thought of asking his brother about the unbidden happenings in his body even more of an impossibility.

He was still thinking about it all the next morning, even though he tried hard to push it all out of his mind. And the biting chill of early morning was enough to send away any thoughts other than the need to stride out, his borrowed boots flattening the morning-sweet carpet of grass, in time with Mick's tuneless whistling. Whatever else Peggy did, she put Mick in fine good humour the morning after. And Gabe turned his eyes towards the ribbony dykes, finding the gleam of gold on their glassy surfaces as pleasurable as ever, with no intruding visions of Peggy's buxom curves bursting over the top of her dress like rolling rain-clouds to excite him. Mick paused by the Brays' cottage.

'You go on in there, Gabe. One of us had best be on time.'

'All right. I'll catch up later.' He tried to sound cheerful, without admitting the fact that those glowering male eyes of the Bray family could turn his stomach to water. He wasn't going to admit that to Mick or anyone . . . but the two elder brothers were already off to their river job, and Da and the younger one had left the cottage as well, to his relief. The river job sounded interesting, according to Fred, where the horse-drawn barges busily ploughed their way between the towns, delivering a variety of goods from King's Lynn as far south as Cambridge. He had no idea what work Da and Ted were concerned with, but Gabe was mightily relieved to see they weren't at the cottage, and in consequence his accursed dimples were deeper than usual in his morning-scrubbed face when Marnie opened the door to him just as if she'd been hovering behind the window-glass waiting for him to arrive. The warm damp smell of soapy water oozed from the kitchen.

'Ma said to tell you your clobber's dry and in the boys' bedroom,' she said importantly, her own face dimpling back at him.

He really was a beautiful boy, Marnie thought, with a shiver of excitement running through her. More beautiful than any of her brothers or the fair-haired farm boys that came here chin-wagging with them into the small hours so that she and Jenny couldn't get to sleep for the loud buzz of noise from the parlour beneath their bedroom.

It was on such a night when she'd first crept out of their room, preparing to hiss down the stairs at them and tell them to shut their traps and let her get to sleep. She was surprised her Ma and Da hadn't yelled down at them before now, because she'd heard them come upstairs ages ago . . . when she'd paused with her hand on the bannister, suddenly stilled by the sound of the most extraordinary noises coming from her parents' room. A mixture of bed-creaking, panting, grunting, strangely exciting and completely unknown noises that had sent her original idea

28

fleeing from her mind and sent her creeping back to bed, to lie there in the darkness and ponder over it. Whatever it was that was happening, it wasn't worrying them that they might waken Davey, who shared their bedroom.

But since that first time, a long time ago now, Marnie had crept out on the landings on other occasions to stand listening, and sometimes to be rewarded by the same extraordinary ritual of sound she didn't altogether understand, but which added a peculiar spice to the long night hours which had to be wasted in sleep. And about which, since her Ma's somewhat garbled and inadequate explanation of future bodily functions on her own account, she'd arrived at her own skimpy conclusions.

'Same room as yesterday then?' Gabe was grinning at her with that dimpled smile that could make her heart feel as if it was turning over in her chest. He was feeling more affected by the sight of her too than he'd expected to be. She was the most beautiful creature he'd ever seen, even apart from Peggy, with her huge brown eyes that all the Bray family seemed to have. Gabe remembered the splintered heel he'd helped to relieve yesterday, and enquired quickly after Jennifer.

'Jennifer!' Marnie mocked, her eyes flashing with derision. 'Has she been preening herself again? Well, *Jennifer's* still in bed, the lazy thing, and Ma and me have been at the washing this past half-hour.'

She nodded her head towards the stairs, but not before he'd seen and noted the small pink fingers she waved about as if they had lives of their own. Slim pink fingers softened with the hot washing-water . . . and wondered briefly how it would feel to take them in his own long tapering hands.

'Don't go in the wrong room now, or *Jennifer* might throw a blue fit!'

He felt her eyes following his progress up the stairs, and changed his clothes quickly in the room he'd been in yesterday. He'd hardly noticed it then, with Ted glaring at him, but now he saw there was one huge bed that took up nearly all the space in the room, where the three brothers slept together. The rest of the space was taken up with an untidy jumble of shirts and breeches and socks, and he added his borrowed clothes to the pile before he left the bedroom.

Another door on the narrow landing opened, and the smaller girl appeared, rubbing the sleep from her eyes. Gabe's mouth twitched at the sight of her, hair even more tangled than it had been yesterday, and practically enveloped in a nightshift several sizes too large for her. Her small feet peeped out from the hem, one of them bound inexpertly in a thick bandage of the same coarse linen slopping material as his working smock. The twitch on his lips broadened into a smile.

'Good-morning, Jennifer-sleepy-head! How's your foot today? Is it still paining you?'

She gave him an adoring look which made him feel sort of swelled-up inside, and the fact that Marnie was still hovering about at the foot of the stairs with an impatience that was flattering, made him linger a moment more to chat with this elfin child. Gabe hadn't yet learned the subtleties of playing one female off against another, but in his case it was hardly something that needed to be learned–it was instinctive.

'It feels much better today, as long as I don't press too hard on it,' Jenny said, suddenly shy at meeting him so close like this on her own landing outside her bedroom door. She unconsciously smoothed down the wild tangle of hair that was topped incongruously by the rose-pink ribbon, and Gabe grinned at the sight of it.

'You keep your hands on that ribbon so that sister of yours doesn't get it,' he whispered conspiratorially. 'It looks better on you!'

Jenny giggled loudly.

'I'll see you again sometime, Jennifer-sleepy-head,' Gabe grinned down at the adoring tawny-coloured eyes, so alight with pleasure at seeing him. 'Be good now.'

Oh, she would, she would, if he said so . . .

'Ma says you're to have this.' Marnie was waving a

30

packet of food at him from the bottom of the stairs. 'She says you look no bigger than a scarecrow compared with our boys.'

Gabe bristled. He was wiry and strong. Not so brawny as the Bray boys, perhaps, but his shoulders were broad, and he had a few years to go to catch up with them yet. He knew the dyke digging was putting muscles where he'd had none before. But by the time he reached Marnie, ready with a sharp retort, her eyes too were smiling at him, and whatever cutting remark he'd been going to say went flying out of his head. Anyway, it was a real treat to have somebody else fixing them up with some tommy, and he took the packet gratefully out of her hands.

'Thank your Ma for me, will you?' he was suddenly awkward, as awkward as Jenny had been a moment ago. For some reason he couldn't take his eyes from that gleaming hair that fell almost to Marnie's waist. He felt an urge to touch it, to run his fingers down its length, parting its perfection and splitting the silky smoothness of it. She saw him looking at it, and it was just as if she knew exactly what was in his mind, Gabe thought, with a kind of anger. He didn't like to have his feelings exposed the way Marnie seemed able to manage it. He swerved his eyes away from her and clicked his teeth instead at Davey, sitting enquiringly in his high chair in the corner of the parlour.

In answer the baby threw his crust on the floor and banged his feet on the foot-rest, and Marnie bent to retrieve the crust with a quick grumble at him. Her hair fanned out in silky strands as she did so and the illusion of perfection was broken. Gabe sighed with an illogical feeling of relief. She was only a girl anyway, and he was stronger than she was any day of the week. He moved towards the door and edged out of it into the cold crisp morning.

'I'll be getting on to the dykes then.'

She was suddenly at the door before he'd taken his hand from it, the soft pink fingers curling over his.

'Meet me at the old mill by Kettle's farm after supper,' she breathed. 'I have to deliver the washing for Ma. Say about half after seven.'

The door was shut behind him before Gabe could make any kind of reply. He heard the occupants of the cottage calling to one another. Marnie grumbling at Davey again for flinging his crust about the room. Ma yelling at Jenny to come downstairs if she wanted any breakfast at all, and then she could be folding some of yesterday's washing ready for the ironing. Jenny answering in that soft young voice of hers as she clumped unevenly down the stairs with her bandaged foot.

And then he went, striking out across the fields to where Mick would have already started work at the claying and wondering what was taking his brother so long. The other clay gangs shouting ribald remarks to each other and asking if young Gabe had had too much ale in his belly last night. Everything the same as every other day . . . except for the sudden surging excitement spiced with irritation moving inside him.

She thought she only had to say the word and he'd come running like a little lap-dog. Marnie, with the too-knowing eyes and the provocative tilt to her chin and that glorious hair . . . a child with a woman's look about her. Commanding him to be at the disused mill by Kettle's farm at half after seven as if she was bestowing a great favour on him, and never waiting for him to say yes or no. Just expecting him to be there.

The strange irritation pulsated round his body as he strode across the dew-fresh fields and settled somewhere in his groin. Well, if he did decide to turn up, he'd show her who was bestowing favours, he thought loftily, and if he gave her a few kisses and cuddles it would be because he wanted it, not her. It wouldn't be the first time he'd kissed a girl . . . not that there had been that many, but on the occasions it had happened it had been a very pleasant sensation to press his mouth against soft yielding lips that slightly parted beneath his . . . yes, he might turn up, he decided. He just might.

The day seemed longer than usual, and he got a teasing from Mick about the packet of tommy Ma Bray had given him. But they both enjoyed the homemade crusty bread, soft cheese and raw onions, and at the end of the day Gabe remarked casually that he didn't think he'd go to the Duck and Drake so early that evening, but that he'd see Mick there later. His brother gave him a broad wink as he left Gabe at their hut on his way for a few ales and another session with Peggy.

'Got something spoiling, have you? Mind you don't get your feathers singed, Gabe. I'll see you later then.'

Mick talked in riddles sometimes, but Gabe couldn't be bothered to worry out his remark. He had other things on his mind as he sluiced the day's clay from his face and hands, put on his tidy shirt and breeches and set off for the old mill with fifteen minutes to spare.

By the time the distant church clock from the village struck a quarter before eight, he was fuming and cursing at himself for bothering to come out here on a fool's errand. Marnie wasn't coming and that was obvious. She'd been teasing him and he'd been daft enough to fall for it. He hung about by the doorway of the mill, straining his eyes towards Kettle's farm in the darkening light and thinking he may as well go on to the Inn after all and enjoy a grumble with Fred about girls . . . when he suddenly saw her running like a will-o'-the-wisp through the moon-whitened field, and she didn't stop running until she fell into his arms, her thin chest heaving and her heart beating fast.

'I thought you weren't coming,' he heard the affront in his voice and the answering laughter in hers.

'Did it worry you, Gabe?' she teased, and planted a damp kiss on his mouth, but before he could pull her close and prove who was master in this situation, she'd twisted out of his arms and clattered up the wooden ladder to the top platform of the mill. He ran after her, suddenly exhilarated, and caught her to him while she pretended she didn't want to be caught, but paused just often enough for him to touch her shining hair, her soft flushed cheeks, her full red mouth . . .

She flopped down on the musty, straw-strewn floor, still laughing and panting. Laughing at him. She was a hundred years older than he and he raged inside, wanting to match her maturity. Her skirt was all rucked up as she leaned back on her elbows, her brown eyes mocking him as they gleamed in the moonlight, her long hair hanging straight as a dyke behind her shoulders. It was as light as day in the mill with the top open to the weather, and the hexagonal patch of sky above them, from where the full moon shone directly down on them. It could have been placed there specifically to light the mill, Gabe thought, truly at that moment the parish lantern of the Fens. His eyes slowly travelled over Marnie's slight body and paused, and he sucked in his breath.

'You ain't got no drawers on!'

A peal of laughter greeted his words.

'It ain't Sunday, is it?'

She suddenly lay back on the straw, hands behind her head. She could see him watching her and it was such a sharply exciting feeling. She wanted him to look at her, to touch, to hold . . . her thin legs moved slightly apart. She discovered she was holding her breath as Gabe tentatively moved one long tapering finger to smooth the silky mound topping her thighs, a mound hardly sprinkled as yet with a down of golden brown hair. She felt a shiver at his touch, but not of fear. Marnie could hear the sudden rasping breathing coming from his throat, and it reminded her instantly of the times she'd listened outside her parents' bedroom door. Her legs spread wider almost without her knowing, as if they moved of their own free will.

Gabe sensed her shiver beneath his fingers and felt himself begin to grow. Instinct told him there was a warm deep chasm there, and the memory of farm animals mating provided the final answer to the question of just what to do. He fumbled and found himself and then he was lying across her and pushing home . . . he saw the startled hurt in her eyes for a moment, but by then it was too late. He hardly even heard her small scream because he was sailing gloriously on a voyage of discovery more exciting than anything he'd ever known. A voyage that culminated in shooting golden spasms that almost took him to the stars.

His hands, that had been pressed to the small flat buds of her breasts, now loosened, because suddenly there was nothing left. He rolled away from her and lay on his back beside her, staring up at the fullness of the moon and letting his quivering body and his feelings subside. It was like being reborn. He couldn't even think of her as a person at that moment because the emotions that claimed him were so all-consuming. He'd done it. He'd had his first sweet taste of a woman . . . well, Marnie . . . he'd done the secret thing he and Fred were always so curious about. He'd done it before Fred. The thought filled him with pride and a kind of triumph.

'That's what makes babies,' Marnie said positively.

Sweet Jesus, what was she saying? Gabe's stomach tightened into a thousand knots. His head jerked sideways so fast it cricked his neck, and he shot up into a sitting position, leaning on one elbow to look down at her. She gave that mocking little laugh of hers again.

'Oh, don't worry, Gabe. It won't happen for us. I ain't had the curse yet, so it's all right.'

The curse? What in God's name was that? The scent of witchcraft was suddenly strong in Gabe's nostrils and he had a job not to flinch away from her like a frightened rabbit.

'I–I–what–' but suddenly he couldn't ask her. It galled him to admit he was ignorant of something that seemed to be in some way fundamental. But she told him anyway.

'I know all about it from Ma. When a girl gets the curse, it bleeds–down there–and once she gets it she can make babies, but I ain't had it so I can't make 'em yet, see?'

Her voice was satisfied, complacent. To Gabe's ears it was greedy, wanting more, tomorrow, next week, next month . . . all the swift pleasure he'd found in her was diminishing as fast as the limp, useless string between his legs. It bleeds–down there–she said. That gleaming, inviting

35

chasm . . . the thought suddenly made him sick, and his head swam as dizzily as if he'd consumed too many jugs of ale at the Duck and Drake with Fred. He stood up and righted his clothes with shaking hands and then pulled her to her feet.

'We'd better go,' he said roughly. Mick would be wondering where he'd got to. Mick . . . did he manage to do this thing for an hour with Peggy, the way Fred had hinted? An *hour*, when his own inexpert, energetic performance had lasted barely thirty seconds? It was one more thought to demoralise him, to fill him with a kind of sweet horror at the idea of pounding away for so long, and to engulf him in his own inadequacy.

'Listen.' Marnie put her hand on his arm and lifted her head to listen. Away in the distance he heard a male voice–almost certainly one of the Bray men. He froze inside, not wanting to guess at the reception he'd get if they came to the mill and found him with Marnie. Yesterday had been bad enough when he'd been innocent . . . Marnie clutched at him and spoke quickly.

'We ain't been here that long, Gabe.' Her words were an innocent barb to his manhood. 'You stay put and I'll cut across the fields to meet Joey. He'll think I've just come from the Kettle's farm. Nobody'll know about our secret.'

She leaned against him and gave him a last quick kiss full on the mouth with her eager lips. And then she was gone, her feet hurrying down the wooden ladder again and out across the fields, and the knots in Gabe's stomach slowly untangled as there was no other sound in the disused mill but his own heartbeats.

It was going to be all right. The Bray brothers weren't about to throw themselves on him and punch him stupid. Marnie wasn't going to be telling anybody about what had happened, that was for sure. It was their secret, and as the minutes passed and nothing happened, he slowly uncurled from the ball into which he was crouched in the straw, and the surge of triumph began to well up inside him again. If anything, this last hint of danger had spiced the whole procedure, dulling his horror at Marnie's calm explanation of the bleeding, making him feel one hell of a fellow after all. It was their secret, but a secret he couldn't bear to keep entirely to himself when it was so deliciously important and exciting. He'd have to tell Fred.

Gabe moved down the ladder carefully, and out into the night. His legs, that had felt as if they were filled with jelly, were recovering fast, and long before he reached the Duck and Drake he was swaggering as he walked. The Inn was warm and welcoming with the smells of ale and humans and animals reaching out towards him as he entered the taproom. He saw Mick in a corner, deep in conversation with a couple of farmers, and Peggy winked at him from across the other side of the bar. Mr Jackson, Fred's Da, smiled at him with the same rosy cheeks as his son.

'You're on your own tonight, bor,' he said cheerfully. 'You should have got here sooner if you'd wanted to see our Fred. He's gone off to Lynn to see about gittin' a job on one of they lighters on the river.'

Gabe stared at him, sick with disappointment. When Fred had mentioned working on one of the barges he'd thought it was just a way of dreaming, like he dreamed of going on a boat to America, and Mick dreamed of owning his own farm. He hadn't expected it to happen so soon, if at all, because he'd thought Mr Jackson would want to keep Fred at the Inn as long as possible. But apparently Fred had got his way, and Gabe felt suddenly betrayed because he hadn't been here to know about it beforehand, and Fred had just gone off to King's Lynn without the two of them mulling over it the way they always did about everything. And just when he was bursting to tell Fred about him and Marnie too. Fred should have been here. Gabe was definitely put out, even though his friend couldn't have known what was so important about tonight, and for a few seconds he just stood in the middle of the taproom floor, uncertain quite what to do.

'Gabe, come over here, will you?' Mick was waving to him, and he moved across the smoky room, relieved not to be standing there like a lark all ready for roasting. *She'd* been ready ... Marnie ... he pushed the memory of her thin, widespread legs and the secret place between them out of his mind and joined his brother and the keen-eyed, brawny farmers puffing away on clay pipes with a foul-smelling mixture fit to rot their socks.

'This him, is it?' one of them looked him over as if he was some kind of specimen. 'He's strong enough, by the looks. How'd you fancy working a farm, bor? Your brother here's been telling us you're partial to animals. Got quite a way with 'em, he says, and we've got more'n enough to keep you busy, long as you ain't averse to a bit o' mole-catching as well as tending the cows. Not a'feared of cows, are you?'

'Of course not,' Gabe said indignantly.

What was all this about anyways? He'd thought he and Mick were all set up for the winter with the dyke digging and any odd jobs they could find if needs be. They'd managed all right in previous winters, and it suited him to be free-willed and not hog-tied to any particular master, even if it sometimes meant a bout with the fists on occasions when they were taunted with the name of Irish tinkers. He was no tinker and never had been, and his Pa back in Ireland would have been outraged to hear his sons called such a thing.

But Pa was dead and unable to stand up for him any more. And he didn't often think of his Mammy now, gone to live in the city with his sister Maureen and her stick of a husband. He knew Mick still sent money regularly every month from the both of them, just the way he'd promised when they left Ireland, with the usual note to say they were well, and one day soon when Mick had his own farm he'd send for her. It was one more futile dream in Gabe's eyes– at least, he'd always thought so until now. But the gleam in Mick's eyes as he leaned towards his young brother across the ale-slopped table at the Duck and Drake was anything but dream-filled.

'Mr Dan and Mr Lester Pinnock are offering us living-in jobs, Gabe, for as long as we do good work. We'll have reg'lar meals we won't have to cook ourselves and decent beds to sleep in. We can start just as soon as we like, because their other help has just upped and left. What do you say?'

'There'll be rabbiting a'plenty in a few weeks' time,' Mr Dan put in enticingly. 'And as many rabbit stews as my good woman can put in your belly, bor.'

'And if you please us, we'll let you have a gun for bird-scaring later on,' Mr Lester added. 'You ain't never tasted nothing till you've tasted Effie's bird pies.'

Gabe listened to their persuading voices with a sick dread inside him. They were offering him a chance he knew he must take or split with Mick, and he wouldn't want to do that. He and Mick were partners. Where one went, the other went, and right now he could feel the unspoken pressure from his brother, willing him to accept, probably having hinted to the Pinnock farmers about his love of animals as an added incentive. But it was love of them . . . not a desire to shoot at free-spirited birds in the grey Norfolk sky or to lay traps to catch the squealing moles or set the dogs and ferrets on to defenceless rabbits and see the guts ripped out of them and spilled on to the wintery ground. Gabe swallowed, knowing some might think him soft, but it wasn't soft not to want to hurt things . . . they were all waiting for his answer, and there was only one he could give. He owed it to Mick who'd looked after him these past two years since they left Drory with as much care as if he'd been their Pa, and he found himself nodding his agreement.

'That's a bargain then,' Mr Lester Pinnock slapped his jug of ale on the table and called for Peggy to bring one over for Gabe.

Minutes later she came across to them with the swaying walk of hers that often aroused coarse comments from the customers of the Inn, winked at Gabe and then in a more meaningful way at Mick. Suddenly Gabe felt himself grow hot as a swift burst of curiosity held him. Wondering just how Peggy would look in a similar situation to the one in which he'd gripped and writhed against Marnie in the old mill. With more substance beneath his hands than the hard tight buds he'd held, and a thick, bushy fleshiness Marnie didn't yet possess. He caught Mick's eyes smiling at him and drank deeply of the cool, rough ale, but there was a fire lit inside him that couldn't be quenched so easily. And he was already demoting the childish battles between wooden armies in the cellar of the Duck and Drake to being the second best game in the world.

CHAPTER THREE

'I don't know what's got into you tonight, girl,' Ma grumbled at Marnie. 'That's twice I've asked you for the washing money from the Kettles. Are you going deaf or something?'

'Sorry Ma.' Marnie tipped the money out of the plush drawstring bag she kept round her waist and smiled a secret smile at her Mother's words. Because *she* knew what had got into her tonight. It had been Gabe O'Brien, and though she hadn't really intended or expected *that* to happen, it had to happen someday, and it was good that it had been with someone as beautiful as Gabe.

She hadn't even minded that it was all over so quickly, even though she knew from her breath-held listening at her parents' door that it wasn't always so. But it was better so tonight, because she hadn't time to be really scared or hurt, for by the time Gabe had got past the hurting bit and filled her to bursting until she thought she'd split right in two, he'd been jerking and pressing and gasping as if he too was in pain, and then it had all been finished.

She never paused to wonder if it had been Gabe's first time too. She just admired him tremendously for not prolonging it, even though he seemed a bit vague when she'd told him about the curse, when she'd thought a clever bor like him would have known all about it. She hoped fervently she'd get the chance to do it again with Gabe before the curse appeared, so there wouldn't be the worry about babies.

Marnie decided to ask Mrs Kettle a thing or two about that next time she had to go over with the washing. It was best not to worry Ma about it. Ma had been red-faced enough telling her about the curse, just as if she didn't have every right to know about the happenings in her own body.

It was all very interesting, and she wasn't afraid of the sight of blood the way Jenny was. It wasn't going to frighten *her*. Mrs Kettle would know all about stopping babies, she was sure. As for the way of getting 'em, well, she didn't need to coax Ma into telling her that any more. She knew it all.

And she felt infinitely superior to that soppy little sister of hers, for all that she had the glorious curls Marnie yearned for so much. She was so envious of them, and of the way her Ma and Da clucked over them sometimes, that she spent even more time brushing her own straight hair until her scalp tingled, and never once offering to untangle Jenny's for her. It wasn't fair that Jenny's should be so curly, while hers was so straight.

Still . . . Marnie's brown eyes sparkled, remembering the way Gabe's look had lingered on her waist-length hair as if he couldn't quite believe it was real. And a look like that, that made a curdling of her insides thicker than any butter-churn, was enough to make all the brushing worthwhile, and all the cracks her Da made about her vanity being the death of her vanish like the heat-haze on a summer's day.

But vain she was and always had been, and she'd dearly like the rose-pink ribbon Mrs Kettle had given to Jenny. She smiled winningly at her little sister as she let her beat her time and again at Happy Families that evening when she got home from the old mill.

'I'll bet you the rose-pink ribbon against my pack of cards in the next game,' she said sweetly, knowing she could beat Jenny hands down any time she chose.

Jenny shook her head decisively, the tawny curls bobbing up and down on her shoulders, the ribbon agleam in the lamplight.

'It's mine,' she said. She patted it self-consciously, remembering Gabe's whispered words not to let Marnie get her hands on it.

'I know it's yours, you silly little cat,' Marnie hissed under cover of the family's gabbing. 'But you can have my green one in exchange. It's much wider.'

'I don't want a green one. I want this one. Gabe likes it,'

Jenny's words added to Marnie's irritation.

'Gabe. Gabe. What's so wonderful about him?' She managed to sound scornful, just as if she hadn't known the feel of him inside her and felt his hot demanding mouth on hers. At least, it had been hot and demanding after she had teased him with her own.

'Ma, I don't have to give Marnie my ribbon, do I?' Jenny suddenly turned to her mother at the ironing table. 'It's mine for always, isn't it?'

'Of course it is, Jenny. Stop baiting her, Marnie, and help her get undressed. She should have been in bed this last half hour since.'

Marnie's lips pressed tightly together. She pulled Jenny's apron and smock over her head, nearly pulling her ears off with them. It was always the same, she brooded. As soon as Jenny appealed to Ma for help she always got her way and there was an end to it. Anyway, Jenny had to go to bed a full hour before she did, and then she could have Ma to herself, apart from the intrusion of the ironing and the continual thud of the flat on the table and the growing pile of uncreased linen ready to be tied up for delivery tomorrow. But at least while she was tying them it was something she and Ma did together, without Jenny forever trying to help when her fingers weren't nimble enough to fasten the string or her arms strong enough to carry the bundles across the fields. All she could be entrusted with were the pies her Ma baked, and if it hadn't been for delivering one of them, she might never have got her foot stuck with a splinter and had Gabe O'Brien fetching it out for her.

Jenny just *would* have to have seen him first, Marnie thought, with an unreasonable burst of jealousy. But she hadn't seen him like *she* had seen him, a triumphant voice inside her whispered, and her fingers suddenly caressed the rough fabric of Mrs Kettle's voluminous apron as if she touched the smoothness of Gabe's skin.

She was impatient to see him again, and for the next few days she hung around the fields where the clay gangs worked the dykes, until Joey happened to see her lurking there and reported her to her Da, and she had to stand in the parlour in front of everybody and listen to him ranting on at her. It was even more mortifying because she hadn't even seen a sign of Gabe, or his brother.

'I've told you times a'plenty to keep away from they navvies,' Da glared at her when she'd been hauled back to the cottage in a fury at Joey for sneaking on her. 'They're nothing but trouble for a young girl, and I'm not having my young 'un coming home here with a pack of trouble in her belly.'

'Da . . .' Ma glanced warningly towards Jenny, gazing goggle-eyed at this tirade.

'I didn't even talk to 'em!' Marnie tossed her head so that her hair gleamed like bronze.

'Talking's not what I'm on about,' her Da said meaningly. 'You're half-grown already, and with a look about you that'd make any navvy hot under his belt for you if he got the chance for it. Watch on for what I'm telling you, girl, and don't let me see they Irish navvies around here again neither. I seen the way the pretty one looked at you, and don't think I missed it.'

His hard eyes raked up and down her body until Marnie felt as if he knew, just by looking at her, what she and Gabe had been up to in the old mill. And it was all so infuriating, knowing how Gabe and Mick seemed to have vanished off the face of the earth since the night she'd asked him to meet her after supper. It was just as if Gabe had had his fill of her and didn't want to bother with her any more. And though she hung about the clay fields, she knew better than to ask any of the other navvies about the Irish brothers, for all that her Da thought she was such a fool.

In her temper she rounded on Jenny, who was supposedly feeding Davey with his supper, but in reality listening with open mouth to the unfathomable exchange going on between her Da and Marnie. All Jenny knew was that it had something to do with Gabe, and therefore she

44

wanted to know what it was all about since he'd been kind to her and she'd liked him so much.

'Why don't you shut your stupid trap before a fly buzzes in?' Marnie hissed furiously at her.

Jenny's eyes filled with tears at this sudden attack for no reason at all.

'Ma,' she wailed. 'I ain't done nothing . . .'

'Nor you have, my duck,' her Da replied. 'Marnie, you can get off to bed this minute, and stay there until you learn to control that temper of yours. And think on all that I've said while you're up there. I'm thinking a spell in service might be what's needed to damp down the spirit in you a bit.'

Marnie flounced out of the parlour in a fury, knowing better than to try arguing with him. But to be sent to bed before Jenny was the worst possible indignity, and she took off her clothes with trembling hands and put on the cotton nightshift, lying cold and shaking between the icy sheets, wild with rage.

They all preferred Jenny to her. They always took her part because she was the youngest girl and those big soft baby eyes. It wasn't *fair* . . . but Gabe hadn't preferred Jenny, had he? She tried to console herself with the thought that he'd come running to the mill when she told him to, and he'd shown her he liked her then all right.

She suddenly remembered the feel of him, hard and pushing . . . and here . . . she put the palms of her hands over her small breasts. He'd seemed to like doing that. Marnie looked down to where they made hardly a bump above the night-shift and pushed them together, wishing they'd grow bigger overnight since Gabe liked them so much. And he'd liked the other part of her . . . one hand went protectively to her groin as if to reassure herself of the secret place he'd entered, and she suddenly jerked it away as she encountered the hot wetness there. And stared down at herself with fury and damp-eyed despair, because the curse had caught up with her before she was ready, and she wept tears of frustration into the unyielding pillow. Oh, it wasn't fair . . . it wasn't *fair* . . . no-one would want her now.

'Marnie?' she heard Jenny's whispering voice a while later when she came upstairs to bed. 'Are you crying, Marnie?'

'*No!*' It was a muffled sound from the depths of the bedclothes.

'You can borrow the pink ribbon tomorrow, Marnie,' Jenny was saying quickly. 'I don't want it if it's going to make you cry. You have it one day and I'll have it the next day.'

You have it one day and I'll have it the next day . . . Marnie mimicked the high-pitched, childish voice in her head, but her eyes involuntarily flew open to see her sister standing by the bed they shared, dangling the rose-pink ribbon in her hand. Tantalising, smooth and satiny . . . Marnie swallowed. She wanted it so much. She was quite sure Gabe would like to see it crowning her gleaming hair . . . if he wanted her at all now that she had the curse.

How long did it last, she wondered? She had no idea, and the days of bleeding seemed to stretch ahead into infinity like a horror-strewn battle-field. She blinked away the sudden blur from her eyes, and Jenny's innocent, eager, wanting-to-please look only made her angrier. Jenny was so *pretty*. The pretty one, she'd heard some of the farmers' wives refer to her. Just because of her big soft eyes and heart-shaped face and those awful messy tangled curls. Right at that moment Jenny's face was in shadow with the flickering candle behind her on the shelf, and the dark contours of her face were a shadowy perfection, the deep brown-gold curls framing it like a gilt-stranded halo. Her small arm was stretched out towards Marnie with the ribbon in her hand, but in a sudden petulant mood, Marnie shrugged away from her sister and huddled up in a ball on the far side of the bed with her back towards her.

'I don't want it now,' she said angrily. 'It's too short and too slippy to stay on my hair properly, and the colour's all wrong.'

She didn't need to look round to know Jenny would be staring down at the rose-pink ribbon, all her pleasure in it gone. Because if it was the wrong colour for Marnie it was supposedly the wrong colour for her too. And she wasn't yet old enough to appreciate that a ribbon that would slide out of gleaming straight hair almost as soon as it was tied, would sit like a coronet in the middle of a riot of curls.

Marnie heard her sister blow out the candle and pad across the rag-rug on the floor to climb in the creaking bed behind her. Usually she let Jenny's small cold feet rest against the back of her legs for a while, quite liking the tingling shivers they sent through her. And was happy to let Jenny snuggle up against her in the darkness. But not tonight. Tonight Marnie kept as close to the edge of the bed as she could manage, her body stiff and tense, and aching more because of it as she lay carefully not touching her sister.

Ma should have warned her about the ache in her belly, Marnie thought, with a rush of self-pity. She wished now she'd thought to ask Mrs Kettle more about the curse than the sparse information Ma had told her. Mrs Kettle would have told her without getting the closed-up look on her face that Ma did whenever the talk got around to more intimate things. Mrs Kettle didn't have daughters of her own, but she lavished all her love on the little Bray girls. She was about the only person in all the world who talked to Marnie as if she was grown-up. *Really* talked, and for some reason Marnie found herself remembering the terribly interesting conversation they'd had not long ago, all about birthsigns.

'You're a Gemini then,' the farmer's wife informed her. 'The sign of the Twins.'

'I'm not twins!' Marnie said in astonishment.

Mrs Kettle laughed. 'I know you're not, lovey, it's just your birthsign, because you were born on 1st June. It controls a lot of things about you, like the way you're sometimes pulled in two directions and have to decide for yourself the way you want to go in life.'

Marnie pulled a face. 'Ma and Da decide that!'

'Well, one day you'll be deciding for yourself, and it's not always easy when part of you wants one thing and the rest of you wants another. Do you know what time of the day you were born, Marnie?'

'It wasn't day at all. It was the middle of the night, and Ma once said it was a good job there was extra light from the full moon for the midwife to see what she was doing or I might not have been here at all. Da said it was shining specially for me that night.'

'Is that so? I'd have laid odds you were born at the time of the full moon. You mark my words, lovey, because all the important things in your life will occur at such times. You're a real moon child and no mistake, headstrong and wayward, and sometimes as cold and remote as that great big ball in the night sky, but always with the capacity to bring light and joy into somebody's life.'

Moon child. Moon child. Marnie had rolled the words round her tongue all the way home across the dew-fresh fields after that conversation, loving the sound of them. Feeling important because she had a birthsign she'd never even heard of before, and that night she'd stood at the bedroom window smiling up at the yellow moon riding high on tufted white clouds as if they shared a special secret. Moon child . . . moon child.

Remembering that interesting talk with Mrs Kettle now, Marnie suddenly caught her breath between her teeth as she stretched carefully in the bed to ease her tense muscles. All the important things in her life would occur at full moon, Mrs Kettle had said in that deliciously mysterious way of hers. And so they had: the tremulous discovery of how it felt to be kissed and held close in Gabe's arms and to know the feel of him inside her, and now this, this other thing, while bright moonlight edged the branches of the tall trees outside the window, silvering them as they shivered in the night breeze. Throwing beams of light on to the patchwork counterpane covering her and Jenny, beams along which flecks of fine dust danced in a golden shower whenever her sister moved restlessly the way she

48

always did until she got herself comfortable.

Jenny. The unreasoning jealousy flooded through her again. Even the little bandaged foot brushing against Marnie's leg reminded her that Jenny and Gabe had shared a moment of intimacy when he'd removed the splinter and made Jenny his adoring slave. A moment preceding and therefore almost overriding in her mind the ultimate intimacy she herself had shared with Gabe. She turned her face into the pillow, willing sleep to come, but when it did it was dream-filled and disturbed, and she was thankful when daylight finally came.

Jenny was already awake, telling her impatiently that Ma had been calling them both for some time, and waiting for Marnie to get up.

It hadn't been necessary to be alone before, Marnie realised, but now it was. She had things to attend to, womanly things, and she didn't want Jenny's gawping, cow-like eyes watching. She swung her legs carefully over the side of the bed, holding them closely together.

'You go on downstairs,' she muttered. 'And ask Ma to come up here a minute while you have your breakfast. I want to ask her something.'

Jenny's curiosity was halted by the glare in Marnie's eyes and she did as she was told, and a few minutes later Ma came into the bedroom.

'What is it, Marnie?' she said irritably. 'The tub's almost boiling and if you think I'm going to soft-soap your Da on account of last night, you're too late. He's gone over to Larksby to see if they'll take you in service. There's no changing his mind now, and you've only brought it on yourself by your flouncing about.'

Marnie felt a choking in her throat. She'd forgotten her Da's threat of last night and paid no heed to the storming words she'd heard beneath her bedroom from the parlour for long after she was sent so ignominiously to bed. Nothing had been so important as the unwelcome discovery in her own body, but now her Ma's words just added to the unwanted feelings burning inside her. And she so wanted to be *loved*, she did, she did . . . Ma was hovering by the door, already preparing to go down and get on with her work again.

'Ma!' Marnie's voice was a sort of croak, and she seemed to cross the room in one great bound without realising that she moved at all. 'It's happened, Ma. Last night, just like you said, only you didn't tell me it would hurt.'

Innocently she produced the soiled piece of linen for which she had substituted a clean piece, and shoved it in front of her Ma's eyes. And incredibly, gloriously, for the first time ever, it seemed to Marnie, Ma's eyes softened imperceptibly towards her elder daughter and she patted her awkwardly on the shoulder. It wasn't as warm as a kiss, but to Marnie it was ecstasy.

'Well now, so it hurts, eh? You're a woman now Marnie, and a woman's made for hurting. It'll not last long, 'specially this first time, and the bleeding will stop in a day or two. But you mind yourself now, my girl, and keep yourself clean. We want no trouble brought home here.' She hesitated as if she'd say more, and then turned towards the door. 'I'll let you off the scrub-wash this morning, and you can set yourself to the baking instead.'

Then she was gone, and Marnie was alone, still with the soiled cloth in her hand. She had no idea what to do with it, but presumably it had to be washed, so she stuffed it inside the old pillow-case with her other dirty clothes. Ma had sounded quite stern at one point, she pondered, but there had still been that unexpected softness in her eyes as if she recognised something in Marnie that was new and shared.

And what had she said? The hurting wouldn't last long and the bleeding would stop in a day or two. So it wasn't going to go on for ever after all, and suddenly Marnie felt as if there was a singing in her veins because she wasn't some kind of circus freak after all either. She was a woman, Ma had said, and as a prize for being so clever she was going to be let off the scrub-wash that day. The curse wasn't so terrible then. In fact, far from making her less desirable to boys it should make her more special. More special than Jenny,

50

because she was too little to make babies yet, but now Marnie could make one whenever she wanted to. Only she knew Ma wouldn't want her to yet, and she'd have to tell Gabe so the next time she saw him.

The brief regret at not being able to repeat the exciting performance in the old mill until she found out about stopping babies from Mrs Kettle made her pause in her dressing. Her agile mind was leapfrogging ahead. Perhaps it would make Gabe all the more eager for her if he had to wait.

And how extraordinary to be thinking about the ways of stopping babies just when she'd discovered the delights of making them. There were suddenly lots of things to think about that hadn't occurred to her yesterday, because yesterday she hadn't been a woman and now she was.

Her spirits were rising rapidly and being restored to their usual brashness as she inspected her face in the mirror, expecting to find some miraculous change in her appearance. There was none, except for the redness around her eyes from last night's crying. She could laugh at herself for getting in such a state about it now. A woman was made for hurting, Ma had said. It sounded noble and dignified, and far removed from the world of little girls in which Jenny still moved.

By the time she was ready to go down for breakfast, Marnie moved with exaggerated slowness and grace down the wooden staircase as befitted a woman, regardless of the fact that no-one took the slightest notice. It didn't matter. *She* knew of her new status, and so did Ma, and she had already completely forgotten where her Da had gone, and that she was unknowingly on the brink of a very different world.

CHAPTER FOUR

It was time to take stock of himself, Mick decided. He'd been a bit uneasy for some while now, worrying about Gabe. But not entirely about Gabe, he admitted. About the two of them. And somehow the brief meeting with the Bray family had pin-pointed his growing sense of failure in the fine hopes with which they'd come to England two years previously.

Two years . . . and what had they accomplished? They had had such a fine send-off, with almost the whole village turning out to wish them well, including Father Flynn, when it was well known he firmly believed in the Irish staying in Ireland and not crossing any water, whether it be narrow or vast. And the tears in the Mammy's eyes had made Mick determined that one of these days he and Gabe would return with money jingling in their pockets to make up for the long hard months of hardship and anguish they'd just come through.

Only the family had seen them on to the boat though, and Mick had been glad of that. He couldn't have stood seeing all those people waving and waving and getting smaller and smaller on the quayside while the lump in his throat had got bigger.

'It won't be for ever, Mammy,' he'd hugged the spare, quivering frame of her to his chest. 'And it's a good life you'll be having with Maureen and Jack.'

'But the town, Mick,' she whispered back. 'All that noise, and so many people rushing about as if the devil himself was after them. People I don't know, and never a blade of grass to be seen.'

He just managed to stop himself reminding her there was hardly a blade of grass to be seen around Drory any more.

Mick had been almost seventeen, already the man of the house since his Pa had died of pneumonia the previous winter. Now, the morning after the potato blight struck its final blow at Drory, he had stared in blind panic at the blackened stubble stretching away from the cottage window as far as the eye could see. Wondering how he was going to be man enough to face this, with Mammy and Maureen and Gabe, and the two skinny little twin sisters, Kathleen and Nora, looking to him for help.

But he didn't know what to do! How could he know? He'd hated their anxious eyes looking to him, wanting to run, to bury his head in the sand and hide—only there was nowhere to run to, and no golden, welcoming soft sand, only the sickening blackness of decay. And the stench of burning as the farmers began the heart-rending task of firing the useless crops on which they had depended so completely. In yesterday's sunlight the fields had been a rich emerald. Now the smoke that reared up into a grey sky was black and choking, and it was the end of hope.

Mick only had to get a whiff of stubble burning, even now, for his stomach to lurch nauseatingly, remembering those first bewildered, weeping days. And the later ones, when days had turned to weeks and then months, and there was no food to be bought or begged or stolen, and the cow had gone dry. And then the final anguish that had taken the two little sisters in a sudden influenza epidemic that had torn through the starving village just as the famine had done.

They had struggled on at Drory for a year, and only Maureen was able to go about with stars in her eyes, because a young man from the town who was a boot-maker wanted to marry her and take her away from the village. For everyone else, the light of hope had long gone out. Except for the few who had fled to America like many from the other villages.

'Jack would take Mammy to the town with us too, Mick,' Maureen told her brother one afternoon when the Mammy was away at the church lighting candles for Kathleen and Nora. 'But there's no room for all of us. Not for you and

53

Gabe as well. I'm sorry, Mick, but that's the way of it, and it's best I speak it plain to you like we always have. Only Mammy won't leave you here.'

Gabe suddenly spoke up from the corner of the room where he'd been staring out of the window. His eyes were hard and bright.

'I don't want to live in the town anyway. I'd hate it there.' His voice was harsh, already knowing at ten years old that this prospective brother-in-law wouldn't want the two clod-hopping brothers in his smart little house. And resenting it angrily, while knowing the truth of the fact that there really was no room for him and Mick at Jack Haggerty's house. Only for Maureen and Mammy.

'I don't want us all to split up,' Maureen went on quickly. 'But there's nothing for us here any more. The land's finished.'

'It's never finished,' Mick snapped. 'Don't ever think it, Maureen. It looks dead now, but in time it'll be just as green and fertile again as it was before.'

'She hasn't *got* time,' his sister said urgently. 'How long is it since you took a good long look at Mammy, Mick? Take a good look at her now, today! She's an old woman. Since Pa went, and then the potatoes failing and then our Kathleen and Nora dying so quick ... God knows how she'll take another winter at Drory.'

'God doesn't know or care,' Mick's voice had hardened, and he ignored his sister's gasp of horror. 'He's a fairy-tale, a myth, put about by men in frocks for children and anybody else gullible enough to listen.'

'Mick, stop it!' Maureen crossed herself quickly, her eyes wide and horrified. 'Is it you I'm listening to, talking like this? If those are your own true feelings, and I can't really believe that they are, then think of Gabe here, and don't be confusing the boy's mind with such blasphemies!'

Mick rushed on, hardly sparing a glance towards his young brother.

'What I believe is that we've all got to get ourselves out of this pit,' he said grimly. 'And I agree with you on one thing. We need to get away from Drory. There are too many bad memories here for all of us now. I think you should marry your Jack just as soon as the arrangements can be made, and take Mammy with you. You say she won't leave Gabe and me. Well, I've got plans for us both. There are a plenty of farms in England that aren't dead, and money to be made by those willing to put their backs into it . . .'

'England? You'd go there?'

'Why not? I'll take their money as well as anybody else's.' He looked across the dimly-lit cottage towards his brother. 'Nobody's heard a word from you yet, Gabe. Come on now, let's have your up or down on it.'

Gabe's face had been rosier than it had been in weeks.

'I'd rather it was America, but if Mick says we go to England, I'm up to it.'

Maureen gave a snort, but there was a tinge of relief in her eyes as well.

'That boy! You've stuffed his head with ideas to match your own, Mick O'Brien. America indeed! And where would we be finding that kind of money?'

'Nobody's asking you to find it,' Mick said curtly. 'America's another fairy-tale for children, and we'll be glad enough to find work in England. Is it agreed then, Gabe?'

'It is indeed!' Gabe's eyes shone as Mick shook his hand on it as if they were both grown men. If he had but known it, as he gazed delightedly into his brother's handsome face, Gabe was feeling more optimistic and grown-up than either of them, for all Mick's fine words.

But it was the only way. It meant security for Maureen and a better life for Mammy. Mammy wasn't that old, she only looked it because of the bad times they'd all gone through. With a bit of genteel living and good food in her belly, she'd probably outlive them all. And as for Gabe and himself, well, they'd just have to throw themselves into the lap of fate and see what happened. His hand was half-raised to cross himself, but he dropped it again. This time he was relying on no-one but himself.

So there had been a wedding in Drory with as much excitement poured into the celebrations as the family could muster, while knowing it meant the end of their being together. Maureen became Mrs Jack Haggerty and Mammy wept a few tears for Kathleen and Nora because her darlings hadn't been here to attend their sister. But the tears and the laughter had to wait, for Mick and Gabe were off to England the very next day, and when they all finally faced each other–he and Gabe with their backs to the sea as if they didn't want to face it until the very last minute–and Maureen with her new husband, and Mammy looking so small and frail between them ... well, it was all Mick could do then to hold on tightly to his own emotions, and not squeeze her in his arms and say it had all been a mistake and they must all go back to Drory again this instant.

Instead, he had held her close and promised to take good care of Gabe and see he came to no harm.

'You'll see he remembers his faith, Mick? And you'll write me letters? Father Flynn has promised he'll come to see me every month and read them to me, if Maureen's too busy.'

Mick's throat had thickened, remembering how proud she'd been when Pa had taught them all to read, even though she always said she never had time for book-learning herself, and was too busy just being Mammy.

'I'll write,' he'd said in her ear, his words for her alone. 'And listen, Mammy. You let Father Flynn read you the letters. When Gabe and me are settled with jobs, I'll send you money every month and you're to save it, you hear? Our Maureen can keep you for the present, but one of these days when there's enough money saved, we'll come back and buy the finest plot of land in Drory for you and Gabe and me. Only it's best that you put the money by, in case we have to move about a bit at first. It's not all for saving though. You're to use however much of it you want to buy any little comforts. You understand now, Mammy?'

'You're a good boy, Mick,' her voice had trembled. 'And I shall tell Father Flynn so. He was worried for you.'

'He needn't worry on my account. Come on now, Mammy, let's see a smile. You'd not send me off to England without a smile for me to remember, would you?'

Now, two years and more later, Mick was remembering that promise to take care of Gabe, and wondering just how far short of it he had fallen. Gabe had certainly run wild since they came to the Fens, and neither of them had set foot in a church since Maureen's wedding. He knew Mammy would grieve if she even guessed at such a thing, and he was careful not to mention it in his monthly letters home. He'd kept faith with the letter-writing anyway, he consoled himself, and a proportion of all the money he and Gabe had earned, whether in good months or bad, had gone across the sea to Maureen's smart town address. He heard back from Mammy occasionally through Father Flynn, and his sister Maureen wrote from time to time in her quick, impatient handwriting to assure him that Mammy was well and looking a deal more fit than she had in a long while. And hinting too that he'd best mind out what he said in his letters home because Father Flynn was still having grave doubts about what he and Gabe were up to in England. Mick frowned, his thoughts back with Gabe again.

He knew well enough that his brother was happy to be at the dyke digging, if only because he loved the open-air life they led. But just lately Mick himself was becoming restless. What had they accomplished after all since coming here? They lived like tramps, they wore filthy clothes and did a dirty job, and they were often taunted by shouts of 'tinkers'. It riled him and troubled him too, and he could just imagine his brother-in-law, Jack Haggerty, turning up his nose even more than its natural shape at the state in which they sometimes trudged home to their mean little hut. Particularly since Maureen had written recently that Jack had now rented a small workshop for his boot-making and had a sign above the door with his name on it in big black letters.

'Haggerty and *son* in a few months' time, God willing,'

she wrote, 'for you're to be an uncle by Christmas, Mick. Uncle Mick and Uncle Gabe. How does that suit you both?'

Mick was pleased if she was pleased. It only surprised him that Jack Haggerty had taken all this time to put a child in Maureen's belly. Surely even Jack Haggerty couldn't be so slow as to have needed so much time to think about it? Thinking of his prim, snub-nosed brother-in-law lying with his rosy sister Maureen, Mick had shaken his head slightly at the incongruity of them together, and let his thoughts wander instead to Peggy.

Perhaps one set of circumstances had set off another, but maybe one of these days he was going to be thinking of taking a wife himself, and how could he offer any girl a share of a rickety hut he shared with a thirteen-year-old boy? Not that marriage was imminent in his mind, but a man needed to prepare for it and to have a proper home to offer a woman. Even if it wasn't Peggy . . . And the first step was to get him and Gabe away from the dykes and their gypsy way of living and find a living-in job with a regular wage. Things could always lead on from there.

He'd been telling himself he was worried about Gabe, but he freely admitted he didn't cut a very spruce figure himself. For some daft reason he remembered the frightened look in little Jenny Bray's eyes that day Gabe had got the splinter out of her heel. Girls had thought him a handsome fellow when he left Ireland, but Jenny Bray had clearly thought him to be a tramp, or worse.

Not that he was over-bothered by the thoughts of little girls, but still, little girls grew up to be bigger ones.

He mentioned none of this to Gabe the morning after they had spoken to Farmer Dan and Farmer Lester Pinnock in the Duck and Drake. He merely announced that they were off to look around their new prospective home, and there'd be no more filthy dyke digging or scrubbing away the smelly, clinging clay from their skins until they were red and raw every night, provided the interview went off all right, and the Missus approved of them.

58

'You are happy about the idea, aren't you, Gabe?' he glanced at his brother, whose face was strangely remote as if he was off somewhere in a world of his own.

Gabe shrugged. He'd rather be walking in the other direction towards the dykes, where there was a glimpse of the Brays' cottage in the distance and always the chance he'd see Marnie again. Or even pretty little Jennifer, whom he could persuade to pass on a message that he wanted to see Marnie in the old mill. Wanted, needed, he wasn't sure which, he only knew he had to repeat the pulsating performance they'd shared, to see if it was all that he remembered and not just another dream. It had all been over so quickly, but he had already passed the point of self-blame, remembering the satisfied look in Marnie's eyes, and eager to prove he was in control of his body and capable of this spectacular happening whenever he wanted it.

'Gabe?' Mick was looking at him anxiously.

'Oh, it's all right,' he felt his face go hot at his brother's searching look. 'Just so long as nobody's going to be scrubbing behind my ears for me every five minutes like Mammy used to.'

'Do you miss her, Gabe? And Drory?'

'I can't really remember Drory, except for the black fields. I remember Mammy, but I don't often think about her. What's the good?'

'What's the good?' Mick echoed. 'She's your mother, Gabe. You can't just stop thinking about her!'

'Why not? You stopped thinking about things, didn't you? Like going to church and all the things Father Flynn taught us!' His voice was accusing. 'I liked Father Flynn. He was fun.'

'All priests are fun to children.' Mick chewed his lip, realising his own bitterness was still brooding away inside him, but until that moment he hadn't guessed it had made such an impression on his brother.

'We can go to church sometime if you want to, Gabe.'

'Maybe. I don't know. How far is it to the Pinnock farm?'

It was an abrupt change of subject, and it troubled Mick,

because he could sense Gabe's embarrassment. Back home at Drory there had never been any embarrassment at discussing religious matters. It had all been open and natural within the family and with Father Flynn, and he felt uneasy at knowing he had been the unwitting cause of turning Gabe away from his beliefs. It was something else he'd have to rectify if he could. Anyway, he was even more convinced that he was doing the right thing in getting the two of them away from the dykes and into a proper living-in job. Gabe was growing up fast and the life of a gypsy could only do him harm. In answer to his brother's question he pointed out the huddle of farm buildings ahead, with the surrounding fields dotted with black and white cows as if they'd been stationed there against the green of the fields like a page from a child's picture-book.

'It's not so far if you want to get back· for a game with Fred Jackson,' Mick said encouragingly. Nor for him to reach Peggy's arms . . .

'Mick, do you know about the curse?' Gabe said suddenly.

'What curse? Has somebody been putting some old country superstition into your head? I know there are a few tales of ghosts hereabouts, and the little people don't only inhabit Ireland.'

'No, not them. The curse.' Oh God, he wished he hadn't started this. He hadn't expected Mick to be so stupid. 'You know—the women's curse.'

Mick stopped suddenly. 'Holy Mother of God, what a question! If that's the sort of discussion you and Fred get up to in the cellar of the Duck and Drake, I'm thinking you'd be better staying in the taproom with me.'

'It wasn't Fred,' Gabe muttered. 'Anyways, do you know about it? Is it like she—is it like I've heard?'

'It all depends what you've heard.' Mick was suddenly gentle. And on who told you . . . just who was it, he'd like to know? But he decided not to pursue it for the moment in view of Gabe's scarlet face, and anyway his brother blurted out the stark facts Marnie had told him in a sudden rush of words.

'That's about it,' Mick nodded. 'Except that it happens once a month.'

'For ever?' Gabe was appalled.

'Well, from the time a girl begins it until she's about fifty, or past the age for child-bearing. Why do you want to know all these things?'

But why shouldn't he know? Mick asked himself immediately. He was the age to be curious and Mick was being neglectful in his duties by not telling him the basic facts of procreation. If Pa had been alive he'd have seen to it, or even Father Flynn, Mick thought. Though why a celibate priest was expected to know all about an activity in which he was never supposed to participate, was yet another enigma of the Catholic Church Mick was finding hardly credible.

But he wasn't going to worry his head about that now, and he was thankful Gabe's attention was suddenly held by the sight of a couple of rabbits scampering away from them across the stubble field, hell-bent for their burrows.

'Did you see them, Mick? Big plump ones and all!'

'Aye, Farmer Dan said there's plenty of them about, and well-fed on his own winter-feed too. He'll be glad to be rid of a few if you fancy setting to with the ferrets, Gabe. You'll have to forget your fine feelings and remember they're vermin. If they eat all the winter-feed, the cows won't get it, so they won't produce so much milk, nor butter nor cheese, so it's us that suffer in the end.'

Mick had always had a logical brain. He also knew how partial his brother was to dairy cheese, and he could see the conflicting emotions on his young face. But Mick won the day, and Gabe finally nodded slowly, seeing the sense of it. Even though back at Drory a rabbit had been a cuddly, furry creature to be petted, over here they were either to be killed or eaten. That was the way of it, and there was no room for sentiment just because he'd once made a hutch for Kathleen and Nora's pet albino and they'd thought he was enormously clever.

That kind of sentiment was for children, Gabe thought,

with a funny kind of lump in his throat, and he wasn't a child any longer. He'd passed that test in the old mill with Marnie, and he unconsciously squared his shoulders and pointed out the long-eared, bronze-coloured dog loping towards them and barking excitedly, followed by Farmer Dan, red-faced and beaming at them.

'Come along then, me bors, my good woman's waiting to take a look at you, and I daresay she'll put some breakfast in your bellies if you ain't had any yet. How d'you fancy eggs still warm from the hens and a slice of bacon that's hardly left the pig's back, young 'un?'

For a second Gabe thought he was going to throw up, but as they neared the long low farm buildings with the neatly thatched roofs, a tantalising smell of bacon frying wafted out across the morning-fresh fields towards him. A smell that made him forget every other consideration save the fact that it seemed like a hundred years since he'd had any sort of breakfast other than thick hunks of dry bread softened with honey, and his taste-buds yearned to be pampered. There was a watering in his mouth, and minutes later Farmer Dan and his brother Lester were urging them to sit at the kitchen table and wrap their lips round the good wholesome food in front of them and then they'd talk business.

And a round-bodied, bustling countrywoman with apple-cheeks just as red as her husband, was clucking at them and saying it was time the little 'un had a woman looking after him by the look of the bones sticking out all over him. He wasn't that thin, except compared to the Pinnocks, and he wasn't that little, but he was too bemused to protest, because of the snowy-white cloth on the table and the matching cups and saucers, and the warm welcome that made his eyes sting.

'It's a fine breakfast, Missus, and more than welcome,' Mick was saying, and Gabe smiled his agreement. Mrs Pinnock beamed at them both, but especially at Gabe.

'Well now, it's nice to be appreciated, and by such a dimpling smile and all. I'm glad you can smile, bor. I was beginning to think a scowl was all we'd be getting from you. Do you think you can bear to live on a farm then?'

Mick was looking at him anxiously, and Gabe saw at once that Mick knew just how churned-up he was inside, even if he didn't know the real reason for it. How could he, when Gabe wasn't too sure of it himself? It had to do with being their own masters–and staying close to Fred to share their growing-up secrets–and Marnie. It had a lot to do with Marnie. He turned quickly from his brother's gaze and smiled again at Mrs Pinnock.

'As long as I can take the dog out sometimes,' he said hopefully, and Farmer Lester laughed out loud.

'Bless us, the lad's putting his own terms to us now. Aye lad, you can take Red out any time you like. He's only a young 'un himself and he'll be glad of a young bor who can stride out a bit with him.'

'That's all right then,' Gabe said. They all laughed again as if he'd said something clever. He'd never known three people laugh as much as the Pinnocks did.

'If you've finished eating, you can come and look at your rooms,' Mrs Pinnock said.

Rooms? A room for each of them? It was true, even if they were tiny and so close to the roof the smell of straw from the thatch was musty and almost overpowering with the windows closed.

But neither of the O'Brien brothers minded about that, and Mick peered through the small square of window-glass to the great flat stretch of land leading away to the South. They had come a good distance from the edge of the Fens where they had lately worked, but the shimmer of water ahead of them took Mick by surprise. Surely they were not that close to the sea? Gabe was the one who asked the question in both their minds.

'Is that one of they broads, Missus?' he said eagerly.

'Well, not one of the big ones,' Mrs Pinnock smiled. 'We're not that far down into the county, Gabe. But it is a little 'un, and big enough to attract whole flocks of birds and wild geese and there are plenty of nests among the reeds. And come the hard spell there'll be ice thick enough to go skating if you've the legs for it.'

Gabe listened, spellbound, as a whole new world unfolded in front of him. Fred must come over, he thought instantly, when he wasn't away on his old barge. And Marnie, there must be a way he could get Marnie to come out here once winter froze the broad . . . he could just picture her dainty feet skimming across the ice, and that long, beautiful hair streaming out behind her in the breeze she created.

'I think you've said the magic words, Missus,' Mick grinned at the farmer's wife as Gabe stared with faraway eyes through the bedroom window, seeing not the panorama in front of him, but Marnie slipping and sliding and laughing into his arms, and her bright-cold cheeks pressed to his own, and his body warming her. Already the bleak dykes were forgotten and the idea of sleeping in a warm bed every night became more attractive by the minute.

'Come next summer, if you're interested, you may get Farmer to take you down the proper broad for the water frolics, Gabe.'

'What are they?' He'd never heard of them and nor had Fred, he wouldn't mind betting.

'Why, all kinds of sailboats racing, and swimming contests and water sports. We generally make a day of it, with Farmer and Lester drawing straws to see who gets left behind to mind the stock.'

As long as Mick and Gabe knew her, Effie Pinnock never referred to her husband as anything other than Farmer.

'You'd best come downstairs now, and Farmer'll show you round outside. I take it the inside is to your liking?'

It was obvious that it was, and they followed her downstairs and out into the yard, where Farmer Dan took over, showing them the chicken coops and the piggery where six fat pink sows stared back at them with disinterested eyes. Then to the milking sheds and the dairy with its churns and butter-making equipment, and the sprawling outbuildings, stacked with straw or farming implements and equipment. And the enthusiastic setter yapping at their heels the whole time to show he was pleased at the arrival of these two new faces.

'Didn't you have a dairy maid once?' Mick suddenly remembered the tales going round the Duck and Drake about her going off with the butcher's boy from the town.

'Aye we did,' Farmer Dan grunted. 'But no more. We've had enough of young women making sheep's eyes all the time whenever a brawny lad appeared. From now on my good woman sees to the dairying.'

It had been on the tip of Gabe's tongue to say he knew a young girl who might suit . . . not that he knew if Marnie would be interested or not, but the thought of them living and working under the same roof was a pleasant one. At Farmer Dan's words, however, he stopped himself in time. He poked around among the interesting pieces of equipment and the fierce-looking scythes, while Mick and Farmer Dan agreed the working arrangements.

'We'll start tomorrow then, Farmer,' Mick nodded. 'We'll need today to sort out our own affairs back yonder and bring over all our belongings. It's not much, but it might take a couple of trips.'

'Take the horse and cart and do it in one,' Farmer said generously. 'I don't want you tired out before you get started, me bors.'

'A couple of walking trips wouldn't tire us out after working the dykes!' Mick grinned. 'But we'll accept the offer of the cart and thank you. We'll be back by sundown.'

They hitched up the horse and cart and a short while later rode back towards the Fens in style, and Gabe was trying frantically to think of a way to persuade Mick that he should be the one to go over to the gaffer at the dykes and tell him they were quitting. He didn't particularly relish the job, but he might get the chance to see Marnie. However, Mick had already decided differently.

'I'll leave you at the hut, Gabe, and you can load everything into the cart while I go on over to the dykes.

The gaffer won't pay you our dues, so there's no use sending you. He'll think you're just playing tricks and trying to get away with the money.'

Mick was right of course. The gaffer wouldn't hand over the money to Gabe unless he produced a deathbed signature from Mick, so there was no help for it. He'd just have to clear out the hut instead, but he watched Mick walk away towards the dykes with a tightness inside him, because by tonight he was going to be miles away from Marnie and how was he ever going to see her again?

'Gabe! Hey, Gabe!'

He swivelled round from piling the hair blankets and the battered carpet-bag containing his and Mick's clothes into the bottom of the cart to see Fred Jackson swaggering towards him, his moonface alight with interest.

'Where'd you get the cart, Gabe? You been thieving on the quiet? Don't you know horse-thieving's a hanging offence?'

'Shut up, Fred. I didn't pinch it. It belongs to the Pinnock farm. Mick and me are working there now.' He felt an unexpected ripple of pride run through him. 'I'm packing up our stuff and Mick's gone to get our dues from Gaffer.' He stared at his friend. 'I thought you'd be working on the river by now. Didn't you get the job on the lighter?'

'Yeah. I start next week. I'll be working with Kenneth Bray.' Fred pulled a face, not overkeen on the bossy way Kenneth had ordered him about as if he was an idiot who knew nothing. He started grumbling about Kenneth, but suddenly realised Gabe wasn't listening and that he had a broad smile on his face.

'I've got something to tell you, Fred. You remember the night you went off to see about that river job? Well, I met Marnie Bray in the old mill by Kettle's farm after supper that night.'

'Yeah?' Fred's eyes widened. 'What did you do then? Did you kiss her? I bet she didn't let you!'

'She let me do more than that,' he said scornfully.

The memory of it came back to him in a rush of heat in

his loins, but for once he didn't try to smother it in an agony of concentration, but let the sweet, quivering sensations do what they would while he told Fred of the delights of seducing a woman.

'By God, Gabe, you're a lucky devil!' Fred's pretence at being the worldly-wise one was momentarily shaken. He couldn't doubt the conviction in his friend's voice, and Gabe felt like Christopher Columbus and Francis Drake all rolled into one at the reception to his news.

'What was it like, Gabe? Was it as good as they say? Did it hurt? Did it last all night?'

'Well, not quite all night! And of course it didn't hurt– well, not exactly–not me, anyway. It was like–like gliding into a smooth warm sunlit pond with no clothes on.'

'Didn't you have any clothes on?' Fred squawked.

'Of course we did–some of 'em, anyways.' He was going to expound a bit further on that, when he suddenly caught sight of Fred's attitude as he sat closelegged on the grass beside him, and the kind of tortured expression in his eyes. And knowing exactly the reason why, Gabe suddenly threw back his head and burst into loud peals of wild coarse laughter.

'Oh you pig, Fred. You horny pig!' he hooted, as soon as he could get out the words. He didn't need to add any more as he saw the sick grin on Fred's face, but then it was happening to him too, and it was warm and lovely and horrifyingly uncontrollable, and he really didn't know whether to be glad or sorry because of it.

CHAPTER FIVE

It was Christmas Eve when Da and Marnie walked up the great driveway of the imposing house called Larksby. No amount of crying and pleading and winding her arms around his neck had shaken her Da's resolve to put her into service and tame her wildness a bit. He'd tried to keep his patience and to explain as calmly as he could in the face of her swimming brown eyes and red-blotched cheeks that it was for her own good and she'd soon learn to enjoy living in such fine surroundings, but to Marnie it was nothing less than another rejection.

She'd been unwanted since birth, her tormented mind wept. The three brawny brothers were the useful ones, and then she had arrived to plague her Ma with the weakness in her chest that still affected her sometimes. Jenny's birth had come at another Christmas-time, while her Da was fuddle-headed with drink, but Marnie had been old enough to remember the way he'd held the new baby high in his arms and laughed with delight over the way her dark-gold hair had grown long and damp and curly from the moment she arrived in the world. His favourite, his darling–even if he rarely showed his affection–and Marnie knew full well to whom it was directed.

And then later, sweet dumpling Davey, who was another boy, and therefore desirable. *She* was the rejected one, the outcast, the one they could well manage without, and *that* was the real reason Da was marching her over to Larksby in the late afternoon of Christmas Eve with her eyes so blotchy and smarting she didn't even notice which way they walked, until they entered the driveway over the frost-crunching ground with the tall trees looming up on either side of them, making it dark and gloomy and oppressive.

So much so that when the trees suddenly gave way to the broad façade of the house with the stone steps climbing towards the front door edged with grotesque, staring-eyed stone gargoyles, the sight was so stunning it caught at her breath and almost made her gag with fright.

Surprisingly, her Da's big hand closed over her own small cold one for an instant.

'They're only people, Marnie,' it was an awkward, late attempt to reassure her. 'Always remember that, no matter who you see here, even if the Queen herself decided to pay a visit. They're people, same as us. They cry when they're hurt and laugh when they're happy.'

He'd never spoken so considerately to her before, and she felt a lump in her throat, even though he'd got it all wrong. Straightforward Da, with his simple country ways, to imagine for one moment that the Queen of England could possibly share the same kind of feelings with such humble subjects as themselves, or to think that she was terrified at the thought of meeting the people who lived here. A surge of bravado spun through her mind. Oh yes, she was, she thought as the surge quickly subsided, and yet there was an undercurrent too of an undeniably leaping, excited, tingling anticipation of what was behind that great door and the myriad windows with the wintery sun probing every facet of sparkle out of them that it could.

Marnie had never been one to dwell too long on past disappointments if something new and exciting was dangled in front of her, and suddenly Larksby was like a great golden key of opportunity, even if she was to be merely a kitchen maid. Her natural optimism streaked far beyond the day, and nothing was impossible . . . and anyway, today was only an interview. Perhaps the Larksby folk wouldn't like her and she could just take a good look round and go right back home again with Da. Her spirits rose by the second.

'You do just as you're told now, and be a credit to your Ma and me, Marnie. There's a big party going on here tomorrow, so Mrs Caine will be specially glad of an extra pair of hands. She's the housekeeper and will keep you in order.'

They were skirting the back of the big house to move round to the servants' entrance at the back, where it was far less grand, but still a palace compared to the cottage on the Fens. She was suddenly aware of the awkward note in her Da's voice, and then she knew. Marnie stopped walking, a horrible sinking feeling gripping her stomach, her mind shrieking in protest. It was a betrayal and she knew it. He was leaving her here today, *now*.

'You're taking me back with you, aren't you, Da?' her voice was shrill. 'You can't leave me here at Christmas–and with Jenny's birthday tomorrow. You said it was just to meet Mrs Caine . . .'

'If I'd told you any more you'd have thrown a tantrum and upset everybody even more,' he said grimly. 'Mrs Caine needs you today and there's an end to arguing. What does a couple of extra days matter anyways?'

Her world was falling apart. Everything familiar splitting and yawning in front of her. Nothing and no-one wanting her, needing her, except the unknown Mrs Caine, whom she hated already. The breath in her chest was a tight ball of hurt.

'They matter to me! You'll all be there without me! Kenneth and Joey and Ted and Davey and you and Ma, all singing happy birthday to Jenny and joining in the Christmas songs without me! It'll be the first time one of us hasn't been there. How could you do it to me! I don't need your bossy Mrs Caine telling me to fetch and carry for a lot of stupid, smarmy toffs.'

'Good gracious me, is that what we are?' an amused voice broke through the choking storm of words that no amount of her Da's shaking could hush, and Marnie glared through hurt, furious eyes at the young man who'd suddenly appeared on horseback at their sides as if from nowhere. He looked down haughtily from his great height as he sat astride the pawing mare, impeccably dressed in riding habit, arrogantly smooth.

70

Marnie was suddenly aware of her Da's strangely deferential voice as he addressed the stranger and that made her madder than ever.

'I beg your pardon, Mr Darryl.' He touched his forehead even though he wore no cap. 'It's my daughter, Marnie, who's come to work in the kitchens. I'm afraid she's got a bit of a hasty temper.'

'She'd better learn to control it then, hadn't she, or she'll be giving Cainey a heart attack before she's been here five minutes.'

He nodded slightly to Da and turned the mare away from them with the merest flick of the reins and pressure from his heels. He sat stiff and straight and elegant, and in that moment of fury Marnie knew both the feeling of being snubbed and the burning desire to make that superior young man beg for her favours. But the spirit in her was soon squashed again, because her Da was railing into her, and no matter how much she raged back she had no choice but to do as he said. She was still a child and had to obey.

She was hauled inside the biggest kitchen she'd ever seen, with a scrubbed wooden table covering most of the floor space. It was loaded at one end with cooking utensils and crockery and silverware, while the pine dresser that took up nearly the whole of one wall was similarly stacked, as well as with the plain thick pottery for the servants' use. The gleaming range glowed with hot coals on which pots and kettles simmered and sang and filled the air with a glorious aroma of cooking. Marnie's startled eyes tried to take it all in at once, along with the silent row of bells above the farther door in sharp contrast with the two red-cheeked women facing each other like verbal duellists across the width of the kitchen table. But their angry voices died down as the newcomers entered with a blast of cold air.

'Let the new girl see to all this silver,' one of the railing voices said triumphantly. 'It's what she's employed for, and I'll need my girls for other duties this evening.'

Marnie swallowed as the two women glared at her, and then the one who hadn't spoken cracked her mouth into a thin smile.

'Well, and it's good news the girl's arrived, Hal Bray, before there's blood spilled here.'

'Now then, Mrs Caine, you know full well you thrive on a bit of healthy ragging with Cook. It wouldn't be Christmas without more feathers flying than the goose's, would it?'

The teasing note in her Da's voice was even more astonishing to Marnie. He never spoke that way at home, and neither did Ma treat him to such talk as this handsome woman who was the housekeeper. A forthright woman, by the looks of her, but more welcoming than Cook, who was by now pushing the sleeves of her overall farther back up her podgy arms and slapping dough on an empty square of table in a fine floury spray, kneading it as if it was Mrs Caine's neck she had under her thick squat hands.

Mrs Caine's chin quivered with indignation and she swept towards another door and jerked her head to Marnie and her Da to follow her through it.

'There's a bit of quiet in here at least, while I look the girl over,' she snapped, slamming the door shut behind them and looking keenly at Marnie, who gaped all around her. 'Well, girl, haven't you seen anything like this before? I thought you were used to washing and ironing, or have you brought her here under a false nose, Hal Bray?'

'I have not!' Da said indignantly. 'She's a fine little laundry maid and she'll do you proud.'

Praise from Da brought the tinge of colour back to Marnie's cheeks as she gazed round her, for truly it was like no other room she'd seen before. One whole wall housed an enormous ironing board with shelves above it holding an array of irons, separate ones for pleating and curling and goffering, all in different sizes and weights. There were several wash-tubs and scrub-boards, dollies and maidens and a huge ornate wringer in gleaming black, brushes and pails and a coal-fired boiler to heat the water. And a proper sink with a tap, instead of having to fetch all the water from the well in an unending procession of back-breaking journeys. A splendid room, and how grand not to be doing the washing and baking all in the same poky room!

'You'd best look at the scullery as well, and then tell us if you think you'll be staying, Miss!' The rancour had gone out of Mrs Caine's voice and she was looking at Marnie with twinkling-eyed amusement at her reactions. A scullery too, instead of the one bulging dresser at home that had to hold everything. Marnie gasped when they went inside the Aladdin's Cave of gadgets and ornaments and implements such as she never knew existed. All shining and polished by diligent hands, it was a place she was never to tire of visiting, examining butter pats and cheese moulds, steak bats and food warmers, aspic jelly moulds and spice boxes, all rubbing shoulders with a hotch-potch of sweet moulds and fish kettles and gleaming copper pans and pottery figurines, fairings and spill holders and match strikers.

'Well girl?' Da's voice said softly..

Marnie nodded slowly. A new world, the thought whispered inside her. Away from the prison of the mean Fen cottage and the ribbing of her brothers and her parents who had no time for love, away from irritating Jenny and adorable Davey. Away from home . . . she felt the lump in her throat again, but she had to make the best of it, and surely this *was* the best of it. She managed to nod at Da, since he seemed to expect it, though she didn't know why he sought her approval, as she was being left here anyway. But Mrs Caine's next words banished the feeling of bitterness, at least for the moment.

'Good. You'll be paid eight pounds a year and given a dress and apron to wear which you'll be expected to keep clean and ironed. You'll share a room with the under housemaid, and if you've any complaints make sure they're genuine before you come bothering me with them. We've no time for cry-babies,' she finished briskly.

Marnie was still reeling with all she'd seen and heard when her Da bade her an awkward goodbye without touching her and told her to be sure to come and see them on her day off.

'One day a month and one evening a week as long as she's indoors by ten o'clock–maybe it had better be nine o'clock for a start,' Mrs Caine assured him. She motioned to him to leave quietly.

Marnie barely heard her. A dress and apron to wear and a room to share with the under housemaid sounded very grand. But it was the other bit of information–payment of eight pounds a year! Money of her own, when she'd had nothing but odd coppers until now. The dizzying thought of eight pounds a year put a sparkle in her eyes that aggravated Cook for some reason when she came into the scullery to fetch some pastry crimps and found her still standing there. Giving herself airs with that shining hair hanging right over the cooking implements as she smoothed the contours of the patterned butter pat with her soft fingers, and her Da still out there yakking in the garden with Mrs Caine in the flirtatious way he had! Cook snorted.

'You'll need that hair cutting off and your nails trimmed before you're going to work in my kitchen, girl!'

The glow fled out of Marnie's eyes. She gasped. Not her hair, not her beautiful hair! She'd die first before she let them touch it. Mrs Caine seemed quite approachable, but she didn't like this old cat who glowered at her over the vast white bolster of her bosom.

'I'll braid it up out of the way,' she said frantically. 'Da wouldn't want me to have it cut. He'd raise a terrible fuss about it. He likes my hair the way it is.'

Their eyes clashed. Marnie trembled from head to foot, but she wouldn't give way in this, she wouldn't. Finally Cook's lips compressed and she tossed her head as she snatched up the pastry crimps and went back to the kitchen.

'See that you do then. We want no carrot-hairs in the soup.'

Left alone, Marnie sagged as if someone had pulled a cork out of her. A young girl, a few years older than herself, poked her head round the scullery door, a girl in a plain brown dress covered by a starched and frilled apron and cap in gleaming white that livened up her sallow complexion and mouse-coloured hair dragged back into a wispy bun at the back of her neck. Her wide mouth smiled with relief at Marnie.

'Are you the new kitchen maid? Thank goodness you've come, or I swear I'd have been scratching Cook's eyes out before the 25th was over. I'm Sal, the under housemaid. Mrs Caine says I'm to show you where we sleep. It's right at the top of the house, of course, so I hope you've got a good pair of legs under that skirt. But at least we can talk as long as we like once we put the candle out without fear of disturbing anybody.'

She was an incurable chatterbox, but from that moment on they were close friends, in league against Cook, the common enemy, partners against the world and the superior attitude of Theresa, the upper housemaid whom Marnie met at supper. Theresa rarely deigned to speak to Marnie, and it suited them both.

The attic room she was to share with Sal seemed a hundred miles away from the kitchens, up the back stairs covered in cheapest cord carpeting–not for the servants' comfort, but so they wouldn't disturb the Larksby family by clattering up and down them. It was a small room with an iron bedstead at each side covered by a straw mattress and a pile of bedding. Beneath each bed was a box for clothes or other possessions. A single chest of drawers separated the two beds, and there was just room for an iron washstand in the space that was left. Marnie didn't mind about the lack of comfort, for she had a friend of her own for the first time in her life and didn't have to share a bed with anybody, and through the uncurtained window she would be able to see the stars at night.

'You're to wear this, Marnie.' Sal handed her a brown dress similar to her own, but with a plain white coverall to put over it instead of the more fancy apron she herself wore. 'That's an odd name you've got, isn't it?'

'It's short for Marina, but nobody ever calls me that. I don't like it anyway.'

'I do. Still, mine's short for Sarah, and I don't like that either, so it's tit for tat, isn't it?'

The little lull in the chatter sent the doubts rushing back into Marnie's mind again.

'Sal, what do I have to do here?' she asked helplessly. 'I don't know what it means, being a kitchen maid. And I've never even seen Mr and Mrs Larksby.'

Sal laughed. 'I shouldn't worry about them, though it's Colonel Larksby, not Mr. You won't come up against them much. Miss Geraldine comes down to the kitchen for a chinwag sometimes. She's the most human of the lot of them, a very pretty young lady with lovely manners. I can't say the same for her brother, Mr Darryl, who's a prize pig when he wants to be.'

Marnie gasped, startled to hear Sal speak so forcefully about the haughty young man she'd seen astride his mare, but warming to her new friend, because it had been her opinion exactly. It was a relief she wouldn't see too much of the Larksby family anyway, but Sal leaned forward conspiratorially.

'You watch out for that one, Marnie. Our Mr Darryl is oh, so correct whenever his family is around, but just let him get you on your own, behind the shrubberies or in a dark passage, and he'll have your skirts up round your head before you can say not today thank you milkman. Still, that's not telling you what you're expected to do in the kitchens, is it?'

She gazed at Marnie thoughtfully, her voice tinged with pity as she went on.

'Just do whatever is asked of you. There'll be grates to be blacked and cleaned, and fires to be riddled and laid. Washing up, silver to be cleaned and polished, kettles to be filled, floors to be scrubbed, anything and everything Cook and Mrs Caine require, including daily duty in the laundry room.'

Marnie almost reeled back in shock. The new life

sounded far more of a drudgery than helping Ma at home, without even the clean fresh air of the fen country, the fields surrounding the cottage, the criss-cross of dykes and the ghostly disused windmills that were so familiar to her eyes. The sudden prickle of tears blurred her vision, remembering one particular windmill and Gabe's arms closing round her. These sweet heady moments were gone for ever, and no amount of money could ever compensate.

'You don't have to do it all on your own, you goose!' Sal's hand was on her arm, her voice full of teasing laughter. 'And I'm sure Mrs Caine will see to it that Cook doesn't put on you too much. She's partial to your Da, Marnie, and she won't want his little girl upset.'

She still teased, even though the idea of anyone being 'partial' to her Da was a comical one to Marnie and she couldn't really believe it. A bell suddenly jangled out in the attic room, making her jump half out of her skin. Sal slipped off her bed and moved towards the door.

'That'll be Cook, thinking we've been up here long enough. Get changed quickly, Marnie, and get back to the kitchen. You can find your way, can't you? Just keep on the same stair carpet and you can't go wrong.'

In time Marnie grew to hate the feel of cord carpet under her feet, though she didn't realise then how it separated 'Us' from 'Them'. It appeared luxurious to her that first day–before she glimpsed the magic world beyond the family doors. But ten minutes later, back in the kitchen and following Cook's hot and flustered instructions, she polished silver and washed plates and dishes and tureens, and ironed a mountain of gleaming damask table linen ready for the grand party the following day. On and on and on . . . and by ten o'clock she was fit to drop and hardly able to drag her feet up the endless stairs to the attic room at the top. Every bit of her ached, and the sound of Cook's waspish tongue at her nervous clumsiness was still ringing in her ears. She flopped down on her bed without removing her dress, just wanting to sleep and sleep and sleep.

'You'd better get undressed before you crumple your dress

and apron,' Sal's voice came to her a few minutes later. 'We've all got to look presentable tomorrow, because on Christmas Day the Colonel likes to include the servants in the family prayers in the morning, and we're all given a little extra something according to our status.' She looked at Marnie dubiously. 'I don't know about you, seeing as you've only just started, but I got sixpence last year and that was my first Christmas here.'

Marnie was too weary to care, but she undressed obediently. Sal offered to help loosen the heavy bronze braids of hair and they cascaded down her back in glorious rippling waves that she didn't even notice. It seemed her head had hardly touched the rough pillow when the hateful bell jangled out again and the process of dressing and rebraiding her hair began all over again. She had a job to stop her lips from trembling in the cold dawn of the attic room, outside which a soft fall of snow was making its first flurries against the window and icing the trees and gardens like spun sugar. For it was Jenny's birthday and Christmas Day, and for all that it was so mean and crowded, she yearned to be there among all that was dear and familiar and home. She missed home and Ma. She missed them all so much . . .

But there was no time for such longings. There was too much to be done, and it seemed she had done a day's work already by the time Mrs Caine inspected them all and herded them upstairs to stand in an awkward row at one side of the plush drawing-room. As well as the female staff there were others Marnie had not seen before–a gardener and his assistant, and two stable-lads. But it was the other occupants of the room and the room itself that numbed Marnie into a feeling of awe. The room was so large that even with its clutter of jardinières and potted plants, heavy drapes and pelmets and every inch of the walls covered with tapestries, family portraits and groups of miniatures, it still gave the appearance of being light and airy by its very size.

On one corner of the heavily patterned carpet stood an

enormous Christmas tree, decorated with gilt-painted fir cones and white-dusted sprigs of holly and mistletoe, small candles that looked dangerously precarious, and the like of which Marnie had never seen before. At the far end of the room was a small railed balcony high above, which Sal told her later was where the musicians played for dancing. If Marnie had been meant to speak at all, it was doubtful whether any sound would have forced itself through her dry lips, but the servants' role and family alike was clearly to be silent and listen dutifully to Colonel Larksby's ponderous voice as he intoned the family prayers.

Marnie looked beneath her long dark lashes at the company assembled opposite them with a mixture of awe and curiosity, never having been so close to the gentry before. They were like opposite sides of opposing armies, the Colonel was a big, bluff man with a huge curling moustache and a jovial sparkle in his eyes. Over his rough tweed-covered paunch he sported a heavy gold watchchain. His trousers were baggy and of the same rough tweed, giving him the appearance of a large shaggy dog. His wife was of nondescript appearance, dun-coloured hair matching her dun-coloured dress, small and dutiful and looking as if she had no mind of her own whatsoever.

'And on this happy Christmas morning, we give thanks to our Lord for the food we eat and the good cheer among us all . . .'

Colonel Larksby droned on while Marnie's feet shifted uncomfortably until Sal nudged her to be still. She continued her perusal of the family since there seemed nowhere else to look. Miss Geraldine Larksby looked about seventeen years old, a year older than her brother, and with more animation in her face than her mother. She wore a green morning dress and her hair curled in pretty fair tendrils around her face. She suddenly caught Marnie's eyes on her and gave her a secret smile that said she was just as bored as anybody else. The smile changed her face to one of exceptional prettiness, and Marnie smiled back, only to replace the smile on her lips by a hasty flattening of her features as she caught the cool, disapproving blue stare of Mr Darryl Larksby on her face. She stared back, unaware that such a performance would be interpreted as insolent, and slotted his appearance into her mind for future reference. Not too tall, stocky, fair of hair, blue of eyes, an out and out toff. There was no doubt of that. Splendid but remote, and she could hardly believe the things Sal had told her about him. Perhaps she had been making it up to tease her.

She relaxed thankfully as the family prayers came to an end and the Colonel approached the servants with a small packet for each one. The rest of the family stayed just where they were, as if there was a gigantic gulf across the expanse of patterned carpet, and Marnie felt a stirring of resentment bubbling inside her that not even the discovery of sixpence in her packet quite removed.

'Is it always like that?' she asked Sal later, letting out her breath in an explosive sigh in the big kitchen, as if she'd been holding it for days.

'Like what?'

'Them–and us. The difference.'

Sal laughed. 'Of course there's a difference, you goose. Why shouldn't there be? I prefer ordinary folk anyway. You wouldn't want a snotty chap like our Mr Darryl sniffing round you anyway, Marnie. A proper dandy he is with his jewels and tie-pins with such spikes in the back it's a wonder he don't stab himself sometimes, and the times he gets Theresa up in his room to help him with them would make his Mama's hair curl if she did but know. Not that Theresa says much, but I've seen her red face when she's come down here again, and I'll bet he's had many a feel there. And the next minute you see him stalking out with one of his fancy walking-sticks, all ebony and silver and never a look in anybody's direction, as if butter wouldn't melt in his mouth. Oh, he's a rare one, is our Mr Darryl.'

She shut up hastily as Mrs Caine came bustling into the kitchen having caught the name on Sal's lips, and telling her tartly not to talk so much about her betters.

'Betters!' Sal shot a glance at Marnie. 'Well, what else is there to talk about?'

'There'll be plenty if you don't get on with your work and leave Marnie to prepare those vegetables. The house guests will want clean glasses to drink from tonight, so I suggest you apply yourself to turning them out and giving them a polish, my girl.'

'We might be allowed to watch the party games, Marnie, if we're good all day, isn't that right, Mrs Caine?' Sal said sweetly as she got down to the task industriously. Mrs Caine snorted, and said she'd see, and muttered as she went off that that girl could charm the birds off the trees if she put her mind to it.

They were kept so busy all day there was no time to be wishing she was somewhere else, Marnie discovered. No time to let her thoughts stray to Gabe and to realise he didn't have any idea where she was, nor she him, nor to wonder if she'd ever see him or his brother again–he'd looked at her so oddly that night in the cottage as if he didn't quite believe her hair was real. No time to brood on the past or dream about the future, for the all-pressing need was to make things run smoothly for those upstairs, to scurry and carry and polish and clean, hot of cheeks and burnt of fingers, for hour after endless hour until at last Mrs Caine said she and Sal could take a glimpse at the party through the rails of the musicians gallery, while the players took their much-needed rest and a glass or two of hot punch to revive them for later efforts.

'But keep out of sight, mind. The guests don't want to see two little brown birds peering down at them.'

They scuttled up the cord-carpeted staircase and through one of the sepia-painted doors leading off it, Marnie following Sal in a fever of suppressed excitement. The thought of watching the elegant company she'd seen arriving in smart carriages some hours earlier and now enjoying themselves in the Larksby drawing-room was almost as good as being part of the festivities, and she had a job not to exclaim out loud at the magnificence of the sight that met her eyes as they knelt by the rails of the gallery and peered down below.

Sparkling jewels and brilliant colours almost assaulted their eyes in the dazzle of the candelabra studded with hundreds of candles for the occasion. A swirl of silks and satins as the ladies moved around the room in a kaleidoscope of colour, a tinkling of well-bred, musical laughter, the deeply flattering voices of gentlemen bedecked like peacocks creating a scene that never left her memory, for it was the first time she had known of its existence. She couldn't quite hide the smothered gasp as she moved an inch or two, and discovered Darryl Larksby's cool blue eyes looking up directly into hers. And saw them looking her way again and again during the half-hour they stayed in their crouching position until the musicians returned and they were forced to go back to the kitchen.

That was the new world then, Marnie thought dizzily. The world upstairs, not this one that was alternately strange and yet drearily familiar, and it was a world she wanted for herself, even if it was as futile a dream as that of Gabe O'Brien yearning for a land of opportunity across an ocean.

'We can't go to bed until they've finished eating and all the clearing away's been done,' Sal said prosaically as they went back downstairs. 'And that'll probably be well into the small hours, so if you get the chance for a quick nap, you'd better take it, Marnie.'

How could she sleep? She was too excited to sleep, too full of all she'd seen, even if Cook was snoring gently by now in her rocking chair by the kitchen range and threatening to spoil the mood of the evening, her small mouth half-open and sagging and wrinkled without her teeth.

'Like a hen's ass,' Sal whispered eloquently. 'Let's go outside and get a breath of air. There are a couple of shawls in the cupboard here.'

Outside the moon was full, smiling down from a clear velvet sky. The snow had stopped long since, crisping the

82

ground into a diamond carpet that sparkled away into the distance. From the back of the house where they stood, the ground sloped away slightly, before resuming its familiar flatness for mile after mile of countryside. Far beyond the grounds of Larksby a few outlying farms and cottages were just visible by their white-painted shapes and the curl of smoke from their chimneys, and there was a glimmer of glassy water that would freeze into a splendid pond for skating once the winter freeze set in properly.

'I could be in a different country for all that I know where I am,' Marnie burst out resentfully. 'It was bad of Da to leave me here the way he did without giving me any warning.'

'You're not sorry, are you? You've got a solid roof over your head and good food in your belly. And there are plenty of lads who come calling at the kitchens,' Sal winked, and then looked at her sharply. 'You are old enough for lads, aren't you, Marnie? About fifteen, are you–same as me?'

'About.' She avoided the question cheerfully. Well, she was tall for her age and most folk thought her older than she was, so why argue with them? But kitchen lads weren't at the top of her mind right then, not after what Sal had told her about Darryl Larksby, and she remembered the cool, appraising look he'd given her that had the sudden power to excite her.

'I've had a romp in the hay with Ben, one of the stable-lads, a couple of times,' Sal was suddenly confidential. 'But he's a bit too grabbing with his hands if you get my meaning. Not much finesse, if that's the right word. Miss Geraldine's always using it, and I think that's right.'

Marnie didn't know if it was or not, but she wasn't interested in Ben the stable-lad. She was wondering about the son of the house, Darryl Larksby, and if his hands were as cool and languorous as his eyes, slowly looking her over, unwilling and yet unable quite to resist showing the interest they felt. Wondering how they'd feel holding her, suddenly wanting to see if she could stir up a blazing excitement in those cool eyes the way she had with Gabe. Both of them had blue eyes, but so different, so different.

'We get the farm boys calling quite regular,' Sal went on. 'Down there near the broad is the Pinnocks' farm. A rum pair of farmers they are, Farmer Dan and Farmer Lester Pinnock. Brothers, so they say, but if one of 'em didn't have a wife you'd think they were more like lovers the way they laugh at each other's jokes and carry on. Still, it's no business of mine, is it? They've just taken on a couple of new hands, and you just missed seeing one of them yesterday when he came with the eggs and milk. A bit young for my taste, but lovely-looking for all that. Black curly hair and dimples in his face when he smiled, and the bluest eyes you ever saw–and the cheek of the devil with his Irish nonsense. Got round Cook in no time, he did, and went off with a huge piece of pie in his hand . . . you're shivering Marnie. We'd best get back inside before you catch a chill.'

Marnie followed, but it wasn't the cold December night that made her shiver from top to toe, nor the heat of the kitchen range that put the glow on her cheeks and the excitement in her heart. It was discovering that she was unknowingly so close to the Pinnock farm, where a new hand with black curly hair and blue, blue smiling eyes that could make her toes curl up, apparently made frequent visits to Larksby. And it was Gabe, of course it was Gabe! It could be no-one else!

And all thoughts of Darryl Larksby and the swift longing for a way of life she had never known vanished as if by the sleight of a magician's hand. She was entirely consumed with longing to see Gabe again. It mattered not one jot that Sal had seen him too and thought he was lovely looking. Marnie gave the coals in the range a jab with the poker without being asked, heedless that she would be the one to clear up the mess from the showering sparks when they cooled . . . she didn't care about anything any more.

The blood was suddenly singing in her veins because Gabe O'Brien hadn't gone out of her life after all, and outside a full yellow moon smiled benignly down on her, just as it should on the important moments of her life. Like a father ... man in the moon ... moon child ... she could almost hear Mrs Kettle's mysterious undertones at that moment. Oh no, it didn't matter what Sal or anyone else thought of Gabe, she thought exultantly, because he's mine, he's mine, he's mine.

CHAPTER SIX

Fred Jackson kept asking himself furiously how anybody could be seasick on a river barge? The humiliation of it stuck in his throat almost as painfully as the gagging bile as he retched and spewed over the side of the lighter drifting on the tide.

They were fastened up at their third calling-place, and the horses nuzzled greedily at their feedbags on the tow-path, pawing the snow-covered ground and probably as anxious as Fred was for them to be under way, tied up to the boat again and trotting along at a fair pace to the next port of call. The queasiness in his stomach seemed to let up a bit once they were moving, but this goddamned bobbing on the tide turned his guts inside out. He lunged for the side of the lighter again, discharging still more of his stomach's contents and sending them floating down river.

'More fish fodder, me bor?' Kenneth Bray's jeering voice was right behind him. They were as antagonistic towards each other as ever, and the other brother, Joey, was only a mite more civil to him. Fred had given up any attempt at making a friend of either of these two. They merely tolerated each other. But he bitterly resented the derision in Kenneth's eyes right now when his stomach felt as raw as sheep-dip and he knew his face must be greener than the grass hidden under the snow.

'Less ale and more victuals is what you need, young Fred,' Kenneth went on relentlessly. 'Just because your Da's an innkeeper don't mean you've got the stomach for it no more than anybody else. Look at you, only half-grown and half-way to being a tippler already.'

'I'm no tippler,' Fred said angrily, the more so at being

looked on as a child by the tall Fenman lounging against the rail as if he owned the boat and the river besides. Damn it, he was well past fourteen and a working man, and if he chose to spend his dues on ale it was his own business. Kenneth Bray wasted enough brass at the Duck and Drake anyway, so he had no room to talk. And if the throb in his head felt like thunder every time a voice was raised or a boat's timber jarred against the bank, that was his problem too, and nothing to do with the ale he'd drunk last night. More likely to do with this bloody freezing weather that was fast taking the charm out of the job for him and making him long for the cheery warmth of a smoke-filled taproom and the musty cellar of the Inn where he'd spent his childhood.

'Suit yourself, bor. Anyway, if you want some food to line your stomach before we move on, there's some hot stew down below.'

The mere thought was enough to make the gorge rise in him again, and the next minute it had forced its way to the surface and he was throwing up what was left of his last meal and the acid liquid contents of his stomach, to the accompaniment of Kenneth's raucous laughter, and that of his brother and the other hands as they caught sight of his convulsions.

But by evening Fred had managed to forget most of the morning's discomfort, and when the lighter had tied up for the night, the twinkling glow of a nearby Inn a short distance from the tow-path beckoned and welcomed him, reminding him that in such a place was warmth and jawing and laughter, songs to be hollered and jugs to be drained till the ale felt as if it was coming out of his ears. And a pleasant muzzy haze to envelop him as he made his unsteady way back to the lighter, to clamber on board and flop on his bunk in a stupor, to dream about girls with soft warm bodies.

Not that he could do much about it if he had a dozen of them all naked and dancing in front of him, with the amount of ale he'd drunk rendering him just about useless. But it didn't much matter. Out here on the river there was little chance of picking up a girl, and those who were on the look-out went for big blokes like Kenneth and Joey and never gave him a second look. They had all the pickings while he had to be content with his dreams, and afford his own newly-discovered relief when the ale didn't diminish him completely.

He wondered if Gabe knew about that one yet. He often wondered about Gabe and how he was getting on at the Pinnock farm with those two old fruits. And about Marnie Bray too, and whether she'd be as willing to open her legs for him as she had been for Gabe. Some buggers had all the luck, Fred thought, and as usual the resentment at his lot resulted in him swaggering about at the Inn that night and spending all the dues in his pocket on more ale than was good for him.

'Time you was leaving, bor,' the landlord was friendly, but firm, by the time it came to slinging out the hard tipplers, the Friday-nighters and the river lads. This one was soon to qualify for the first category, the landlord thought, with a keen look at Fred's ballooning red face that would almost assuredly be turning pea-green by morning.

Fred lurched to his feet obligingly, mellowed by the ale and the company, calling a loud goodnight to anyone who'd answer, and steering as straight a course as possible towards the door. The Bray brothers appeared from another room a few minutes later, and Fred could hear their ribald remarks following his progress along the tow-path alongside the river. He gritted his teeth, needing all his concentration to balance on the slippery ground on legs that didn't fully belong to him any more, and with the glittering, shifting water at the right of his line of vision already making the stomach-heaving sensations begin.

'Hey you, Fred, why don't you try steering a course by the stars? Their lines are about as straight as yours,' Joey's hooting voice called after him.

'I should forget about the lighter for tonight if I was you, bor. You'd do better sleeping it off under a hedgerow. At least they keep still, and with luck we'll be moved off before you come to in the morning,' Kenneth put in his penn'orth.

They weren't going to rile him, Fred told himself, even though he was hot with fury inside. He needed to keep his wits about him. A cold stinging pain suddenly caught the side of his ear as Joey hurled a ball of hardpacked snow at him. It exploded like dancing white stars about his head and so did Fred's temper.

He wheeled round, dragged up a handful of snow and flung it back at the Bray brothers. There was no impetus behind it and the other two merely ducked and pelted him with more snow. Their laughter was loud and aggressive, their catcalls rousing him to a wild rage. He suddenly slipped on the tow-path and hauled himself to his feet again, smarting with humiliation and fury.

'Where are your sealegs, bor?' Kenneth taunted him. 'I heard you was sniffing round the landlord's daughter tonight. It'll take more'n a piddling weak-kneed boy to do a man's job there.'

'It didn't take more'n a boy to take a good poke at your Marnie!' Fred yelled out the words almost before they were formed in his head, and the next minute he was hauled to his feet by his coat collar and Kenneth was shaking the innards out of him till his teeth rattled and his eyes rolled around in his head. The immediate area in front of him was filled by Kenneth's face; hard, dark, incensed, his lips dragged back over his teeth as if they were held taut from somewhere behind his head, and the fumes of ale he breathed out made Fred want to retch even more than the fear wetting his trousers.

'What was that you said?' Kenneth roared in his face. 'You little snot-rag, have you been with our Marnie? I'll kill you inch by bloody inch if you have, and starting with this so you won't find it such a pleasure next time!'

His big right hand suddenly made a grab at Fred's crutch, squeezing tightly and twisting at the same time. Fred let out a scream of agony as pain shot through him like a knife. He kicked out wildly, catching Kenneth on the shin, but nothing was going to make him loosen his hold. Nothing but the truth.

'Not me!' he screamed. 'It wasn't me! It was Gabe O'Brien if you must know, in the disused windmill by Kettle's farm. Ask her yourself if you don't believe me . . .'

'That bloody Irish tinker!' Joe yelled. 'That grinning, smarmy bugger. He's the one we want, Ken, not this little piss-bag.'

'Where is he?' Kenneth demanded, his eyes glittering. He shook Fred's throat with one hand and twisted the damp mass in his crutch again for good measure. Even if he hadn't done the deed, the little snot-rag had known all about it . . . been gloating over the thought of his sister and that Irish bastard and coming all over his pants in his bunk at night. His fingers tightened.

'At the Pinnock farm,' Fred screamed. Red and black spots danced in front of his eyes at the excruciating pain in his groin, sending him half out of his mind and not caring about what he said. The words gushed out of him. 'Gabe and Mick are both there now, working on the farm. That's where you'll find 'em, only don't let on that I was the one who told you! Don't tell 'em!'

The grip on his body slackened, and Fred stumbled to his knees, weak with relief as his private parts began to resume their proper contours. His eyes flooded with water despite himself, and all he could do was kneel there in the snow, rocking back and forth with his hands clutching his groin, praying for the pain to subside and hoping to God he wasn't damaged for life. God help Gabe too, when these two got hold of him–any thoughts of warning him were squashed when Kenneth suddenly grabbed hold of him, by the hair this time, and put his face close to Fred's again.

'All right, you snivelling bastard, but if you know what's good for you, you'll sling your hook on to another lighter. Me and Joey's going after the Irish scum and you'd best not be aboard when we get back.'

He let him go suddenly, sending Fred sprawling. He scrambled to his feet, scarlet-faced and wanting to lash out verbally, since he'd never get the better of these two by force. He backed away, preparing to run along the tow-path to the lighter and the protection of the other deck-hands.

'You should've paid more mind to what your girl was doing on the nights you weren't at the Duck and Drake, Kenneth Bray,' he yelled out in a last burst of bravado. 'Gabe O'Brien ain't the only Irishman knows how to lay a girl, and Mick sure had his fill of your Peggy any time he wanted. She was randy as hell for him . . .'

He wasn't quick enough. With enough noise to rouse the dead the two Bray brothers were on him, punching and kicking and yelling.

'Over the edge with him, Joey. Tip the little bastard in the drink. He'll make good bait for the fishes.'

The water was icy. It penetrated his bones as they sank him time and again, holding him under until his lungs were fit to burst and then yanking him, spluttering and choking and spewing, to the surface again. When he was more drowned than alive, they called a halt.

'All right, that'll do,' Kenneth ordered. 'That'll show him we mean business. We'll get started for the Pinnock farm, Joey. We can pick Ted up on the way and should make it nicely by daybreak. And then there'll be two more smarmy Irish tinkers who'll wish they never crossed that bit of water.'

As their voices receded, Fred tried to see through eyes half-drowned with river water, and to claw his way to the bank. His hands were so cold he could barely get a grip on the reeds, and he was almost too exhausted to haul himself on to the tow-path. The alternative was drowning, and though the idea of just floating off to oblivion after the agonies he'd suffered was strangely sweet, he had no intention of ending up as fishbait on account of Kenneth and Joey Bray. He finally managed to heave himself over the edge of the bank and lay there shivering and panting with the water running out of him as if somebody had turned on a tap.

At that moment he decided he was finished with the river. He was well enough acquainted with the workings of an Inn to find himself a job in some other taproom well away from here and from the Duck and Drake. He could never go back there again, because even if the Bray brothers didn't let on that he had told on Gabe and Mick, he'd never be able to look them in the face again without betraying himself. Nor Peggy either. He suddenly convulsed and spewed up the remaining ale and river water all over the clean white snow, sobering up completely with the final paroxysms that shook his body.

The idea of working indoors, on dry land, in an atmosphere of constant conviviality was suddenly more welcome and desirable than the arms of the most alluring female. Girls were trouble, Fred decided once and for all. He dragged himself to his feet and slouched along to the lighter to change into some dry gear and effect his immediate disappearance from the river for ever.

The following morning there was a heavy ground mist on top of the snow, but the peculiarly brilliant blue of the December sky was dispersing it rapidly as Gabe and Mick crunched over last night's virgin snowfall, across the Pinnock fields to the perimeter of the land they owned. The setter, Red, ran madly along in front of them, scattering snow in wild, excited flurries; showering the two of them as he yapped and barked, jubilant at setting off on such an early start for another morning's rabbiting. The fields hereabouts were honeycombed with warrens and the months before and after Christmas were the season for rabbiting, to line the farmers' cold store with a plentiful supply of meat for stews and pies, and to sell the excess at a handsome profit shared by farmer and catcher.

Mick strode along as eagerly as Red, his tall figure muffled in a thick sweater and jacket, collar turned well up over his ears. Over his shoulder was a long-handled rabbiting spade, from which hung the handbox containing the evil-smelling ferrets used for searching out the prey. Gabe carried the nets and gamebag and a stout stick, and a sick feeling in his stomach, for there was something particularly repugnant to him in setting small animals to catch bigger ones, and then the horrors that followed.

There was much about farming that appalled Gabe. It wasn't just the rearing of fluffy cuddly baby animals and the growing and harvesting of golden wheat and healthy green crops and the warm egg-collection in wicker baskets beloved of storybooks. It was the harsh reality of sorting out livestock that was expendable and dealing with it in the quickest way possible, whether it was rats in the chicken run or a sickly cow past her prime. The ruthlessness with which the seemingly bland and cheerful Pinnock brothers dealt with such unsavoury tasks was sadistic and savage to his mind, and he despised himself for his softness, wishing he could be more of a realist like Mick, because he knew full well it had to be the way of things in order to survive.

That morning his stomach heaved as usual as he and Mick reached their destination and he watched his brother lay the ferret box on the ground in readiness for coping them. Red lay down patiently, chin touching the snow, knowing well enough the need for quiet now the real business was about to begin. At least Farmer Dan hadn't insisted on Mick coping the ferrets by his own method of stitching their mouths up for the duration of the hunt so they could only- attack the rabbits with claws instead of tearing them to pieces before they were retrieved. Even so he had to hold each of the stinking, squirming animals tightly while Mick tied the twine cruelly tight round each vicious mouth and head, trying to ignore the frantic scratchings on his own hands from the needle-like claws. When it was done he pegged down the nets over the likely escape routes and the ferrets were set down the main rabbit runs.

'Should be worth a bob or two today, Gabe,' Mick whispered as they waited while the ferrets went underground. There was no knowing how long it would take, but they were optimistic for a good killing, as the frosts were traditionally supposed to fatten wild rabbits and the temperature had been biting cold for days now.

'With luck it'll be as short and sweet as a donkey's gallop

and we'll be back with a full bag by dinner-time. That'll suit you, heh, Gabe?'

It should do. If only it didn't mean the hulking and legging had to be done before they went back to the farm for their midday meal. The rabbits' bellies had to be slit and gutted and their back legs folded so that they all fitted neatly into one another like spoons in a box for easy carrying. It meant they carried the stench of blood on their hands and clothes for the rest of the day. And the nauseating sound of the clamouring ferrets, released from their coping as they savaged the discarded innards to satiate their greed until the next day when the ritual began all over again. Gabe had no stomach for his own food by the time Effie Pinnock slapped a steaming plateful in front of him, and if it wasn't for the long cool draught of ale that preceded each meal to steady his nerves, he doubted whether he'd eat enough through winter to last till summer.

Drinking ale in the cellar of the Duck and Drake with Fred seemed like part of another world to Gabe now. Then it had been done with the delicious knowledge of something forbidden. Now, it was sheer necessity on his part to keep himself sane. Farming wasn't really the life for him, he admitted, as he and Mick waited motionless for the first rabbits to appear above ground—only to have their necks snapped and their bodies tossed aside until later while the nets were reset for the next catch. He tolerated it for his brother's sake, for Mick seemed born to the land, but Gabe loathed every minute of this part of it at least.

'They're taking their time,' he muttered, as the minutes went by and there was no movement from the warrens. He let his eyes wander around the vast whiteness of fields and hedgerows, towards the small mirrored surface of the broad to the South of them, glittering in the winter sunlight till it made his eyes hurt from looking at it. He continued scanning the horizon, watching the grey puffs of smoke from cottage and farm-house, wishing he was inside one of them now, warming his hands at a log fire instead of crouching in the snow with ears cocked for the slightest sound. A horizon in which any building was something of a relief, and the greystone mass of Larksby in the distance to the North, the most notable one. A fine big house, Gabe acknowledged, and with a Cook who made apple pies to rival Effie Pinnock's. His mouth watered a little, remembering the great wedge she'd treated him to last week, with the hot soft apples oozing out of pastry flaked in mountainous layers, and the hint of cloves to tantalise his tongue.

Red's head suddenly lifted from the snow and his ears flicked up. The sick thrill of the hunt becoming the kill churned Gabe's stomach for a moment, and then the dog began to growl and to scramble to his feet in a flurry of snow.

'Shut the bloody thing up,' Mick hissed. 'Mother of God, what's the matter with him?'

Gabe didn't answer. Or couldn't, through a mouth gone suddenly dry as bone as the sight of three tall figures advancing menacingly towards them blotted out everything else. As if they came out of nowhere. They must have been skulking along in the lee of the hedgerows, hoping to take them by surprise, and so they had, so they had . . .

'Mick, look out!' He suddenly found his voice in a loud yell as he caught the gleam of a knife in Kenneth Bray's hand and saw the stout sticks the others gripped in theirs. Red leapt to his feet properly then, barking furiously and lunging forward, but Joey lashed out with his stick in a vicious blow to the setter's head. The dog fell to the ground without a whimper, his battered head bleeding in a scarlet circle that stained the white ground. All thoughts of rabbiting were forgotten. And it was no time for asking questions as the Brays spread out around them with murder in their eyes. Mick grabbed up the long-handled rabbiting spade, and Gabe grabbed the stick on the ground beside him and braced himself.

'Get 'em, me bors,' Kenneth the leader suddenly bell-owed like a bull. 'Kill the fuckin' swine who got at our

Marnie, and the other bastard for showing him the way.'

The knife flew down towards Gabe's chest. He threw himself sideways, catching the edge of the blade on his left arm. It sliced through his sleeve and seared his flesh. Blood gushed out in a hot tide, making his senses reel. But somehow he held on to them, knowing he couldn't leave all the fighting to Mick, not when the shock of Kenneth's words made him realise it was him they were after. He made a superhuman effort not to retch or faint or sob with terror. He saw Mick swing the rabbiting spade round his head and bring it down with a crack on Joey's shoulder that knocked him cold at once and must surely have broken bones.

'We're even now, you buggers,' Mick roared back, all the Irish in him boiling up like a volcanic eruption. 'God knows what it's all about, but you've been spoiling for this since the first time we saw you, so let's have you. Come on, who's first for having his skull split open and his brains splattered in the snow like pigs' chitterlings?'

Gabe saw Ted glance uncertainly at his oldest brother. With Joey unconscious on the ground the younger one had lost a lot of his spunk. They could almost smell the fear in him. The stick hung loosely from his hand, and with a sudden swift movement Gabe swung his own stick hard across it, knocking it to the ground and snatching it up before Joey could make a grab for it.

'Well done, Gabe. So now there's only one of 'em worth a penn'orth of salt, is there?'

But there was still the silvery gleam of the knife in Kenneth's hand. He poked and prodded it towards Mick, but keeping his distance from the spade wheeling round Mick's head.

'Throw it, Mick! Get him!' Gabe yelled, still with a sharp look-out for Ted. It was one for one now, and he'd back his own brother for wits any day, despite the Fenman's bristling muscles. But the two of them seemed suddenly wary, fencing with each other as if the scent of death was in the air, each pair of eyes watching the other face for the slightest flicker.

'I hear you been visiting the Duck and Drake a few times,

you Irish shitbag.' Jab jab with the knife.

'Jealous, are you?' Mick taunted, the spade still threatening. 'What's up, hasn't our Peggy been too accommodating lately then? It's hardly surprising after what I've given her. She won't be satisfied with a strutting turkeycock who's all words and no action.'

The knife whistled through the air.

'Look out, Mick,' Gabe screamed, but there was a clash of metal as Mick met the knife with the scoop of the spade, and Kenneth made a dive to retrieve it. Mick lunged towards him, but the knife was back in Kenneth's hand, its wicked point directed straight at Mick's heart, and the Fenman was snarling at him.

'By the time I finish with you, you'll have nothing left to offer any woman, nor that randy little bugger over there. Poking little girls in windmills is how he spends his spare time, in case you didn't know it, and I'm not having my sister's belly filled with Irish trash, nor my girl's neither.'

'Let's get Da, Kenneth,' Ted's voice was shrill. 'I'll go for him, shall I?' He looked nervously at Joey, groaning in agony now as he regained consciousness, his arm hanging uselessly by his side, his left shoulder lopsided and flattened.

'Shut your noise, you bleedin' coward,' his brother roared. 'I'll deal with these bastards on my own if you've lost your guts.'

His jaw tightened as if he'd decided to risk the hammering on his skull from the wheeling spade and come in for the kill, when a deafening shot rang out across the stillness of the fields, and the snow suddenly skidded up in their faces from the impact of it. The solid, running figures of Farmer Dan and Farmer Lester loomed up a short distance from them, and Ted hauled Joey to his feet, screaming at Kenneth to get out of there quick before they all had their heads blown off.

Kenneth evidently saw the sense of it and backed away as fast as his brothers. He kept the knife directed towards Mick for a minute longer and then turned tail and ran, with Joey practically dragged along between the other two as they hauled him away from Pinnock land.

'I'll see you again, you bastards,' he yelled back. 'Don't think I've finished with you yet!'

Gabe was already on his knees beside the dog, his own wound forgotten, even though the blood still trickled on to the snow and he'd begun to feel extremely lightheaded. He'd fully expected Red to be dead by now, but the animal's side was still heaving, and the gash in his head wasn't as lethal as it had first appeared. Gabe packed the snow against the wound to stem the bleeding, talking in a low voice all the time and stroking Red's back, while Red's tail wagged feebly and his tongue slid out to lick Gabe's hand.

'You'd best give your arm the same treatment, bor,' Farmer Dan's voice was gruff. 'The dog will live, I've no doubt. He's as tough as couch grass, but I don't know about you. You're as white as the weather. Have you two taken up fighting as a new sport, because I'll not have it if you're going to act up this way too often? You'd best get off and try some other job if you can't abide by the rules.'

'It won't happen again, Farmer,' Mick said thickly. He crossed himself without thinking and muttered 'God willing' under his breath. Because he was bloody sure the Bray brothers *would* come looking for them again, and he had a few things to sort out with young Gabe once he was recovered enough. He felt a sudden anxiety. The boy did look bad–real bad–and Farmer Dan was busy tying his own kerchief round his arm while Gabe assured him through lips pinched and blue that he'd be able to walk back to the farm all right.

'A good hot drink and some food is what you need,' Farmer Dan insisted. And then the sudden commotion at the nets reminded them that this had started out as a rabbiting day and the coped ferrets were going frantic trying to claw into the trapped and terrified rabbits.

'You take the boy back and I'll see to the catch with Mick,' Farmer Lester said, to Gabe's intense relief. 'As long as one of us is here with a gun, there'll be no more intruders likely to come stealing. Maybe we'd best let Mick carry a gun in future, if we're gettin' poachers hereabouts.'

If that was what he thought, Mick was thankful to let him go on thinking it, and to let Farmer Dan help Gabe. make his unsteady way back to the farm with the setter plodding along at his side, from then on his faithful companion. He and Farmer Lester got on with the necessary job of sorting the day's catch, making it presentable for cooking or selling. No need for the whole day to be ruined, and there would be time enough to deal with Gabe and to stew over the accusations Kenneth Bray had made.

Half an hour or so later, Gabe's arm had been washed and salved and tightly bandaged to allow the flesh to knit together. Effie was fussing round him like a mother hen, and talking indignantly about putting man-traps in the fields if there were poachers abroad again.

She was every bit as bad as her men-folk, Gabe thought sickeningly, even though the thick hot soup she put under his nose tasted sweeter than nectar, and he devoured every last drop of it and drained the jug of ale at his side until the colour began returning to his face and the strength to his limbs. Then Effie left him alone to have a rest by the fire, and never mind what Farmer said and whether he thought the boy should be getting back to work or not, because she'd have the last word or her name wasn't Effie Pinnock!

But being inactive only gave him time to think and for the bitterness to grow and fester inside him, because the leaping flames from the logs were like the fire of her hair that he'd wanted so desperately to hold. And how he'd got himself burned . . . she was a prize bitch after all, his beautiful Marnie . . . splitting on him and running to her brothers with their precious secret.

She was one of a breed that wasn't to be trusted–never again as long as he lived. He tipped more ale into his jug and let the cool liquid with its hidden fire run down his throat and relax him a little. This was the true friend, this and the faithful brown eyes of the animal at his feet. The only brown eyes he wanted to see gazing up at him. He pushed away the sudden sweet memory of her arms winding around his neck and the salty tang of her skin touching his . . . never again would he get caught up in that trap. Unwittingly he echoed his one-time friend, Fred Jackson's thoughts. He was done with girls.

CHAPTER SEVEN

It seemed to Marnie as if she spent every spare minute she could straining her eyes across the white expanse of land between Larksby and the Pinnock Farm. Why didn't Gabe come, she fumed? Sal had said he'd been several times with the milk and eggs from the farm. She kept picturing the surprised delight on his face when he discovered where she was. Planning further clandestine meetings maybe on her evening off, and the whole day she was to have once a month. She ached to see him, if only to bring something familiar into this strange life into which she had been plunged so unexpectedly. She pushed her fingers into the tight braided hair at the base of her skull, wishing Sal hadn't pulled it quite so tightly that morning—but there was an extra bonus in the fact that Cook had insisted on her having it braided, because when Marnie pulled it loose at night it cascaded down her back into long loose waves instead of the dyke-straight gleaming hair she'd tried so hard to crimp.

And she wanted Gabe to see her like that. Marnie turned away from the kitchen window with a little stamp of frustration as she heard Cook calling sharply to her to stop star-gazing and attend to the mountain of breakfast dishes waiting to be washed up, or she'd be feeling the weight of her hand across her shoulders. Marnie had learned already that it was no idle threat. The thought had flicked through her mind that maybe Cook was 'partial' to her Da as well as Mrs Caine, and that she resented the way her Da was more flirtatious with the housekeeper. Whatever the reason, it was as well not to incense Cook and feel those lashing hands deal her a stinging blow.

She had been at Larksby a couple of weeks now, and back

to the cottage on her two evenings off. The first time she was still filled with a burning resentment against her Da, but the welcome she got from little Jenny and the subtle difference in Ma's attitude towards her now she was no longer dependent on the family, softened her first intent to rail into the lot of them.

Jenny had been kneeling on a chair at the cottage window, obviously waiting for her sister to arrive home, her fingers tracing the lacy patterns made by the frost on the outside of the glass. As soon as Marnie appeared she waved frantically, and almost threw herself into her arms when she got inside the door.

'I kept asking Ma when you'd be coming home. I wish you hadn't gone away, Marnie!' Her young voice was petulant and complaining. 'It's not fair. The boys aren't any fun any more. Joey sits around all day 'cos he hurt his arm on the river and Ma says he's gettin' in everybody's way.'

Marnie stared in surprise at Joey, who sat glowering at her from his chair near the fire. His arm was strapped up to his side and he looked in a sore temper.

'How did it happen, Joey?' she said sympathetically. She moved towards him and stopped in her tracks as he gave the impression of flinching away from her though he barely moved. But there was definitely something in his attitude that deeply resented her presence, she thought. As if it was *her* fault, and the familiar unwanted feeling seeped into her.

'It's like she says,' he growled. 'I hurt it on the river and I don't want to talk about it.'

He turned abruptly away to stare broodingly into the leaping flames, hating the feeling of uselessness his injury imposed on him, and filling his time with even more useless ideas of how to get his revenge on the O'Brien brothers.

She scooped little Davey up in her arms and nuzzled her face into his fat little neck, hoping for the usual ecstatic response, but he was overtired and not in the mood to be hugged, and he squirmed to get out of her arms, yelling and screaming, just as if he'd forgotten her already. She dumped him down on the floor. Well, at least Jenny seemed pleased

102

to see her, she thought sinkingly. Only somehow it wasn't a thought that pleased her terribly. Jenny was just Jenny. And where were the others?

'*Why* do you have to go away to work, Marnie? Why can't you stay here and work?' she was still stamping about.

'You know full well what your Da told you about that, Jenny,' Ma came into the room with her arms full of stiff, frost-dried washing, ready to be pulled and folded and ironed. She looked at her older daughter. 'It's good to see you, Marnie. Your Da and the other boys won't be back tonight, but this one here's been itching to hear all about the big house. So if you've a mind to help me with this folding you can tell her all about it.'

It was her way of saying she wanted to hear about it too, Marnie realised, and perversely she wasn't going to damn well tell them—not right away anyway. She took the other corners of the coarse cotton sheet her Ma was holding, recognising it as one of Mrs Kettle's.

'Work's work anyway,' she commented tartly. And she was still doing it here, even on her evening off! But it never occurred to her to refuse. Joey suddenly threw down one of Davey's battered wooden toys he was trying to mend with one hand and making a worse mess of it. His inactivity was clearly frustrating him beyond measure.

'She's better off where she is,' he snapped. A sudden surge of pain from his impatient movement sent his free hand to his broken shoulder, and he winced, despite his determination not to let on how badly his body and his pride were hurt.

'Is it bad, Joey?' Marnie hated to see her brother like this, but her Ma told her shortly to leave him be.

'It's done and finished with, Marnie,' Ma went on. 'They say it was a crate of bottles that fell and smashed his shoulder. At least he's alive and it'll mend in time, and what concerns us now is paying the doctor's bill. That's more important than worrying over past history and he asks for no sympathy.'

Nor gets it, Marnie thought. But there was something

about Ma's attitude that told her she didn't fully believe the story no doubt corroborated by the other brothers. And if she could have read Ma's mind at that moment, she'd know she was correct. Ma knew her sons well enough to guess there was more to that broken shoulder of Joey's than they let on, especially when you added to it the fright in Ted's eyes on the day it happened, and the clamped lips of the three boys that told more than words. But she knew too that when they put up a solid front of secrecy there was more chance of hell freezing than getting to the bottom of it.

'Tell me about the big house, Marnie,' Jenny was wheedling now, her soft brown eyes large and beguiling. 'I'm going to ask Da to let me work there when I'm big enough.'

Marnie laughed out loud. 'Fancy asking to work there! You're a silly ninny, Jenny. There's a big fat woman who's the Cook, forever bossing me about and another one called Mrs Caine, the housekeeper, who's always arguing with her. You wouldn't like to be in the kitchen when those two set their tongues against each other! There's my friend, Sal, who shares my bedroom. She's all right.'

It occurred to her that she'd never had a real friend before. And it was nice to be able to use the word, to savour it and roll it around her tongue experimentally. Friend. My friend Sal. Not as sweet perhaps as saying my boy Gabe, –but something of her own all the same. Something she didn't have to share with Jenny. She suddenly smiled at the little sister, waiting expectantly for news of the big house, suddenly feeling important at knowing Ma was itching to know something about it too. She came down from her high horse and began telling them everything.

'You should see the kitchen and the scullery, Ma, as full of different implements as there are stars in the sky. And a special room for doing the washing and ironing so the steam don't get into the baking tins and turn them rusty in no time. It's like–like playing at work in a way.'

Ma snorted a little. Work had always meant red raw

104

hands and an aching back and precious little time for cuddling and kissing. And whether the baking tins were rusty or not, they still had to be scoured and used until they were so thin they fell apart in the Bray cottage.

'What about the fine ladies, Marnie?' Jenny breathed. Her eyes sparkled as she listened. 'Do they wear silk dresses all the time and pretty shoes?' She wriggled her own bare feet about in front of her, clearly longing for the day when she would own shoes.

'What is Colonel Larksby like, Marnie?' Ma couldn't contain her own curiosity any longer. 'And his family? Do you see them at all?'

'Oh yes,' her voice was faintly patronising. 'Colonel and Mrs Larksby are quite nice. There's a daughter called Geraldine. She's very pretty with fair curly hair and blue eyes the colour of the sky. She's quite friendly really.'

'Friendly?' Ma stared. 'You don't mean she talks to you?'

'Yes I do!' Marnie felt the small mounds of her chest swell with importance as Ma's hands paused in the folding of the washing. 'She comes down to the kitchen sometimes, and especially when Cook and Mrs Caine are busy elsewhere. She talks to Sal and me—and Sal says she's taken a liking to me.'

'Well I never.' Ma didn't conceal her astonishment, and Marnie felt a stab of anger. Was it so surprising that somebody should like her, for goodness' sake? She prattled on recklessly.

'And the other day I asked her what a word meant. It's a French word, and she knew it!'

'She must be a very clever young lady.'

'Oh, she had a governess until quite recently, but now she's gone Miss Geraldine feels bored. That's what Sal says anyway, which is why she likes to talk to us.'

'What was the word?' Jenny said eagerly.

'What word?' Marnie's thought had already gone off at a tangent, remembering how delicious it had felt for the three of them to be sitting round the kitchen range, her and Sal in their coarse brown dresses and aprons, and Miss Geraldine in a stiff rustle of green silk. Sitting there as friendly as you like.

'The French word, ninny,' Joey's voice from the fireplace reminded them that he was still there, and unable to resist listening.

'Oh–it was "finesse".' It sounded so elegant, needing to be said slowly, the way Miss Geraldine spoke.

'All right then. Tell us what it means, Miss Cleverclogs.' Joey sounded real nasty for some reason, she thought. She lifted her head.

'It means having good taste and being refined in the way you speak.' Unconsciously, she did just that, which resulted in an explosion of sound from the fireplace chair, and a snappy retort from Ma to Joey not to use foul language in her hearing or he could scrub his mouth out with soap. Marnie reddened, knowing she'd put it on a bit. 'Anyway, you could improve a bit by hearing the way Mr Darryl speaks, Joey. He's only sixteen, two years younger than you, but a proper gentleman in the way he dresses and talks. You should see him when he's dressed to go out riding with his whip and all.'

'Great stupid ponce!' Joey spluttered, outraged at the way his sister was sneering at him. 'I'll bet I could beat him in a fight right now, one-handed as I am.'

'Is that how you came to be laid up?' Ma whipped at him, eagle-eyed. 'Fightin' and swearin'.'

'No it ain't,' Joey snapped. 'We already told you about that.' He glared at Marnie, mimicking her attempt at rounded vowel sounds. 'Mr Darryl's a proper gentleman when he's all dressed up, is he? You'd best see he acts like one and all, unless you want to get landed with a heap of trouble. They fancy people just sling you out on your ear if you try laying anything at their door, mind, no matter how big your belly swells, and I'll wager the Larksby blue eyes can be as cold as anybody else's when it comes to sticking together.'

'Joey, you just stop that kind of talk,' Ma butted in again, her face tight and angry. In front of Jenny too, with her saucer-eyes gaping, and her baby mind trying to get the hang of it all. And Marnie looking as if she knew only too well what all the talk was about. Ma looked at her sharply.

'This Mr Darryl is a gentleman's son, and he wouldn't be taking up with a kitchen maid, would he?' she said, in a voice that demanded reassurance.

' 'Course he wouldn't,' Marnie tossed her head. The waves rippled in the copper sheen of hair cascading loosely down her back. 'You are stupid, Joey, saying such terrible things and worrying Ma like that.'

She was suddenly vastly superior to her brother, even though he was eighteen years old and already a man.

'Anyway, if this is the way I'm going to get bawled at when I come back home, I shan't be so eager to come another time. I don't know why you're so angry with me, Joey. It ain't my fault you got your shoulder all busted.'

'That's all you know,' he muttered under his breath, but before she could demand to know what he meant by that stupid remark, Ma was asking if she wanted some hot soup with them before she went back to Larksby because the time was getting on and it was a long walk. Marnie turned her back on her brother and ignored him for the rest of the evening. As it was, Jenny and Davey had been allowed up far later than usual, and Davey was dropping with sleep on the rug in front of the fire. She offered to put him up to bed before she left the cottage.

He was like a cuddly little butterball, she thought, as she undressed him. Plump rosy cheeks and a thumb permanently enlarged from sucking it, no matter how many times it was pulled from his sleeping mouth at night. Marnie adored him, and he seemed to have recovered his bad temper sufficiently to throw his arms tightly round her neck while she carried him up the rickety staircase to her parents' room and laid him in his cot.

He was so tired he was asleep almost at once, while she stroked the soft hair back from his cheeks. Marnie straightened, watching him sleep, the incessant sucking on the soft thumb a rhythmic, soothing sound. Her eyes were soft as she looked at him, loving him.

Her eyes moved across to the other bed in the room. Her parents' bed, the patchwork quilt hastily thrown over it. Virginal, unused, betraying none of the frantic scufflings and squirmings and gruntings she knew went on there. She shook her head slightly. She could no more relate the beautiful act she and Gabe had performed under the light of the moon in the old mill with her own Ma and Da in their everyday world of work and poverty, than she could relate to the man in the moon.

Not that she could really believe it had ever happened between her and Gabe any more. It all seemed like a hazy dream now, and sometimes it was even difficult to picture his face, at least in the way she had seen it then, above her, with that glowing, spectacular look that she'd never seen on anyone's face before.

'Marnie,' Ma's voice hissed at her from downstairs, and she jumped, realising she'd just been standing here, motionless except for her fingers smoothing the patchwork quilt on her parents' bed, her mind a million miles away.

She hurried out of the room and down the stairs, to where Ma was dishing up four bowls of hot, tasty soup. Suddenly she didn't want to look at Ma, and imagine her with Da that way. She spoke hurriedly as she took her place at the table.

'Miss Geraldine says she'll teach me to read a bit if I like,' she said. 'Seeing as I'm so interested in words.'

Joey snorted. 'What do you want with book-learning? You'll end up marrying some farmer's boy and having a fat little litter of your own. Who're you going to read to then–the cows and pigs?'

Marnie looked at him icily.

'Why shouldn't I learn to read? Just because you're not much good at it, it don't mean I can't be. Anyway, there's no reason why a girl can't read books as well as bring up babbies, is there?'

'I suppose it might be a safer way of passing the time,' he grunted.

108

He was in a funny mood tonight, Marnie thought irritably. She didn't like him tonight. And when Ma suggested he should walk part of the way back to Larksby with her, she hoped he'd say no because of his busted shoulder. But he agreed that it might be a good idea. Jenny clung to her before she left, pressing damp kisses on her face, while Ma merely nodded and told her to mind and keep wrapped up this cold weather.

She strode along beside her tall brother, suddenly tongue-tied. Suddenly glad to get out of that claustrophobic little cottage and realising with a start of surprise that she'd be pleased to get back to her own little room she shared with Sal and have a bit of peace and quiet. She hadn't expected to feel like that.

'You mind on what I said, Marnie,' Joey's voice barked out at her after they'd walked in silence for a while.

'What was that then? You've done nothing but snap at me or talk in riddles all night,' she said crossly.

'About this Mr Darryl,' he growled. 'Don't go letting him touch you. You're not a baby any more, and you know well what I'm on about. You've got a knowing look about you, and there's many a fine gentleman hot for a bit of kitchen sport, despite what Ma thinks. You mind and keep out of his way if he looks like cornering you anywhere.'

Marnie kept her eyes in front of her. It was the first time any of her brothers had spoken to her as if she had anything to offer a man. And though it made her warm with embarrassment, it made her feel good too. Because it meant Joey at least was thinking of her in terms of being a woman and not a little girl. It made her feel important.

For his part, it was on the tip of his tongue to tell her he knew all about her and that bloody O'Brien boy, but something about the proud tilt of her head and the decision he and his brothers had made to keep the knowledge about it strictly to themselves, stopped him. Anyway, he reasoned, perhaps it had been so awful, she wouldn't want to try the experience again in a hurry. He couldn't imagine the Irish boy having much between his legs to boast about.

'I'm all right, Joey, honest,' Marnie said suddenly. 'You don't need to worry about me.'

'That's all right then.' The subject was best forgotten, he thought, with relief. This wasn't his job anyway, only it seemed somebody had had to warn her, and when the opportunity arose, he'd felt obliged to take it. He was glad it was over, and probably this poncey Darryl Larksby would be more interested in riding his horses than riding a kitchen maid. He might even be more interested in his stable-lads. By the time Larksby came into sight, Joey had reassured himself, and watched Marnie walk on until she was safe within sight of the gates. And then he turned and walked off in the direction of home, pushing her out of his mind and concentrating instead on getting back to the cottage and sitting down to take some of the appalling ache out of his shoulder.

But he was never going to feel a twinge there, he thought savagely, without swearing to get his revenge on that bastard Gabe O'Brien for cocking his sister, and the other one for crashing the rabbiting spade down on to his shoulder and putting him through this purgatory.

Marnie had swung on through the gates of Larksby that evening with her chin held high, trying out the smooth, swaying walk that Miss Geraldine had, and wishing she could be like her. She noticed the curtains twitch behind one of the tall windows on the ground floor of the house, and scuttled quickly round to the kitchen door, before anyone came out to chastise her for parading about like one of the gentry.

'Had a good time, Marnie?' Sal looked up from the pillowcase she was mending by the kitchen range.

'All right, I suppose. Is there a cup of cocoa going, Sal?'

'Help yourself. Cook's retired to bed with one of her heads, so I'm hanging on here in case anyone's needed. Mrs Caine's gone off with her gentleman caller.' Sal grinned, winking her eye at Marnie. 'A great hulking blacksmith he is, from the town. Wouldn't fancy him laying across *me* of a night!'

Marnie tried to keep the expression on her face laconic, and not to go pink at Sal's frankness. Though she could hardly imagine Mrs Caine getting up to such antics. Still, she shrugged. It was no business of hers. She made herself some cocoa and suddenly felt extremely sleepy. She gave an enormous yawn and told Sal she thought she'd go to bed as well.

'I'll try not to disturb you when I come up,' Sal said cheerfully. 'Though I doubt if it will be for a couple of hours yet. Keep the fire in our room stoked up, there's a love. It's cold enough to freeze a brass monkey tonight.'

Marnie made her way up the cord-carpeted staircase to the attic room. The fire was low, and once it went out the room was as cold as ice. She picked up the coal bucket, exclaiming as she saw there were only a few nubs of coal there. She put them on the fire. They might keep it going, but they'd need more for the morning. She'd have to go all the way back down to the coal cellar to fetch some out of the servants' allowance. There was no help for it, and Sal would be cold by the time she came to bed, and wouldn't want to bother fetching any.

She put a shawl round her shoulders and made her way back downstairs again and through the narrow dark passage to the coal cellar. She didn't like coming down here, and she shovelled the lumps into the bucket quickly and made her way back out again. Her heart was thumping. Even in daylight it was a gloomy part of the house, but at night it was a hundred times more spooky. She hurried back to the top of the house and into her room.

She stopped immediately she'd closed the door. Something was different. When she'd gone downstairs she'd left the candle burning. Now there was only the smell from the burnt wick, and the only light came from the dying embers of the tiny fire in the grate. Maybe the wind had blown the flame out, but even as the thoughts tumbled over themselves in rapid succession in her mind her eyes grew accustomed to the darkness and took in the humped shape on her bed. She gasped and dropped the bucket of coal, turning frantically for the door handle.

But the shape on the bed suddenly leaped off it and sprang towards her, pinning her against the door. She couldn't see who it was at first, and she was too frightened to scream. The saliva had dried up in her throat, and who was there to hear anyway? Cook just might, but her 'heads' usually resulted in her taking a sleeping draught, and she would probably be insensible by now.

Anyway, she was too busy fighting off her assailant, with his hands roaming all over her body. What did he want of her, she thought hysterically? Who would try to rob a servant girl? She had nothing.

It dawned on her instantly that he wasn't here to rob her. His hands were squeezing the small buds of her breasts, his chin nuzzling into her throat, and then one hand left the top half of her body and was fumbling beneath her skirts until it felt the soft dampness there.

'Come on then, my beauty,' a hoarsely excited voice said in her ear. 'I watched you strutting up the drive tonight, and I decided you'd had long enough to be fancying yourself. Time for me to be doing a bit of fancying instead.'

'Mr Darryl!' She stuttered out his name, knowing that she hadn't been imagining the curtains twitching when she came back to the house. 'Please, no . . .'

'Please *yes*!' He laughed coarsely. 'On to the bed with you, wench. And you just keep on fighting if you've a mind to. I like a bit of a fight.'

He almost threw her on to the bed. It creaked and groaned beneath their combined weight, and Marnie was more frightened than she'd ever been in her life before.

'Let's have a look at you then.' He threw the brown dress over her head so that she shivered in the cold night air. She felt his hands stroke their way towards her groin. She pulled the dress down frantically from her face, humiliated and furious that he should treat her just as an–an object in this way. She clawed at his face, but he merely laughed, and jerked her hand out of the way. His own hands were pawing all over her body, no matter how hard she fought against him.

'I told you I like a fight, wench,' he panted coarsely, as if her resistance excited him even more. 'And don't think I've not seen the way you've looked at me. I'll wager you've been along this road before. It's a pity someone's got here before me, but that'll not stop my pleasure, nor yours!'

His type wouldn't stop to think about giving a woman pleasure, her mind screamed. She suddenly found her voice, and shrieked loudly. 'Get out! Get out of here. Don't, please, don't . . .'

The words tailed off in a loud gurgle, because his one hand clamped down over her mouth, and when he removed it his mouth covered hers, forcing hers open and probing inside it with his tongue in a way that made her want to gag. He smelled of perfume and powder, but if it was supposed to affect her sensuously, it was having the very opposite effect. It was so pungent it sickened her.

Suddenly he moved his weight from her, but her brief moment of relief was soon over. Before she knew what was happening he had slipped out of his breeches and was covering her with his warm body again. It was going to happen, and she could do nothing to stop it. She wouldn't even know how to stop it, and in the light from the moon she could see his cool blue eyes glittering down at her. They held nothing but lust in them.

And it was a lust that shamefully excited her even while it frightened her. She still had wits enough about her to recognise the feeling and hated herself for it. And she knew all too well what came next, but with Gabe it had all been so different. Then, she had wanted it with a child's curiosity and a woman's longing. He was suddenly aware of the gasping sobs that were still throbbing in her throat and looked at her with satisfaction.

'Well, well, wench, so your education hasn't been too complete, has it? It's time we put that to rights.'

'Please,' she gasped, the fear uppermost again. 'Sal will be back soon.' She struggled to half sit up.

'No she won't. And if she was, do you think she's not had plenty of the same and knows when to keep her mouth shut? The lot of you are only good for one thing.'

With a swift movement he pushed her down on her back again and forced her legs apart with the weight of his body. He pressed down on her so hard she could hardly breathe. It was a nightmare beyond belief, and all thought of this act being pleasure had long since gone. Her body had not been prepared to receive him, and his flesh dragged against hers. The springs on the bed screamed out in protest as if in accord with her, and she could only think hysterically that surely it must end soon. Gabe had only taken seconds, and the pain had been over before she had really noticed it, so that she remembered only the excitement and the pleasure, but this went on and on and on until she prayed that she would faint and that if it had to continue she would be insensible.

How could it continue like this? she sobbed, the tears running down her face and into her mouth and ears. He took no notice, seemingly in some kind of trance as he pounded away, grunting and heaving, the sweat glistening on his pallid body. She loathed him for the way he used her, and she would never forgive him for this night . . .

'You're a fine little wench,' he panted against her hair. 'Just ripe and begging for it, weren't you? We'll have plenty of nights like this, so don't you go blabbing your mouth off or it'll be the worse for you. Nobody will believe your word against mine, you hear, so you just lie back and enjoy it.'

Enjoy it? Her mind screamed out in agony at the way her body was being abused. And she knew he could have her any time he wanted her. She was only a servant and had no rights, and she'd be too afraid to tell, anyway. Maybe he thought she was older, she thought suddenly, as he pounded away above her. Maybe if she told him.

'Please, Mr Darryl . . . ' she sobbed. 'I'm barely thirteen.'

He gave a kind of whoop of pleasure and lunged against her in a way that felt as if it must rip her in two.

114

'Even better! The younger the better, I say. Like breaking in a new mare!'

He suddenly raised his head and gave a grotesque imitation of a horse's long-drawn-out whinny, and then he shuddered to a stop and withdrew himself from her. Marnie clamped her legs tightly together, sore and uncomfortably wet and horribly ashamed, as if she had been the one to commit the whole vile act by herself.

She kept her eyes shut, hearing him move about and pull his breeches on again. She just lay there, curled up into a ball on top of her bed, praying he'd leave her. But before he did so, he came back to the bed and yanked hold of her chin, forcing her to look at him. He was so handsome in the light from the window, his eyes glittering and his sensual mouth smiling coarsely down at her. Like a devil, she thought wildly. So handsome and so evil.

'Remember what I said, wench,' he said softly. 'Not a word to anyone, and we'll have some fine times together. You've the makings of a game little filly and there's nothing like a night ride. I'll be calling on you again, wench.'

Somehow she dragged up a semblance of dignity.

'I have a name,' she muttered. 'I'm called Marnie.'

'And I'm *Mr* Darryl,' he jeered. 'And don't you ever forget it!'

Seconds later she heard the door click shut behind him, and she went weak with relief. She moved very carefully, undressing quickly and slipping beneath the covers on her bed. If Sal wanted more coal on the fire she would have to see to it when she came to bed. Marnie closed her eyes with shame. What if Sal had come upstairs a little while ago and seen her writhing about with Mr Darryl? Her face suddenly burned. Did Sal suspect that this would happen? Had she had to suffer his pawings and disgusting perversions before Marnie arrived at Larksby? The idea sickened her, and she turned her face into her pillow, the tears pouring down her cheeks, knowing how she'd been used and would continue to be for as long as Darryl Larksby chose.

Oh Gabe, she wept, I've betrayed you. This was for *us*, those magical moments in the old mill had been destroyed for ever by the lust in Darryl Larksby's body. But Gabe didn't care, she thought bitterly. He hadn't ever tried to see her again, not in the way she'd wanted so badly to see him. He hadn't bothered to come to the cottage again, and he hadn't even told her he was going to work at the Pinnock Farm. Maybe he was embarrassed at what they'd done–or maybe once he'd had her he didn't want to bother any more.

Perhaps there was a reason why he hadn't come to Larksby since her arrival, and only that red-faced farmer's wife had appeared with the provisions they needed. Such as hearing that she was working there, and deciding he didn't want to see her any more, and somehow getting round Mrs Pinnock so she'd go instead. That Gabe could get round anybody with his Irish charm.

Marnie's stomach felt as if it was tightening with hurt and disillusion as the possible reasons for Gabe's non-appearance in her life began to swim into her senses like a great tidal wave. He didn't want her any more when he'd had his fill, the thought screamed into her head. But Darryl–*Mr* Darryl–he'd liked his first taste of her and wanted more–and she was there for the taking, like a lamb to the slaughter.

They were hateful, the whole bastard lot of them, she sobbed into her pillow. Her Da for putting her here in the first place, her high and mighty brothers who thought they could tell her what to do, Darryl Larksby with his superior ways and his nasty little perverted habits, Gabe, on whom she'd lavished all her young love ... bastards, bastards ... and she was never going to trust a single one of them again, as long as she lived.

CHAPTER EIGHT

'Is it true?' Mick demanded.

The smell of the ferrets still clung to him as he faced his brother in his bedroom at the Pinnock farm. Gabe lay sprawled out on top of his bed where Effie Pinnock had finally insisted he should be when faintness kept swamping him.

Normally, Mick was careful to wash away every trace of the ferrets and the clinging fur and blood of the rabbits in the outside wash-house before coming indoors, but today was an exception. He looked down at Gabe with eyes that were as troubled as they were angry. For if Gabe had been doing as the Bray brothers had hollered, then he, Mick, had been sadly lacking in the care of his brother.

It was just as he had feared before they came to work for the Pinnocks. Gabe was growing wild and lawless, and if Father Flynn ever got wind of what had happened in the fields here today, and the cause of it, he'd condemn Mick as being every bit as bad for breaking his spade over the Bray boy's shoulder, and wash his hands of the pair of them.

'If you mean did I meet Marnie in the old mill, yes, it's true,' Gabe said sullenly.

'Well, thank you for not lying to me on one count,' Mick's voice was curt. 'And the rest–the fornicating?'

Gabe couldn't stop his mouth flickering into a brief smile.

'This sounds like being a lecture, because you're using the longest words you can find, as you used to say to Mammy . . .'

'Leave Mammy out of it, Gabe. She'd not be proud of you this day. *Well*?'

The smile faded. 'All right. Whether you use long words

or Kenneth's favourite one, it amounts to the same. Yes, I did it. *We* did it. It takes two for that particular game, remember? You should do, Mick. You and that blowsy barmaid at the Duck and Drake . . .'

He was blustering, his insides turning to jelly at the incensed look on Mick's face, and suddenly his brother's arm lashed out and clipped him on the side of the head. It was the first time it had ever happened, and it rocked Gabe's senses for a minute.

'You silly young bugger,' Mick snapped. 'You can talk about doing a man's job when you're a man and not before. And what do you suppose would have happened if the girl had got in the family way–got caught for a babby, you numskull? It can happen, even to young girls like that one.'

'No it couldn't. She said it couldn't, because she hadn't had the curse.'

Mick stared down at his brother, with everything shifting into place like the pieces of a jig-saw puzzle.

'So that was why you wanted to know all about that on the day we came to see about the jobs here,' he said at last. His anger was quickly evaporating at the defensive, sullen look on Gabe's face. Because if anybody was at fault it was himself, because he'd missed out on an important piece of Gabe's education.

Sweet Jesus, what was more important on this earth than learning about procreation? Everybody had a right to know all there was to know, and it was up to him to tell his young brother, since that was part of the undertaking he'd given to Mammy when they left Drory. To look out for Gabe, and that meant taking on the responsibilities of a father, however embarrassing he found it. He had failed him, and therefore he was partly to blame for all that had happened. He cleared his throat.

'Look Gabe, we'd better talk about this. If you're going to go around the country–uh–fornicating–you'd best know about certain things.'

His attempt at levity faded out as Gabe turned a cold bright stare on him.

118

'I don't need to know anything because it's not going to happen again. Never again!'

'Oh, come on, Gabe, so you got your ass kicked and it's smarting a bit, but never's a long time, and the world's full of pretty girls just as sweet as Marnie Bray. You'll go through plenty of them before you decide on the right one.'

'Shit on them! Aren't you listening to me, Mick? I'm speaking, so listen. Words are coming out of my mouth and I mean what I'm saying. I'm not having any more to do with girls.'

'All right, all right,' Mick placated him as his voice rose angrily. 'Only just remember there are a lot worse things than marriage.'

'I've got no ideas about ending up an old fruit, in case you're worried on that score, nor a priest neither,' Gabe snapped. 'And I don't plan on being answerable to anybody but myself from now on.'

Mick felt suddenly helpless.

'Have I been such a bad brother to you all this time, Gabe? It pains me to think so after the way Mammy gave us her blessing . . .'

'Now *you* leave Mammy out of it, Mick. And get out of my room, will you? You stink of those bloody ferrets and it turns my stomach.'

He rolled over on his side, away from Mick's worried gaze. He'd fully expected his brother to come storming into the farmhouse and lay into him for causing all the trouble between them and Bray brothers. He'd had all the answers ready, and somehow the tables had been turned, and it was Gabe who was bristling with self-righteous indignation, and he wasn't quite sure how it had happened. It wasn't often he got the better of Mick, but his brother's anger had disappeared so quickly it was almost a let-down.

Gabe winced as the weight of his body started the gash in his left arm throbbing again, but he kept his teeth clamped tightly together until he heard Mick clumping downstairs before he let out a low groan of pain. He turned over on to his back again and stared up at the ceiling. It still made him lightheaded if he moved too fast, and the stink of those ferrets really was making him want to retch.

He got up carefully and went across to the window, opening it wide and breathing in great gulps of fresh air. It blew into the room in a clear frosty blast, but it cleared the smell and it crystallised his thinking. You had to be crafty to survive in this world, Gabe decided, and since he was now so firmly established in Effie Pinnock's favour he was in half a mind to get her to put in a word with Farmer, letting him help with the beasts in the fields instead of forever setting those bloody wicked traps.

Only by the time Effie came calling for him to come down for supper that evening, and the talk around the big scrubbed table was man's talk in which she played very little part except in serving up the food and clearing it all away, his nerve failed him. He didn't particularly fancy getting stuck with the label of being an old woman, and anyway, delivering the dairy produce for the farm took up a deal of his time, so for now, he'd settle for that. One of these days the time would be ripe for him to get away and do the things he really wanted to do. Only for the life of him he wasn't too sure just what they were yet.

'I'll not have the lad taking the eggs and milk to Larksby and into the village until that arm's fully healed,' Effie declared once supper was cleared away and Farmers Dan and Lester were filling the farmhouse with fumes from their evil-smelling pipes. Now was clearly the time for her to say her piece, when the men were sated in belly and mind from the day's work. 'There's no sense in sending him out while he's in danger of collapsing with weakness and dropping all my eggs, nor while the gash is likely to split open again. I'll do it myself for a week or two.' Her eyes dared anyone to challenge her.

Gabe let her argue the toss with the men, but the objections were few and they all knew Effie had won the day. He didn't much care whether he was sent out or not, though he couldn't be rabbiting while he was delivering, and the season for it would soon be over. He'd quite liked going up to Larksby. He'd enjoyed the glances the girl with mousey hair had given him, the one they called Sal. And Cook's succulent apple pie could still make his mouth water whenever he thought of it, but he was in no mood to let any woman, young or old, make up to him. For the present, at least, he'd meant what he said to Mick. And it was two weeks later when he took the pony-cart through the snow-crisp fields to Larksby, rapped on the kitchen door and waited for it to be flung open, clapping his hands together to beat off the cold.

Afterwards, neither he nor Marnie could have said who looked more surprised when she opened the door. She'd run to open it at Cook's irritable request, expecting to see Mrs Pinnock again, and there in front of her was Gabe. Her beautiful, black-haired Gabe, with those dimpled cheeks and that devastating smile that lit his blue eyes as if he had a hundred candles behind them.

But they weren't smiling today. They gaped in disbelief at first, taking in her appearance in the brown servants' dress and white coverall, her gleaming hair braided tightly behind her head, her long slim hands dirtied from black-leading the kitchen range.

A wild colour rushed into her cheeks, and a delighted smile widened her mouth as Marnie looked into his eyes, forgetting in the space of a moment every bit of her resolution to hate him for ever.

'Gabe,' she breathed his name in a long sigh. 'I thought you'd never come. I thought I was never going to see you again!'

He recovered himself quickly, reminding himself that she was trouble, to him and to Mick. Because of her he'd got the gash in his arm that still pained him and gave him sleepless nights. Because of her his brother watched every move he made like a hawk, as if he was about to rape Effie Pinnock as soon as look at her. Because of her Mick had changed almost overnight from somebody he could look up to and envy, to a man who professed almost as much piety as Father Flynn, and because it sat so unnaturally on

Mick's lusty shoulders it made him a somewhat comical figure in Gabe's eyes.

So she needn't think she could gaze at him with the sudden glow in her brilliant eyes and expect him to come running again whenever she lifted her little finger. Even if the sudden sight of her had caused his heart to leap in his chest and bang uncomfortably against his ribs–she was trouble. He kept repeating the phrase to himself as he pushed past her into the Larksby kitchen, humping the milk pail into the corner, and the egg-boxes on to the table.

'Well, so it's you again, is it?' Cook smirked at him. 'We were beginning to think you'd abandoned us, hadn't we, Sal?'

'We had!' Sal's eyes flirted mildly with Gabe, sending a searing stab of jealousy through Marnie. Not that Gabe appeared to notice any of them over-much, nor did he seem anxious to linger and partake of the fresh-baked bread and plum preserve that Cook pressed on him. But it was more than he could do to resist it, even though it was obvious he was avoiding her eyes, avoiding talking to her, as if she was nothing, non-existent. She would have been furious if she hadn't been completely mystified.

How could he be like this, after what had happened between them in the old mill? Or was this the way all men acted? It was certainly the way Darryl Larksby did. There had been more occasions since that first time, using her in the same contemptuous way. Needing her for his own pleasure, and treating her to the utmost indifference if he happened to come face to face with her during the course of the day. It was the ultimate in humiliation. But she had never expected Gabe to be like that. Not *Gabe* . . .

When he finally left to go on to the village with more of the Pinnock dairy produce, Marnie made up some pretext to go outside and raced after him before he set off, putting her hand on the pony's bridle to steady her shaking nerves.

'Gabe, what's wrong?' she burst out at once. 'Why won't you talk to me? What have I done? Is it because of all of them in there? We could meet anywhere you say, Gabe.

I'm working here now, but I get one evening off a week and a whole day off every month.'

'What makes you think I'd want to meet you anywhere?' His voice was so harsh and cold and distant she involuntarily stepped back a pace. She stared up at him, her first sweet young love, at the hard, angry contours of his face, and the warmth in her own suddenly left it, leaving only two patches of humiliated colour staining her cheeks.

'Why are you being like this?' her voice was shrill. 'There must be a reason, Gabe.'

She let go of the pony's bridle and clutched at his arm, his left arm where the pain inflicted by her brother's knife still burned, and the indignity of it inflamed his senses even more. He jerked his arm away from her.

'Get away from me, you little bitch,' he snapped. 'I don't want anything more to do with you, understand? Just keep out of my sight and don't try to speak to me when I come here again. And you know the reason well enough, so don't pretend you don't.'

'Gabe, I swear I don't know what you're talking about . . .' she could hear herself becoming hysterical, but he looked so strange, so vindictive, as if he truly hated her.

'Oh yes you do,' he suddenly shouted. 'Whore! Kitchen whore!'

He gave a jerk on the pony's reins and yelled at him to move, and minutes later he was driving the frightened pony furiously away from her, needing to put as much distance between them as he could, as if only by doing so could he rid himself of the sight and sound of her and refuse to believe that she was imprinted in his heart and soul for ever. He would not believe it. No woman on earth could have that much power over a man. But because he was so afraid of the kind of power she held in her femininity, in the gleaming strands of her hair that had wound themselves round his heart almost without him realising it, he had hurled the worst insult he knew at her. And all he wanted to do at this moment was to get away and to pretend he'd never seen her again. But he wasn't turning tail and running either. He wouldn't let them think they'd won, those Brays, and driven him away from the Fens. He just needed time to get himself used to the idea that whenever he went to Larksby she'd be there. And he would totally ignore her.

Marnie watched him drive the pony cart at breakneck speed, fighting down the sudden nausea that filled her. She was stunned. It couldn't be happening, she thought wildly. He had turned against her as if no love between them had ever existed. As if he had never wanted her the way she knew he had, as she had wanted him. She swallowed the great lump in her throat and blinked back the tears welling up in her eyes. What had she done to deserve his fury? And that terrible thing he'd called her that had made her flinch as if he'd struck her. Why, why, why?

The only explanation that she could think of was that somehow, in some devious way, Gabe had got to hear about Darryl Larksby's visits to her room. Kitchen gossip . . . but no-one knew of it, as far as she knew. She had said nothing to Sal, and she was too ashamed of it to confide in anyone. But she supposed Darryl Larksby could have blabbed on about the new kitchen maid while he was at some tavern, drinking himself into a stupor. Maybe somewhere that Gabe had been—or his brother, Mick. The new kitchen maid at Larksby, who was something to be sniggered about and discussed in the smoke-filled taproom of an Inn, and her assets bandied about.

Marnie's face burned as she stood as if frozen while the thoughts whirled around in her head. It could have been Mick, innocently bringing home a spicy piece of gossip to chew over with Gabe at the Pinnock farm, not knowing who the new kitchen maid was . . . and then, when she had flung open the door so delightedly to see Gabe standing outside, all the tales he'd heard would have come rushing into his mind. About her and Darryl Larksby. It all seemed to fit. Whore, he'd shouted at her, kitchen whore.

'Marnie, what on earth's the matter with you?' Sal's voice was suddenly drumming in her ears, and the other

124

girl's hands were shaking her. 'You'll catch your death of cold standing here, and you're shivering? Cook's been yelling at you for the last five minutes, and grumbling about you chasing after the boys. She'll not stand for it unless you're more discreet.'

She made an enormous effort to calm herself, knowing Cook would be as lief to box her ears as anything else if she didn't pull herself together.

'I'm not chasing after boys,' she said through chattering teeth. 'I hate boys if you must know.'

Sal began smiling. 'Oh yes! I've heard that kind of talk before. Our Mr Darryl giving you a bad time, is he?'

Marnie stared at her sickly, and then Sal put her arm round her shoulders and walked her back towards the kitchen.

'Don't worry, love,' she whispered. 'He'll tire of his new sport soon. Just grit your teeth and let him get on with it. It's not so bad if you can make your mind a blank and think about something else. He soon got tired of me anyway.'

She gave Marnie's arm a squeeze, but there was no chance to say any more because Cook was wrenching open the kitchen door and bawling at the pair of them.

'Is this some kind of conspiracy between you two young skivvies? Marnie, get in here and put these eggs away, and what was that young lad shouting about? Were you baiting him? Because I'll not have goings-on in working time, so just you remember that.'

Marnie bit her lips tightly, deciding not to risk a battle of words between her and Cook just then. She was too tense, too vulnerable, and she wouldn't want to dissolve into a mass of weeping jelly in front of this obnoxious woman. Sal winked approvingly and went about her own jobs.

But later, when they had got through the never-ending day and lay side by side in the narrow beds in the attic room they shared, and the candle was snuffed out, Sal leaned up on one elbow and looked across the space between them.

'I should have warned you about Darryl, Marnie,' she said sadly. 'I meant to–but I didn't want to frighten you–and you did imply that you knew all about it, didn't you?'

Marnie felt the slow tears trickling down the sides of her face.

'I didn't know it could be like this,' she said in a small voice. 'So hateful and to feel so–so used. Sal.' She twisted her head to look at the other girl. 'I let you think I was fifteen, the same as you, but I'm not. I'm only thirteen, and before–before I came here it had only happened once. It was very different. With him–Darryl–it's a nightmare.'

She turned her face into the rough pillow and wept, feeling the touch of Sal's hand on her own.

'Does he know you're thirteen?' Sal demanded.

'Yes. I told him. It made no difference.'

'It wouldn't!' Sal said indignantly. 'It would make him all the keener. Somebody should tell on him, Marnie. He shouldn't be allowed to get away with it. You've got years here yet, unless you decide to leave Larksby, and he'll just make use of you whenever he chooses.'

'You said he'd soon tire of me,' Marnie's voice was suddenly frightened.

'Well, I expect he will,' there was no confidence in Sal's voice any more. He liked them young, he'd told her that when she had been the object of his perverse activities. But Marnie was still a child, for all her knowing looks.

'Perhaps we should tell Mrs Caine,' Sal began dubiously.

'Oh no! I couldn't bear it if anybody knew!'

'It's the only way of stopping him, isn't it? I'm bloody sure the Colonel wouldn't allow it to go on any longer.' She sat up in bed properly, her voice suddenly excited as she looked at Marnie. 'Miss Geraldine. We'll tell her about it. She'll think of a way of letting her father know, and she's taken such a fancy to you I'm sure she'll be as indignant about it as anybody.'

Only when the time came, on one of the occasions when the three of them were ensconced in the kitchen and Miss Geraldine was laughing indulgently over Marnie's earnest attempts to read and tripping over the simplest words, it wasn't such an easy matter. How did you say casually to a young lady of quality that her brother was a randy pervert with a nose for the youngest, freshest servant girls he could find? It was impossible.

'What's the matter with you two today?' Geraldine said, when Marnie suddenly threw the children's story book down on the table in disgust at being unable to concentrate and spell out the shortest of words successfully. Her brain seemed to be addled today. Geraldine looked from her to Sal, her delicately-arched brows drawn together in a frown.

'Is there something wrong?' she said quickly, in her high, cultured voice. 'You look very flushed, Marnie. Are you sickening for something? Perhaps you should ask Mrs Caine to give you a draught to settle your stomach.'

'My stomach's all right,' she muttered. She glanced at Sal. Why didn't she help? This was her idea, and now she was a bundle of nerves. Supposing they managed to get the words out and Miss Geraldine didn't believe them? It was a terrible accusation to make about a gentleman, even though she and Sal both knew full well that it was true. But Miss Geraldine might think it was a trumped-up charge to extort money from the Colonel. The implication could so easily be made that they were good-time girls, and by this time tomorrow they could be thrown out of the house. Marnie licked her dry lips, uncertain what to do next.

'How do you spell pervert?' Sal suddenly asked. The other two stared at her red face.

'Good heavens, what a thing to ask,' Geraldine's face was as red as theirs.

'All right then. How about servant? That's a word Marnie ought to know. Perhaps you could make a list of interesting words that would be more useful than a children's story book, Miss Geraldine. Let's see . . . I've mentioned pervert and servant . . . then there's brother . . . ' her voice grew bolder and more reckless. 'How do you spell your brother's name? Darryl, isn't it? And, um, oh, I've said pervert, haven't I . . .?'

Geraldine jumped to her feet, spilling the books she'd

brought with her on to the kitchen floor.

'I think you've said quite enough,' her voice was shrill and tight. She looked from one to the other of them, clearly upset as well as angry, the muscles in her throat working visibly, and her hands shaking. She turned and hurried out of the kitchen with a swish of her skirts, and the other two sagged in their hard chairs.

'Oh Sal, that was terrible,' Marnie's voice trembled. 'What do you think she'll do?'

'God knows, but I couldn't see any other way of doing it. We couldn't just *tell* her, could we?' Sal looked thoughtful, though she too was shaken at her own daring. 'I'll tell you what though, Marnie, she didn't look disbelieving or scandalised as if it was a horrific shock to her shell-like ears, did she? She didn't pretend not to understand or reach for the smelling-salts.'

'She could hardly fail to understand when you kept on saying pervert.'

'Exactly. Makes you wonder if she'd had some inkling already, don't it?'

'I bet she won't come down here again,' Marnie said miserably. 'She was so sweet and pretty, better than the two old trouts forever arguing and snapping at us. She'll hate us now, even if it is all true, for making such a slanderous attack on her brother.'

'I expect you're right, Marnie. Never mind, we've still got each other. Come on, let's pick up these books before Mrs Caine gets back from the village. You know she thinks you're acting above yourself by wanting to learn to read, and Cook will probably shove them in the fire. Anyway, cheer up. Miss Geraldine will probably come down some time or other to collect them, so we'll put them safely in a cupboard until she comes.'

They busied themselves with their allotted tasks for the rest of the morning, putting up with Cook's irascible tongue when she began picking fault with everything, from Marnie's haphazard stacking of the baking trays to Sal's uneven stitching on the family pillow-cases. Mrs Caine

128

arrived back, hot and breathless from the village, and sailed about her duties with a stony expression on her face.

'She's probably had words with her blacksmith friend,' Sal giggled to Marnie. 'Did you see how flushed she was? I bet he wanted to tickle her fancy behind the anvil.'

Marnie giggled back, the thought of anybody wanting to tickle the likes of Mrs Caine as unlikely as her Da relenting and coming to Larksby to bring her home. The sudden giggling ended up as a kind of choking sound in her throat. He'd never do that, of course. She'd even toyed with the idea of telling him about Mr Darryl, but she'd end up getting the roughness of his tongue and his stick for leading him on, no doubt . . . and if she dared to tell her brothers, they'd be up here in a murderous rage and she didn't care to think of the consequences, not for them or for Mr Darryl.

She couldn't seem to get her mind off the situation, nor the worry that Sal may have done irreparable harm this morning.

She and Sal were giving the silver an extra rub up when Mrs Caine suddenly burst into the kitchen, her handsome face agog with excitement, clearly bursting to tell some interesting tit-bit of news.

'There's such a rumpus going on upstairs,' she gave Cook's arm a shake to waken her, their usual differences forgotten in the importance of her announcement. 'There's the four of them in the drawing-room, with the Colonel as red as a turkey-cock and Mrs Larksby in tears and swooning off every ten seconds and ringing the bell for Theresa to bring her the smelling-salts. Poor Theresa–the minute she gets in the room, the Colonel's roaring at her to get out, and she's gone scuttling upstairs in a flood of tears herself now.'

Marnie could spare only a passing thought for the upper housemaid who was as snobbish as any of the family, and rarely deigned to sit with her and Sal in the kitchen. She caught Sal's eye, aware that her heart was pounding inside her.

'Go on then, Mrs Caine,' Cook urged, her little eyes glistening as the scent of scandal filled the air. 'What's it all about? Has she found him out in some lecherous doings?'

'Of course not, you ninny. No, it's the young 'un! The dandy! Been caught out playing about with village girls, I wouldn't wonder, and not for the first time. Remember all that fuss a while back, Cook? Oh ho, he was on the carpet this afternoon and no mistake.'

'And the Colonel allowed Miss Geraldine and her mother to stay there and listen to it all?' Cook was clearly affronted, despite her own eagerness to hear everything there was to hear.

'It appeared it was Miss Geraldine who made the accusations as far as I could tell,' Mrs Caine frowned. 'Not a pretty thing for a young lady to do, I must confess, but if she had the well-being of some poor wretched girl in mind, one can only commend her. It really threw the cat among the pigeons upstairs.'

'Did you hear any names mentioned?' Cook said eagerly. Marnie held her breath, aware that Sal was doing the same.

Mrs Caine snorted. 'No,' she said regretfully. 'They shut up every time I went in the room, but I heard enough to get the drift of it, and this time the Colonel's had enough. He's packing Mr Darryl off to some fancy college until he goes to the university and then talking of sending him abroad. It's clear he don't want no kind of scandal around here nor young strumpets with swelling bellies trying to worm their way into the family fortunes!'

Marnie felt a flood of relief at Mrs Caine's words. If Mr Darryl was really going to be sent away she could breathe easy in her bed without the hateful thought of him touching her again. Miss Geraldine *had* believed it then, and there had been 'a fuss a while back', apparently with some village girl, so maybe the Colonel had half-suspected his son's weakness long before now.

'You two had better close your mouths before the flies get in,' Mrs Caine said briskly to her and Sal. 'And perhaps this will serve as a warning to you both, never to get entangled with young gentlemen, for it'll end in nothing but disgrace on both sides. Not that any young gentleman would be looking twice at either of you, but you'll see now how the gentry stick together and defend their own, and quite rightly too. Now stop gawping, and put some tea in the pot, Marnie, and make us all some refreshment. I'm quite parched after all that excitement, and I'm sure Cook is as well.'

They were united for once in a common interest, and gossiped the next half hour away while they sipped noisily at their tea, indulging in a wedge of seed cake and allowing Marnie and Sal to do the same. The two of them managed to escape to the laundry room a little while later whilst the two women were still nodding their heads together, and danced round the room gleefully, their eyes shining.

'It worked, Sal! You clever thing. I had visions of being hauled up in front of the Colonel and being given our marching orders for daring to slander his precious son. And instead of that, he's the one who's leaving. It's like Christmas all over again!'

Sal laughed at her jubilation.

'He hasn't gone yet, mind. But you're right, and the thought of never having to see his snotty face looking down on us when we know damn well what goes on in that sick mind of his is better than all the presents under the tree. Hooray for Miss Geraldine. Dare we thank her, do you think?'

Marnie shook her head. 'Better leave it. Let her come to us if she wants to. She won't want to face us yet. He is her brother after all, Sal, and she must be sick at heart at having had to expose him like that.'

'There's a lot of horse sense in that noddle-head of yours, isn't there, love? You're quite sure you're only thirteen, I suppose, and your Da hasn't been having you on all these years?' she said teasingly.

Marnie laughed, knowing she meant it as a compliment. All the same, she wished Sal hadn't used those particular words about her having horse sense. It reminded her sharply of Mr Darryl and his peculiarity . . . and she was remembering the strange way he reared his head and whinnied. She gave an uncontrollable shudder.

CHAPTER NINE

He came to her room one more time before he left Larksby for his fancy college.

He'd been so distant to stable-lads and servants alike since his humiliating reprimand from his father in front of his mother and sister, that Marnie began to believe Darryl was actually ashamed of his behaviour and cutting himself off from all contact other than his horse, on which he rode furiously every morning. Not that she glanced his way any more than she was obliged, for the very sight of him could make the sickness creep into her stomach again, and she was counting the days until he left at the end of January.

It was Sal's day off, and she had begged permission to stay away all night because she was visiting her family east of King's Lynn, and it was such a journey there and back in one day.

'You mind and get back here early tomorrow morning,' Mrs Caine told her sternly. 'If you don't get your work done properly, you'll just have to stay up half the night tomorrow night to make up for it. We've no time for idlers.'

'Yes, Mrs Caine,' Sal spoke demurely, sticking her tongue out behind the housekeeper's back as soon as she'd swept out of the kitchen. 'Silly old trout. Acting as if she's the Queen bestowing a great honour on me! Anyway, I'll see you tomorrow, Marnie. Enjoy the luxury of having the room to yourself!'

It would be a novelty anyway, and the first time it had ever happened, Marnie realised. And it was her own day off tomorrow, so once Sal got back she'd be going off home to the cottage to tell what it was like to have a room of her own at a posh house like Larksby. It struck her as she was pulling the brown dress over her head at the end of that day, when she was nearly dropping with weariness at doing Sal's work as well as her own, that her little sister Jenny had their own room at the cottage all to herself now. Trust Jenny to get the better bargain, she thought sulkily. But she didn't have the plush surroundings of Larksby, even if it was only viewed through a servant's eyes. She crossed to the window and peered out at the moon-white landscape outside. Not quite as stark as it had been recently, now the snow was beginning to melt in the slow thaw, and patches of green grass and shrubs were pushing their way through in the lawns and gardens.

She sensed the opening of her door rather than heard it. Her heart gave a giant leap in her chest as she swung round, all her nerves tingling, to see Darryl Larksby's shape outlined against the door, his hands behind his back as he lounged there watching her.

'What do you want?' she stuttered. The sound of her own heartbeats was suddenly deafening as she heard his coarse laugh, and he slowly advanced towards her.

'Now there's a silly question, wench,' he spat out the words. 'Didn't you expect me then? Surely you knew I'd want to thank you for arranging for my education to be finished in such style.'

'Thank me?' her eyes were huge and dark with fear. She backed against the chest between the beds, but there was no escape and she knew it. He shot out a hand and yanked at her white shift, splitting the front seam to expose her small high breasts. He fondled them roughly with one hand.

'On the bed,' he commanded. 'Quickly!'

He brought his other hand round in front of him and Marnie gasped as she saw he had a riding whip in it. He pushed her on to the bed, flung the whip down and stripped off all his clothes. His white belly was flabby, but nothing else about him was slack. He climbed across her without ceremony, spreading her thighs with his body and driving into her. She gave a wild scream of pain but he clamped his hand across her mouth.

133

'Shut your noise,' he snarled. 'And make the most of it, for it's probably the last time for a while. Now don't tell me you're glad to hear that? Not after all the good times we've had!'

He thrust into her brutally, and in desperation Marnie sank her teeth into his shoulder, tasting the blood on her lips as he swore at her and slapped her face.

'I'll scream the house down,' she gasped through stinging eyes. 'Your father will flay you alive if he knows you've been up here again.'

'Who's to tell him? The same one as before by dropping little bits of poison into my sister's ears?' he snapped. 'Not you, piss-pot. And there's nobody going to hear you if you yell all night. The walls at Larksby are thick enough, and that fool of a cook was snoring soundly when I passed her room. So we've got the whole night for me to give you something you'll remember, haven't we?'

She couldn't control her terrified sobbing at his words.

'You're–you're hurting me,' she managed to say between her sobs.

He laughed cruelly, and she saw that that was what he intended. He was making her pay. She should have been on her guard and expected this to happen. And from the look on his face she knew there'd be no pleading with him. And no help from anyone. There was nothing she could do but lie there and endure it, just as before.

It almost made her retch to hear his grunts of satisfaction, but she knew from past experience that if this appalling ritual had to go on it would be easier on her to be quiet and pray that it would soon be over. And at last she thought he'd had enough when he suddenly rolled off her.

'Turn over,' he ordered.

She looked at him fearfully, and he pushed her on to her face with an impatient oath. She lay there, hardly able to breathe for the fear and loathing she felt for him.

'Not like that, you halfwit. Stick your ass in the air.'

He pushed her knees forward and then mounted her from behind, while she gripped the pillow in terror. And suddenly it seemed as if he went wild. He gripped on to her long hair with one hand, while with the other one he slashed the riding-whip back and forth across her back in a frenzy.

'Giddy up, giddy up, you clod-hopping mare! I'll show you who's master. You'll remember me when I'm gone, won't you, whore?'

She could hardly catch her breath between the beatings, and she was half afraid he was going to break her neck with his jerkings on her hair, and in the end all she seemed able to do was make incomprehensible gurglings in her throat as he speared into her. Then she felt him suddenly go rigid as it ended, and there was the disgusting sound of him whinnying in triumph.

She didn't even notice him leave. She was too concerned with the pain that seemed to envelop her everywhere. She stretched her legs slowly from their tight, cramped position, and tried to lay perfectly still on her stomach. Her head and neck ached appallingly, and her throat was parched and dry. Between her thighs was an agony of burning, and her back . . . the tears that seemed to have been in her eyes for ever were blurring them again. Her back throbbed from the lashings of the whip, and if she tried to ease the cotton shift away from it she sucked in her breath at the stinging of it.

She was probably going to die, Marnie thought dully. The pain was too much for anybody to bear, and when Sal got back tomorrow morning and came up here, she'd find her cold and rigid on her bed. No-one would know what had happened. No-one would care, no-one in the whole world, because she was a nobody. Her parents had cast her out and Gabe didn't want her any more. That hateful Darryl Larksby had treated her as an animal, nobody would want her after this anyway . . . she might just as well be dead. Shame and self-pity welled up inside her in shuddering sobs, and the panic of being so completely alone quickened her breathing so that she truly thought her last moments had come, and when the room appeared to swim about in front of her, she didn't try to fight it. She welcomed the sweet oblivion of unconsciousness.

'Marnie! Oh God, Marnie, wake up! What's he done to you?'

She was aware that her eyes were open, but it wasn't easy to focus them on anything. She could hear a voice, Sal's voice. It was frightened, bordering on panic, and it was very close to her ear. She tried to speak, but her lips were chapped and swollen where she'd been breathing open-mouthed, her nostrils clogged. Slowly she began to bring Sal's hazy shape into her range of vision, and saw the surge of relief come into the other girl's eyes.

'Thank heaven! I thought you were dead for a minute. You look terrible, and your back, oh my God, your poor back! He needs . . .'

'If you say horse whipping, I'll strangle you,' Marnie said huskily.

'He needs locking up,' Sal said viciously, her eyes moist. 'I should fetch someone to see you, to prove once and for all what he is.'

'No! Don't tell, Sal, please don't tell!' The shame of it was almost as bad as the agony she felt at moving every muscle. 'I'll be all right if I stay up here today. Cook and Mrs Caine will think I've gone home as it's my day off, and if you can sneak up a drink for me now and again, I'll manage.'

'You'll need food, and that back needs medical attention. Your shift is stuck to it where the weals have opened. They could be infected if you don't have a doctor to see to them.'

'Sal, please!' Marnie begged her. 'If you could just leave me to sleep, I'll get over it. I've had a few whacks from Da in my time, and I heal quickly.'

'None like this, I'll wager,' Sal said grimly. 'Well, if you won't let me get help for you, at least let me bathe the weals and put some salve on them. I've got some excellent stuff in my drawer the doctor gave me once when I scraped my leg badly in a fall. It'll maybe hurt a bit, but you can't let them stay like that with your shift sticking to them.'

It hurt so bad it was all Marnie could do not to scream out loud as Sal got on with the job. But it had to be done, and fairly quickly, or Mrs Caine would come storming up here to demand to know why Sal wasn't about her work, and she would be discovered. She gripped the pillow while Sal worked as gently as she could on her back, stuffing it in her mouth to stop from crying out, telling herself no pain could be as bad as the pain of last night . . . and at last Sal said she'd do.

The day passed somehow. She drifted in and out of sleep with no notion of time. When Sal brought her hot drinks and a carefully hidden bowl of broth she obediently drank, and by the time it began to grow dusk she was beginning to feel a little easier and aching from lying face down for the last twenty-four hours. She eased herself on to her side, finding some relief in just changing her position, and managed a smile when Sal came up to see how she was feeling.

'Not so bad,' she said huskily. 'Sal–thanks. For every- thing.'

Sal shrugged away her thanks. 'I've lain the seeds downstairs, Marnie. I've told them you came in a little while ago, shivering and feverish, and sneezing all over the place. Cook's terrified of illness and spreading germs in her kitchen, and she's snapping to Mrs Caine that she won't let you set foot down there until you've got rid of your fever. Mrs Caine may look in to make sure I'm not lying, but as long as you're in bed and sniffing a bit, she'll not come through the door, so you can stay up here for a few days with their blessing and I'll bring your meals up. Oh–and Mr Darryl's leaving first thing in the morning, and they're having a little party for him tonight, for appearances' sake, I suspect, so he won't try bothering you again. I thought you'd like to know.'

The weak tears ran down her face as soon as Sal went out of the room. Thank God, thank God, thank *you* God, was all she could think. And thank you Sal. Only another woman would do what she had done, she thought with gratitude. One who knew what it was like to be used by a man. At thirteen, Marnie already felt as old as the hills.

And thank God she didn't have to make her way unsteadily down the cord-carpeted staircase until her pretended fever was gone. It was good to have someone who cared about her and not to feel completely abandoned and alone.

Mrs Caine looked in briefly during the next morning. She was half-asleep, her face flushed from a bout of self-pitying weeping, and sufficiently dishevelled for the housekeeper to believe Sal's story. She hovered near the door.

'Your father's in the kitchen, Marnie. He can come up to see you for a few minutes if you wish.'

Da here? To see her? The flood of joy she felt subsided a little as Mrs Caine went on to say he'd called delivering some flour from the mill where he'd been working a few days. Of course he wouldn't call specifically to see *her*, but still, he was here, and she'd be glad to see him. He was still her Da.

When he appeared, dusty and white from the mill, and filling the room with a dryness that made her cough a little, he stood well away from the bed for fear of catching the imaginary fever and taking it back home to the little ones. With Joey not bringing in any money until his shoulder healed, they wouldn't want to spend any more on doctor's bills, she acknowledged.

'You're going on all right then, girl?' he said gruffly, with the awkwardness of one not used to sick-visiting.

'Yes thank you,' she mumbled. 'Sal looks after me.'

'Right. Well.' The silence yawned between them. 'I'll let on to your Ma that you ain't too sick then. She'll be glad to know it.'

Marnie turned her face away from him, filled with a rush of disappointment in him that he couldn't be more loving, more concerned, more ready to stay with her a little while instead of edging already towards the door. Ridiculously embarrassed at seeing his own daughter in bed and ailing. For a second she wished she had the gall to hurl the real truth of her indisposition at him in a torrent of words, to see if that would bring a spark of emotion to his face, but she knew too well the holocaust that would bring about if she did.

'I'll be all right in a day or two, Da. Will you ask Sal if she can bring me up another drink when she has the time, please?'

It was his excuse to leave her, and they were both relieved to snatch at it.

'You'll be better when the spring comes, my girl,' he said finally. 'Everything looks different in the spring.'

She heard him clattering downstairs in his heavy boots. Spring seemed a hundred years away; warmth and sunlight, everything new and young and green, and the daffodils growing in great profusion, just waiting to be gathered in golden, glowing armfuls–she loved the spring. And there was one sure thing about it, it would come again, however dark the days seemed at present. She'd never expected her Da to be the one to remind her, or to be the one to trigger off her natural optimism, but they were of one blood, after all, so maybe he did understand her a little, despite his inability to express himself competently. Marnie was oddly comforted.

And by the time the winter snows had slid away under the cool March winds and the thin warmth of April sunshine, the weals on her back, if not her heart, had healed. She had become accustomed to life at Larksby, especially now that Mr Darryl was safely away at college, and Miss Geraldine had recovered her equanimity and started revisiting the kitchen when Marnie and Sal were there alone. The only thing that still had the power to twist a knife within her was the utter indifference she received from Gabe O'Brien when he came once a week or more. It was as if he'd put up an invisible wall between them, and she was too proud to try and break through.

But it hurt to see the way he flirted with Sal, and even teased the haughty upper housemaid, Theresa, when she happened to be anywhere around. He was a favourite with Cook and even Mrs Caine frequently commented that the boy had a way with him that would charm the halo off a saint. But with Marnie he was cold and brusque, and her hurt gradually changed to bitterness. She told herself resolutely that if he didn't care about her, she certainly wasn't going to waste her affections on him–a resolution that didn't always take effect, no matter how much she tried to enforce it, because she was always wondering if it was time for him to come by, thinking that maybe this day would be different, and the smile that lit his eyes would be all for her.

But there were other things to think about besides Gabe O'Brien. One afternoon towards the end of April, Miss Geraldine came into the kitchen, and Marnie glanced up in embarrassment at Mrs Caine. The housekeeper still disapproved strongly of the fact that Marnie was progressing quickly with her reading under Geraldine's instruction, considering it undignified for the young lady of the house to spend so much time and trouble on a servant. Truly, Geraldine often sighed, Mrs Caine cared more for dignity than did the Larksbys themselves. But it was not to bring one of the reading books for Marnie to study that she appeared that particular afternoon.

'Father has decided we shall all spend a day at the water frolics next month,' she announced. 'It will take us some time to journey there, so we shall have to make an early start, probably about six o'clock in the morning. We shall go in the carriage, of course, and Father will put the big trap at your disposal, and he expects you, Cook and Mrs Caine to make the picnic arrangements. The grooms will each take charge of a conveyance, and the stable-lads may ride alongside.' Her voice suddenly lost its somewhat pompous tone, and a smile enlivened her pretty features. 'It will be such fun, Marnie! All the boat races and the picnicking along the banks, and the firework displays afterwards!'

'It sounds exciting,' she said eagerly.

'Exciting!' Cook snorted. 'It sounds like a lot of hard work for some, begging your pardon, Miss Geraldine.'

'Oh Cookie, don't be so cross. You know you enjoy a day out as much as the rest of us,' Geraldine laughed at her.

'I wish my little sister and brother could see it,' Marnie's voice was suddenly wistful. 'Still, it will be something to tell them about the next time I go home.'

Within half an hour Geraldine had talked to her parents and returned to the kitchen, saying gaily that if Marnie wanted her brother and sister to come with them, her father must deliver them to Larksby by ten minutes before six o'clock in the morning of the day of the outing. Marnie gaped with pleasure, never expecting to hear this, and went a fiery red as she thanked Geraldine profusely.

'I told you she'd taken a fancy to you,' Sal grinned, when they were on their own again and attending to the family laundry, hardly able to see across the room for billowing steam and bubbling cauldrons of soapy water. Marnie laughed.

'Wait till I tell them! Jenny will be wild with excitement. And Davey–you'll love Davey, Sal.'

'Probably. Not that I care much for little children. Sticky, damp creatures, the ones I've ever come in contact with,' she said carelessly. 'Still, I daresay I'll manage to like him since you seem to think he's so wonderful.'

She flicked soapy water at Marnie to let her know she was only teasing, but nothing was going to squash the feeling of elation inside Marnie right now. It was almost the first time she'd felt anything other than lethargic since the terrible night Darryl Larksby had come to her room and raped her. Her wounds had healed except for a certain stiffness and soreness, but there were scars in her mind and memory that would never heal.

On her next evening off she went to the cottage and told the family that Jenny and Davey were to be allowed to come along if Da would get them there on time. She looked at him anxiously, but to her relief he nodded agreeably.

'Oh aye, it will do them good to have a day away from home.'

He said no more because of the whoops of delight from the youngest Bray children, who danced round and round the room, leaping over Marnie and hugging her until she begged for mercy, but with a pleasurable feeling running through her at being the cause of so much adoration. It was a long time since she'd felt anyone's arms around her like this, and she extricated herself reluctantly when Ma said Davey must be got ready for bed.

'I'll undress him,' she said quickly, not wanting to lose the soft warmth of him, and thinking how lovely it must be to have babies who looked up at you with such trusting, adoring eyes.

'I'm in Jenny's bed now,' he shrilled importantly. 'I don't have a cot now I'm a big boy!'

And if she'd still been at home she might have shared the morning sweetness of his warm little body, Marnie thought enviously. But she pushed the familiar empty feeling away from her, for this was no time to brood about being sent to Larksby, when by anybody's standards, she should consider herself lucky to be in such good employ, and she wasn't unhappy, was she? If she examined her situation dispassionately, she couldn't honestly say that she was. There were a good many things she still yearned after, but she wasn't actively unhappy . . .

She'd stayed later than she meant to at the cottage that evening, and she hurried through the dewy fields, remembering with a stab of nostalgia the way she'd run so eagerly to the old mill near Kettle's farm to meet Gabe. It seemed like centuries ago. A dream that was only in her imagination, and when she caught sight of a stumbling, black-haired figure moving towards her in the cool twilight, she thought she must still be dreaming. She suddenly stood quite still, because it was no dream, no apparition, no longed-for image of her mind lurching towards her across mist-blanketed fields. It was Gabe, and he was hopelessly drunk by the look of him. Drunk or ill.

'Are you all right?' she spoke nervously, not knowing what to say to him, and yet unable to brush right past him as if he was a stranger. He was flushed as if with fever, but the moment she stepped near to him she could smell the drink reeking out of him.

'I'm in splendid form, wouldn't you say?' he slurred the

142

words, throwing his arms about extravagantly. 'Isn't that what your gentry folk say? Splendid form, what?'

Marnie swallowed. He made no move to pass her. He stood in her path, swaying slightly, his feet apart to keep his balance. Where was his brother, she wondered frantically? She couldn't imagine he'd sanction this kind of behaviour.

'Is Mick with you?' she asked quickly.

He pretended to peer all around him, inspecting blades of grass and searching in his pockets. At last his face relaxed into a brilliant smile.

'No,' he chuckled. 'Must have forgotten to bring him with me. Or did I leave him behind at the Duck and Drake? That'll be it! He was going off upstairs with Peggy last time I saw him. Know Peggy, do you? Big girl, you know, big . . . ' He made expressive movements with his hands, but Marnie wasn't listening to him any more. That smile of his would always be her undoing, she thought desperately, and she missed him so much.

She moved closer and put her hands on his swaying arms.

'Gabe, don't be unfriendly to me any more,' she said in a tremulous voice. 'I don't know what I've done, but I can't bear it when you look at me as if I'm an insect or something. Didn't–didn't it mean anything to you–in the old mill?'

His smile slowly faded, like the sun going behind a dark cloud. Suddenly he pulled her to him, his arms closing round her in a vice-like grip, pressing on the scars on her back. She gasped, and then he pressed his mouth to hers in a savage kiss that held no resemblance to the loving embraces she remembered. And as suddenly he let her go.

'Is that what you wanted?' his voice was rough. 'Well, it's all you're going to get to brag about this time, whore.'

Shock ran over her like a dousing of cold water.

'Why do you call me that horrible name?' she said hoarsely. 'Don't you know it was the first time in the mill?'

She bit her lip. But not the last, her mind shrieked. He saw the shamed expression on her face and turned away from her in disgust, completely misinterpreting it. She had *told* on him, told her brothers, and he was never going to forgive her for that.

'Bugger off back to your poncey friends,' he shouted furiously.

He stumbled on across the fields, heading in the general direction of the Pinnock farm, intending to be in bed and sleeping it off long before Mick got back to rail into him for drinking too much at his tender age. Any age was all right when you had something to forget, he thought savagely, and he wasn't likely to forget the fight with the Bray brothers in a hurry, nor the threat that they weren't done with the O'Briens yet.

Marnie practically ran the rest of the way back to Larksby, sobbing hysterically at the way he'd treated her, her pride smarting and her back stinging where he'd pressed against the scars. It was the last time she would bother to ask after his well-being, she vowed. He was nothing to her, nothing, nothing . . .

As the time drew near for the outing to Hickling Broad and the water frolic, Marnie found it less troublesome to push Gabe O'Brien out of her mind. There was too much to think about and prepare to waste time on futile dreams, and on the days he was due at Larksby, she purposely found other work to do so that she was out of the kitchen. When the day arrived–a sparkling sunny morning that promised to be hotter than most so far–she scooped her young brother up in her arms as soon as her Da deposited him and Jenny at the kitchen door.

'Now you mind and do as Marnie tells you,' he admonished them. 'And don't go getting into no trouble. I'll be back for you tonight.'

'Better make it very late tonight, Hal Bray,' Mrs Caine put in. 'We'll not be back from Hickling afore ten o'clock at the earliest, and probably later than that.'

Jenny and Davey were so much in awe of her and of

144

Cook's vast bosom riding in magnificent brown serge above a tight-waisted black skirt, that they were tongue-tied for the best part of the journey, despite Marnie and Sal's easy chatter as they pointed out the various villages and the splendour of Norwich as they rode on towards the Broad. And even Theresa unbent enough to give them a few sweet-meats and chucked Davey under the chin a few times. But at their first sight of the Pleasure Boat Inn alongside the Broad, its staithe fringed with willow trees, bustling with people, and the jostling, straining boats of all sizes and shapes with their sails hoisted and flapping in the breeze, the excitement overcame their shyness, and they jumped up and down in the trap until Mrs Caine had to tell them to stop before they threw everyone out.

There were carts and carriages of every description, and horses tethered to any available post. The boat races had already started, and a small troupe of players was assembling beyond the Inn to entertain those who were more interested in music and mime than in water sports.

As each race started a gun cracked out to herald the off, and a great roar went up from the crowd. Sal laughed as Davey joined in hysterically, his brown eyes shining with excitement every time two boats sailed dangerously near to one another.

'He'll not be happy until a couple collide,' she shouted in Marnie's ear above the hubbub. 'And I reckon he won't have to wait long!'

There were several accidents and near-accidents to have the onlookers catching their breaths with excitement during the morning, and half a dozen fights breaking out to take the interest away from the huge, boat-infested sheet of water.

'The Colonel won't be too pleased if the stable-lads get caught up in fights,' Sal commented. 'Just look at Ben, swaggering about inside the Inn. Making up to the local barmaids, I shouldn't wonder.'

Marnie looked. And felt her heart give a lurch as she saw two other dark heads she recognised inside the Inn, where pint-pots thumped down on wooden tables and raucous laughter bellowed out incessantly. Of course, Gabe and Mick would have heard about the water frolic–everyone from miles around was gathered here today–and she felt sickened at the way he was downing the pot of ale and shouting for another. He'd be rolling drunk before the day was half-gone at this rate. What was wrong with his brother, that he didn't try to stop him? It was a pity her own brothers couldn't have been here today, she thought wistfully. It would have been nice to see them, but they were busy on the river and couldn't spare the time for such frivolities, according to her Da. Or else they thought such things were beneath them, when they used the waterway for a living and not for sport.

Mrs Caine was bustling about and ordering them to come along and have some food as she and Cook unpacked the enormous hampers.

They were sitting on a grassy patch where other parties were gathered to eat their picnics. The Larksbys sat a little way apart from them, with Mrs Caine moving between the two camps as if they were opposing armies. Geraldine gave Marnie a conspiratorial wink, as if to imply that she'd rather be sitting with the servants.

'Hand the food round, you girls,' Cook said sharply. 'Don't sit there expecting to be waited on, and those children look as if they could do with a bit of fattening up.'

They ate huge platefuls of Cook's beef patties and bread and cheese, onions, pieces of cold chicken and tongue, washed down with mineral water or bottled ale according to age and temperament. Wedges of fruit pie and seed cake all disappeared as if by magic, and afterwards they lay back in the warm May sunshine, lulled by the satisfaction of full stomachs and the unusual idleness of the day compared with the unending cleaning and polishing and cooking and laundering at Larksby.

The races had stopped for lunch and were due to start again in half an hour or so. Time for a snooze, Cook commented, and Marnie could see her brother and sister

146

giggling behind their hands at the sight of her bolster-like bosom rising and falling with every wheezing breath she took.

'Stop it,' she hissed at them. 'Go away and play if you've finished eating–and mind, not too near to the water.'

They skipped off with Jenny holding tightly to Davey's hand. The Pleasure Boat Inn was spilling out some of its customers to make room for others, and Marnie saw Gabe come lurching out with the stable-lads from Larksby, heads together, sharing a lewd joke that had them roaring with laughter seconds later and causing the straightfaced Mamas seated around to tut-tut and turn their backs on such vulgar creatures.

He must know she was here, Marnie thought. If Ben was so much in league with him today, he must know all the Larksby servants had been brought on this outing, but never by a glance did he acknowledge it, and it infuriated her to see how he smiled across at Sal, and even passed the time of day with Theresa, who merely tossed her head and ignored him. She wished he hadn't come, she thought, in a fury. Why did he have to be here when she was doing her best to put him firmly out of her mind? He was like a thorn under her skin.

There was a sudden commotion alongside the bank some little distance away from the picnickers. Gabe and Ben were striding out that way, laughing so stupidly and practically holding each other up. Marnie watched them scornfully and then she caught sight of her little sister running towards Gabe and throwing herself into his arms, where he swung her round and round to her delighted screams. Gullible Jenny.

Marnie suddenly realised Jenny's screams weren't those of delight, and that she was pummelling against Gabe's chest and screaming out Davey's name.

Davey, in God's name, where was Davey?

Marnie leapt to her feet, hardly realising that she was covering the ground in a frenzy of panic as she saw Gabe drop Jenny to the ground and start sprinting to the bank where the reeds grew thick and lush, swaying and slushing

147

back and forth against the mud which all the activity had stirred up in the Broad today.

'Davey!' She screamed. 'Davey!' Oh God, if anything had happened to him . . . She was supposed to be responsible for him, and she had sent him off to play with Jenny while she dozed in the sun, and he was so little, oh God, he was so *little* . . .

By the time she reached the spot Jenny was crying hysterically and Gabe had waded in with Ben following him. They were still half-laughing, still too merry with ale even for the shock of the cold water to make their reactions sharp, and they kept falling over, losing their footing on the muddy bottom and stirring it up all around them. Laughing and slithering and throwing great gushes of water up in the air so that the small crowd of onlookers, who'd wondered for a moment if there was some cause for alarm, wandered away and put it all down to youthful high spirits.

'Where's Davey, Jenny? Where's Davey?' Marnie was shaking her sister until her teeth rattled, willing her to say he was being cuddled and fussed over by some doting Mama who'd taken a fancy to him, but Jenny sobbed and pointed, hardly able to speak.

'In the water,' she screamed. 'Davey went in the water. Gabe's going to find him. *Gabe*! *Please* find Davey!'

The two boys suddenly stopped their antics and began scrabbling amongst the mud-choked reeds, and instantly it seemed, the bank was crowded with people, all shouting instructions or wailing or just standing around helplessly, some of the men jumping in beside Gabe and Ben, as they finally realised it wasn't all a game.

And then a hush fell over everyone as Gabe emerged with a small body covered in slime and mud, and somehow stumbled out of the water with it in his arms with the help of the onlookers, his face streaked with tears and grief, his legs threatening to fold up beneath him until one of the men took Davey away from him and laid him gently on the ground.

It couldn't be true, Marnie wept. It *couldn't*. Not Davey,

not her darling, her cuddly little butterball. She could hear Gabe's stuttering words somewhere behind her as he tried to explain to anybody who'd listen.

'I thought she was making it up. Jenny . . . she's always one for telling stories and we couldn't see no child in the water. We thought she was having us on.'

'Hush now bor,' she heard somebody say kindly. ' 'Twasn't your fault and none would say it was. You did all you could and nobody's blaming you.'

For one agonised moment Marnie raised her blurred, swollen eyes from Davey's limp body, ignoring the arms that held her and tried to comfort her and looked across straight into Gabe O'Brien's eyes. And no hatred could be more tangible than the look she gave him then. Oh, somebody blamed him. Somebody would always remember this day when the ale had fuddled Gabe's senses so much that he couldn't tell the difference between a child's excitement at seeing him again and a cry for help. Oh yes, somebody would always blame him for this, and he knew it.

She pushed away the arms that held her and gathered her baby brother up in her own, as if the warmth of her body could bring some spark of life back to him. She was vaguely aware of voices all round her, decisions being made, help being offered. Sounds that grew close and then receded and meant nothing, the sound of Gabe crying and vomiting over the edge of the bank into the Broad, Jenny's frightened sobs as Sal and Theresa tried to console her, the rustle of Miss Geraldine's silk skirts as she knelt beside her, and the Colonel's gruff, caring voice.

None of it helped. How could it? She was entirely alone in her grief, and everything that had happened in her life before was meaningless compared with the finality of this. This was growing-up then, her distraught senses cried out inside her . . . this moment when you looked death in the face for the first time.

PART TWO

CHAPTER TEN

Marnie pulled a face at her reflection in the dressing-table mirror of Miss Geraldine's bedroom. Surely someone of barely twenty-two summers shouldn't have such lines around the eyes and such a haunted, shadowed look in them, she thought? But of all days in the year, this was the one that always affected her most deeply, the one on which she invariably awoke with a sick, churning feeling in her stomach, as the memory of that other hot, sparkling summer morning surged into her mind.

Black Friday was the way she always referred to it in her thoughts, the day on which her little brother Davey had drowned. And the nine years between that day and this had done nothing to lessen the horror of remembrance.

Things had changed in nine years, Marnie acknowledged. Colonel Larksby's wife had died as colourlessly as she had lived, and to all intents and purposes the household carried on as if nothing had happened. Mr Darryl had come home briefly for the funeral, but to Marnie's enormous relief had been completely indifferent to her and the rest of the staff. And Sal had said slyly that he'd probably discovered a new kind of sport to feed his appetites in the fancy male college he attended before going to university.

Marnie didn't care what he did as long as he didn't bother her. She was so coldly aloof to him and any other young man who made tentative approaches towards her that it froze them off immediately. She had no wish to become any man's plaything, ever again, and now that she was elevated to being Miss Geraldine's personal maid, she had a new status. She was no longer a mere kitchen maid at everyone's beck and call. She could read and write and was Miss Geraldine's confidante. She had lost her old friend Sal, several years ago, when she'd moved on to another position in King's Lynn, and there were two new girls in the Larksby kitchens who suffered the jibes and cuffs from Cook and Mrs Caine, a small pasty girl called Dolly, and her sister Jenny.

Marnie stared thoughtfully at her reflection. By rights she shouldn't be wasting time day-dreaming like this. She should be laying out Miss Geraldine's afternoon dress ready for her to change into when she came home from her morning's visiting with her father. She should be tidying round the pretty rose-pink bedroom that was the lightest in the entire sombre house, and which reflected Miss Geraldine's personality. But times such as these, when she had a moment to ponder, were precious to Marnie.

Fond as she was of Miss Geraldine, it was pleasant not to be constantly at her bidding, to feel she was still her own person for a little while. And to let the small feeling of satisfaction she felt at her position at Larksby have its way.

Not least of the pleasure it gave her was knowing that she was elevated far above Jenny. Pretty Jenny, who really was a beauty now, at sixteen, even in the drab brown servant's dress, with her glowing curls that had Mrs Caine for ever grumbling, but which would never be entirely tamed. There were ties of blood between Marnie and Jenny that could make her fiercely defensive on her behalf should anyone threaten her young sister's well-being, and yet she could never quite smother the jealousy of her that always smouldered in her mind.

She despised it, but she was mature enough by now to recognise it, and to keep it firmly under control, at least for most of the time. And she had been extraordinarily pleased when it had been decided that Jenny should come to Larksby to work in the kitchens. It was almost like being part of the family again to have Jenny there, instead of always knowing the sinking feeling of having been cast-out because of her disgraceful tantrums in the fen cottage. Over the years, Marnie had learned to control the tantrums, along with most other emotions. In fact, Geraldine Larksby was very

154

often puzzled and exasperated by Marnie's dead-pan expression whenever she came home excited from a party or a ball to where her maid would be lolling with sleep, but still obliged to stay up and help her mistress get ready for bed.

'Aren't you interested to know about the latest fashions, and all the fine houses I visit, or the string of beaux I'm collecting?' she frequently exclaimed impatiently. She and Marnie conversed quite freely now, and Marnie answered bluntly.

'The fashions, yes, and the houses, I suppose. Not that I shall ever see the inside of them! But as for the young men ...' Marnie wrinkled her nose, to Geraldine's annoyance, who would then proceed to sigh and preen in front of the mirror, pouting prettily at her animated face to judge the effect it had, just to irritate Marnie at having to wait patiently while the performance continued. Finally she would flounce away from the mirror and instruct Marnie to unfasten her dress and help her out of her many petticoats.

'You aren't natural, Marnie,' Geraldine often grumbled. 'Any healthy young girl should be interested in young men. Don't you want to marry and have children of your own some day?'

'If I could have the children without the necessity of giving myself to a man in marriage, it would be a different matter,' Marnie said crisply, thinking longingly of the sweet baby softness of Davey as she remembered him, and with no other meaning intended. But Geraldine stared at her, and a tart note came into her voice.

'And a fine position you'd be in if that happened. An unwed servant girl with a baby on the way would soon discover the world a very lonely and alien place, Marnie. If that's the way your thoughts are going, you'd better be looking round for a suitable lad as soon as possible to wed you!'

Marnie flushed deeply, and the words poured out before she could stop them.

155

'You mistake my meaning, Miss Geraldine. I've no intention of making any kind of attachment with a young man, and nor do I ever want to marry. The fact that I love children is unfortunate, because it seems únlikely that I shall ever have any of my own. Not if it takes a man to give them to me!'

Geraldine continued to stare as she stood by the bed in her long white drawers and camisole. If the atmosphere between them hadn't been so tense, Marnie would have found the sight of her quite comical. But Geraldine's eyes suddenly softened.

'My poor Marnie. So the scars have still not healed after all this time. I will pray for you on Sunday, that you may come to believe that not all men are alike. I assure you that some men can be the sweetest, gentlest of creatures.' She gave a small, self-conscious smile, and badẹ Marnie hurry up and get the bed turned back, for she was weary with dancing and talking and needed to get her beauty sleep.

And on that particular night, Marnie lay sleepless and wide awake in her own small room at the end of the corridor where she now slept, to be within easy access should Miss Geraldine require her during the night. She realised that her mistress had assumed mistakenly that all her bitterness was because of Darryl, Geraldine's own brother, but the nightmare of the nights he had assaulted her mind and body had dulled, because he had meant less than nothing to her. The real festering scar was the knowledge that Gabe O'Brien had once called her a kitchen whore, and clearly still believed it. Marnie was still convinced that somehow or other it had been Darryl's indiscretion in some tavern that had caused the idea to get into Gabe's head, but even that was incidental, compared with the fact that Gabe had believed it so readily and had hurt her so badly when she had loved him so much.

After Davey had drowned she had been quite demented for a long while, and somehow the love she'd felt for Gabe had become a twisted hatred. Somehow it had resolved itself into the belief that Gabe could have saved her little brother if he'd really tried, and that it had been a vindictive way of revenging himself against Marnie that had made him pretend not to realise the seriousness of the situation at the broad until it was too late.

It was surprisingly easy to hate, Marnie had discovered. And once the hard shell of hatred was wrapped securely round her, she told herself he would never hurt her again, and nor would any other man. But her eyes were often damp by the end of the day as she turned her face into the coarse pillow and tried to sleep, for in one respect Geraldine was perfectly accurate. It wasn't *natural* for her to be so filled with a cold hate. She'd had to work at it. She was basically warm-hearted, loving, eager for all that life had to offer, and she'd thought she'd discovered it all, long ago in the old mill by Kettle's farm. She was basically a romantic, the moon child that had seemed to beautifully describe the way she wanted to be ... but she'd learned a hard lesson through Gabe O'Brien, the dreams had turned sour, and there was nothing to believe in any more.

The click of the bedroom door handle made her flinch as always that sunny morning, and for a few seconds Marnie's eyes dilated as she watched the door open through the dressing-table mirror. Then Miss Geraldine entered in a flounce of petticoats and a cool morning breeze. Marnie came back from her reverie, for this was an important day for her mistress, who was receiving a young gentleman caller for afternoon tea and would want to look her best.

'What on earth are you doing there, Marnie?' she said irritably. 'You should have my clothes out by now. You look terrible. If you don't brighten yourself up I shall have to think about letting your little Jenny take your place. I can't stand the sight of long faces around me–oh, for goodness' sake, I didn't mean it! Here, you silly girl. Blow your nose and stop snivelling.'

She tossed a wisp of fine lace handkerchief across to Marnie, whose eyes had suddenly filled with tears at her sharp words. And the shock of discovering she could still cry when she hadn't cried in years thickened her throat and

157

reddened her eyes still more. She blew her nose hurriedly, and after a moment's hesitation thrust the handkerchief into the cuff of her smart maid's dress for laundering. Whoever the young gentleman caller might be, he hadn't sweetened Miss Geraldine's tongue with love, and the unexpectedness of hearing her suggest so callously that she might be replaced by Jenny was like twisting a knife in her heart. She forced a light tone to her voice.

'I'm sorry, Miss Geraldine. It won't happen again. It's just today–being the day my little brother drowned. It always puts me in the doldrums.'

'Oh. I didn't realise.' Geraldine was all sympathy now. 'But you can't live in the past for ever, Marnie. Your sister doesn't mope about the place in this way. I heard her laughing and chattering to one of the stable-lads when I came in. She's such a pretty little thing!'

'Jenny wasn't old enough to know the full horror of it,' Marnie muttered. 'And she finds it easier to forget than I do.'

'And to forgive, perhaps,' Geraldine said sagely, though she couldn't have guessed how right her words were. 'Come along, Marnie, it's too fine a day for soul-searching, and what good will it do? It won't bring him back! Please help me out of this stuffy outfit before I suffocate inside it. And once I'm in my finery for Mr Lacey's visit you must take a couple of hours off this afternoon. Don't come back until it's time for dinner, do you hear? Go and visit your parents or something, or whatever you people do in your free time.'

'Thank you, Miss Geraldine.' Marnie's voice was wooden.

She didn't particularly want time off, but when it was offered, it just wasn't done to refuse it. All the same, she hoped to get a glimpse of this Mr Lacey who could get Miss Geraldine in such a tizzy. She was definitely of marriage-able age–some might say past it, at twenty-six–and she had been invited to plenty of weddings of her contemporaries over the past few years. It could be that she was beginning to get anxious about her own prospects, and it was that

that made her more vinegary than of old. But Marnie knew well enough that if she wanted to keep on her post as personal maid here, even if Miss Geraldine married, she had better watch herself, especially with Jenny's pertness catching her mistress' eye. Marnie pushed down the familiar tug of jealousy and moved quickly towards her mistress to help her to change her clothes.

'Go home, Marnie,' Geraldine said suddenly, with her hand on Marnie's arm, her eyes not unkind. 'You hardly ever go now, do you? Don't they miss you?'

'Nobody misses me. They see Jenny often enough, and Ma doesn't need anybody to help her now she's finished with the scrub-wash of folks. I don't get on with my brothers. They all turn on me for no reason, so it's best I stay away when they're at home.'

It was said without malice, a statement of fact, but the look on her face stayed with Geraldine Larksby. It was lonely and remote, and not the look that should be seen on a young girl's face. Geraldine had her maid's welfare at heart, but in Marnie's case there was just no reaching her when she chose to close her mind, and she frequently gave up trying.

But by mid-afternoon Marnie was making her way through the summer-strewn flowers in the meadows on the outskirts of Larksby. She had seen Mr Andrew Lacey arrive, and had helped Miss Geraldine deck herself out in her frills and furbelows to await him in the drawing-room. She wondered briefly how anyone could fancy a future lifetime with such a wishy-washy dandy as he appeared, with a long pale face and a thin-lipped smile, but it was no concern of hers, and she concentrated instead on enjoying the sunshine, and hoping desperately that her brothers wouldn't be at home; that her Ma and Da would be in a mellow mood and not overrun with grief because it was the anniversary of Davey's death-day; and most of all that they'd be glad to see her.

Her heart sank when she heard raised voices as she neared the cottage. She couldn't hear Ted, so she assumed he was away from home at present, but Kenneth and her Da were going at it hammer and fire-tongs, and every now and then Joey was in on it too. She hesitated, listening, before she pushed open the cottage door.

'How many more times do I have to warn you to keep away from those Irish scum!' Da roared. 'The pair of you make me want to puke. They're worthless gypsies, for all that those fruity Pinnock brothers treat them like prodigal sons. They ain't worth the tangle over a blowsy piece of skirt, and the older one's never abroad in the fields without a gun, and well you both know it. If you get your heads blown off, it'll be nobody's fault but your own. If there's trespassers on the Pinnock land, they're entitled to shoot first and ask questions later, and that's just what they'll do. And if you two bors ain't got no more sense than to keep baiting them all the time, you want your heads cracking together. And there's Joey with a stiff arm and unable to defend himself properly from years back, and I'm still wondering about that an' all!'

'Oh Da, that's past history,' Joey said angrily. 'I'm not a halfwit just because of a busted shoulder that never healed properly, and those river crates are heavy enough to bust anything.'

'If it *was* river crates,' Da said meaningly. 'I ain't such a simpleton, me bor, not by a long chalk.'

Marnie pushed open the cottage door. Da wasn't young any more, she thought fearfully, but he still ruled the chicken-roost, and when she went inside she saw him towering over her two brothers, his brows drawn together in a fierce glare in his gnarled old face, with her brothers, for all their size, seeming to cower before him. It was uncanny, and she knew they'd hate for her to have heard the row between them and their Da. She forced a smile to her lips and pretended not to have noticed anything amiss, though her body was suddenly chilled, and she was aware of her heart pounding because of her Da's reference to the Irish scum–which meant Gabe and Mick O'Brien.

'Miss Geraldine gave me some time off, because she's

entertaining a gentleman friend this afternoon, so I've come to see you,' she said brightly.

The boys ignored her and Da grunted, still too wrapped up in their fury to bother with her.

'And not before time,' Ma came in stiffly from the scullery, face flushed from the baking as usual. 'We don't see as much of you as your sister. Too busy to spend much time with your family now, I suppose, now you've taken up with that Miss Geraldine Larksby!'

Marnie looked at her in exasperation.

'I haven't taken up with her, Ma! I have to wait on her hand and foot!'

She could have added that there didn't seem to be much reason for coming home any more when nobody seemed pleased to see her. In fact, Joey looked downright furious at her appearance for some reason, and totally refused to look at her. Kenneth muttered something about it being a lucky day for her when she landed such a good position, and it was a pity poor little Jenny had to be content with skivvying. Ma said tartly that while she was here she might as well give a hand with turning the beds, and Da sat down heavily with a brooding look on his face, wreathed in clouds of black, evil-smelling smoke from his clay-pipe.

Everything here was the same. Everything familiar, from the swaying candle-lantern, not yet lit though it was already dim in the cottage, to the musky bodily smells and the rancid whiff of the river on Kenneth and Joey's clothes. Familiar and unutterably depressing, because there was not one vestige of warmth and comfort here, not even as there had been when they were all children and Davey and Jenny had clung to her skirts and thought she was grown-up and wonderful. Strange how in those days she had always yearned to be loved, and now she suddenly realised that those two had given out all the love and warmth there was in this cottage. And now Davey was dead and Jenny had grown away from her, and it was mostly her own fault, Marnie knew, because of her own damnably jealous nature.

161

She followed Ma upstairs, wondering if she remembered what day it was, and if she should mention it, Ma was getting old too. Her arms were thin as match-sticks, and didn't look as if they'd ever yearned to hold a child to her flat bosom. Yet she'd borne and suckled six of them.

'I don't forget, you know, Marnie.' The suddenness of Ma's voice made Marnie jump as they stood on opposite sides of the lumpy mattress she and Da shared. 'It was a day just like today when the Lord took my babby. It's not given to us to know the reason why, but He gave us feelings along with everything else, and sometimes it makes me wonder just what my poor Davey did that made the Lord want him all choked up with muck and weeds. If He had to take him, why couldn't He just have cracked his skull with a flash of lightning instead of spoiling him like that?'

'Stop it Ma, for God's sake,' Marnie said raggedly.

'For God's sake?' Ma's voice hardened again. 'That's blasphemous talk. I hope my Jenny ain't getting into no wicked ways up at Larksby.'

My poor Davey. My Jenny. Wasn't there one person in all the world who'd look at *her* and call her 'my Marnie'? Miss Geraldine had, briefly, but that didn't count. And hadn't she kept insisting to Miss Geraldine that she wanted no-one? That she hated all men and to none but herself, and then only rarely, would she admit that her heart wasn't really frozen, that there was one man who could touch her soul, and that man treated her like dirt. She despised herself for still wanting him, even now after all this time. But she had seen him many times at Larksby over the years, and the years had been good to Gabe O'Brien. The beautiful black-haired boy of thirteen, with the tangled gypsy curls and the dimpled charm guaranteed to make female hearts beat faster, had emerged like a chrysalis into a lithe, handsome man with the ability to stir Marnie into almost uncontrollable emotions whenever she saw him. Sometimes rage at the way he snubbed her; sometimes grief when the longing for him swept over her; sometimes love, and when she admitted her love for him she invariably loathed herself for her weakness and forced the loving to turn to hate.

'Are you going to help me turn this mattress or aren't you?' Ma's voice was irritable now as Marnie's hands paused over her task. 'It used to be Jenny who wasted her time dreaming. I thought you were too hard-headed for all that nonsense.'

Oh no, Ma. Not hard at all, only on the surface. Soft as butter underneath. Soft as butter.

'A young man on the horizon, is there?' Ma went on shrewdly. 'About time. You'll be past your prime if you don't think on getting wed, girl. And a pursed-up mouth and frowning eyes are no ways to make yourself attractive.'

'I've no wish to wed.'

'Why ever not? Do you want to stay in service for ever?'

Marnie shrugged as they flipped up the patchwork counterpane together and patted it into place.

'What else is marriage if it's not being in service of a different kind, and without benefit of wages?' she said scathingly. 'I'm not that willing to give up my freedom to wait on some man for the rest of my days.'

'And what freedom is there in waiting on Miss Larksby?' Ma glowered at her, clearly not understanding this kind of thinking at all.

'Freedom of spirit,' Marnie muttered.

And Ma would never understand what she meant by that! And nor she did. But she had one final taunt to throw at her daughter before they went down the wooden stairs.

'You always did have that pouty look about you, Marnie. I must confess it troubled me at one time when you were younger. Now it's more like to put men off, and I reckon it'll be left to our Jenny to give Da and me our grand-babbies, since the boys don't seem overkeen to make a legal job of it. There'll be plenty of followers for Jenny, I'll guarantee.'

Marnie clumped down the staircase behind Ma, a sudden bereft feeling shooting through her. She was suddenly as vulnerable as a child again, yearning to be wanted, to be petted and loved the way everybody loved her sister Jenny, and it seemed Jenny could have everything Marnie always wanted without even trying. It wasn't fair, it wasn't fair.

By the time she left the cottage after helping Ma prepare some tea and then helping her clear it all away again, she was telling herself not to be such a fool. She was mature enough now to laugh at herself and not to let things hurt her the way they used to, wasn't she? There was always a favourite in every family, and if Davey had lived it might very well have been him, instead of Jenny. She gave a sudden determined swallow, remembering Geraldine's grumpiness with her and the half-teasing suggestion of replacing her with Jenny and knew it was up to her to put a better countenance on it if she didn't want that very thing to happen.

It wasn't that she didn't like Jenny, she argued with herself, after she'd bade her parents and brothers goodbye with a feeling of relief a while later, because it was almost impossible for anyone to dislike Jenny. And she certainly wouldn't want any harm to come to her. Jenny was artless and open, without a jealous bone in her body, and Marnie sometimes felt even more ashamed at her own unworthy nature in comparison. But she couldn't help her own nature, and she thought waspishly that Jenny's sunny nature and the aura of goodness surrounding her sometimes seemed to be unreal and not part of this world at all.

For some reason Marnie suddenly remembered back to that delicious time with Mrs Kettle, and the phrase she'd used for Marnie that she'd thought so romantic and beautiful. Moon child, moon child. She hadn't appreciated then that there was a dark side to the moon, and in her case it was the soul-destroying jealousy that consumed her–and if she was the moon, then Jenny was surely the sun, she thought ruefully.

'Marnie! Why didn't you tell me you were coming home today? I thought you'd have been in attendance on Miss Geraldine and her young man. Is it true she's hoping to be wed quite soon? Cook says he's a milk and water dandy, but

164

none of the rest of us has seen him. Did you get a glimpse of him today?'

The object of her thoughts was standing in front of her, the quick, light words tripping out of her in her eagerness, and Marnie blinked away the dark musings and forced a smile to her lips as Jenny's flushed face and sparkling brown eyes came sharply into focus. She must have appeared through a gap in the hedge, and her sudden appearance startled Marnie into being sharper than she intended.

'You'd do better to mind your own business, and not go tittle-tattling below stairs with Cook and Mrs Caine and that simpering Dolly.'

'Oh, Marnie, we don't tittle-tattle. Only you can tell me, can't you? Just me. Is it true? Will Miss Geraldine wed him, do you think? I'll not tell a soul if you let on to me, I promise!'

God, but she had a wheedling way with her, Marnie admitted. It would be the death of her if she wasn't careful, or would it? With a sudden flash of intuition Marnie surmised that with that so-innocent beauty and the eager freshness about her, and that glorious cascading red-gold hair falling over her shoulders that Marnie could never quite forgive, Jenny could rise to any heights she chose with no more than a glance in the right direction from those expressively beautiful eyes of hers. She was wasted as a kitchen maid, Marnie thought, in a rare moment of dispassionate appraisal.

'I'm not that much in Miss Geraldine's confidence,' she said tartly. 'But my guess is that she'll take him if he offers. She's not had any other offers to my knowledge, and she's not in her first bloom any more, though I'd thank you not to repeat what I've just said, and it's only for your ears, Jenny.'

'How calculating you make it all sound,' Jenny sighed. 'Have you no romance in your soul?'

'That's for children,' Marnie told her. 'If it's marriage you're after, it's best to settle for a fair-minded man who's

165

not entirely repugnant to you, I reckon.'

Jenny shook her head slightly, obviously not agreeing with her sister's views at all. And maybe wondering for a minute who had put the sourness into Marnie's face when she was once so happy and eager, and Jenny had looked up to her so much.

'I'd best get on home or they'll think I'm not coming,' she said in sudden embarrassment in the little silence between them.

Marnie let her pass, and it was some minutes later before the frown clouded her face as she realised that Ma certainly hadn't been expecting Jenny that day or she'd have said so. And that the meadows stretching away in front of her towards Larksby like a flat green daisy-starred carpet were unbroken by hedges or gates just here, and that she'd certainly have been aware of her sister's approach before she popped up in front of her like a golden apparition if she'd come straight from Larksby. Her footsteps slowed and then stopped, and she turned full circle to gaze back the way she'd come.

The footpath from the cottage had skirted a long low hedgerow, thick with may blossom and humming with the drone of bees searching for nectar. At right angles to it was another winding footpath, trodden by many feet, between two banks of overgrown vegetation, leading towards the dykes and the old mill and Kettle's farm.

Marnie frowned again. It could only have been from that way that Jenny had appeared, and she suddenly remembered her sister's flushed face, her sparkling eyes; the quick speech as if she wanted to cover up her appearance with conversation, before she was asked any questions; the cascading, ruffled hair, which Cook would never have approved if she'd just left the Larksby kitchens.

The little fool had been meeting some village lad, Marnie guessed at once, and was making a token visit home in case anyone should ask, and from the look of her the meeting had been entirely satisfactory.

It shouldn't make the slightest difference to her, Marnie

166

told herself sharply. Why should it? She certainly didn't expect her sister to live a nun-like existence just because she herself had become embittered towards men.

It was just . . . something completely illogical within her seeing Jenny like that, with a look about her that was like an exquisite echo of Marnie herself, a bitter-sweet ghost of the past to haunt her mind of the one and only time she'd been held in Gabe O'Brien's arms in the old mill and known she was loved. Not wondered, *known*. And loved for herself, because she was Marnie and desirable and not second-best.

And from somewhere deep inside, the old, hateful jealousy was rearing up and uncoiling like a serpent in her gut, because if Jenny had been meeting a village lad anywhere that day, it was almost certainly in the old mill. *Her* place. Hers and Gabe's. And all the years between might never have been as the searing jealousy took hold of her again in a shuddering red anger.

CHAPTER ELEVEN

Jenny's step was light as she walked on towards the fen cottage. It had been quite a shock to come out of the shady footpath and find herself face to face with her sister, but the moment of surprise had been covered successfully, she told herself, and if anything, added an extra excitement to the deliciousness of the past hour. A smile curved her soft full mouth, and the beautiful honey-gold eyes that matched her hair sparkled with the memory of it.

Once, she'd have been able and eager to share the delight of her assignation with Marnie, and relive it all over again in the telling, but those days were gone and Marnie seemed to be always out of patience with her lately. Besides, she didn't really want to share it with anybody, it was too personal and private, and to have a young man falling over himself for her favours was still new to her.

Not that he was exactly falling over himself, she conceded. In fact, if she was truthful, she supposed she had been the one to do most of the chasing, if gazing at him with adoration oozing out of every little bit of her could be called chasing. With a promise in her eyes of which she was hardly aware, so that no lusty young chap worth his salt could stay immune for ever. And neither had he. Jenny suddenly laughed out loud for sheer happiness, and because the air was soft and humming with bees, and the scent of may flowers was heady in her nostrils, she bent and picked a daisy and began pulling off the petals one by one, intoning gaily as she walked.

'He loves me, he loves me not, he loves me, he loves me not . . .' until she had stripped the stem of all the white petals and pulled a face at the result, tossing the stem away and telling herself airily it was all superstitious nonsense anyway. And who needed such things to prove something she already knew? Hadn't she just lain in his arms and heard him whisper the words of love she'd so wanted to hear? Hadn't he said she'd driven him mad with desire so that he couldn't hold out any longer even though she was little more than a child and he a man?

'A child?' she'd echoed softly in the dimness of the old mill. 'How can you call me a child? Is it a child who welcomes you like this? A child who dreams of you night and day and aches to see your smile and feel your arms around her? This is no child!'

She was still amazed at her own daring at speaking to him that way when he was her first, her only lover. At having had the nerve to encourage him so brazenly, and going more than halfway to letting him know she was quite willing to be seduced. She wasn't ready yet to admit that she had done most of the seducing, because when it came to the ultimate end, it had to be the man who took charge, didn't it? Without his willingness and ability to co-operate, nothing was possible.

And it was not before time for it to happen, Jenny had argued with herself. Even that simpering Dolly in the kitchen had told her tales of rompings in the stables and made her green with envy because it was a world she didn't yet know and yearned to discover. She was impatient not to be left behind. And had thought with some distaste that it had to be somebody special for this momentous happening in her life, and not one of the sweaty stable-lads or village louts with their rough hands and hot eyes and lewd jokes who was going to deflower her.

There was only one . . . the sun was dazzling in her eyes at that moment, and like everything else, it was all a little unreal, and she still couldn't quite believe this wonderful thing had happened, not just today but for the past couple of months. The exciting meetings in the disused mill near Kettle's farm, and knowing she belonged to someone of her own. Hugging the secret to her through every minute of the working day and long into the night when she slept in the austere room with the snoring Dolly, the room that used to be her sister's at Larksby.

She could put up with Cook and Mrs Caine, who had got even more irascible towards each other and everybody else recently. She could put up with the skivvying and the long hours, and the uncomfortable lumpy bed with the squeaking springs that were forever prodding her back. She could forget them all to relive the golden times she shared with *him*, and then she was transported from the coldness of the little attic room to the old mill again, dusty and dank and yet the best place on earth when he folded her in his arms and breathed her name.

'Jennifer . . . Jennifer . . . my sweet, pretty Jennifer. You're like a breath of spring itself, so you are,' he'd murmur in her ear as his hands roamed freely over her body. She thrilled to his touch as always, for he was the only person who ever used her full name as if she was *somebody*, and she ignored the faint smell of ale that was always on his breath and the unsteadiness of his voice, as if he came to her half against his will, despite himself. She knew he wanted her, he *did*, and she'd been in love with him since the first moment she saw him, even if she hadn't recognised it then as love.

'Gabe,' she'd sigh his name, winding her arms round his neck and caressing the black curls that had always fascinated her. 'Oh Gabe, love me, love me . . .'

She'd hear his smothered groan as they sank down on the dusty floor of the mill, and she'd wriggle while he spread his jacket beneath her, and he'd be muttering that it was more than any man could do to resist an invitation like that.

She'd expected pain, the first time, but there had been very little, and anyway it hadn't lasted long. Almost before she'd started glorying in this marvellous new feeling that was pulsating through her body, he'd rolled away from her and was breathing heavily beside her.

But that was only the first time. Since then there had been others–once a week on her evening off, she'd hurried to the mill before going to the cottage and he'd been waiting for her. There was a piquancy to their relationship that spiced it even more than the thrill she knew when he was with her. And that was the vague certainty that her sister Marnie had once wanted Gabe for herself, before she turned against men altogether. Silly Marnie, Jenny laughed to herself, for letting herself turn into a sour old maid before her time, and denying herself the joy of lying in a man's arms the way she lay in Gabe's.

She felt the impatience rise within her as she heard Da and her brothers shouting at each other when she was within sound of the cottage. They were always shouting. Her brothers were forever fighting somebody, and she knew full well a lot of the resentment among the fenmen was because of the Irish navvies who took their jobs and their girls. And their sisters, she thought. For some reason she couldn't fathom her brothers hated the O'Briens even more now they'd done well for themselves by landing jobs at the Pinnock farm a lot of years ago instead of still working the dykes. Now they practically ran the Pinnock farm between them.

Jenny could hardly remember a time when they hadn't worked there. Not that she had seen much of them over the years, since the time Gabe had taken the splinter from her foot which had been the cause of the first fight between her brothers and the O'Briens, and one that stuck in her child's memory. But that was past history, and she couldn't see the sense in raking up past mistrusts, or continuing a feud for which there seemed no cause. They lived here and worked the land, and why shouldn't they? But even Gabe had made no bones about keeping their meetings secret, and had been very insistent on it, Jenny remembered, her brows meeting in a frowning line in the middle of her forehead.

'You're to tell no-one of this, Jennifer,' he'd said the first time, when she was still in a half-stupor of love for him, and the realisation that she'd given him the most precious possession she had, and that therefore they belonged together for all time in her mind.

'Oh, I wouldn't,' she breathed, but he'd looked at her sternly, and ran his finger along her full lower lip, still heavy from all the kissing.

'No-one at all,' he'd repeated deliberately. 'Definitely not your sister and none of your family. They hate me and Mick, and there's no love lost between any of us. If they ever got wind of you and me, they'd come gunning for us for certain. You wouldn't want that to happen now, would you, sweet Jennifer?'

'Oh, no! Oh Gabe, I'll say nothing, I promise! It's our beautiful secret. Oh, I love you too much for me to do anything that might hurt you, you know that!'

She threw herself into his arms and pulled him close, feeling the way his body moulded itself to hers, pressing her soft eager lips to his mouth and thrilling to his instant response, and then hearing him say regretfully that he must get back to the farm before he was missed, and that she mustn't be too late going to the cottage and arouse suspicion. She never saw the sudden bleak look in his eyes as he held her and looked beyond her shoulder at the bright blue hexagon of the sky above the mill and thought briefly of how it was once bathed in moonlight, nor heard the catch in his breath before he buried his face in the softness of her burnished hair. She never realised that he never said he loved her, not once.

The cottage door crashed open and shut again as Kenneth and Joey came storming out, their faces black as thunder. Kenneth's cleared a little as he saw Jenny coming up the path towards him.

'It's good to see you, girl. Go in and see if you can smooth Da's tongue and temper, will you? for you're the only one that can. Our Marnie's been here, but she just manages to rub Ma up the wrong way, and today especially they need cheering up.'

Her heart lurched. It was Davey's death-day and she'd completely forgotten it except in the moment of waking that morning. She hoped apprehensively the good Lord wouldn't punish her in some way for enjoying the pleasures of the flesh when she should have spent the day in sober mourning. But perhaps He wouldn't condemn her, because it had happened so long ago, and she couldn't even remember Davey's face any more. She consoled herself by assuring her brothers she'd try to put Ma and Da in a good humour by the time they got back.

'Be sure you do,' Joey grunted, and Jenny knew by his expression that his shoulder was paining him. 'We're off to the Duck and Drake for a few jars and a yarn or two, so mind how you go, Jenny, and get off back to Larksby before dark.'

'I will,' she smiled at him, touched as always by the way she never failed to give her the same warning, as if something bad might befall her and more than a little anxious in her heart because she knew Gabe was meeting his brother Mick at the Duck and Drake that evening too. But then she shrugged. They were all grown men, and it was time they acted like it. They all needed a good shaking for carrying on like children the way they did. Wasn't that the way wars were begun, over smouldering hatred that suddenly burst into flames? Jenny shivered and went into the cottage to placate her parents with her sunny smile.

And Gabe O'Brien was preparing to sup his way through another evening at the Duck and Drake and still asking himself how in damnation he'd got himself into this situation?

Ever since the fight at the Pinnock farm when he'd learned the fickleness of women to his cost, he'd vowed strictly to leave the whole female sex alone to the end of his days. He wanted nothing more to do with a single one of them, and Marnie Bray could take her swaying hips and her knowing eyes and soft pouting mouth and stew in her own juice for all he cared. But the hell of it was she had wormed her way into his heart and he couldn't seem to shake her completely loose no matter how hard he tried. Not that he'd have anything more to do with *her*.

But over the years his natural lusty instincts had been stronger than his will, and he'd asked himself angrily why he should deny himself the right of every man to have a bit of

173

fun now and then because of the likes of *her*? It was only proving that she meant something to him, and he wasn't prepared to admit that, but he wished furiously he didn't see her as often as he did–every time he went to Larksby from the farm. Eventually he'd picked up a willing dairy maid and found a kind of forgetfulness between her fleshy white thighs, thus proving something else to himself–that the needs of his loins could be entirely satisfied without his heart ever being involved at all.

He'd hoped then that he'd severed all connection with the Bray family, physically and emotionally, and maybe wiped clean the memory of the terrible fight with the Bray brothers and the scene with Mick that followed. He'd suffered agonies to try to forget them, especially after the accident at the broad, when he fetched the babby up out of the water, choked in mud and slime, and met the accusing eyes of Marnie Bray, just as if he'd let the child die on purpose. Sweet Jesus, even now he could still taste the bile in his mouth, remembering the look in her eyes.

And then Jenny had come back into his life. Sweet, pretty Jennifer, with such a look of Marnie about her as he remembered her at the old mill it had stunned him into a furious rage for days. Marnie had been mature for her thirteen years; Jenny was innocent and fresh for her sixteen; in his mind they were one and the same, desirable, provocative, ripe for loving, and the ache in his loins was hot and familiar every time he looked at her or thought about her or imagined laying with her. Although he'd still had to fortify himself with ale before he suggested to her that he could meet her sometime, by the old mill by Kettle's farm, maybe, near to the cottage, but not too near, knowing it was mad, trying to step back into the past and when she came, full of love and eagerness and wanting, and he finally took her, murmuring her name in full because he knew she liked to hear it; whispering words of love that were meaningless and had been repeated in the same way to anyone who'd spread her legs when the need took him; knowing finally that whoever lay beneath his body when

174

he performed the act, it was *her* that he held . . . not Jennifer, nor any willing dairy maid or village girl, but Marnie, his Marnie.

And he despised himself still more for knowing that something stronger than himself, something twisted inside him, gloried in the fact of Jenny's likeness to her sister. In the fact that he was getting some kind of sweet revenge against the Bray brothers for all the hurt they had done him and Mick, even if they were unaware of the way he was doing it, and a certain revenge against Marnie herself by taking her sister and putting her in her place.

Sweet Jesus, he thought in his sober moments, was this what a woman could do to a man? Destroying every decent feeling in his soul and filling him with the urge to get his revenge any way he could? And maybe that was one more reason why he spent so much of his time with his brain fuddled with drink–so he wouldn't feel sickened at himself for the way he was using sweet little Jennifer Bray.

'I thought you were never coming,' his brother Mick looked up from the table in the taproom of the Inn when Gabe swaggered inside. 'Have you been stuffin' your head with them ships' posters again? It'll do you no good, me boy. You'll never get that kind of money the way you spend it all on ale!'

And what have you been stuffin' this fine and dandy afternoon, Gabe taunted silently? The same as me, I'll be bound, even though Peggy was half-betrothed to Kenneth Bray by now, according to some, but Gabe knew full well she was still dallying between the two of them.

Aloud he said, 'Farmer Dan brought me back another poster from the shipping office in King's Lynn today. It does no harm to anybody to hang them on my bedroom wall. It does no harm to find out about things that interest you, does it?'

'It'll do no good either,' Mick muttered, as Peggy slid a jug of ale towards Gabe, with a smile of her eyes and a roll of her hips.

'It improves your education. Mammy'd like that.'

'Oh aye! You know all there is to know about the fine ships and the ports and distances from here to America, I'm sure. If you were going to sit some kind of test for knowledge on it I'm sure you'd win hands down. But it don't feed the cattle, nor get your work done.'

'When there's any complaints about my work Farmer Dan or Farmer Lester can make 'em, not you,' Gabe said angrily, his face fiery. 'You may be my brother, but you're not my keeper!'

'Shut your arguing, you O'Briens, or else sling your hooks,' roared the red-faced Mr Jackson from behind the barrels of ale. He ailed with gout and was rarely free of pain any more. All he wanted was a peaceful life, and he was still angered because his son Fred should be here with him now to help make his lot easier, instead of working some other tavern God knew where on the other side of the river, according to vague reports he'd heard.

Mick raised his hand in brief acquiescence and looked across at his brother gravely. There were more important matters to discuss than Gabe's pipe-dreams and getting old man Jackson's dander up. The pipe-dreams Mick himself had once dreamed about America had long since vanished, and he was more than content to work the Pinnock land.

'There was a letter from Maureen while you were out. Mammy's ill, and it looks bad.'

'Oh?' Gabe drained the jar and rattled it for more.

Mick felt the irritation stab inside him again. Mother of God, but the lad could sink it. And some days more than others, as if he had some special reason, like something to forget.

'Can't you show a proper interest in Mammy's welfare? I said she's ill, and she's an old woman.'

'She's been ill before and always survived. She's as strong as the earth. It's only Maureen fussing the way she always does!'

Mick glowered at him. 'I'm thinking perhaps one of us should go to see for ourselves. How long is it since we went home? Only once in the last five years. It's not the way

176

loving sons should behave, is it?'

Gabe looked sharply at his brother's troubled face. Mick was always one to carry the worries of the world on his shoulders. He should know by now it was an impossible task to expect of anyone. And he was still unwilling to admit that Mammy could be in any real danger, putting his head in the sand because the alternative was something he didn't want to consider. Anyway, he told himself, Mick was just reacting to Maureen's letter with typical guilt feelings, which was probably just what their sister intended with her usual caustic references to Mammy's desire to see them both again before she died. Such references had occurred with monotonous regularity in every letter she sent them, and he couldn't think Mammy spent all her days thinking about the two of them after all this time.

At least in one respect she must be happy. Two years previously Jack Haggerty had moved his boot-making business back to a fine big house at Drory, where the fields had grown sweet and green again, and the potato crops flourished.

'You know it's not practical for us to go off to Ireland whenever Maureen says the word, Mick! We owe that much to the Pinnocks, don't we?'

Mick stared at him thoughtfully.

'You've a fine sense of loyalty when it suits you, Gabe.'

'And haven't we been loyal to our promise to Mammy all these years?' he said passionately. 'We've sent her money and plenty, more than could be expected of any sons. Enough so she'll have had no need to be beholden to Maureen and her stick husband at all.'

Enough and plenty so there was none left for Gabe to even think about taking the hazardous journey to America. It was also an excuse to keep him exactly where he was, though he never chose to see it that way.

'There's more to promises than money,' Mick sighed. 'There's gentle hands and the sound of a loved one's voice at the end of the day, and bonds that mean more than all the comfort the priests and doctors can bring. But you're right about the Pinnocks, Gabe. We can't both go off together at a minute's notice. I'll write back to Maureen and find out exactly what Mammy's trouble is, and maybe see about going myself if I think it necessary.'

'And say a few hail Marys for her when you've a mind,' Gabe said glibly before he could stop himself.

Next minute he felt the back of Mick's hand cuff the side of his face.

'Don't mock the faith, Gabe. Mock me if you must, but not the faith. You might have need of it one day.'

'Changed your tune, haven't you?' he hissed, seeing the warning glare from the landlord. ' 'Twas you who spoke of men in frocks and had no time for them, I seem to recall!'

He rubbed the side of his cheek resentfully, but knowing by the gleam in his brother's eye it would be best to leave it. And as the door of the Inn opened to let in a gust of night air with the newcomers, he slewed his chair round so his back was towards them, for once having no wish to bait the Bray brothers this night, even though there were only two of them, and one of them Joey with the stiff shoulder Mick had busted. And it seemed the Brays were content also with insults and cat-calls for one evening, that were returned in full measure across the width of the taproom to the entertainment of the rest of the Inn's clients, who watched their long-running battle with keen interest.

Gabe smiled into his jug of ale with secret enjoyment, wondering what the Brays' reaction would be if they knew how their little sister had spent the hour before going to the cottage, with the deceptive air of innocence about her. The knives would be out then all right, and he remembered suddenly how she had sighed beneath him with pleasure in the old mill. His eyes were suddenly bleak, thinking of the paradox of her knowing his body so well and yet not really knowing him at all. Not the essence of him and hoping with a momentary feeling of remorse that at least he *did* give her pleasure.

If he could have seen her at that moment, he'd have been satisfied on that score. From the minute she'd walked in the

178

door of the cottage, the tense atmosphere had lightened. She was Da's favourite, his darling, the least complicated of his children, and she brought the sunshine into the cottage, even though he was not articulate enough to voice his feelings so flamboyantly.

But there was a glow about her lately that minded him vaguely of the way Ma had been when he'd first wed her. He sat beside his Jenny at the scrubbed wooden table while Ma brought them her home-concocted fruit drink and seed cake, and asked about her life at Larksby. Jenny answered gaily, tossing her tangled curls behind her shoulders, and Ma's eyes suddenly narrowed at the sight of her, more perceptive than Da, sensing more than a mere satisfaction in doing a job that put regular meals in her belly. Ma rose from the table as soon as they'd finished and told Jenny to follow her out to the scullery. The younger one had always been less trouble than Marnie, less eager to discover worldly things, more content to remain a child, but suddenly Ma wondered. She turned to face her daughter, her mouth tightening with embarrassment.

'There are things we should talk about, Jenny,' she muttered. Jenny waited nervously as Ma paused.

'What things, Ma? The way I came in today, perhaps? I'm sorry. I remembered the day, truly I did.'

'I don't mean the day, girl,' Ma brushed it aside just as if she herself hadn't brooded on it half the day. 'I mean things you should know that I should have told you about long since.'

Jenny waited anxiously while Ma forced the words out, plain and simple, about the wickedness of a young girl knowing a man's body without benefit of marriage and churching, and the awful consequences that could follow. Because it was so alien to her to speak of such intimate things, Ma chose the most pompous words she knew to add dignity to her warning, and to remove the suggestion of anything personal in it. It was merely something that needed to be said, and finally she'd said it, with her eyes fixed determinedly a foot above Jenny's glossy head until she'd finished. Only then did she meet her daughter's eyes, confident of a job well done, to meet the stark white cheeks and trembling mouth, and to note with surprise the way Jenny's hands were clenched tightly at her sides as if in sheer terror.

'Come now, girl,' Ma said roughly. 'I had no wish to frighten you, and there's worse things in life than to be bedded by a good man and bear his children in due course. When you're fully grown you'll remember all I've said and be glad to know of it in advance, so that certain happenings in your own body won't alarm you. And now you can put it all to the back of your mind, and come back for a chinwag with your Da and me before you make the walk back to Larksby.'

But she couldn't put it to the back of her mind at all. Ma's words stuck there like a gag in her throat all the while she teased Da about his foul-smelling pipe and told him how Cook had got into a fury last week when she'd forgotten to take the fruit pie out of the oven until it was a sticky blackened mess. She brightened her parents' evening with her pretty chatter and made Da forget the irritation he felt over his son's continual feud with the Irish scum. She lulled Ma into forgetting the moment of anxiety she'd felt at Jenny's glowing appearance. She could persuade anyone that the whole world was rosy, except herself.

And on the long walk back to Larksby worry started to gnaw away at her like a rat with a chicken carcass. Ma's talk, pompous and wordy as it was, might have resulted in private sniggers of amusement at her ill-concealed warnings, had they not struck a horrible chord of realisation in her stomach. She could read and write and count, since Miss Geraldine had decided to take on the job with pretty little Jenny as well as her sister . . . and she found herself counting days and weeks, and turning over a horrible possibility that was stirring in her mind. And remembering the dire prediction of what could happen to an unwed young girl should certain unfortunate events take place–cast out by family and friends, disgraced in her place

180

of employ, and shunned in all probability by the young man concerned–she gave a sudden uncontrollable shudder.

She was relieved when Larksby came into view and she could hear the sound of familiar grumblings in the kitchen–Dolly was getting the rough edge of Cook's tongue! She pushed open the door and was immediately enveloped in the warm, steamy atmosphere, and found Dolly surrounded by a mountain of pots and pans and crockery after the family dinner, and that of the servants. Jenny pushed through the grumbling women and offered to help Dolly, even though it was her evening off, but all the pleasure in the hour she'd spent with Gabe O'Brien had long since evaporated like will-o'-the-wisp, and in its place was only a gnawing anxiety. She felt a great need to be doing something with her hands and to engage Dolly in the trivial conversation of which she seemed capable, and to hope she could ignore the suspicion growing inside her.

But she began counting days and weeks in her sleep, and none of them added up any differently. She made endless inspections of herself, and after another three days of uncertainty she could keep the worry to herself no longer. While Miss Geraldine was out riding she sped up the cord-carpeted staircase into the plusher corridors of the house, and knocked frantically at her sister's door.

'Jenny, what do you think you're doing up here? Miss Geraldine will be back soon, and she'll not be pleased to see a kitchen maid here, whether you're my sister or not!' Marnie glared at her, thinking she should know better, and knowing she'd be the one to be reprimanded if Jenny was caught up here. Then she took a closer look at her sister's face. Seeing that it wasn't sunny as was usual, that there was a pinched look about her nostrils and dark shadows beneath her eyes, she pulled her inside her room and closed the door behind her.

'What's wrong, Jenny? You look terrible. It's not Ma, is it? She looked thin and ill last time I saw her. Or one of the boys getting into another fight? They should have more sense. I swear they only come to life when there's trouble and somebody to fight, especially if they're Irish!'

She almost spat the word out, as if it was as hateful to her as to her brothers, and Jenny looked at her with the look of a frightened child in her eyes, combined with the fear of a woman. And somehow even before she'd said a word, Marnie knew. And felt an unexpected surge of maternal feeling, coupled with a wild fury at her sister's stupidity as Jenny stumbled across the room to throw herself into her arms and hide her face in her shoulder, so that Marnie's hands went automatically to the shining curls still tumbling down her back.

'I don't know how to tell you,' she stuttered. 'But I've got to tell somebody! Not that it'll do any good!'

CHAPTER TWELVE

On the same day, a second letter arrived at the Pinnock farm from Ireland.

'Now will you come home?' Maureen wrote passionately. 'All she ever wanted was to see her boys, and you denied her even that. I watched her pine for love of you both, and you couldn't even repay her love with a visit now and then. Jack and me took her as often as we could to the coast because she loved it so, but I know why. It was so she could look across the water towards England where her boys were. And now she'll see them no more and I'm not sure I can forgive you for the hurt you caused her. Her boys! Will her boys come home for the funeral? It's this day week, and Father Flynn will be sore displeased if the O'Brien family is not complete again.'

'She's a rare way of puttin' it,' Gabe spoke roughly to hide the fact he had a lump the size of a rock in his throat. 'All together is something we'll not be again, not now.'

Mick's hand rested briefly on his brother's shoulder.

'We'll be united for this one last time,' he affirmed. 'Like Maureen said, she pined for her boys, and her boys won't let her down. She'll still be there with us, never fear, while she makes the crossing,' he crossed himself as he spoke, 'and then she'll have the comfort of Kathleen and Nora and Pa. The wee one won't be alone, Gabe. You've to tell yourself that.'

'There's no room for more than one in a wooden box, and the ground's a cold hard place for lying in, and she was always too thin and weak to withstand the cold,' Gabe said wildly. Next minute he found a glass pushed into his shaking hands, and when it was guided to his lips he felt the sting of spirits coursing down his throat.

'You'll not give way like that when we reach Drory, will you, Gabe? Maureen and Jack will want supporting in their grief, since they've been the ones to tend Mammy all these years. And their young 'uns won't want to be frightened by the sight of near-strangers weeping and wailing. Maybe we'd best call on Father Flynn when we get there to ask for strength.'

'What's all this then? A renewal of faith?' Gabe muttered. 'I'd a feeling it was going this way with you. You'll be wearing frocks yourself next and swinging a rosary.'

'I won't clobber you this time, Gabe, because I know it's your grief that's talking, so go ahead and get rid of it any way it pleases you, just so long as you don't go upsetting things when we reach Drory. I'm blaming myself for not going sooner. Mammy needed us and we failed her, but at least I'll see her laid to rest properly in the place she loved best, and if there's any money left out of what we sent her, she'll have a fine big headstone to mark the spot. I'm away to Farmer Dan to tell him we have to go right away, so start getting your things together, for there's no time to be lost in reaching Drory.'

Gabe heard him clumping heavily down the stairs. And thirty seconds later he was lying full-stretch on his bed and blubbing like a baby. It wouldn't bring her back, but it lifted some of the pressure from his brain, and by the time Mick came back upstairs to pack his own belongings in a travelling bag he'd borrowed from Missus, Gabe was flushed and shaken, but ready to make the journey home, as if Drory was a penance he'd always known he'd have to make.

Farmer Dan and Farmer Lester were gruffly agreeable to their leaving, finding embarrassment in any talk of grief or death. It was something peculiar to the English, Mick decided, for at home they'd had many a lively discussion round the kitchen table with Father Flynn on the wonders of the hereafter and the miracles that were all around if a body cared to look for them. Only just now he was in no mood to search for miracles or anything else. Farmer Dan had been good enough to loan them a horse and cart to take them to the boat at Bristol, which was right the other side of the country, and they were to leave it at the Inn where they'd put up for the night before the crossing, until their return.

'You *will* return, won't you, bors?' Farmer Dan eyed them keenly. 'We rely on you two more'n enough, and we know it. But I'd remind you that you've had a good living here wi'us, and there's duty to the living as well as the dead.'

'Farmer, that's no way to talk, with the poor bors' mother just lying dead,' Missus said in a hushed voice, but Mick shook his head slowly.

'He's right though, Missus. We can't help Mammy now, except to be there at her burying, but we owe you all a lot and we'll be back as soon as things are settled. You'll not begrudge us a few days with our family though?'

'Take a week,' Farmer Lester's voice didn't hide his relief at Mick's assurance. The pair of Pinnock farmers were aging rapidly, and without him and Gabe the farm would have deteriorated long ago. They owed them a good living and a roof over their heads–and anyway, what was there for them in Drory? The last real tie was gone with Mammy's death–Maureen had her Jack and her brood of children. Their first-born had died at birth and it had been three years before she conceived again, but then the four little Haggertys had been born within five years, so Maureen would be far too busy to spare too much time worrying her head about two wayward brothers who'd gone to England and stayed there. He hardly admitted to himself that he hoped she'd be too busy to give them a lecture the minute they set foot in Drory again, to make him feel even guiltier than he did already.

'We'll be off then, Missus.' Mick was the one to be embarrassed when the time came for leaving. Goodbyes were always tricky, especially when all had been said, and after all, the Pinnocks had never known Mammy. Gabe said very little on the journey West to Bristol, seemingly sunk in depression, and Mick found his mind wandering as they passed familiar landmarks; the Duck and Drake; the Bray cottage; the ribbony dykes gleaming in the thin sunlight like yellow silk. He thought briefly of Peggy, remembering how he was supposed to be seeing her that evening, and that she'd be put out at not knowing why he didn't turn up.

But there was no time to be thinking of such things now, and he was getting a bit anxious about the strong hints Peggy was giving out about getting wed. She was supposedly practically tied up with Kenneth Bray, but he was sure she'd change her mind without a qualm if Mick was to say the word and marry him instead. Only he wasn't sure he wanted it that way after all, not even for the sweetness of taking something one of the Brays wanted. Peggy was all he needed when the call of his loins got the better of him, but he'd·a feeling she'd be a shrew of a wife and he was content to let things stay as they were for the present.

Besides, how could he suggest stopping on the way to Drory on such a mission? It would seem slightly blasphemous to delay his arrival for Mammy's burying on account of his own desires to keep Peggy sweet towards him. No, it couldn't be done. He knew in his heart Mammy would never have approved of a blowsy wench like Peggy, and perhaps subconsciously that was one more reason why he'd never got around to asking her to marry him over the years. And until now, Peggy had liked things the way they were–playing the field, he suspected.

'You mind and get yourself a good catholic wife one of these days, Mick,' Mammy had told him often enough in the days before he left Drory. 'Don't let your head be swayed by any wicked scarlet woman and let down Pa's good name. The O'Briens have always had a proud name, and I'd not want you to be the one to spoil it. You mind on what I say and on Father Flynn's teachings, and you'll not go far wrong.'

Holy Mother of God, was he hearing things now? Her thin voice seemed to wander in and out of his senses as if she was sitting here beside him in the cart, so that once or

186

twice he turned his head sharply just to prove to himself that there was no ghostly apparition seated there.

But he knew, without the telling, that Mammy wouldn't have considered Peggy in any way a suitable wife for him, and even though she never knew of her, he felt he'd let Mammy down. And in more ways than one. For hadn't he promised to come home to Drory one day to buy her the finest plot of land that money could buy? Mick's eyes filled, for the plot that would be ready for Mammy now was a cold and lonely place, not green and fertile as he had envisaged. He *had* let her down, and none knew it like himself, and not all the money he and Gabe had sent across the Irish Sea all these years could have made up for it, not then, not now, not ever.

'Are we stopping for some food soon, Mick?' Gabe's gruff voice broke into his brooding when they'd travelled for some long time and they were both feeling stiff and tired. 'Missus packed us a rare feast, so we might as well eat it if we feel like it or not. We'll not be doing Mammy any favours by starving ourselves.'

'You're right,' Mick agreed. He reined the horse to a stop near a shady tree and gave him his nosebag while they ate the provisions Effie Pinnock had provided. Neither felt much like eating, but each did it to please the other. Neither felt much like talking either, but when they talked they talked of *her*, and when they'd drained their jugs of ale and Mick had watered the horse, he looked at his brother thoughtfully.

'You know something, Gabe? We've talked more about Mammy this day than in a long time, and talked as if she's still here, still someone to be respected and loved. It's strange—or is that part of the faith, do you suppose? Discovering that we don't lose touch with our dear ones even when they cross over?'

'Mammy hasn't crossed over anywhere. She's *dead*!' Gabe said brutally. 'Dressing it up with fancy words won't change things, and I wish I was going anywheres in the world except Drory! I don't want to see our Maureen with her accusing eyes because we've stayed away too long, nor that snotty-nosed husband of hers and their crowd of good catholic babbies! I don't want to see Father Flynn greeting us like black sheep come down from the mountain at last, or else treating us like lepers for staying in England all this time. And most of all I don't want to see Mammy all thin and green and mouldering in her coffin.'

He was shuddering so violently Mick had to slap him hard to bring his glazed eyes back to normal and rid them of the look of horror they held. Mick held on to Gabe's arm with a grip of iron and looked hard into the haunted blue eyes.

'Now you listen to me, Gabe. They'll not say we came home slinking in the back door with our tails between our legs, nor like a pair of tinkers. We'll hold our heads high and act with dignity the way Mammy would expect. And we'll look on her face in the coffin and touch her hand and kiss her cheek so her spirit won't haunt us, and not flinch from it to have Maureen snapping our heads off for being less than men afterwards. Is it understood?'

Gabe nodded slowly, the colour slowly filling his cheeks again after their momentary whiteness. Sweet Jesus, but he'd need fortifying with something stronger than ale if he was to get through all this without disgracing himself. He'd not faced death, except in animals, since he'd held little Davey Bray in his arms nine years before, drowned from the broad, but the horror of it had never left him. And in his worst nightmares he'd still be holding that soft, limp little body and trying frantically to clear the muck and slime from his nose and eyes and mouth. He resisted the sudden urge to retch and muttered to Mick that he'd be all right.

'Good. Remember all I've said then. This is the last thing we do for Mammy and we won't let her down.'

They started off in the cart again, and Mick found himself repeating his own words over and over as the journey continued, needing a strength to sustain him as well. But if the two of them bolstered each other's spirits, they'd get by. And by that same evening they'd put up at the Inn on Bristol's waterfront and would make the crossing at first light the following morning. They'd be at Drory by midday.

Afterwards, Mick couldn't have said who was the uneasiest at the burying and the wake that went before it. Jack Haggerty was more pompous than they remembered, though Maureen could clearly see no wrong in the man at all, which was the way a good wife should be. The four Haggerty children seemed completely overawed by the fact of two new uncles none of them remembered fully; the house was hushed and overflowing with black-clad friends and relatives, and Father Flynn scurried about among the lot of them, full of his own importance and looking not a whit older than Mick and Gabe recalled him, and he was clearly a great god-like figure to their nieces and nephews. And not least to add to the children's apprehension was the white-lined coffin that lay in state upon its trestles in the front parlour where the pallid shell of their grandmother lay.

'Sweet Jesus, but I'll be glad when this day's over,' Gabe muttered to his brother as they followed in walking procession behind the small coffin to its last resting-place, to the accompaniment of wailing and sniffing and noisy sobbing.

'Bite your tongue, Gabe, and keep your nerve steady. 'Twon't be long now, and it'll all be over.'

He was trying hard to disassociate himself from the very reality of it all. Making his mind a blank, because, honest to God, he'd be a blubbering wreck like the rest of them if he wasn't careful, and it was bad enough to see Gabe near falling to pieces. One of them had to be strong . . . though for every agonised second it took for them to lower the coffin into the ground and to hear the wailing rise louder as Father Flynn's intoning voice went on and on and on, Mick was reliving his own private horror.

Last night he'd gone to the parlour to kiss Mammy a last goodbye, while the watchers stood round about the room, talking together in whispers. It had to be a trick of the light from the flickering candles, he'd told himself desperately, but he could have sworn Mammy's mouth had tightened by the merest fraction when he leaned over her, trying not to breathe too deeply because of the smell, and that there was a tiny glistening in her almost-closed eyes that frightened him near to death himself. He'd stumbled out of the parlour when he'd kissed her, knowing the watchers would consider it his natural grief, and knowing himself that the truth of it was he thought Mammy was condemning him for his lack of filial duty and his attachment to such as Peggy, even from the other side. For being now on the other side, she'd know all there was to know about him and Gabe. He'd clung to the wall outside the parlour, his fingers like leeches on the dark wood panelling, until his brother-in-law Jack had proved himself human after all and told him to follow him into his den where there was brandy waiting for him. He breathed deeply and hard and drank deeply, ignoring the way his head swam. It was what he needed.

'By God, Jack, it was a shock and all, seeing her like that.'

'Then try to forget it, man. Remember her as she was. That's the way she'd prefer it, and wouldn't you yourself? None of us wants their last memory to be as a shrivelled wraith.'

Mick had tried to forget. All night he'd tried, but now as the earth was scattered over the coffin her face rose up to haunt him, grotesque and accusing. And yet he'd done all for the best, he raged. He'd taken Gabe to England for Mammy's sake, so she'd have a good life with Maureen and Jack. He'd sent money back for her comfort every month without fail. He'd tried to be a good son in all but the thing she most desired–to have him and Gabe with her, and for that he was a failure.

Someone was nudging him to follow round the open grave, and he moved mechanically, hardly knowing what was happening any more. He was supposed to be strong.

He was a man, and he felt as bewildered as a child, and the only person he needed in all the world at that moment was lying beneath the cold earth of Drory and he'd never see her again. The hot tears blinded his eyes as he felt a hand rest firmly on his arm.

'I'll see you and Gabe as soon as you've an hour to spare, Mick,' Father Flynn's voice washed through the blur of his mind. Oh Jesus, was he to be censured still more?

'Father, I've not been to confession in a while,' he muttered. 'I'd be taking up a deal of your time.'

' 'Tis not the confession I'm wanting to see you about, Mick. 'Tis a personal matter and one of great importance to the two of you. But this is neither the time nor place for discussing it, nor while we're back at the house for the feasting. I'll see you both privately, tomorrow perhaps, and we can have a good long talk. Your Mammy wished it this way, God rest her soul.'

'Amen,' Mick's response was automatic. 'Very well, Father. Tomorrow.'

'Good. Come during the afternoon and we'll share a pot of tea together. 'Tis a long while since we did that, Mick.'

'So it is,' Mick inclined his head. 'We'll be there tomorrow afternoon, Father.'

What was this then? Some last-ditch attempt that Mammy had dreamed up to get him and Gabe secured back in the faith again? If so, it just added to the horror he felt that she could still reach out to him from the grave. He'd loved her, wanting always to enfold her frail body in his arms and protect her from all ills, and yet now he was afraid because of her. It didn't make sense. So it was with trepidation that he went with Gabe to Father Flynn's house at the top of Drory Hill.

'So he can look down on us all from his priestly position,' Gabe commented as they walked. 'What's the point of this meeting anyways? He'll not persuade us to stay, will he?'

'Would it be so bad if he tried?' Mick said curiously.

Gabe looked all round him. There was a remembered familiarity about the place, a feeling of peace and coming

191

home that couldn't be denied. A tugging at his heart–but it had the air of always being the place in which you began or ended your days, and the real excitement of living that happened in the middle, had to be lived out elsewhere. He shrugged, knowing it was nothing he could readily explain.

'There's nothing for us here, Mick. And we promised to go back. The Pinnocks need us. Drory doesn't.'

It was a statement of fact, but more than that. A severing of old ties that they both recognised, and in each of them was a sudden urge to get this meeting with Father Flynn over and done with, and to get back across the water to England.

They sat awkwardly in the priest's front parlour that overlooked the hill and the sprawling village below.

'Of course I've kept very much abreast of all your doings because of the letters you sent your Mammy, Mick, and it's pleased she'd be to know you'd both grown into strong, healthy men.' It was the mildest of reproaches, because she hadn't seen it for herself. 'And have you kept the faith all these years, Mick?'

Mick looked into the swirling bubbles at the top of his tea cup, filled with embarrassment and hating himself for it. He couldn't lie to a priest, but neither did he feel obliged to confess all.

'It's hard to explain, Father,' he began.

Father Flynn sighed. 'Ah, then you don't need to, Mick. But if the faith is still in your heart, God will know it, never fear.'

'What was it you wanted to see us about so specially, Father?' Gabe said quickly, knowing it would be his turn for being questioned next. His face flushed slightly as the priest gave him a sorrowing look, as if he could read right through the skin and into Gabe's head and knew Gabe O'Brien hadn't been a good practising catholic all these years either, had engaged in brawling and drinking and fornicating. Gabe flinched away from the penetrating look as if he'd been struck, but Father Flynn took on a more businesslike tone, and the brothers each gave a small sigh of relief.

'Your Mammy never left a will, nor anything so fancy,' he

looked at them both keenly. 'But your sister Maureen knew full well what her intentions were and approved of me seeing you both like this to explain them to you.'

He went across to his big desk and took out a box from a locked drawer. When he opened it, Mick stared to see a great bundle of letters inside, all his letters to Mammy written over the years.

'She kept them all!' he said huskily. He stared at them, and it was as if all his past–and Gabe's–was tied up in those thin twine-bound envelopes, and he didn't want to touch them. They were hers. But it was clearly Father Flynn's intention to give them back to him. There was another long envelope in the box which the priest tapped between his two hands.

'Aye, she kept them, Mick. They were more precious to her than gold. What use did she have for gold when her daughter and her good man took care of her so well? They're true catholics, the pair of them, as was your Mammy. True upholders of the faith, all of them. And your Mammy was more concerned with her boys' future than her own. Worldly matters meant nothing to her, which was why she instructed me to save all the money you two sent her and put it safely in the bank in my name, so that when the day came I should be able to deliver it straight into your hands with no fuss, which is just what I'm doing now. This is the day, Mick, and this is your inheritance, yours and Gabe's.'

He pushed the envelope into Mick's shaking hands. For a few minutes he couldn't get his thoughts together, or slide his nail under the seal of the envelope. He was as reluctant to open it as if it had been a barrelful of rats, but he was suddenly aware of Gabe's rapid breathing alongside him, and he ripped the envelope open.

The amount on the cheque danced in front of his eyes. It couldn't be so much. Had she spent nothing at all on herself? Nothing at *all*? That hadn't been their intention. The tears started into his eyes as he remembered urging her to spend as much as she needed, and he'd fully expected her to have given some to Maureen each month, to have donated a fair portion to the church, and for there to have been a modest little sum for both him and Gabe. But this . . . it was riches, he thought, stunned.

Gabe took the cheque from his shaking fingers and gasped. He didn't know what he'd expected really. He'd hardly thought about it, thinking like Mick, that Mammy would have needed plenty for living expenses, and there'd be a nice bit for them both when the accounting came. But he'd never imagined anything like the figures that dazzled his eyes now.

'If you'll take my advice you'll see that cheque gets safely into an English bank as soon as you get back, and draw on it when you wish.' Father Flynn went on calmly as if such riches came to the O'Briens every day of the week. 'But there are several more things to be said. Your Mammy wanted Maureen and Jack and the children to have most of what she possessed, which seemed right and proper after they'd given her a home all these years, but she was anxious there should be a tree planted by the church in Mick's name, for which she provided, and I'll see to that in due course. For Gabe, her baby, she said, she left this.'

He handed over a small envelope, inside which was Mammy's wedding-ring. Gabe nearly choked over it, and hardly knew whether thank you was the appropriate thing to say at the moment. He stuck it on his little finger and curled his fingers into his palm, and the priest nodded with satisfaction at the action.

And a few days later they were on their way back to England, the goodbyes said, and assurances made for keeping in touch, and with Maureen becoming emotional and hugging them both tightly at the quayside as if she'd never let them go. In their minds as the boat slid away from the Irish coast was the realisation that now they could buy anything they wanted. For the first time in their lives the O'Brien brothers could hold up their heads in the community.

'Listen Gabe, 'tis best we say nothing to anyone about

this money,' Mick said warningly. 'Once the news got out 'twould spread like wildfire and we'd be at the mercy of all the rogues in creation. As soon as we get the chance we'll get off to King's Lynn and put the cheque in the bank in two separate accounts, so we can each use it as we see fit. That makes sense, doesn't it?'

'Oh aye,' Gabe said at once. 'Have you plans then, Mick?'

'Well, the Pinnocks can't go on farming for ever,' he said slowly. 'I'm thinking the time may be ripe for buying them out if they'll agree, but it's something to be suggested cautiously, and I wouldn't want to turn them out in their lifetime. Maybe we can work out an arrangement. I think 'tis something Mammy would have approved.'

Gabe let his brother dream and work out the easing of his own conscience. There was a dream stirring in his own mind too, that he wasn't prepared to share with anyone yet, not even Mick. But it was far removed from any idea of buying up the Pinnock farm.

CHAPTER THIRTEEN

'Are you absolutely sure, Jenny?' Marnie demanded. 'You haven't got mixed up with your times and forgotten when it should have happened?'

'How could I forget?' Jenny spoke through shivering lips. 'It's true, I tell you. What am I going to do? Ma's been going on at me only this very day about being an outcast should anything like this happen to a servant girl. It was just as if she had some idea of it. I can't tell her, nor Da! Nor the boys!'

She was near to hysteria and Marnie shook her shoulders. There was no sense in wasting words, and she spoke bluntly.

'Da will kill you if he finds out, and you know it. There's only one answer, and that's to get you wed as soon as possible. Who's the lad?'

Jenny stared at her sister with huge, frightened eyes, the trembling words suddenly stilled on her lips. Don't tell anyone, Gabe had said, least of all your sister . . . and didn't she know just what her family's reaction would be if they discovered it was Gabe O'Brien who'd put the child in her belly? Unconsciously her hand went to cover it, as if to protect it.

'I'll not tell,' she said in a low voice. 'I'll never tell. It wasn't his fault no more than mine. Why should he pay?'

'Why should you! Don't be such a fool, Jenny. Is there some reason why he can't marry you? Is he married already? Good God, you haven't been up to that game, have you?'

'He's not married, and I'm sure he'll do right by me when he finds out. But I haven't had the chance to tell him yet, and he should be told first before I say his name. It's only fair.'

With childish logic she stuck out her lower lip, and Marnie felt a stab of compassion for her.

'All right. But don't forget it's your child's name too, and don't let him get away with it, you hear? You're no more than a child yourself!'

She suddenly caught hold of her trembling sister and pulled her into a swift, embarrassed embrace. Gullible little Jenny, to fall for some man's sweet plausible voice and enticing charms. Marnie felt a brief pang, because she knew so well the way it could be, but she'd chosen to turn her back on all of that—and look where it had got her sister, anyway! It was a heavy price to pay for a few moments' pleasure, and at sixteen there were a lot of years to go on paying.

'I'll keep your secret, Jenny, but this is one secret that can't be kept for ever. In time it will be obvious, and you must get things settled as soon as you can. When will you see the lad to tell him?'

'I don't know for sure,' Jenny stuttered. 'But very soon now.'

Another week before they met at the old mill. Another week in which the situation might change, she thought desperately. When the curse might even yet decide to pay her a visit, and it wouldn't be so much a curse then as a blessing—or she might try to see Gabe before then. He'd be coming to Larksby with the eggs, and sometimes she managed a few words . . . only it would take more than a few words to sort out this tangle. But she loved him and she was sure he loved her. It would be all right, it *would*! She felt the touch of Marnie's lips on her cheek, and the sudden smoothing of her hair, and her eyes blurred, knowing what a mess she'd got herself into, and that the worst of it all lay in front of her.

'I'll help any way I can, Jenny, but when all's said and done, this is one game you started on your own, and one you've got to get out of yourself, with the lad's help. He's got to wed you, and quickly.'

'I know it.'

But when egg-day came, it was Effie Pinnock who arrived in the kitchen at Larksby, red-faced and puffing, to dump the egg-boxes on the kitchen table and sit awhile to catch her breath and spin a few yarns, while Cook told Jenny to fetch the farmer's wife a glass of barley water to cool her down. And then she heard Effie explain through short panting breaths how it was she was delivering, instead of the farmhand.

'Gone over to Ireland, the pair of them, for their mother's burying, and proper cut up they both were too. Farmer had to let 'em go, of course, though things couldn't be worse at the farm at present, with Farmer Lester complaining of pains in his belly the whole time, and keeping Farmer and me awake at night with his groaning in the next room. I'm thinking it's something worse than just the colic that ails him, and a sorry state we'd be in if they O'Brien bors decided not to come back. Farmer depends on 'em like his own sons, and no mistake.'

She took a long drink of the cooling barley water while she paused for breath. And by the stone kitchen sink, Jenny's hands remained frozen over the pile of baking tins she was supposed to be scouring, her face a white mask, her stomach tying itself in knots as she heard Effie Pinnock's rasping words.

Gabe had gone away, the thought stabbed into her brain. And Mrs Pinnock had hinted that he might not come back. Dear God, what would she do if that happened? He must come back, he *must* . . .

'They wouldn't leave you in the lurch like that, my dear,' Cook was saying comfortably. 'They know when they're well off, and the young 'un always seemed content enough when he came here.'

'Oh aye, I'm not truly worried,' Effie Pinnock agreed, to Jenny's enormous relief. 'Though Gabe's always been one for having stars in his eyes, and you should hear him go on about America sometimes when he's got a bellyful of ale. You'd think the streets were paved with gold to listen to him, but Mick's heart is in the land all right, and I reckon they'll be back soon. A week is what Farmer told them to take, so they should be getting back by this week's end.'

This week's end. So she wouldn't be able to see him

before then, Jenny thought. And her next evening off wasn't until Wednesday, when he'd be meeting her at the old mill. If he turned up, she thought suddenly. If he was as upset by his mother's death as Effie Pinnock said, maybe he wouldn't want to see her so soon. She'd just have to pray that he'd be glad to see her to take his mind off things for a little while . . . only when he did, he'd have more worries to think about. But she couldn't concern herself with sparing his feelings, she thought desperately. He had to know, and all that mattered was seeing him and telling him, and hearing him say that of course they'd be wed and everything would be all right, and he'd smooth the path with her family . . . and Wednesday wasn't that far away.

After all, he was still in mourning. He needed a little time to recover from one ordeal before facing another, even though she couldn't give him too *much* time. She heard Cook snapping at her to get on with the scouring, and plunged her hands into the greasy water as if her life depended on it.

Marnie would want to know if she'd seen her lad, she thought frantically. She'd have to be careful how she got round the fact that he wasn't here at present, so that Marnie shouldn't put two and two together. It would soon filter round that the O'Brien brothers had gone off to Ireland, and Marnie might begin to wonder. She'd have to invent some tale about her lad being ill, but that she'd arranged to see him at the earliest chance.

'See that you do then,' Marnie said, when she'd spun the tale. She was troubled for her sister, seeing the dark shadows deepen under her eyes, and the quick, nervous movements she made with her hands. Incredible though it seemed, this trouble of Jenny's had drawn Marnie closer to her than she'd have believed possible, and the old, hateful jealousy had been smothered in the anxiety she felt on her behalf. She hoped desperately Jenny would soon get things settled, and wished she'd tell her who was responsible for her condition, finding it oddly irritating and endearing at the same time, as she recognised Jenny's determination and loyalty in letting the lad know first.

She'd tried to fathom it out for herself. None of the Larksby employees, she guessed, or Jenny would have informed him before now. Somebody she'd met through Dolly, perhaps, or at the cottage with her brothers. Marnie frowned, knowing the circle of acquaintances had to be small, and yet wondering if she really knew her sister at all. Though they both lived and worked at Larksby, their worlds revolved independently, and she knew a sharp feeling of guilt for the lack of interest she'd always shown in her sister's affairs.

She'd make up for it now, she vowed. Poor little innocent, to be facing all this alone. She remembered Darryl Larksby, and the way he'd forced himself on her when she was just such an innocent, and shuddered. At least Jenny seemed sure of the lad's reaction to her news, which was something for which to be thankful. She couldn't imagine how the so-called gentry would have greeted it, had it been one of them on the receiving end, particularly one such as Darryl Larksby. It made her blood run cold just to think of it.

It still surprised Marnie to find how much she'd mellowed towards her sister since learning of her plight. As if by proving that pretty little Jenny was not beyond being besmirched and in need of protection, all the latent protectiveness of which she was capable had suddenly surged to the surface of Marnie's character. Instead of filling her with anger and contempt for the lad responsible, the knowledge that both of them would be like wide-eyed innocents floundering in a sea of matrimony had somehow softened her, especially when she'd listened to Jenny's stumbling words about how she truly loved the father of her child. How she *wanted* him . . . she'd looked at Marnie as if not really expecting her to understand, but oh, she did, she *did* understand, and ached to comfort her.

She found her expansive mood spreading to feel sympathy for the ailing Farmer Pinnock when Jenny remarked on it casually after Marnie had seen Effie toiling back down the driveway towards the horse and cart, and then heard her comment equally casually that the O'Brien brothers had gone home for their mother's burying. Poor Gabe, Marnie thought, with a rush of sadness for him. He did so hate for anything to be hurt or to die, and he must really be feeling this. And never for a moment did the slightest suspicion cross her mind . . .

She was walking through the meadows on her own free day on Tuesday, and musing over how the gods had at least been kind to her on one count, and never let her be with child, neither from Gabe's inexpert lovemaking, nor Darryl Larksby's hateful attentions. The knowledge was tempered with a renewal of the feeling that perhaps she was barren, and her body would never know the feel of a child growing within it the way Jenny's did. It would have filled her with regret for the future if she hadn't been too fervently grateful that it had never happened in the past.

She looked up suddenly as a shadow lengthened over the soft young grass at her feet, and the colour flooded into her face as she encountered the clouded eyes of Gabe O'Brien. He swayed slightly on his feet, his mouth tightening as if bracing himself for their usual caustic exchanges whenever they met.

But Marnie was enveloped by a swift remorse for all the time they had wasted in hating each other, when the feeling burning inside her now had nothing at all to do with hate. And surely he must see it, he must know it. Impulsively she put her hand on his arm.

'Gabe, I'm so sorry about your mother,' her voice was breathless, her brown eyes pleading for him to relax his usual aggression towards her and be friends. And glory upon glory, after a few seconds his mouth softened into a half-smile, enough to mark the dimples in his cheeks and crinkle the sides of his eyes so that their blueness was dazzling, the way they used to be.

'Aye, 'twas a shock,' he nodded slowly. 'Stupid how we expect our parents to live for ever, isn't it? When it stands to reason they'll go first, mostly anyway.' He looked down

201

at the ground between them, his own need for comfort accepting her need to give it. And maybe now would be as good a time as any for putting old ills behind them, now that there were plans to be made. 'Are you still blaming me for Davey, Marnie? Even now?'

She felt the sting of tears at the backs of her eyes. The pressure of her hand was still warm on his arm, and she found herself shaking her head slowly.

'I thought I was, but I gave up blaming anybody a long time ago, Gabe, if I did but admit it. I'm adult enough to see now that it was fate that was to blame if anything, only it's hard to find the words to say sorry when a thing's gone on for so long, isn't it?'

'So it is. But maybe we've both grown up since those days. Maybe it's time we saw each other as two different people, not as two children who ran wild across the fens and didn't really know what time of day it was, let alone be capable of handling adult situations.'

She realised he had one arm around her waist, and that the other was touching her hair, let loose from the habitual braid she still wore at Larksby, and falling in gleaming waves to the small of her back. She heard the sound of her own breathing, shallow and ragged and waiting.

'Oh Gabe, I never wanted the hurt between us to go on so long,' she said all in a rush. She looked up into his face, her heart in her eyes, and the man in him was stirred by the sight of her soft trembling mouth, so that it was more than he could do to resist kissing it. He felt her arms tighten round his neck and her body shape itself to his as if she couldn't be close enough to him—and why should he resist what was offered, and when he was so in need of comfort?

'Come back to the farm with me, Marnie,' he said thickly against her lips. 'There's nobody there and they'll not be back for hours. Mick's gone with Farmer and Missus to the infirmary to see what ails Farmer Lester, since the doctor's so puzzled. We'll not be disturbed, and you can see how I've come up in the world with a room of my own and all.'

He was persuasive, his voice deep and sensual, still with

the delicious Irish lilt that had always fascinated her. And she needed little persuading, for he'd always held her heart in his hands, even if he never knew it, and when he opened them to let her in, she went gladly and willingly. Yet she still felt somehow as if this was all a beautiful dream she'd dreamed so many fruitless times, and that his tenderness had grown out of his vulnerability just now, when he was still grieving for his mother. And she on her part wanted so desperately to comfort him, the need for him suffusing every other emotion; the need to touch and hold and love, to let him know she cared and had always cared, and always would, till the end of time. She was caught up in such a tumultuous rush of love for him she'd have followed him anywhere, done anything, as long as he continued looking at her as if he was really seeing her again, with none of the hardness that had glittered in his blue eyes towards her for so long. If she had ever believed in miracles, Marnie thought humbly, it was now, when Gabe O'Brien was making it very plain that he wanted her.

But when she finally lay in his arms on his narrow bed and she could feel the maleness of his body beside her as his fingers caressed the roundness of her breasts when they were freed from the restricting bodice of her frock, the exquisite longing to belong to him, body and soul, was almost like a physical pain inside her. It was a long while since she'd felt such fire in her veins, or known such eagerness to know a man's body in such intimacy, and the childish remembrances of that one fumbling time of discovery with Gabe in the old mill, and the nightmare of Darryl Larksby's assaults on her were finally blotted from her mind for ever as the new pulsating sensations claimed her with the mounting passion between them.

'Oh Gabe,' she heard herself moan as he slid gently between her thighs. 'Oh Gabe, let this really be happening. Don't let me wake up tomorrow to find it was all a dream. I couldn't bear it, not now!'

And then she stopped talking as his mouth covered hers, as the rhythmic movements began and she matched every one with her own, going to meet him in a shared ecstasy that was drowning her senses and sending her into an almost trance-like state, until he suddenly held her more tightly, gathering her up in his arms as she felt the explosion of his climax inside her. They lay there without moving for long afterwards, his mouth still on hers, his body still fusing with hers; as if both were reluctant to move away, to break the spell that held them captive.

'I've always loved you, Gabe,' she whispered at last, with a catch in her throat. 'Always . . .'

'And I you. Even when I knew . . .'

Her eyes opened slowly as he stopped, bringing the room into focus, bringing her back to reality, seeing the blur of the ships' posters all round the walls of his room; their clothes scattered about haphazardly; the sun shining in through the window. It should be the moon, she thought illogically. All the important times in her life were supposed to happen at the time of the full moon, weren't they? She smiled indulgently to herself. Moon child. The moon child was a child no longer, but a woman loved, and in love.

'When you knew what?' she said lazily, bringing her gaze back to Gabe's beautiful face again. And saw that it wasn't quite as smiling as it had been just now . . . dear God, was he going away from her again? She reminded herself swiftly that he might suddenly be feeling guilty at pleasuring himself so soon after his mother's burying. She swung her legs off his bed and picked her clothes up from the floor, covering her nakedness hurriedly.

'Please don't try to explain anything, Gabe. It's all right,' she said softly. 'But I think I'd best be getting back to Larksby now, before they get back from the infirmary.'

She wanted to say she was glad–so very glad–they'd found each other again, only somehow she felt such words wouldn't be quite right at such a time if he did indeed feel as she supposed. Words were inadequate anyway, for all that needed to be said had been said between them in the act they'd shared, and he was truly hers again. That much was certain, she thought exultantly, and all else could wait.

They both knew the truth of it and that was all that counted. When they were both fully dressed again, she leaned across the bed and touched him gently on the mouth with her fingertips.

'She wouldn't have begrudged you this, Gabe,' she said softly. 'She'll be resting in peace, never fear.'

He looked a little startled for a minute, and then she was clasped in his arms again and he was kissing her hard as if to make up for all the lost kisses between them.

'She'd have loved you,' he said huskily. 'I know she would. Will I come with you to the end of the lane?'

Marnie shook her head. She suddenly wanted to be alone, to mull over the stupendous thing that had happened so unexpectedly. The whole world was suddenly a joyous place again, and she and Gabe O'Brien were lovers. *Lovers.* The word had a beautiful sound, and she repeated it often to herself all the way home, knowing that her whole being glowed because of it. Because of him. She didn't want to see or speak to anyone, and she shut herself in her room at Larksby, gazing at the face in the mirror that was suddenly alive again, wanting to laugh and sing and cry all at the same time, because she was so happy, and wishing everybody in the world could be as happy. She sobered quickly, remembering her sister Jenny, but even Jenny's problem couldn't diminish the joy of remembered passion she and Gabe had shared so spontaneously. Nothing on earth could take away the memory of that.

For Gabe too, the memory was very sweet, even though he was asking himself a while later just how it had happened, when he'd firmly told himself he'd never give himself so wholly to a woman again. Enjoying the pleasures of the flesh was one thing, but to have known such a perfection of unity with her, to have felt it as much a spiritual experience as a physical one, had left him shaken and slightly afraid, as if no woman should have that kind of power over a man's feelings and emotions. The very maleness of him protested at the idea even while he had exalted in possessing her. But who possessed whom, he wondered now? as his tingling senses returned to normal.

And that Marnie should have this power over him, when he'd vowed never to let her entangle herself in his heart again, and had told himself angrily that she was trouble? He was still enough in control of his emotions to want to cling on to his convictions, even when every part of him remembered the softness of her ... and there had been a sweet inevitability in their coming together this day. She was as he remembered from his first inexpert attempt at love-making, remembered and yet different, so different ... it had had a glorious familiarity and an exciting newness at one and the same time.

'Gabe, are you anywhere about?'

He started as he heard Mick's voice calling him from below. He'd been so lost in dreaming he hadn't heard his brother and the Pinnocks returning, and he ran downstairs guiltily, hoping his unusually high colour would go unnoticed, and that no-one could guess that he'd spent the last hour lying upstairs with Marnie Bray in his arms.

But there were other things to occupy the minds of the three people in the big farmhouse kitchen. He saw at a glance that Missus had been crying, and Farmer looked crumpled, suddenly old.

'The news is bad for Farmer Lester, Gabe,' Mick said briefly. 'They've kept him at the infirmary, but they don't give out much hope. Maybe if they'd got him there sooner ...'

He shrugged, and Gabe stared at him disbelievingly, not wanting to credit that someone else close to them was dying. The Pinnocks were closer to him and Mick than family now, and he felt a sharp grief that one of the genial brothers should be facing the end. How would the other one react to it, he wondered? One look at Farmer's face confirmed that his own will to live wouldn't last long without his brother. They were like two sides of the same piece of cloth.

It was all wrong to be so dependent on another human being, Gabe thought angrily, and suddenly he couldn't stand there making mumbling platitudes in a house that seemed to be already mourning before there was even a corpse. And he'd had enough gloom at Drory. At least Marnie had helped him forget for a little while. He stumbled out of the kitchen, saying he had things to attend to, and Mick found him a little while later, with his forehead pressed hard against the coldness of a milk churn on the stone table. Mick put his hand on his brother's shoulder in shared sympathy.

'This won't change things, Gabe,' he said gruffly. 'In fact, while they were all at the infirmary, I went to the bank and saw the manager and deposited our cheque. They'll want your signature too, so I suggest that you're the one to take Farmer and Missus in to see Farmer Lester tomorrow, and attend to it while they're visiting. I've made the overtures towards buying them out, and I think they'll be very agreeable.'

'What kind of ghoul are you to be talking about such things when a man's dying?' Gabe said angrily. His own brother to be so insensitive . . .

'Not ghoulish at all,' Mick said calmly. 'It took their minds off the immediate trouble, and eased their worry for the future, I'm thinking. Farmer Dan seemed to welcome the suggestion, and you can see for yourself he'll have no stomach for the place without his brother. You have to be realistic, Gabe, and I made sure they realised they'd always have a home here, and that things would go on very much as before, with Missus doing the cooking and cleaning and all. Damn it, man, I'm as sorry as anybody that this has happened, but somebody's got to be practical, and those two look as if they've been pole-axed.'

Gabe had to see the sense of it, though it seemed bloody callous to him to be thinking about money and buying land when Farmer Lester's life hung by a thread. He agreed to taking the Pinnocks into the infirmary the next day, and he went to put his signature to the forms at the bank, and heard himself called Mr O'Brien with a note of deferential respect in the bank manager's voice.

What a difference money made, he thought bitterly. And if only it could buy good health, there'd be even more incentive to earn it.

The Pinnock farm seemed to be awash with tears all the rest of that day, and by evening Gabe could stand it no longer. He strode out across the fields, intending to make for the Duck and Drake. Intending to drink himself near insensible to blot out the sight of Missus and Farmer pathetically clinging on to each other like so much flotsam after a shipwreck. He couldn't stand the sight of their grief. The softness in his heart couldn't take any more, and if anything could block the memory of it, temporarily anyway, it would be Mr Jackson's good strong ale that had acted as a panacea time and enough.

But before he was halfway there he heard running footsteps behind him, and heard his name being called breathlessly and urgently. He turned with reluctance, knowing he'd completely forgotten about her, knowing she'd been totally out of his thoughts ever since going home to Drory; since yesterday with Marnie; since the happenings at the farm; he'd certainly forgotten any idea of going to the old mill today . . .

'I'm glad I caught up with you, Gabe,' Jenny's voice was quick and strained and nervous, and he registered vaguely that she looked less sparkling than usual, her prettiness dimmed, her beautiful eyes anxious and heavy. She held on tightly to his arm, and he had to resist the sudden urge to shake her off like an unwelcome insect. She intruded into his sorrow at that moment.

'Farmer Lester's dead,' he said flatly.

'Oh!' She stood quite still, seeing that he was on a different plane of consciousness that she couldn't reach. All this just after his own mother had died. She licked her dry lips, knowing she *had* to reach him. The dead were beyond help, but the living proof of her need for him lay in her belly, and her hand covered it in the oddly protective way she had begun to adopt when thinking of the child.

'I'm sorry about Farmer Lester,' she rushed on, 'but I've

something of importance to tell you, Gabe, something that concerns the two of us. Gabe, I'm with child, I'm positive of it. There's been no sign for these past two months, ever since we've been together, and you know as well as I do there was no-one else before you!' She heard her voice grow shrill as he said nothing, but stared dazedly into her eyes as if she'd suddenly grown two heads. The look on his face frightened her, and she grabbed hold of both his arms and shook them.

'Gabe, you must help me! I don't know what to do! All I know is my Da will kill me if he finds out, and you as well. You've *got* to help me, Gabe!'

He suddenly came to life as the panic in her voice transmitted itself to him. Dear sweet Jesus, if her Da would kill her, what would he and those three murderous brothers of hers do to him if they found out he was responsible for this! Their sweet pretty Jennifer, spoiled by the likes of him, their hated enemy, who'd already tainted one sister when she was barely old enough by their reckoning to know what she was about! Killing would be too good for him . . . they'd dismember him bit by bloody bit until he was only good for fish-bait. He suddenly yelled at her as he found his voice, sharpened by panic.

'How can I help! I'm no witch-doctor to charm it away, am I? Are you sure it's really there anyway? Couldn't there be some mistake, for Christ's sake?'

Jenny burst into noisy sobbing, sagging against him so his arms had to hold her to stop her from falling.

'There's no mistake. And how can you talk of charming a child away, Gabe O'Brien? I thought you were supposed to be a good catholic, and such talk is wicked. It's a child–*your* child, and it has a right to live now you've put it in me. And you'll have to wed me, Gabe, so I can hold my head up high again and not be branded for ever because of it!'

He held her close to his chest as she started wailing again. His thoughts whirled at the shock of it, and his stomach felt like a writhing mass of worms inside him. Wed her! They'd never stand for that, those Bray men. Even though he'd stake his life on it being his child. There'd been no need for her to plead as heavily on that count. She'd been as pliant and naive beneath him, but he was in no mood to think on such things, and right at that minute he doubted if anything could stir him into sexual passion again. Not if this was the result, this shivering, frightened child who clung to him for reassurance and protection.

'We'll find a way round it, Jenny,' he said roughly against her flushed cheek. 'Just give me a while to think and to catch my breath on all this.'

She lifted her face and stared into his eyes, her own eyes drowning in tears, willing him to want her, to do what was right, and somehow to avoid bringing the wrath of her family down on both their heads. She noted wanly that for the first time ever he'd called her Jenny instead of her full name, as if somehow she was no longer the shining star she wanted to be for him but made of very mortal clay–but none of that mattered as long as he did right by her.

'Don't leave it too long, Gabe,' she stammered. 'We should get things settled as soon as possible, because it can't be hidden for ever.'

She smothered a sob as he pulled her close again, not wanting to see those frightened child's eyes a second longer, and the bleakness stared out of his own again as he looked unseeingly across the wide green fields into an uncertain future. He knew he had to do what was right. It was something that had been instilled in him since birth, by his parents and his church, and however much he kicked against it, he'd have to wed little Jennifer Bray.

So this was his penance, he raged inside, for wanting one sister too much and the other not enough. But he steeled himself not to think of Marnie, not now.

'Just give me a week,' he muttered, almost to himself. 'This day week I'll have got things sorted out and we'll make plans. I promise you it'll be all right, so long as you promise me you'll tell no-one, Jenny. It can't make much difference to wait just one more week, and then I hope to have something to offer you.'

And by then he'd have been to King's Lynn and the shipping office and into the bank to draw out sufficient money, and he'd have put the plan in motion that was spinning round in his brain–the only plan possible in the circumstances.

CHAPTER FOURTEEN

Marnie looked at her sister in exasperation. She'd always thought she was the stubborn one of the family, but Jenny was showing she could dig her heels in with the best of them when she chose. The two of them faced each other in Marnie's room one evening while Geraldine and her father were at dinner. Marnie eyed her sister's still-slender figure where, as yet, there was no real sign of anything amiss except for a fullness in her breasts that hadn't been there before. The situation was soon going to make itself noticeable.

'Why won't you tell me?' Marnie demanded. 'Is the lad still ill? I'll go and see him myself if you're afraid . . .'

'It's nothing like that. I've seen him and told him and he's making plans. In a few days I'll know what he intends to do, but in the meantime I'm saying nothing to anybody. We arranged it between us, so please don't ask me to betray his trust, Marnie!'

She shifted her eyes away from Marnie's scathing stare, knowing she wouldn't think such a lad worthy of anybody's trust. Wishing Gabe were here right now to take her in his arms and tell her he loved her and they'd be wed right away and she wasn't to worry about a thing. She knew he wouldn't let her down, but it didn't stop her worrying. She worried herself sick, and she'd taken to chewing her nails, already softened by the amount of time they spent under water in the kitchen sink or at the washtub, so that now they were raw and bitten down to the quicks.

But Gabe had said not to tell, and she never would. He had his own reasons for insisting on secrecy, and she knew full well the feud between her family and his was a major reason, even if the history of it all was quite obscure to her. But she preferred not to have the holocaust descend on her head until it was absolutely necessary. And having listened openmouthed to Gabe's plan, with luck they'd be too far away for anyone to catch up with them by the time anyone connected their disappearances.

'And he *will* wed you?'

Jenny hid a sigh as she nodded quickly. Marnie was so insistent . . . but he'd said he would, hadn't he? She was sure he'd said so. He must have done, or he wouldn't have taken the trouble to see that she was taken care of like this . . . in any case, he hadn't said he wouldn't. And she was impatient for the days to pass so she could see him again and hear that the plans were under way, even though the magnitude of them still made her feel very afraid. But Gabe had always had a persuasive tongue, and he'd convinced her that this was the only way.

Marnie had spent more hours dreaming about Gabe during that week than in the whole of her life before, only now the dreams were built on substance and not on shifting sand. He loved her and she loved him, and the fact that she knew there must be a great deal of sadness and work going on at the Pinnock farm right now after Farmer Lester's death was the only thing that could curb her impatience to see him again. She knew he wouldn't be able to get away to visit her at all, and his mind would be too filled with the sad business of the burying.

No, of course she couldn't think of seeing him yet, but it didn't stop her missing him, nor dreaming of him to the extent that Miss Geraldine remarked on it caustically early one evening while they were on their way for dinner with one of Geraldine's young lady acquaintances at North Lea, a country house some two miles distant towards King's Lynn, and for which Marnie had to be in attendance.

'If I didn't know better, I'd say you had your head full of a young man, Marnie,' Geraldine commented, as they trotted along in the pony and trap over the grassy tracks.

'Is it so impossible to imagine then?' Marnie said, with the familiarity of a long-time employee. Geraldine laughed.

'I suppose not, with anyone else. You're a young woman still, though I tend to forget it sometimes when you get that prissy look about your mouth. I always feel years older than you then, though you're not much more than twenty, are you?'

'Twenty-two.'

'Well, it's time you were thinking about young men, I suppose, or that pretty sister of yours will be getting married before you do.'

Marnie kept her face a blank, a habit she'd learned to do quite successfully when necessary, though she couldn't stop the sudden leap of her senses at Geraldine's words. Just as if she guessed . . . but of course, she couldn't have done. She didn't have as much contact with the kitchen maids any more, and Jenny was so close about this lad of hers she doubted if she'd even confided in Dolly, let alone let a whisper of it reach her mistress' ears and be in danger of being thrown out of her job in disgrace.

Not that Geraldine and her friend, Miss Ellis of North Lea, would be above indulging in as much tittle-tattling as their servants, Marnie thought. There was nothing much to choose between them in that, and she'd heard many a spicy piece of gossip when she'd been in attendance at the far end of a drawing-room, supposedly deaf and dumb and blind as befitted her station. And many was the tale she could tell, if she chose, not least, the reason why Mr Andrew Lacey never came to Larksby any more, and why the brief attachment between them had died a quick death on Geraldine's discovery that he already had a fiancée, at present travelling with her father in India, but due back in England any day.

Remembering Mr Lacey's wishy-washy manners and long pale face, Marnie couldn't see that Geraldine had lost very much, but her mistress had been swollen-eyed and red-cheeked for days, and snapped her head off every time she opened her mouth, and Marnie was very glad when she'd apparently recovered from the slight to her dignity and announced that in future Mr Lacey's name was not to be mentioned.

And the evening at North Lea was no different from the usual round of endless chatter between the two young ladies after dinner, while Marnie sat with Miss Ellis' maid at a discreet distance away from them, awaiting any demands their mistresses might make on them.

Barbara had been haughty towards her at first, coming from a slightly more elevated background than a lonely fen cottage, but eventually unbending enough to indulge in a little light conversation in low tones, to relieve the boredom of the evening, though Marnie never felt she could take to her the way she'd taken to Sal, and she still mourned the loss of the easy friendship she and the other girl had once shared.

This one, Barbara, was too finicky, and over-conscious of herself as lady's maid to be anything like a real friend. Marnie had no real friends now, she thought with a stab of regret, unless she counted Jenny. She pondered on that while she admired the petit-point embroidery of Miss Ellis' firescreen that Barbara was quick to point out with as much pride as if she'd worked it herself.

It was funny to consider her sister her friend . . . and yet, why not? Presumably Jenny thought of her that way to have come running to her with her trouble, even if she hadn't been confident enough of her reaction to tell her the whole story. But no doubt that would follow soon, and Marnie hoped fervently the episode would be resolved without too much fuss. And in due course, she would be an aunt, she reminded herself, with an unexpected surge of pleasure. And she'd have the chance to hold a baby in her arms again.

'Marnie, you'd best get that silly grin off your face and stir yourself,' Barbara managed to look disapproving even while she hissed the words under cover of a cough. 'Miss Larksby is preparing to leave, and keeps looking hard at you.'

She started, completely lost in her reverie for a moment, the sudden sharp memory of how Davey had felt in her arms all those years ago, soft and warm and sweet-smelling, as vivid in her mind as if it had been yesterday.

She rose quickly to attend to Geraldine, and by the time they were told one of the North Lea stable-lads was ready to ride alongside them back to Larksby, Marnie had recovered herself.

The night was soft, the air balmy and scented with the wild flowers growing in profusion along the hedgerows lining their track. A full yellow moon, the parish lantern of the fens, lit their way as if it was daylight, throwing long shadows ahead of them. There was hardly any need to feel nervous before the grey stone mass of Larksby loomed up in front of them, and the stable-lad took his leave of them with a touch of his cap to Geraldine and a wink and a nod to Marnie. She helped her mistress out of the trap and handed the reins to their own stable-lad who appeared as soon as the clop-clop of hooves announced their arrival.

'There's a bit of a to-do in the kitchen, Marnie,' he breathed in her ear. 'Your Da's been there this long while waiting for you, and the young 'un, Dolly, told me to get you in there as soon as you can manage it.'

Marnie stared at him. A to-do in the kitchen? What was that to her? And her *Da* here? Her heart gave a sudden uneasy lurch. Jenny hadn't been so foolish as to blab everything at home that evening, had she, before everything was properly settled? Or been so reckless as to take the lad home with her on her evening off and blurt out that they were to be wed, so that Da put two and two together and laid into the pair of them?

The possibilities spun round and round in her head. She knew she had no choice but to escort Miss Geraldine into the house and help her out of her visiting clothes, into her sleeping attire and see that she was settled for the night, before she could even think of visiting the kitchen and see what had brought Da here this night. She wasn't too sure she wanted to know anyway, she thought uneasily, because one thing was certain. It couldn't be good news.

'You're all fingers and thumbs tonight, Marnie,' Geraldine complained crossly as she fumbled with the buttons on her dress. 'That's twice you've pinched me. For heaven's sake be careful, girl, or I shall be black and blue tomorrow.'

'I'm sorry, Miss Geraldine . . .'

'And don't stand there hanging your head like a pet dog, stupid! And close the window, will you? I've a fancy to sit up in bed and read for a while, and I don't want to catch a chill. Go down to the library for me and bring up the book I was browsing through yesterday. You'll find it on the small sofa-table.'

But when she'd brought it Geraldine had changed her mind and wanted a different one, and Marnie could have cried with frustration as she sped up and down the stairs, itching to get down to the kitchen by now and see what was wrong. Her imagination had moved away from Jenny, and she was fretting that perhaps Ma was dangerously ill, or one of the boys hurt in an accident, and the breath was tight in her chest and there was a stitch in her side by the time Geraldine had finally done with her and she could hurtle down the cord-carpeted staircase to the servants' quarters. When she entered the kitchen she was so out of breath and panicky she could hardly speak, and stood there pressing her side where the stitch still stabbed at her before she could say a word.

Her eyes took in the group of them. Dolly was cowering by the stone sink, her eyes darting about in fright and obviously wishing she was somewhere else if Da's raging temper had been much in evidence; Cook was banging pots about, her face fiery red as a turkey-cock, her arms ready to flay anyone in sight; Mrs Caine was trying to placate Da and having no more success than if she'd tried to stop the sun rising every morning. And Da . . . Marnie felt the saliva dry up in her mouth. He looked wild enough to throw a fit at any minute, and as soon as she appeared in the doorway he rounded on her at once.

'Now then, girl, what do you know about all this?' he roared at her.

'Know about what?'

She stared back unflinchingly, a look which he defined as insolent, and within two strides he was over the kitchen floor towards her and cuffing the back of his hand across the side of her head.

'Don't play the innocent with me, miss,' he shouted, as she gasped with pain and bit back furious tears at this outrage in front of the kitchen employees. 'Your sister is what I'm on about!'

'It's nothing to do with me. I know nothing!' Marnie shouted back.

Stupid Jenny, she was thinking irately, to have gone home and told them everything, and evidently to have got Da's dander up with her too by saying Marnie had been a party to it all! She could have left her out of it, she thought furiously, and why wasn't she here in the thick of it anyway . . . or had Da decided to keep her at home in the cottage under his eye from now on?

'Where is she?' he demanded. He shook her shoulders until her teeth rattled in her head. 'I'll have the truth of it now. None of your fairy tales, girl!'

She stared at him as if he was stupid.

'How do I know where she is! In bed, I suppose, if Cook's done with her for tonight and she's not at home with you. Where else would she be?'

A horrible certainty took hold of her as the silence between them stretched on, and only Dolly's snuffling breathing could be heard in the kitchen. If Jenny hadn't gone home on her evening off, as seemed likely, and she wasn't here, then it could only mean one thing–that she and her lad had decided to flee together and tell no-one at all of her condition or their future plans. Marnie forced back the momentary feeling of being cheated and not getting the chance to hold Jenny's baby and nurse the child after all, but that was the least of her thoughts right now.

'Didn't she go home this evening then?' she said unnecessarily.

'She did not! And Ma's there fretting to see her, sick and bad with the influenza. So I said I'd call over here to see what stopped her visiting her family, only to find she's been gone from Larksby since early afternoon, and this ninny here says there's none of her belongings left in their room.'

Marnie swallowed hard as she glanced at the shrinking Dolly. It was true then. Jenny had fled with her lad, and even if he'd promised her the earth, she wouldn't give much for their chances if he was as poor as she, for they wouldn't find much work as a couple with a baby on the way. Maybe she'd have fared much better after all to have faced up to Da, once the lad was prepared to wed her, instead of turning tail and running.

In that minute, she lost patience with the pair of them. She'd. tried to help, had wanted to help, but they'd just upped and skidaddled like a pair of scalded cats. But at least Da looked as if he thought her own reaction was genuine, Marnie thought thankfully. He let go of her shoulders at last and she rubbed them tenderly.

'So!' He spoke grimly. 'You had no idea of what she was planning? Nor any reason for it?'

'No Da! I swear I didn't know. I couldn't make out what you were meaning just now.'

And she wasn't going to blab out the reason for it neither. Jenny was a fool, but the child she carried was blameless, and it was for the sake of the child that Marnie wouldn't risk Da's anger if he learned the truth and went after them.

Her Da finally nodded slowly, accepting her flustered words. And then there was a new torrent of abuse towards him from Cook and Mrs Caine for stirring up a hornet's nest in the household and frightening Dolly half to death. He rounded on them angrily.

'Shut your noise, you old fish-wives,' he yelled. 'Any father worth his salt would come looking for his girl, but at least I'm satisfied none of you had a hand in her going

219

missing. Maybe it's the constables I should be seeing next, in case some harm's come to her.'

'No, Da, don't do that,' Marnie said quickly. His eyes narrowed again as he looked at her, and she invented rapidly. 'She has been talking to me about leaving Larksby sometime to get a better position. I know she fancied being a–a lady's maid–like me. Only she wanted it to be a surprise for you, and I reckon that's where she'll be gone. I expect she'll be writing to tell you all about it in a few weeks when she's settled somewhere. Why don't you leave it awhile and see, and not spoil it for her? You know she's always been one for springing surprises to please you and Ma.'

She held her breath, praying he'd believe her. Banking on the way he'd always favoured his pretty Jenny and would accept that she'd done this to prove she could get as good a position as her sister. Unconsciously she crossed her fingers in her palms as she watched the doubts creep over Da's face, and then he shrugged.

'Aye, well, maybe that's the way of it then, though she should have asked me first, since I got her the position here. You young 'uns never did give much thought to your actions, always doing things on the spur of the minute, hasty and headstrong the lot of you. But you'd best come home and see your Ma then, Marnie, if our Jenny's gone off to better herself, for she's peevish and moaning with the aching in her limbs and four menfolk to wait on by herself.'

And no help from any of them, I'll be bound, Marnie thought savagely. And whose fault was it *she* was here at Larksby anyway? It hadn't been her idea to come here, dumped like an unwanted parcel . . . and the loneliness of that first Christmas away from home and the rejection she'd felt then seared through her all over again.

But she knew she'd be going to the cottage as soon as she could–tomorrow, she promised Da, providing Miss Geraldine would let her have a few hours free, and knowing too that by then she'd have invented more of Jenny's confiding in her to become a lady's maid for Ma and Da's benefit; embroidering the tale; smoothing the way; dispelling all suspicion; because once started on the road of deception, there seemed no other way but to follow it through.

And Jenny would once again emerge as the clever one. The bright sun who heartened Da's life . . . and in due course Marnie supposed she'd have to produce a letter supposedly from Jenny to assure them that all was well and that she now enjoyed a good 'position' as a lady's maid. Marnie thanked God for the fact that neither her parents nor her brothers could read or write. At least that simplified things a little, and they'd expect any letters there were to be sent to Marnie and passed on.

'Well! Aren't you going to offer a body a drink of cocoa, after all that gabbing?' Da suddenly demanded of Cook, who snorted loudly.

'Do you think you deserve it, Hal Bray, making enough noise to waken the whole household like that!' She scowled and muttered for a few minutes, and then told Dolly to stop gawping and put some milk on to heat and they'd all have some cocoa. She looked frostily at Marnie. 'How about you, miss? Will your fine lady allow you to stay and drink with the likes of us now?'

'She's not here to stop me, is she?'

Marnie's feathers were definitely ruffled. She'd been feeling perfectly happy and content coming back here tonight in the soft yellow moonlight, dreaming how it would be if she and Gabe had been riding along together towards a place of their own and within an hour it felt as if the sky had opened and rained down all the fury of the gods on her unsuspecting head.

Jenny had no idea what a fuss she'd left behind, she fumed. And what could have possessed the girl to go off into the night like this without giving even Marnie an inkling of what she had in mind? No, she'd been missing since early afternoon, Da had said, so she could be almost anywhere by now, assuming that this lad of hers had a bit of money or at least a horse or cart to take them in. Maybe he was rich after all and had swept her off in an elegant carriage, Marnie thought, with a twist to her mouth. It would be just like

Jenny to come up out of a dung-heap smelling of roses.

She was weary with the scene with Da coming at the end of the day and the boring waiting around for Geraldine at North Lea. And glad when he'd finally finished his cocoa and began stamping out of the kitchen, reminding her not to forget her promise to come to the cottage the next day.

'If Miss Geraldine will let me,' she said huffily. 'It's her I have to answer to, don't forget.'

And that's your fault too, she added silently, as he glared back at her.

'I'll tell your Ma she can expect you,' he was clearly going to accept no arguments. 'She can do with a bit of a hand with some baking and scrubbing while she's ailing.'

Marnie chewed her lip savagely as she watched him go, barely resisting the urge to yell after him that she'd given up skivvying when she'd become lady's maid to Miss Geraldine, but she banged the door behind him in a futile gesture, knowing full well she'd go to the cottage and do whatever was expected of her.

'Now then, we've had enough banging about for one night, miss,' Cook snapped at her. 'And enough upset from your family as well, and now I suppose we're to be looking for a new kitchen maid, since Jenny's decided to leave us in the lurch.'

'It's nothing to do with me,' Marnie said haughtily. 'I can't be held responsible for her.'

'I know somebody who'll take the job,' Dolly butted in eagerly, her eyes hopeful. 'Name of Florrie Tanner in the village.'

'Oh aye, another fly-by-night such as you, I daresay!'

'You'd best tell her to come along tomorrow, Dolly,' Mrs Caine overruled Cook's grumbling objection. 'The girl can't manage two people's work by herself, so we'll see if this Florrie girl will do for a while anyway.'

'Thank you, Mrs Caine,' Dolly shot a triumphant look at Cook, whose lips had tightened into a thin line of anger.

Nobody was missed for very long around here, Marnie thought. Jenny's disappearance would be a nine days' wonder, and then she'd be forgotten as easily as the waters closed over little Davey's head. She gave a sudden shudder as the thought spun into her head almost like a foreboding, and banged her mug down by the stone sink before leaving them to wrangle on without her. All she wanted to do was to fall into bed and sleep, and blot out everything about Jenny and Da and all else. She undressed in her room without lighting her lamp, in the light of the moon streaming in through her window, shivering a little as she pulled the cotton nightgown over her head, and threw back the bedclothes.

She saw the envelope with her name on it at once. It had been placed inside her bed where she couldn't fail to notice it, and she snatched it up, knowing it must be from Jenny. She lit the oil lamp quickly, and ripped open the seal of the envelope.

'Perhaps you'll think we've taken the coward's way out, Marnie,' she read, 'but it seemed the only thing to do, all things considered. We've made our plans very carefully, and I won't even tell you which port we're leaving from, nor which point of land the ship will land in America so you'll not be able to let on to anybody unwittingly. But I wanted you at least to know where we've gone.'

Marnie felt an awful suspicion begin to twist and unravel inside her. A sudden sharp image of a small farmhouse bedroom spun into her mind, the walls dotted with ships' posters, proclaiming the fine passages and opportunities awaiting emigrants who ventured to cross the Atlantic. She was aware of the thudding of her heart, the shaking of her hands and every part of her so that she could hardly keep the paper still to read on.

'I can't face Ma and Da, and I know what the boys' reaction will be if they hear of my condition. So I'm begging you, Marnie, if you have any feelings for me at all, to say nothing about the child in all this, nor that there was a lad involved. Let them think what they will about me . . .'

. . . and about *me* for lying for you, Marnie thought

223

bitterly. She turned the page over quickly, not wanting to know, yet compelled to finish the letter.

'I truly love him, Marnie, otherwise I'd never have agreed to going halfway across the world with him. I'm sure he loves me too, even though my news was a shock to him, coming on top of everything else. So don't think too badly of us, please, and spare a thought for me in the middle of the ocean, for Lord knows I expect I'll be a terrible sailor. The very thought of it makes my stomach heave, and I don't think I'm in the best of health for travelling. I'm petrified at leaving dry land for near on three weeks, but it's what Gabe and me want.'

The letter fell from Marnie's hands on to the bed as soon as she read his name. None of the rest of it mattered at that moment. The words Jenny wrote were burned into her brain. 'Gabe and me', Gabe and Jenny, *her* Gabe . . . she felt as if she was going to choke; as if the room spun in a crazy kaleidoscope of dancing shadows and yellow moonlight seen through a blur of tears; she grabbed the letter back into her shaking hands and forced herself to read the rest of it.

'Please, *please* forgive me, Marnie, for putting so much on you, but you've always been the strong one, and I've always looked up to you right from when we were little, and I know you won't fail me in this. And one last thing–whatever happens, let no-one guess that Gabe and me have gone away together. Nobody else knows about us except you, and I don't have to tell you what Da and the boys might do to Gabe's brother in revenge. I wouldn't want that on my conscience. I wanted to tell you before we left, but Gabe insisted it must be kept just our secret, though I often wondered if you guessed it was him, remembering how I'd always thought him so marvellous when we first saw him, though I never thought then that I'd be his wife. God bless you, Marnie, and God willing, we'll see each other again someday.
　　Your loving sister,
Jenny.'

'Damn little fool!'
Marnie swore out loud, crunching the letter in her hands and feeling the scalding tears run down her face as the

224

enormity of the step Jenny had taken swept over her, combined with the terrible anger and despair that was building up inside her with the force of a maelstrom. She tried to curb the immediate thoughts for herself and to try to guess just how the devil her sister was going to survive in an unknown country with a man who wasn't her husband and being already pregnant. Damn the Bray family for being the way they were so that even pretty Jenny was too afraid to beg their help when it was most needed. Damn fate that had been so cruel to all of them . . . most of all, damn Gabe O'Brien for showing her too late the meaning of fulfilment and then throwing it back in her face like this.

Did she mean nothing at all to him then? *He* hadn't bothered to write to her to explain . . . but how did anybody explain this? And if he was so in love with Jenny, why take *her* that sunny afternoon back to the farmhouse and pretend that she was the only one he wanted and had always wanted? How could he have pretended so success-fully? She wept into her pillow so that it muffled the sound, because if she once lifted her head she knew she'd be wailing and screaming the house down. It was all so cruel . . . so unbelievable . . . and Jenny was so naive as to wonder if Marnie had guessed that Gabe had been the one. Jenny had said he loved *her*, but it had been Marnie he'd held in his arms at the farm, and all the doubts and the hatred between them had been dispelled in a single afternoon. All the years of loving him that had simmered so close to the surface of her hatred had flared into tumul-tuous rapture. It *hadn't* been all on her side, she thought passionately, it wasn't possible. Unless it had been his one final triumphant hour of revenge for some wrong she was supposed to have done him, she thought in bewilderment. Oh, but it was despicable of him. She'd felt an inborn pity for Jenny, but gradually, as the thoughts whirled around in her tortured mind, she began hating them both, knowing that once again in their lives, Jenny had won, and this time she'd got the only man Marnie had ever wanted.

She doubted if the bruises would ever heal. It was too

much to bear, and she didn't know how she was going to face each new day, knowing it took Gabe farther out of her life, knowing he'd made the choice himself. How could he do this? she raged inside, her despair alternating with a wild fury she didn't know she was capable of feeling.

Marnie closed her eyes tightly, not wanting the sharp images of the two of them lying together to surge into her mind, not Gabe and Jenny, their faces transformed by desire . . . it was too unbearable for her to believe, and yet she had to believe it, for the truth ran through every word of Jenny's frightened letter . . .

She opened her eyes to stare blankly at the ceiling, where the shifting patterns of moonlight were cast by the rustling branches of the tree outside her window. She turned her head to see the brilliant orb of the moon edge fully into sight, splendid and cold and remote.

Moon child, she thought bitterly. 'All the important times in your life will happen at the time of the full moon . . .'

And none was more important than now, Marnie cried despairingly, tasting the salt of her own tears as they filled her mouth—now, when her heart was breaking into little fragments and there was no-one in the world who cared or would help her mend it . . . no-one at all.

CHAPTER FIFTEEN

Several times on the road to Southampton Gabe had to stop the horse and cart to hold her head while she was sick at the roadside. She was terrified of being sick, and he was revolted by the sounds, the smells, the gasping apologies, the tears that slid down her face, the traces of vomit that splashed on his clothing, the need to comfort and soothe her when he felt so abominably ill himself.

But his ailment was more an illness of the spirit than of the body, and never for a minute did he let on that he wished himself anywhere but here on the road to Southampton and the ship that was to take them to New York, with Jenny Bray by his side. Never did he betray the fact that he knew in the depths of himself that this was all wrong . . . not their fleeing from the storm that would descend on them if they stayed and faced her family, but the two of them together–Gabe O'Brien and Jenny Bray–*that* was what was wrong.

But the softness in his heart wouldn't let him abandon her when she beseeched him with those great imploring eyes of hers, and he told himself despairingly that it had to be, and that he must forget Marnie completely.

He swallowed the bitter taste in his mouth as the thought of her came rushing into his brain, and he forced her out with an almost physical effort. She had no place there now. His duty was to her sister, the pathetic little waif heaving and spewing at the roadside and clinging on to him as if he was her only lifeline.

He heard her panting as the spasm passed, and felt her trembling limbs, and knew an enormous pity for her at having to go all through this because of him. And he knew full well how terrified she was at the thought of the journey ahead of them. She'd been appalled when he first told her how he proposed to solve her problem, and raised every objection under the sun. She was a bad traveller; she was no good with new people; she'd never survive in a strange land; she couldn't speak the language.

'They speak English, you ninny,' Gabe felt his irritation with her explode into anger. 'Sweet Jesus, I'm trying to do what's right for you, and you're gabbing on about things that don't matter!'

'They matter to me! I'm scared stiff at the very idea! Aren't we going to be wed? That's important too, Gabe . . .' the most important of all . . .

'Of course,' he snapped. 'But there's no time for that before we leave, since you're so insistent about the time going on. I'm going to arrange everything as fast as I can. I'll book the passage for us as a married couple anyway. It'll cost less for us to share a cabin, and I don't suppose you'd want to be on your own half the time. Besides, if anyone started to suspect your condition, 'twould look better. You can wear my mother's ring.'

He'd nearly gagged himself then, knowing it had never been meant for Jenny Bray's finger.

'But we *will* be wed?' she'd said resentfully.

'Look, if it worries you that much, I'll spin some tale while we're on board about our having had a hasty wedding some time back, and you being romantic and wanting another ceremony on board ship. The Captain will think it just a whim because you're pregnant, but I daresay if I pay him the proper due he'll conduct the ceremony, and it'll all be legal then. All right?'

She'd have to be satisfied with that. It sounded reasonable, Jenny thought grudgingly, even though there was little of the lover in Gabe's manner now, and that was another thing that made her anxious. But the thought that he might run out on her if she didn't agree to his plan was even more frightening, and she found herself agreeing to everything, even to the fact of him handing her his mother's wedding

228

ring when she'd finally crept out of Larksby early that afternoon, with her few clothes and possessions bundled into a bag, and had joined him in the country lane where they'd arranged to meet.

'Won't you put it on for me, Gabe?' the tears sprang to her eyes, for suddenly her stomach wouldn't stop heaving and she was so afraid she was going to be sick if he didn't stop looking at her so broodingly. She'd been sick half the night, and Gabe was looking anything but a man on the brink of realising a dream. Her eyes pleaded with him not to make her feel any worse than she did already, and at such a look his bitterness faded, remembering that he'd been the one to get her into this mess anyway. He hesitated only a second longer before he slipped the gold band on her third finger, where it fitted adequately enough.

'With this ring I thee wed, Jennifer Bray,' he mumbled solemnly, dredging up the half-remembered words from Maureen's wedding service. With my body I thee worship . . . well, he'd already done that, hadn't he? And no doubt he'd continue to do so once the immediate assault on his nerves was over. Once they were in the habit of spending every night in each others' arms . . . he pulled his hand away from hers, knowing a moment's horror at the thought, but she was too concerned with admiring the ring on her finger to notice his expression.

'Speaking those words and giving me a ring ought to make me your common-law wife anyway, didn't it, Gabe? Isn't that what they call it?'

'Aye, that's right.'

He didn't know and cared less, but if it made her happy . . . The day was hot and they had a long way to go, and the ship left on the early morning tide the following day. There was no time to waste in mooning over wedding rings.

'We must be moving, Jennifer,' he said roughly.

She gave him a sudden brilliant smile, and he felt his heart turn over. Christ, she was no more than a child, he thought remorsefully, and she was trusting her life to him.

Her life and that of her child's—his child's. He leaned over and kissed her briefly.

'We'll survive—Mrs O'Brien. You'd best get used to thinking of yourself like that from now on, and don't look too surprised if people on board ship call you Missus, or you'll be giving the game away.'

'I feel married now anyway. Mrs O'Brien . . .'

He let her lean her head back and dream as he urged the horse on. They *had* to survive—he'd told Mick so last night when he'd told him what he was going to do, and it had been as bad a moment as any he'd known as he faced his brother on the way back to the farm from the Duck and Drake, his heart pounding, his guts lined with lead.

'You bloody young fool!' Mick's temper had been up in a minute, as he'd expected. 'What in God's name possessed you to take up with a Bray girl in the first place? You ought to have more sense. And to put a child in her belly . . . Christ, man, I could wring the living daylights out of you! Don't you know what her brothers will do to you when they find out?'

'They're not going to find out unless you tell them,' Gabe yelled back. 'Do you think I don't know what they'll do! I've got a scar on my arm now that aches and throbs at times because of them.'

'And that was for poking the other one, you randy little bugger!' Mick lashed out with his arm and clipped his head until his senses rocked. 'Somebody ought to take a knife to you and do a bit of castrating if you can't keep your bloody cock under control. Just how do you expect to keep it from the Brays anyway, or have you dreamed up some stupid idea in that great dumbhead of yours that it must have been a virgin birth? Jesus, she must have been a virgin when you got at her, just like the other one! Are you thinking of making this your life's work, going round poking little girls?'

'Shut up!' Gabe screamed at him. 'Will you listen to me, Mick? The Brays aren't going to know about it because I'm taking her away with me. We've got passages booked for

America, and I've been trying to tell you all evening, only I didn't know how!'

That had really shut Mick up for a while, especially when he learned how Gabe had planned everything down to the last detail, and that little Jenny Bray was quite willing to make the hazardous trip across the Atlantic with him. He was even struck by a grudging admiration for the two of them, even while he thought the whole venture was madness. But he was persuaded by Gabe's desperate explanation that it was the only way open to him, and that no one else must know of it.

'And what am I supposed to tell Farmer and Missus?' Mick demanded. 'And old Jackson at the Duck and Drake–and the rest of them at Larksby? How long before they start adding two and two? And what about the girl? Won't she want to tell her family some tale?' He shook his head. 'It won't work, Gabe.'

'It *will*. It must. Tell them all I decided to go back to Drory,' he said wildly. 'That's believable enough, and as for Jenny, her sister will put things right for her.'

Not for a hundred pounds could he have said her name right then.

Slowly Mick's anger ebbed out of him.

'I can't approve of what you're doing, Gabe, and yet I can see your reasoning. And if you and Jenny love each other, who am I to condemn you for wanting to wed her, though I'd have wished for any other girl in the world for an O'Brien. Still, maybe it's time the feud was buried, even though none shall know of it from me, and you know I'll cover your tracks any way I can, and wish you well.'

His voice had gravelled suddenly, as if remembering all the years they'd shared and that they were to come so sharply to an end. But Gabe had never wavered in his certainty that this was the only way . . . not until now, when he was hot and tired and dusty, and Jenny was heaving up the contents of her stomach yet again.

'I'm sorry, Gabe,' she gasped, wiping the back of a trembling hand across her mouth. 'It's never been this bad before, nor as often. Maybe it's something I ate that disagreed with me. I had some sharp apples yesterday.'

He was tired of her pathetic appeals to him. She nauseated him, and he felt a swift shame that it was so. He wouldn't kick a dog, but he had a great urge to strangle Jenny Bray if she didn't shut her noise. He didn't want to feel that way because he could see the beads of sweat on her lip, and her skin was alternately flushed and then translucent when the sickness raked her guts, and the look of her scared him. But it was only her nerve failing her, he persuaded himself as he bathed her face in the cooling water of a stream. Once they were safely on board ship and steaming away from England with no chance of anyone tracing them, the excitement of the adventure would catch up with them, and Jenny would be fine, and the way he remembered her, little and pretty and dainty.

'It's not far now,' he said encouragingly and gently, because of the guilt he felt on her account. 'I swear I can smell the sea already, and once in Southampton we'll find an Inn for the night. A proper meal will help line your stomach again.'

'You are good to me, Gabe.'

She pressed her face against his shirt and he could feel the heat of it. Christ Jesus, she was like a furnace, even though he'd just splashed cold water on to her skin. The sooner they got to the inn and relaxed the better. He helped her back in the cart and jerked the reins for the horse to get moving. And he breathed a sigh of relief when the milestones told him they were nearly at their destination. He nudged Jenny, who was dozing by his side by then, the weight of her heavy against him.

'Are we nearly there?' her voice was still drowsy with sleep.

'We are that, Mrs O'Brien,' he said, knowing he'd better practise it too, or he'd be forgetting it himself. And he could see it pleased her to have him address her like that. No doubt making her feel she really belonged to him ... it gave him a different kind of feeling. In some odd way it made him think of her as a new person, not the golden Jennifer or the trusting, child-like Jenny. Mrs O'Brien was just one step removed from being so necessarily familiar to him, and he chose to keep thinking of her that way.

They found an Inn and booked in for the night, and the landlord directed Gabe to a local man who bought the horse and cart for near enough what he'd paid Mick for it. When he got back Jenny looked a mite more refreshed after a proper wash, though she barely picked at the food put in front of them. Then there was nothing left to do but go to bed, after arranging for the landlord to give them an early call the next morning.

Gabe followed Jenny up the dimly-lit staircase, feeling ridiculously nervous. Aware that they were to share the double bed the whole night long, and that he was responsible for her from now on. The enormity of it all was turning his insides to water. She undressed without looking or speaking and crept into bed, shivering at the coldness of the coarse sheets. He slid in beside her a few mintues later, and she snuggled up against him. He could feel the weight of her breasts, heavy and soft, and the sharpness of her nipples against his chest as they touched him. And she was suddenly all limbs, he thought in sudden panic, as her legs wound around him and her arms held him close, like a spider spinning a web to ensnare a fly.

Her voice was soft and hesitant and wistful.

'I do love you, Gabe.'

His heart turned over, for at that moment in the warm darkness, she sounded so like Marnie, even acting a little the way Marnie had acted once, so long ago, boldly and possessively, as he felt the sudden touch of her hand at his groin. Sweet Jesus, and he was having to resist the violent urge to flinch away from her, behaving like some outraged Victorian maiden because she wanted more reassurance . . . wanted what she assumed to be her right. And shouldn't any red-blooded Irishman be grateful for the fact of having a lusty wench lying in his arms and begging for it?

'It's all right, Gabe,' there was the little-girl softness about her now, sweet and understanding. 'I know you're tired and anxious, and you drank a lot of ale downstairs.'

She was excusing him now, for Christ's sake, he thought, with burning humiliation. But maybe even that was better than her guessing that the thought of getting his leg across her that night was putting him into a cold sweat. And now she was taking his hand . . . he felt his throat constrict as she put it over the gentle swelling of her belly. He could feel the thick tangle of hair beneath his lower fingers.

'That's our baby in there, Gabe,' she whispered shyly. 'Don't you think the growing of a child is a miracle? I know it's wrong to start it before the wedding, but it's not the child's fault, and the miracle of making new flesh and blood out of two people's loving is still the same, isn't it?'

Her hand was over his, moving his gently over the soft mound, and despite the mild horror he'd felt a few minutes ago, and the copious quantities of ale he'd consumed, he could feel a definite stirring between his legs. He and Jenny were pressed close together in the bed, and he knew by the sudden catch in her breath that she was aware of the hardening of him.

He could tell by the way her nipples suddenly felt as if they stuck into his flesh like needle-points. He heard her rapid shallow breathing. It was warm and it was dark and she was *here*. With a smothered oath he turned quickly, pinning her beneath him, spreading her legs with his body and driving into her with a kind of desperation.

It wasn't really Jenny squirming beneath him in the few minutes he took, it wasn't even Marnie, because he wouldn't let himself think of her . . . it was all women, and he was loving and hating simultaneously until he climaxed with the urgency of a dam bursting, and then he rolled swiftly away from her, hating himself for his need, but unable to deny the relief from it. And thank God she seemed to fall asleep right away and not to notice how long he lay awake staring into the darkness.

Early the next morning they dressed and breakfasted and

234

made their way to the waterfront. Jenny's face was still burning hot, and she'd taken very little food, even though he'd urged her to eat properly.

'I couldn't,' she mumbled on their way to the ship. 'Now the time's really here, I'm too scared to eat.'

'Is that all it is? You're not still feeling ill?'

'No,' she lied for his sake, since he'd been so loving the night before.

'Thank God for that. We can't change our minds now,' Gabe said crisply. He took hold of her hand. 'Cheer up, Mrs O'Brien. Once we're safely in our cabin and we've found our sea-legs, we'll be fine.'

He wished he felt as confident as he sounded. This was his dream, he reminded himself, but in his dream he'd always travelled alone, and he tried desperately to rid himself of the idea that Jenny was a gigantic millstone round his neck.

And if she was, he thought bitterly, whose fault was that? He almost dragged her along the waterfront, their bags bumping alongside them until they found their ship. He wished irritably that Jenny would stop shaking with nerves. Damn it, they were supposed to be a married couple with a child on the way, going halfway across the world on a great new adventure. But from the way she looked, she resembled a cowering child about to be spanked, and for two pins he'd turn her over his knee and do it. He grumbled at her as soon as they were inside their cabin.

'I'm sorry Gabe,' she spoke through chattering teeth. 'I keep shivering one minute and breaking out into a sweat the next. It's so hot in here. There's no air, and it's so dark, and I don't like the way the ship keeps rolling about.'

She made a retching sound and clapped her hand to her mouth, her eyes large and apologetic above it. Gabe's irritability spilled over.

'Sweet Jesus, we haven't even started moving yet, and there's 3000 miles to travel, so you'll just have to get used to it, won't you? There'll be more air when we get under way and the ship won't roll so much then. Why don't you lie down if you're feeling jittery?'

He saw the shine of tears in her eyes and the remorse stabbed at him again. Damn her for always making him feel that way. He suddenly had to get out of the small confined cabin before the sight of her made him throw up as well. He was unbearably claustrophobic in her company.

'I'll go up on deck and find out how long before we leave,' he said abruptly. 'You'll be all right, won't you?'

She nodded unconvincingly.

'I'll unpack our things and then I'll lie down.'

Suddenly she pressed herself against him, her arms holding him, her voice shrill.

'We *will* be all right, won't we, Gabe? It was all right last night, wasn't it–at the Inn? Just like it's always been?'

'We'll manage,' he muttered. He extricated himself from her clinging arms and fled, breathing in great gulps of air as soon as he was outside the cabin. Christ, what was *wrong* with him? She was the one with the shattered nerves, not him. He had to get a grip on himself. After a few minutes he wandered round the ship, getting his bearings, nodding to other passengers, trying to ignore the gnawing anxiety inside that at any minute the three Bray brothers would come roaring towards him as if conjured up by magic, brandishing knives and sticks and knocking him senseless . . .

But they didn't appear, and his taut nerves gradually relaxed as the crew bustled about getting ready for departure, and the rolling of the ship steadied into a rhythmic throbbing of the powerful steam engines. The feeling of power beneath him rekindled something of the excitement in his veins so that just for a while he was able to forget everything but the fact that the day he'd dreamed about for so long was actually here. He was suddenly caught up in the excitement and the noise as the rumble of the engines grew more insistent and the onlookers on shore waved furiously, and at last the ship slid away from the waterfront and out into the English Channel.

For a few moments Gabe was so emotional he could hardly breathe, and he stood motionless at the ship's rail, jostled by other passengers, some in tears, some silent like him, some jubilant and shouting goodbye to anyone who'd listen. He stood and watched the waterfront recede majestically away into the distance, and then he mingled with the crowds on deck, gulping in the salt tang of the air, almost deafened by the attendant gulls screaming and wheeling as they circled overhead, hearing the slap-slap of water as the bows of the ship cut through the rippling waves as she settled on course.

It was a good while later when he returned to the cabin, after he'd located the dining-room and various other parts of the ship. Jenny was huddled up on her bunk. He thought she was asleep at first until he heard her groan.

'Gabe, I feel so ill,' her voice was thin and hoarse. 'My head spins and hurts so, and I feel sick all the time. And I'm so *hot*!'

She threw the covers off her in a wild movement and he bent to retrieve them with an anxious frown.

'All ships roll like this, but you'll get used to it in a little while. It's just a touch of sea-sickness, I expect.'

He tucked the covers round her, and then he caught sight of her face properly. Jesus, she looked as if she was on fire. He touched her skin, expecting it to be clammy as before, but it was dry and burning. Her eyes looked suddenly sunken in her face and her lips were parched. Even her beautiful hair had lost a lot of its sheen and hung lank and lifeless round her small face. She was breathing in thin little gasps as if she didn't have enough strength for anything more.

There was a water jug and two glasses in their containers on the washstand. He filled a glass with water quickly and lifted her head, instructing her to drink. She tried to obey but most of the water trickled out of the corners of her mouth, and then she suddenly began coughing and vomited all over him.

'Holy Mother of God!'

He had to swallow a couple of times himself as the smell reached his nostrils. He tried to clamp them together and reached for a towel to wipe some of the muck off his clothes.

Jenny was crying. Not loudly or even apologetically, just mutely crying, the tears running down over her flame-red cheeks, and the sight of it unnerved him so much he was awash with pity for her.

'Listen, Jennifer, I'm going to see if there's a doctor on board,' he spoke hoarsely, right in her ear. She grabbed hold of him, her arms locking round his head.

'No, don't leave me! If you leave me I'll die, I know it! Stay with me, Gabe, *please*!'

'All right, all right, I'll stay,' he said quickly before she throttled him.

He wrung out a face-cloth in the water and sponged her face, and then he had to get out of his stinking clothes and into some clean ones. The smell still clung to him, but at least he felt a little cleaner. Then he sponged Jenny again, noting that the water had dried almost immediately on the heat of her skin. He loosened her clothing and let the cool water trickle over her throat and the pink-tipped mounds of her breasts. She moaned the whole time. Her neck looked swollen as if the glands were enlarged, and when he touched them she twisted away from him. She seemed to have difficulty in breathing again, and she didn't speak at all except for the unintelligible mumble that broke from her lips now and then.

Gabe suddenly felt a new stab of fear. What if it was *typhoid*? Dear God, they weren't that far out of Southampton. If he did bring a doctor to her and typhoid was confirmed, might not the ship turn round and put them ashore, or pull in to an Irish port to get Jenny into a hospital? He felt the sweat trickling down his back as he stared desperately at her. He had no medical knowledge save that that came from years of tending animals and their ills. He had no way of guessing if it was typhoid or even what the symptoms were, he only knew that whatever ailed Jenny Bray it was bad . . . but he couldn't take the risk of their being put ashore before their journey had properly begun. He sponged her with a renewed devotion, pleading silently with her to get well, and for the malady to be no

238

more than acute sea-sickness combined with the worry of the past weeks.

Gabe leaned over her from time to time to try and catch the mumbled words in case she needed anything, but it seemed to be all delirious nonsense. Her breath was so rancid he felt repulsed every time he came near her. Her tongue was furred, her eyes dull, but he went on doggedly sponging her and talking to her, since the sound of his voice seemed to calm her whenever the violent spasms of babbling gibberish overtook her.

He managed to get her out of her travelling dress and into a cool cambric nightgown during the long hours he sat with her. He dumped the messed clothes into the slop bucket with his own and repeated the sponging process time after time. There wasn't the slightest flicker of emotion in him save pity as he worked the cooling face-cloth over the soft milk-white breasts and belly and the smooth young limbs. She was just a pathetic creature who needed him, and at last she appeared to go off into a shallow sleep.

Gabe flexed his cramped limbs. She'd been a dead weight in his arms, and he realised he was thirsty and very hungry. It must be hours since breakfast, he thought, and he moved carefully to the porthole and swivelled his neck to right and left. Their cabin was on the starboard side, and if they were still within sight of any land it should be visible. There was none.

He glanced back at Jenny, chewing his lips. She must see a doctor and he knew it. Her pulse was weak and, dear God, the mumbling was beginning again. What if she were to die right here in the cabin? He'd be accused of being a murderer then because he hadn't gone for help when it was obvious she was very sick.

He waited no longer. He went out of the cabin and up on deck, registering a small surge of relief that they were indeed well out to sea by now, and there was no hint of land to be seen. He went purposefully towards a crew member and asked if there was a doctor on board who could attend to his wife. The man eyed him cannily.

'Aye, if you're willing to pay for his services!'

'I can pay,' Gabe said abruptly. 'Where will I find him?'

He followed the directions, and finally a gaunt looking man was listening intently to Gabe's frantic description of Jenny's symptoms.

'Has she any spots? Oval in shape, light red in colour?' he said rapidly. Gabe shook his head. Jenny's skin had been unblemished.

'How about her belly? Is it swollen? Painful?'

'No more than with the retching as far as I can tell. She doesn't complain of it. She's expecting a child in six months.'

'And she's raving?'

Gabe was suddenly angry. Why didn't the fool come and look at her and see for himself instead of asking all these questions?

'She's not mad!'

The doctor looked at him keenly.

'I never said she was, young man, though perhaps you're the one who's mad to bring a pregnant woman on a long sea voyage. Let's pray to God it's not the typhoid anyway, or you'll not be popular on this ship. You'd best lead the way to your cabin.'

'I'll pay for any treatment, of course,' Gabe said quickly, in case the doctor thought he was penniless.

'That you will, and pray with all that's in you there'll be treatment I can give her, for if it's the typhoid it's more likely a burial you'll be needing.'

Gabe wondered if he was always this blunt, or if it was merely his way of preparing him for the worst. He walked in front of the doctor to the cabin, his knees like jelly. The doctor wrinkled his nose at the smell that hit their nostrils as soon as they entered, and told him that wasn't doing the patient any good at all. Jenny thrashed about on the bunk, the broken words and half-sentences drivelling out of her dry lips. The doctor lifted her eyelids, felt her pulse, took her temperature, then lifted her nightgown to examine her

240

minutely for the tell-tale spots on her chest and back, and made a brief examination of her belly. He studied her thoughtfully, his eyes noting the ill-fitting wedding-ring on her finger.

'It's not typhoid,' he rapped out. 'Nor anything more than an extremely high fever and *mal-de-mer*, I'd say. But she's very weakened by all this vomiting, and she looks over-young to be pregnant. Shot-gun wedding, was it?'

Gabe felt his anger and his colour rise, but what was the use of denying it, he thought wearily, as the doctor's keen eyes burned into his? He'd probably seen it all before. He nodded, feeling suddenly as young and gauche as Jenny, and the doctor sighed.

'You both need your hides kicked, but the lassie needs more than that just now. If you've enough money, young man, I can arrange for someone to sit with her and sponge her and do all that's necessary for a few days, in turn with yourself. She needs careful nursing, and you need some food in you by the look of you and a change of scenery from this cabin. I've a nurse I can call on, and this lass isn't out of the wood yet by a long chalk. The pair of you will be in a sorry state by the time we reach New York if you're intending to carry on by yourselves in here the whole journey.' He glowered at Gabe. 'You're both still wet behind the ears, and with a child to consider, don't forget.'

'All right, all right!' Gabe burst out when the doctor paused for breath. 'I've money for nursing, and I'd be obliged if you'd see to it, please.' And stop treating me like a raving idiot, he stormed silently.

The doctor straightened.

'I'll see to getting these stinking things taken out of here as well,' he motioned to the slop bucket. 'And the nurse will be here directly. As soon as she arrives you get out of here and get yourself some food before you collapse. I fancy this has taken some of the hot blood out of you, hasn't it? You young fools never think of the consequences when you lay a wench, but it's not so pretty when they're all swollen and vomiting.'

Gabe bolted for the door before he finished speaking. Let *him* wait for the nurse, he thought furiously. He'd had enough lectures to last him a lifetime, and he wasn't paying good money to listen to more.

It was five days later when Jenny's lucid moments lengthened into more coherent speech, but even then any attempt at more than a brief conversation totally exhausted her. By then the stern-faced nurse had become part of their lives, holding Jenny down when the mindless fear gripped her, and helping her sip barley water or boiled milk and the most appalling slops, which were all she could keep down. The doctor had made regular visits, and Gabe was only too thankful to let them take over for a while, finding relief in just being away from the sickroom and finding some consolation in forgetting his troubles in the drink he purchased daily.

There was a great deal he wanted to forget. There was the undoubted fact that any love he'd felt for Jenny had rapidly vanished, and though he despised himself for it he knew it was only pity and a sense of duty that kept him by her side now. There was the feeling of having let Mick down and leaving him to cope with the farm by himself just when he needed Gabe most, even though he never pressed it. There was still the mourning for Mammy and Farmer Lester that had somehow got smothered in the events that had happened since their deaths, but which still dragged him down. There was the longing for Marnie that was locked up in his soul, but which broke into his consciousness from time to time like the remnants of a long-forgotten dream, to tantalise and torment him.

He stumbled into the cabin on the evening of the fifth day to meet the disapproval of the nurse's thin lips as the smell of alcohol preceded him.

'Mrs O'Brien can try some more solid food today,' she informed him. 'Shall I get it sent here? She's certainly not strong enough to go to the dining-room.'

'Why not!' Gabe threw his arms about expansively. 'Let Mrs O'Brien have anything she needs. I'll be buying the whole bloody ship soon!'

As soon as the nurse left the cabin with an outraged swish of skirts, Jenny put out a thin white hand towards him and whispered his name. He went to her at once, ashamed of his outburst, but Jesus, the money was running out at an appalling rate, and the bottles of booze weren't helping any, but they were as necessary to him as Jenny's nurse was to her.

'Gabe,' she whispered tremulously. 'Have I been very ill?'

'Pretty ill,' he said gruffly. *Mal-de-mer* indeed! This fever was more than bloody sea-sickness, or his name wasn't Gabe O'Brien. Her hand went to her belly.

'But the baby–is it still all right?'

'Oh aye, it's all right.' There'd even been a moment when he'd thought that if she lost it . . . but the wickedness of such a thought had been too firmly ingrained in his catholic background for him to allow it proper shape.

'I prayed that it would be, Gabe. It would be terrible if anything happened to a blameless child after all this.' She hesitated for a minute, her voice still thin and wobbly. 'Did I dream it, Gabe, or did the Captain come and marry us like you said he would? I'm so muddled and I dreamed of so many things . . . me and my sister Marnie when we were children and I loved her so much . . . my little brother Davey calling me . . . I remember a man with a sharp voice and hearing people call me Mrs O'Brien lots of times, and something about being wed. You did see to it, didn't you, Gabe?'

His tongue seemed to stick to the roof of his mouth. He swallowed convulsively and bent to kiss her cheek. It was thinner than before, but mercifully cool. He didn't look into her eyes.

'I saw to everything, Mrs O'Brien,' his own voice was thick. 'You and I are as married as we'll ever be, and there's my Mammy's ring on your finger to prove it. Now just stop your worrying and sit up a bit before that nurse sends your food down for you. Let's make you look presentable.'

She did as she was told, obedient as always, and he prayed she wouldn't guess at the way his heart was pounding, and that his guilt wasn't written all over his face. Sweet Jesus, he'd swear on a stack of bibles that he'd really meant it at the time, about getting the ship's Captain to marry them . . . but things had changed since then.

He didn't love her, and wasn't it just as much a sin in the eyes of God and the church to marry without love? He'd already sinned so much he doubted if God wanted anything more to do with him anyway. But by all the saints, he didn't want to be married to Jennifer Bray, not now, not ever, and where was the harm in continuing the deception they'd already begun, since she thought it was now all legal-like?

CHAPTER SIXTEEN

'You haven't been listening to a word this last half-hour, Marnie,' Geraldine Larksby said crossly. 'You're always in a dream world lately, with that stupid shut-in look on your face. I never thought you were all that close to your sister, but it's ever since she disappeared that you've gone all peculiar. I was never fully convinced with the story that was put around at the time about her. It wouldn't surprise me in the least if there wasn't some young spark involved there, with a pretty little thing like Jenny. If you know any more about it, it's your duty to tell me. I can't have you going about with a face like thunder the whole time. Out with it, Marnie, for heaven's sake!'

She leaned forward from the shade of the wide oak tree under which they were sitting, while the pony grazed contentedly into the young grass as he waited for his charges to return to the trap after their picnic. Geraldine had become very fond of the fashion for outdoor eating, and was always cajoling Cook to prepare a hamper of provisions for the two of them.

Marnie sensed the feeling of anticipation in her mistress' face without looking at her, and tightened her mouth. The tale had gone around Inn and mansion alike about the mysterious disappearance of the little Bray girl some two months ago now, and Geraldine was quite certain Marnie held the key to the riddle, and would dearly like to know the truth of it. Even a servant's scandal was of interest to share with her intimates, especially when the servant had been in one's own household.

'Jenny's well and happy in her new position,' Marnie repeated the words woodenly, parrot-like. They'd been said so often she was beginning to half-believe them herself. It was easier to believe them than to think of Jenny and Gabe together, with the coming baby an unbreakable bond between them.

'And where did you say she has this fine new position?' Geraldine persisted, her sharp little eyes never leaving Marnie's face.

'I didn't say. She doesn't want to have Da getting on his high horse and fetching her back. Somewhere in the country . . .'

'Oh, very explicit,' Geraldine said sarcastically. 'But you do know, don't you?'

'Perhaps.' Marnie stared fixedly ahead at the patient crawl of a ladybird down the gnarled bark of the oak.

Geraldine stood up sharply, brushing the crumbs of cake and bread from her wide skirt, tossing back her fair hair with annoyance.

'Really, you can be the most infuriating loon at times, and the tale sounds too far-fetched for words. Do you honestly think people believe it?'

'If they can prove no different, why shouldn't they believe it? Da does, and so does Ma, and that's the important thing.'

Geraldine's scornful look said louder than words that simple folk like the Brays would believe anything if it meant one less mouth to feed in the family and one less sprig to worry about. She had no patience with the lower classes who wore their fierce pride like a banner the way Marnie did, too close for their own good. Independence was for people of quality, and servants should be quiet, pliant creatures, the way Jenny might have been if she'd stayed on long enough to replace Marnie.

There were times when Geraldine could cheerfully have told Marnie to go to Hades, even though part of a young lady's role in life was to be gracious and condescending and minister to a pathetic maid's needs, when the two of them had been more like companions for so long now. In their case, it was more often Marnie who was the strong one, and Geraldine was continually irritated by her, and wondered quite often if it was time they parted company.

'We'll take a trip to King's Lynn next week,' she said imperiously now. 'I want to look around the shops and have a change of scene. I'm tired of the country and never seeing anyone but country clods. I shall see if Papa will arrange for us to stay at an hotel for a night or two. What do you say to that?'

'Whatever you wish, of course, Miss Geraldine,' Marnie knew very well she had no choice, no matter what whim caught hold of her mistress. She began packing the things back into the picnic hamper.

'You aren't afraid one of these elusive letters from your sister will arrive while we're away that should have your immediate attention?'

'I don't expect one . . .'

'I didn't think you would. Well then, we shall see what Papa has to say about our little trip. I fancy you'll be even keener and change the sour look on your face when I tell you my brother and his fiancée are expected to visit us next week!'

Marnie's heart jolted. On the infrequent occasions that Darryl Larksby had come back to the house over the years, she had managed to avoid any contact with him. The mere thought of his groping hands or even the mention of his name was still enough to have the sick revulsion crawling up her spine. And the memory of the night he'd whipped her raw, riding her like a mare with no more thought for her feelings than using her for his own lustful satisfaction could still twist her stomach into a turmoil of fear . . .

'Won't it seem odd for you to be thinking of leaving Larksby just when your brother will be visiting?' she felt compelled to ask.

'There's no love lost between Darryl and myself, and my father is fully aware of it.' And aware of the reason *why*, Marnie thought guiltily, though why she should feel guilt when she was the one who had suffered at Darryl Larksby's hands, was inexplicable.

'Anyway,' Geraldine went on evenly, 'common courtesy

demands that I should be there to meet this French mademoiselle Darryl's got himself engaged to, but once the formalities are over, and I've made my pretty little speech of welcome, you and I can make our escape. I take it you approve?'

There was still the hint of sarcasm in her voice, because they both knew there was no need at all to get her maid's approval. But there was also a brief look of understanding in Geraldine's eyes that replaced the usual frosty look they held lately, that assured Marnie she knew all about her abhorrence. And that the kind of scars her brother had inflicted in a young and innocent girl were the sort· that remained deep in the mind long after the physical ones had healed.

Marnie nodded quickly, a sudden lump in her throat. It seemed a long time since she'd had any kind of consideration from anyone, and in view of Geraldine's usual caustic attitude towards her these days, it touched her to know she fully realised what an ordeal it would be for Marnie when Darryl Larksby came home.

'How long will they be staying?' she asked nervously.

Into her brain came the sudden sharp image of that pale flabby body of his on her narrow bed, his eyes dark with lust, his hands reaching for her. She forced the image out of her mind with a shudder.

'About a week, I believe. That will be long enough. I'm not fond of the French as a race, though I must confess I'm curious to see what kind of floss Darryl has found for himself.'

Marnie found she was curious too. What kind of girl would subject herself willingly to the treatment he meted out? Or had he changed in nine years, with the discipline of his schooling and the tempering that time wrought in his character? It was a generous thought, but one that wasn't completely believable to Marnie, and she knew she'd be on her guard the whole time he was in the house.

'Do you know anything about the young lady?' she asked, when she and Geraldine were jogging along at a fair

248

rate in the pony and trap.

'Only that she's well-connected and the daughter of a French gentleman with vast estates South of Paris. I imagine those facts alone were enough to attract Darryl to her, since anything in skirts or out of them will suit his purposes.'

Geraldine had been given to using more and more coarse remarks over the years when the two of them were alone, and Marnie was quite unshocked by them coming out of that so-sweet little mouth. Besides, in this case she recognised the truth of Geraldine's words, and felt a brief pity for the unknown French girl. Perhaps until now Darryl had been carefully restrained and allowed her to see only the well-bred, considerate English gentleman in him, and if so she was in for a horrible shock on her wedding night, Marnie surmised, when his perverted lust was unleashed in full measure on her unsuspecting body. God help her if she was a virgin . . .

Unless, of course, she was a French trollop already knowledgeable of his quirks. But it sounded unlikely from Geraldine's description of her. And trying to visualise the unknown Mademoiselle Suzanne Dupont at least allayed a little the dread she felt at seeing Darryl again, and even thinking about anything different helped to close her mind to the tragedy in her own life that had been brought about by the two people she'd thought closest to her.

She avoided thinking about them as much as possible, but how did you tell the sun not to rise at the start of a new day? And with every sunrise the thoughts of Gabe milled round in her brain the minute she awoke and the weeping and the longing that was like an open wound inside her would clutch at her and torment her until she threw off the bedclothes, heart pounding, breathing heavy and tortured, while she fought to replace the blank mask on her emotions.

Cold reason made her despise herself for the tears she wasted on Gabe O'Brien. He wasn't worth it, and she told herself so a thousand times. He was rubbish, scum, and a coward to flee with her sister the way he had. As for Jenny, she was a fool and always had been. A silly, simpering, soft-hearted fool, who'd let herself be seduced by a sweet-talking Irishman with blue, blue eyes and those goddamned dimples in his cheeks.

Marnie's hands would be clenched so tightly as the furious thoughts ran on that her palms would be scarred with the curved crescents of her finger-nails, and the pain of it would bring the beads of sweat to her forehead.

'Damn them both,' she'd storm out loud in the seclusion of her room. 'Damn and curse them both to hell, the rotten pair of bastards.'

But she was the one who was cursed and she knew it, because she couldn't forget them. They each had a hold on her heart that was like a silken thread, too strong to break, and they wouldn't let her go. It was impossible to try to put Jenny out of her mind with Ma and Da demanding to know every week if she'd heard from her, and having to produce the letters she'd composed laboriously herself, to read out to them from time to time.

It was like a nightmare. Inventing some great house a good distance from the fens, peopling it with characters conjured up out of her own imagination, and crediting Jenny with delivering the little anecdotes on paper that would make the invented Rayner family seem real to her parents. And then to suffer the satisfaction that spread over Da's face as he praised his youngest daughter for her initiative in finding such a good post all by herself, and knowing that the sun still shone out of Jenny's boots as far as Da was concerned, and that she, Marnie, was feeding the flames of his complacency.

She would dearly love to shriek out the truth one of these days. She sometimes imagined doing it too, and seeing the absolute shock on Da's face.

'She's not a lady's maid at all, you old fool, nor ever has been. She's a kitchen whore, and she's gone off to America with her lover to have his bastard, only I'm the one he should have taken, because he belongs to me. He's *always* belonged to me! I had him first, before I really knew what it was all about, and he took my maidenhead in the old mill under a full moon. He's mine, not hers, but it's your precious Jenny who'll drop an Irishman's babby!'

She was screwing her hands together, almost saying the words aloud in her fury, when the little bell on her wall commanded her to Geraldine's side one morning, and jerked her back to reality. She answered it gladly, knowing she spent too many early mornings in a state of suspended agony before she properly faced the day, and this was a special day at Larksby, the day Darryl and his French mademoiselle were due to arrive.

Colonel Larksby had insisted that Geraldine should not go off to King's Lynn until the visitors had been here at least two days and a night, so they were obliged to comply with his wishes. But Wednesday couldn't arrive too soon for Marnie, and the thought of the hotel booking was like a lifeline to her. Darryl and Mademoiselle Dupont would leave on Sunday afternoon, and she and Geraldine would be back for their last evening. It was only a few days out of her life, she kept telling herself, and they would soon pass.

She and Geraldine were walking in the shrubbery when the sound of carriage wheels clattered on the cobbles. Marnie felt her heart lurch and her senses swim for an instant, and then she heard her mistress say reluctantly that they had best go and greet the new arrivals or that would be wrong.

'Papa's not in the best of humours these days, and I don't want to antagonise him further, or he may decide to cancel our little expedition to King's Lynn out of pique,' she said irritably.

'Is there something I can do for you while you greet them?' Marnie's voice was high and quick.

'You can come with me. Do you think I've any great desire to meet him alone, any more than you have?' It was an oblique reference to the fact that Geraldine had been informed of her brother's attacks on Marnie and had been the one to tell her father, and that they both knew Darryl

251

had never forgiven her for it.

So there was nothing for it but to follow Geraldine into the house to where Darryl Larksby was introducing a plain, slightly-built young lady to his father. She was a pale facsimile of his own mother, Marnie thought instantly, and guessed that this marriage had probably been eagerly sought by the French Papa, who would be glad to get such a gauche, dull creature off his hands to a pretty English gentleman. And Darryl was probably going to profit handsomely from her dowry, but she was hardly going to excite his cravings as Marnie remembered them, and a series of tavern girls would probably be the bane of Mademoiselle Dupont's future life.

Geraldine moved forward quickly and touched her lips to her brother's cheek. Above her head his cold eyes took in Marnie's appearance in the slow, insolent way she remembered, and she had to hold herself very still to resist a great shudder at his look. The next moment he had released his sister and was pulling the French girl forward, who replied in perfect English with barely a trace of an accent.

Marnie wished desperately that she could leave the drawing-room, but for the next hour she was obliged to stand behind Geraldine's chair to attend to every little request, from picking up a dropped handkerchief to closing the window a fraction, to ringing the bell for afternoon tea and seeing Mrs Caine's tight-pursed lips when Geraldine said airily that Marnie could pour. To handing Darryl his cup and saucer with hands that trembled, and knowing he was perfectly aware of it. To wondering what on earth the engaged couple could possibly have in common, especially when the lingering looks he sent towards herself told her clearly he had no intentions of restricting his amorous inclinations just because he had a fiancée.

He frightened her as much as ever. She wished there was a bolt on her door, but servants did not have such luxuries. But surely he would never dare to risk coming to her room again? He must hate her anyway . . . but she knew only too well Darryl's methods of dispensing hate. And perhaps

252

the pale Mademoiselle Dupont would be receiving his nightly attentions? She glanced across to where the French mademoiselle was sending him fond little unspoken messages, and guessed not. So far Darryl would have behaved himself.

At last the tea-drinking ritual was over and she could retire upstairs to set out Miss Geraldine's clothes for dinner that evening, and have a little time to herself. She told herself she was overreacting to Darryl Larksby's presence here, and imagining the awareness between them still existed. She told herself a hundred times that he wouldn't risk trying anything with his fiancée in the house and losing the prospects that were dangled in front of him by toying with a maid, but nothing could take the dread from her mind . . .

By bedtime she was feeling less anxious. Geraldine had decided to go to bed early as she had a headache, and told Marnie she could do the same, but she was in an irritable mood when Marnie went to help her undress.

'They'll be talking downstairs for hours yet,' she complained, as Marnie took the pins out of her hair and began its nightly brushing. 'And all this talk of weddings is so boring except for the main participants.'

Especially when the bored listener was in danger of becoming a soured old maid herself . . .

'Don't brush my hair so hard, you ninny,' Geraldine jerked away, making it worse. 'Didn't I tell you my head aches?'

'Shall I fetch you something for it?'

'No. I'd rather try and sleep naturally than have my brain fuddled by potions.' She eyed Marnie's reflection in the mirror. 'Well then? What did you think of our French floss?'

Marnie shrugged. 'It's not for me to think anything.'

'Oh, don't be such a pompous idiot. Will she do for him, do you think?'

'How would I know?'

'Well, you should know if anybody does,' Geraldine

snapped. 'Tell me what you think of her, idiot.'

A red mist blurred Marnie's eyes as she stared at the discontented face in the mirror in front of her. At the mouth that had once been so pretty and never mouthed such obscenities as it did now on occasions, nor been so insensitive to Marnie's own raw feelings.

'If she's willing to spend every night with her ass in the air while he rides her like a prize stallion, she'll do very well for him,' she snapped back.

Geraldine spun round from her dressing-stool and slapped her hard across the cheek.

'I didn't ask for details like that . . .'

'Didn't you? I thought that was just what you wanted to hear!' Marnie rubbed her face furiously, too incensed to care what she said any more. If Geraldine sent her packing tomorrow, so what? 'Would you like to hear more so you can whisper it to your pretty-pretty friends over afternoon tea? Don't you want to know how it feels to be viciously raped at thirteen years old by a sadistic monster who cares for nothing but satisfying his own lust? Who whips you raw as if you're his most hated mare while he tries to split you in two, and then whinnies in triumph when he shoots his seed into your belly like an exploding cannon?'

The red mist cleared and she suddenly stopped the torrent of words as she saw the look on Geraldine's face as she listened. Seeing the slack, parted mouth, the saliva glistening on her lips. Hearing the laboured breathing; seeing her eyes darkened and glittering as if she vicariously experienced everything as Marnie described it. She suddenly saw that this was exactly what Geraldine had wanted all along, and the knowledge sickened her. She'd kept the memory of it all bottled up inside her head all these years, and now it was out on the surface, throbbing and burning and pulsating as if it had a life of its own.

She gave a choked cry of misery deep in her throat, and twisted away from the girl beside her.

'May I go?' she said tightly. 'If there's nothing more you require of me tonight?'

'Yes, go.' Geraldine's voice was thickened, as if she had just experienced a sexual climax. 'Sweet dreams, Marnie.'

She didn't even remember reaching her own room, just the feeling of leaning against the closed door with her chest heaving and straining against the bodice of her dress, and the tears streaming down her face.

Sweet dreams . . . there were no dreams for her that didn't end up as nightmares. There was either the pain of dreaming about Gabe and Jenny together, or the terror of hearing the click of the attic door all those years ago and knowing Darryl Larksby had come for her again. She wanted to run from dreams where once she had welcomed them with eager open arms. Once, long ago, when she had been young and fresh and Gabe O'Brien had loved her . . .

She stumbled across to her bed and fell across it in an agony of weeping. Oh Gabe, *Gabe*. Her spirit wept, her senses vulnerable as a child's. How could you? How *could* you desert me when I loved you so?

But he *had* deserted her, the cold reason whispered. He hadn't wanted her enough–or else he'd wanted Jenny more. The sobs gradually subsided and the tears dried on her cheeks. Her hands were ice-cold as she finally undressed and lay taut between the sheets with that one thought burning into her brain. He hadn't wanted her enough–or he'd wanted Jenny more.

When the door opened stealthily a long while later she was still lying dry-eyed, staring up into the darkness. She swivelled her head, knowing with an almost fatalistic listlessness that it would be Darryl. She eyed him coldly as he stood there in a long dressing-robe, forgetting her previous fear in her contempt for him and all men.

'Hello whore,' his voice was soft and guttural as he moved nearer her bed.

'Get back to your French piece,' she said crisply.

He hesitated, clearly expecting her to be gasping in terror, in the way that had excited him so much.

'Don't tell me you've forgotten our nights together!'

She couldn't stop the tremor than ran through her then,

and her eyes clouded at the memory of how he'd used her. She could scream and yell and bring somebody running right now to show him up for what he was, she thought suddenly . . . as if he read her mind his hand suddenly clamped against her mouth.

'You aren't going to be a silly girl, now, are you? I can fix it so no-one else will employ you for miles around, bitch, and don't you forget it. And you wouldn't want to spoil a gentleman's sport now, would you?'

She sensed that he wasn't fully roused, that he was just sounding her out. The excitement of the chase was strong in his veins, but he wasn't too sure of her reactions. She pushed his hand from her mouth, suddenly quite certain herself of what she intended to do.

'I'm not a child any more, *Mr* Darryl.'

'Oh, I could see that the minute I set foot in the house. You're a fine little whore now, just ripe for the plucking, and I'll wager a bit more experienced than the last time I laid you.'

His hand suddenly slid under the bedclothes, fondling her breasts beneath the cotton night shift. They were full and heavy, and she heard his intake of breath and then the soft laughter in his throat as her nipples hardened involuntarily. She could feel her heart hammering.

'Get out of here, you bastard,' she said in a low voice.

'That's more like it, bitch. I like a fight, remember? Let's see how you've changed since the last time then. I'll bet the village louts have taught you a trick or two. I'll bet they've given you plenty of practice!'

His hand wrenched her night-shift up to her waist and went to the fleshy mound above her groin. She heard him suck in his breath as the flat of his palm rubbed sensuously against it, and knew he was gazing at her exposed body in the light from the window. Still she lay, unmoving as a statue as he parted her legs and began to stab his fingers into her until the juices flowed. Her body reacted, but her mind remained deathly cold and crystal clear . . . waiting for the right moment.

'Christ, but you're a beauty,' he said raggedly. 'As fine as any French whore I've seen. You'd do a fine trade across the water with a puss like that, and those luscious full moons.'

Don't forget my ass, she added silently.

'All ready for it, whore? Not had it lately, maybe. Well, prepare yourself for a cocking you won't forget!'

His hands left her for a moment and flung off his dressing-robe. He was as naked as the day he was born, and she could see his enormous erection crowning the tangled hair. He climbed clumsily on to her bed, his mouth drooling, ready to drive relentlessly into her, and with every bit of force she could muster she jerked her knees into his groin.

He gave a yell of agony and clutched himself, hardly able to believe what she'd done after her apparent silent submission.

'What tricks are these, bitch?' he shouted as he bent double.

'Try this one,' she hissed, and grabbing his erection she gave it a hard twist, at which he howled furiously.

'Or this!' She yelled back and scrabbled forward on the bed until she was near enough to sink her teeth into the taut flesh in a vicious bite that had him howling again and grabbing himself in anguish.

'You bloody bitch,' he screamed. 'You've probably ruined me for life!'

'I hope so,' she screamed back. 'Then you can't go around poking any more little girls, nor your poor unsuspecting little French piece. Has she had a taste of you yet? She has all my sympathy, for I'd rather share my bed with a toad than with you!'

And she spat full into his eyes.

He lashed the back of his hand across her face, but she didn't care. It was worth it all to see him contorted in agony, his hand still clutching the shrinking thing that had caused her so much pain, with the blood spurting out between his fingers. He'd made *her* bleed, she thought

257

savagely, and it would be some while before he felt like putting that bloody thing anywhere but in his breeches.

'You she-cat, I'll kill you for that,' he roared.

And then the insistent ringing of Geraldine's bell stopped his words. 'What the hell's that noise?'

'That's your sister,' Marnie said pleasantly. 'Shall I go and see what she wants, or wait until she comes in here in a fury to see why I haven't answered immediately the way a good servant should–*Sir*?'

She knew well enough Geraldine's finger would be pressed on and off the bell for as long as necessary until Marnie attended her, if it took all night. But Darryl didn't know that. She stared him out unflinchingly until he slid off her bed and threw his dressing-robe back on and tied it tightly.

'And if you ever come near me again I shall go straight to your fiancée and give her an intimate report of what she can expect in your bed,' Marnie hissed after him.

He stood looking down at her, but she knew she had the upper hand at last. He wouldn't risk being disgraced in the eyes of Mademoiselle Dupont and lose her dowry and her father's riches, she guessed scathingly, and without another word he strode across the room and slammed the door shut behind him.

She wilted like a dying flower. The hot tears bubbled in her eyes and the thickness in her throat threatened to choke her. The bell still rang, but Geraldine would have to wait. For once Marnie couldn't slide out of bed and rush to do her bidding, not until she'd pressed a cooling wash-cloth to her burning cheeks and between her legs where he'd touched her, and not until she'd rinsed out her mouth to rid herself of the taste of his blood on her lips.

By the time she reached the other girl's room, Geraldine was in a raging temper.

'What have you been doing! I thought you were never coming, and my head aches so terribly I must have one of Mrs Caine's powders after all. I shall never sleep without it,' she moaned, her face red and blotchy. 'Get out and fetch it, quickly.'

Marnie turned on her heel without a word. Suddenly she felt that nothing could touch her any more. She'd finally vindicated herself for all the wrong Darryl Larksby had done her, and she could dismiss Miss Geraldine's tantrums as being those of a frustrated female who hung on to a servant's tales of rape as the only thrills she was ever likely to get in her life. They were both pathetic creatures in their own ways.

Ten minutes later she was holding Geraldine's head while she sipped the draught from the glass. She lay back on her pillow as if exhausted.

'I shall sleep now,' she muttered. 'I trust no-one molested you while you were wandering about the house so late?'

'No-one,' she said evenly. 'I wasn't afraid of the dark.'

Nor ever would be again, not in this house.

'Good. And we go to King's Lynn tomorrow, so go back to bed, Marnie. We shall need to be up quite early.'

That was a comforting thought too. And the next day Darryl Larksby kept out of her way. She didn't see him before they left, and learned from Geraldine that he felt slightly indisposed after the sea crossing, and would stay in his room until lunchtime. Marnie allowed herself a small smile, thinking that his 'indisposition' was going to last longer than a few hours.

They left Larksby in the carriage with a groom in attendance and arrived at King's Lynn during the afternoon. Marnie had never seen the inside of an hotel before, nor so many fashionable ladies and gentlemen parading along the promenade to take the afternoon sun. It was the same on the following day, but by then Geraldine wanted to spend some time browsing in the shops as well as to breathe the good sea air that was relaxing them both. Marnie was especially relaxed, knowing that Darryl was well away from her present surroundings, and unlikely to bother her again on this visit home at least.

'I want to rest before dinner,' Geraldine announced on

the second day. 'So much of this sea air is making me sleepy. You may take another turn if you wish, Marnie, since the marine offices seem to interest you so much.'

It wasn't so much the offices as the sight of the posters in the windows that advertised the health-giving voyages to America on splendid steam-ships that were alternately intriguing and tormenting her, remembering the posters Gabe had had pinned to his bedroom wall at the farm that were similar to these. She stared at them as if drawn by a magnet for long after Geraldine had returned to the hotel, and suddenly she was aware of a man's voice speaking to her. She stiffened at once, a haughty rebuff on her lips, when she realised she was being addressed by name.

'Excuse me, Miss. It is Marnie, isn't it? Marnie Bray? I recognised you by the colour of your hair!'

She turned sharply, staring at the florid-faced, rotund young man behind her on the pavement. Not a gentleman, she thought swiftly, yet not a servant either, by his apparel or his manner. She frowned in vague recognition, still not able to place him, and wondering how he knew her. A friend of her brothers, perhaps? Somehow she didn't think so. They had few friends, and she was unable to picture this round fellow at the fen cottage.

'You don't remember me, I think,' he was saying diffidently. 'Well, there's no real reason why you should, I suppose. The name's Fred—Fred Jackson, late of the Duck and Drake Inn. *Very* late, since it's been years since I was there, but I used to be a friend of Gabe O'Brien.'

The wild colour flamed her face at the unexpected mention of his name. She stared at Fred Jackson, who for some reason seemed suddenly embarrassed by her scrutiny.

'Have you heard anything of Gabe lately?' he said hurriedly.

'He's—not around these parts any longer.' Caution made her evasive, and Fred Jackson looked slightly relieved to her surprise.

'Well,' he tried to sound hearty, but it came out clumsy instead, 'if you ever do see him, be sure to give him my best,

Marnie. And–uh–I reckon I owe him a bit of a sorry-un for blabbing on to your brothers that time. It's a long time past, but if you see him, tell him so for us, will you? It's a bad thing to split on your best bor.'

He spoke in riddles as far as Marnie was concerned, and she had no wish to stand here discussing Gabe O'Brien with this Fred Jackson, nor try to fathom out what he was trying so stupidly to explain. She cut him short by saying she must get back to the hotel where she was staying, without mentioning the fact that she was only there on sufferance as lady's maid to Miss Geraldine Larksby. But there was a sudden deferential look in his eyes as he assumed she must have come up in the world, and would have no use for such as Gabe O'Brien anyway.

'That's all right then.' He stood aside to let her pass. 'Just as long as there were no heads broken on account of my blabbing. But I reckon you'd have known if there had been.'

Marnie was tired of his mumbling and nodded briefly to him as she made her way back to the hotel. Fred had said little that made any sense to her, and yet for some reason the memory of his words stayed with her, just because they had concerned Gabe and some youthful indiscretion between him and Fred Jackson. She pushed the words to a small corner of her mind, like a tangled wool-skein to be unravelled at some future date.

CHAPTER SEVENTEEN

Jenny could hear Gabe lurching home long before he reached the miserable shack in which they lived. She tried to stop her lips trembling and her stomach heaving as she stirred the broth simmering on the stove. He'd be drunk again. He was more often drunk than sober these days, and the bright dream that had heralded their arrival in America had long since turned to ashes.

She wasn't even sure if she loved him any more, or that she had ever truly loved him. But he was the only human being belonging to her in the whole of this vast alien country that frightened her by its size, its people, its brashness. She clung to Gabe like a waif, knowing how her dependence on him irritated him, but unable to resist it. She'd made no friends at all since coming to America, and spent many hours alone.

Where was the wonderful life Gabe had dangled in front of her to allay her original fears, she thought resentfully? The fine house, the well-paid employment, the streets running with silver? It had all soured and tarnished in three short months, and though he shouted at her often enough that his money had started running out with alarming speed on the ship with her heavy medical expenses, she was shrewd enough to know that most of it had gone on drink and gambling. And women too, probably, though that was something Jenny deliberately closed her mind against for most of the time.

He certainly didn't turn to her so often in the sultry heat of the night, except on rare occasions when his basic needs demanded relief, and she was the one who was nearest . . . and sometimes it could still be very sweet. But too often Jenny imagined that he wasn't really with her in spirit. His mind would be elsewhere and he made love to a fantasy woman . . . she sensed it, though she never mentioned it. Only once did she protest at the speed of his love-making, as if he couldn't bear to lie on her a second longer than was necessary.

'It's only because of the babby,' he'd said thickly. 'We don't want harm to come to it, do we? Not after we've come all this way to see it born safe and free. Once you've got rid of your lump things will be different.'

He'd lain beside her then with his hands on her belly, and she'd been temporarily lulled into believing him. Everything would be all right when the baby was born. She'd put her own small hand over his.

'I wonder whether it's a boy or a girl, Gabe,' she said dreamily. 'We'll have to think of a name for it soon.'

'Plenty of time for that,' he grunted.

'I'd like a name to remind me of home,' her voice was wistful. 'Perhaps we could call it David if it's a boy, in memory of our little Davey, and it would be nice to call it after Marnie if it's a girl, wouldn't it? Gabe . . . Gabe, you're hurting me!'

His hand had tensed over her, and then it was pressing down as if he had no control over it. He removed it quickly and turned his back on her.

'We've cut ourselves off from the past and we want no reminders,' he said roughly. 'The child will be born American and we'd best give it an American name, and I don't give a damn if it's boy or girl but just let me get some sleep, will you?'

The quick tears had started to her eyes then. He could be unaccountably cruel at times, and always, it seemed to Jenny, just when things were beginning to improve between them, dashing her hopes. And any mention of home seemed to make him close up within himself. It was a point of constant bickering between them, because Jenny wanted to keep the memories alive, while Gabe tried uselessly to push them away for ever.

It was for that very reason that he turned so often to drink for solace, he assured himself time and again. He'd made a mess of his life and Jenny's too, and the wonderful life just waiting on this side of the Atlantic didn't materialise for them. Not the good living he'd pictured anyway, and it was galling to admit that the only thing available to him was work at some nearby stables, so that he came home every night with the stink of horses clinging to him. And that was usually followed by Jenny wrinkling her pretty nose at the mixtures of horse smells on his clothes and strong drink on his breath.

The sight of her finicky manners and wrinkled nose incensed him. And the warm friendly saloons made him forget what he was going home to, and the ladies of the night who frequented them weren't so fussy about lingering smells when he accompanied one or another of them to the accommodating rooms above. When you peeled off all your clothes one body smelled very like another, he thought cynically, except for the heavy cloying perfume his transient bed partners used. But by the time he got home to Jenny he was usually past caring how that clung to him too.

She paused in her broth-stirring as he banged open the door and kicked it shut behind him. He was still a very handsome man, she thought fleetingly, and time was never going to change those dimples in his cheeks or the way his blue eyes lit up when he smiled, but right now he was unshaven and unkempt and the sight of him leaning arrogantly against the door and belching vulgarly suddenly infuriated her.

'I walked up towards the big white house on the hill today,' she said quickly. 'I was going to enquire if they had any work for me, as a kitchen-maid or something . . .'

Gabe burst out laughing.

'Maid? You? With a seven months child in your belly? Nobody'd take you for a maid, my girl.'

'Don't be stupid,' she snapped. 'Anyway, I decided I'd never be able to stand the work and the walk to and fro each day, not with the weakness still in me from my fever on the crossing. I saw a man tending the garden up there and I asked if there was any work that might suit you.'

'You did what! When I want a woman to do my asking for me, I'll be six foot under,' he thundered. 'I'm man enough to find my own work . . .'

'Yes, with the stinking horses and not enough money for a decent home for our baby to be born in! Is that your idea of comfort? If you got a job at a big house like Larksby maybe we could get a little cottage in the grounds.'

'Will you shut your face about Larksby,' he shouted. 'I'm my own man, Jenny Bray, don't you forget it, and *I'll* decide what I do!'

'Jenny O'Brien.'

'What?' he glared at her.

'I said Jenny O'Brien. I'm your wife, remember? And I reckon you should respect me for that, and not come home with other women's perfume on you!' She dared to say it, and her mouth trembled as she tried to hold on to her dignity.

'Women's perfume!' he blustered. 'Is that all the thanks I get for sprinkling it on myself to get rid of the smell of the stables for you then? I thought you'd have realised that, Mrs O'Brien.'

His smile suddenly flashed out the way she remembered it, with the capacity to make her heart beat faster and turn her knees to jelly. He'd get round anybody with that smile, she thought weakly, but he wasn't getting round her so easily. He left the door and came across the room towards her. Despite the seven months' child she carried she was as light as a feather in his arms when he reached her, and despite all her good intentions she leaned against him with a little sigh of resignation as his lips began working their way over every bit of her face and throat.

The sight of her anger had excited him unexpectedly, and so did the feel of her swollen body against him. Within minutes he had pushed her gently back on to the old horse-hair sofa and taken her there and then, with her arms wound tightly round his neck and her soft parted mouth giving him back kiss for kiss.

And he was instantly contrite for the way he'd used and abused her all these months. Not for the fact of just making love to her, because she'd been panting for it as much as he had when it came to it, and maybe it wasn't a bad thing to stir up a row with her now and then, because it sparked off the desire in him that was so often lacking now as far as Jenny was concerned. He moved carefully away from her and pulled her to her feet.

'How about that broth now then? It smells good to a starving man.' He whacked her playfully on the backside. To his surprise she winced and pressed her belly.

'It's nothing,' she said quickly in answer to his enquiring look. 'A twinge that's been coming and going all day, that's all. I expect the baby's moving its position.' Her eyes suddenly glowed as she leaned up to kiss him on the mouth. 'Thank you Gabe.'

'What for?' he started laughing. 'It's the first time I've been thanked for that caper.'

'Not just for that! For letting me know there's still something between us and that we didn't make a terrible mistake coming here. I can face anything as long as I know that.'

'There's something between us all right,' he grinned as he patted her belly, but there was a thickness in his throat as he saw the childlike trust in her soft brown eyes.

And I've brought her to this, he thought guiltily. He watched her clumsy movements as she brought the steaming broth to the table and spooned it into the two dishes, comparing her now with the pretty Jenny who'd come so willingly to the old mill with him to learn the art of seduction.

'I'll go up to the white house later on to see if there's anything going there if you like,' he said grudgingly.

Her smile was brilliant. She put the soup ladle down and threw her arms round him and kissed him again. She tasted of salt from the tasting, but it wasn't unpleasant.

'Oh, thank you Gabe!'

'If you go on thanking me like this I shall begin to think I'm a hell of a good fellow,' he squeezed her thickened waist. 'Get that broth down you before you fade away,' he teased.

'I don't really feel like eating tonight,' she played about with her spoon, fighting down the sudden nausea that was plaguing her again. She didn't mention it to Gabe, knowing how he hated it.

'Well, you've had your share of good things for one evening,' he agreed. 'You can tip it back in the stew pan if you don't want it and leave it simmering for my supper. It's too good to waste.'

She was pink with pleasure as he praised her cooking. All too often she got the feeling she could do nothing right, and she leaned her elbows on the table with no more pretence of eating and watched him enjoy his broth.

'Won't it be lovely when we don't need to save the slops, Gabe? When we're rich and have everything we need.'

She nearly said that when that day came she hoped Marnie could come over and visit them, when they had a decent house in which to invite company, but knowing how Gabe hated reminders of the past she resisted it. Time enough for that when their fortunes improved. She'd wanted to write to Marnie to let her know how they fared, but several things held her back. The fact that she couldn't admit what a hovel they lived in for her own shame, and that there was always the danger of her letter being intercepted and someone giving chase to them. Who would do that she couldn't imagine, but the thought of it stopped her writing any letters home.

Gabe was probably right, and they had a new life to make, but her links with the old were still too strong to forget. She watched him eat until he'd wiped every bit of broth from the dish with his bread and leaned back satisfied. It wasn't yet dark, but he lit the oil lamp for her, sending a soft rosy glow into the starkness of their surroundings. Reminding her as always of the fen cottage where she'd spent her childhood, with the tang of the river coming home with her brothers and Da's pipe sending wreaths of smoke to cloud the ceiling, and little Davey's sweet baby smells that would soon be relived in the joy of her own baby. No matter how often Gabe said there was no use living over the past, the past was part of her and had made her what she was, and at least while the memories lived on in her head she didn't feel so entirely cut off from the familiarity of home.

The memories seemed needle-sharp that evening after Gabe left to go looking for work at the white house on the hill. She knew she wouldn't see him again for hours. If the news was good, he'd have to have a drink to celebrate. If it was bad, he'd drink to recover from the insult to his feelings. Either way, he'd end up at a saloon until the small hours, but at least she doubted if he'd want to sample one of the upstairs rooms after their brief union on the sofa.

Jenny was still smiling at that too as she tipped the broth back into the stew pan for Gabe's supper. The next second the smile was torn from her face as a gigantic pain ripped through her and buckled her knees. She sank on to the rag rug on the floor, her whole body trembling, her hands clutching her belly.

'Gabe! Gabe . . .' she knew she was screaming out his name, but the sound seemed to be strangled somewhere deep in her throat. Choked and silenced by the fear and dread that there was something very wrong inside her, and that she was completely alone.

Gabe had gone too far to hear her even if she'd bellowed like a bull. He'd already decided to call in at the nearest saloon for a stiff drink to give himself some Dutch courage before going up to the house on the hill. He was already half-wishing he hadn't agreed so readily to do as Jenny asked, but she'd stimulated him in her anger, and though her body hadn't been ready to receive him it had responded quickly, and the moments had been very sweet. Not exquisite, as had been some others, but nevertheless deserving of some consideration from him.

Gabe needed nobody to tell him what a bastard he was. He knew it for himself, and all his attempts to put everything right refused to add up the way he'd intended. Sometimes he thought he was just a natural-born loser. But tonight had been good–surprisingly good, since he'd gone home with no lusty feelings towards Jenny that evening, and it had revived his sense of duty towards her at least.

She wanted him to seek out a better job and so he would. He owed her that much. Jesus, the place where they lived was more of a hovel than the fen cottage where she used to live. He veered his thoughts away quickly as images of a girl with a knowing look and a fall of hair like burnished silk spun into his mind, a girl whose image could still send up a stirring in his loins.

Forget her, he instructed his subconscious angrily. She's trouble, and the one he'd got had to satisfy him and that glorious afternoon at the farm was nothing but a dream . . .

Once inside the saloon it was easier to set the forgetting processes in motion. He was known here. Men called out to him cheerfully and the saloon women eyed him provocatively, parting red mouths into teasing smiles and showing more of their voluptuous shapes than was seemly in a decent woman. Gabe had cushioned his head against more than one pair of ample breasts there tonight, but right now he wasn't thinking about that. He needed one drink and that was all. He went straight across to the bar.

'Usual, Gabe?' the barman had the bottle at the ready. He winked. 'There's a special poker game going on in the back room tonight. High stakes. You interested?'

'Not tonight, Joe . . .' regretfully.

'You ain't going chicken on a poker game, are you, boy? I never thought I'd see the day when an Irishman backed down.'

'I'm not backing down.'

'The boys were hoping you'd be in tonight. I told 'em I'd

269

send you in as soon as you arrived. The little woman wearing the trousers then, is she?'

Gabe was suddenly angry, his pride ruffled. 'No woman tells me what to do.' He drained his glass. 'Fill her again, Joe, and lead me to the game.'

He needn't stay long, he told himself. Just long enough to get caught up in the excitement of the game, maybe win a few dollars and then pull out. He musn't stay long. He had to get up to the white house as he'd promised Jenny, and Irishmen looking for any jobs that were going wouldn't be too welcome at a late hour. It was late enough already . . .

By the time Gabe had been at the poker table an hour he was oblivious to time or anything else. He was on a winning streak and expansive with the amount of drink he'd consumed. He was quite sure that if he broke off now he'd never have this much luck again. And he convinced himself very easily that tomorrow morning would be the right and proper time to go looking for work.

His instincts told him his luck would hold. And if he was lucky tonight, he'd be lucky in the morning. It was his own brand of logic that he applied when it suited him, and there was no sense in rushing into something on a whim of Jenny's. She always went on to bed early, and tonight would be no exception. She'd fall asleep as soon as her head touched the pillow, expecting him to waken her with any news. There was no reason for him to spoil a good game of poker. He gave up thinking about anything but the pleasure of pitting his wits against his opponents.

'Gabe . . .' sounds were oozing out of Jenny's throat now, even though it felt tight with fear. Why didn't he come? How long did it take to walk the two miles up to the top of the hill and make enquiries and then walk back down again? She knew it was unreasonable to expect him back within an hour, even without going for a drink, but it was more than three hours now, and it was dark outside, and

270

the remains of the broth were congealing in the stew pan, and the pains were getting stronger.

Surely it shouldn't be like this, so agonising, as if she was in danger of being ripped apart every time they assaulted her? Besides, it shouldn't be happening at all yet . . . unless she'd been wrong in her monthly flows and had miscounted. Jenny was no scholar, and she told herself desperately that if the child wanted to be born then it must be time and everything would be all right.

But there was a deep dark primitive fear inside her all the same. If only Gabe would come, he'd know what to do. He'd fetch somebody, a midwife, a doctor–she'd seen no-one yet. There'd been no need since her fever, and now that she was in the grip of the pains she was too frightened to venture outside the door of the shack herself. Besides, she had no idea where a doctor lived.

Oh God, oh God . . . a searing pain held her in another band of iron. She'd tried standing up when they came; leaning against the table. She'd tried lying on the sofa; upstairs on the bed; back on the sofa again. Now she was down on the floor on her knees, since that seemed the less painful of all the alternatives. She wished Ma were here. She'd been too little to remember Ma's confinement with Davey . . . oh Ma, did it always have to hurt like this?

There was nobody to hear when she screamed in agony. The shack was isolated and they had no neighbours. The pain went on and on, tearing her apart. It extended into her thighs and down her legs. It was everywhere. It enveloped her in mists of red fire that left her panting, her whole body bathed in sweat when the brief respites came.

The rag rug was crumpled where she clutched at it. She crawled across it to reach for a towel to dry her glistening face and body. Her teeth were beginning to chatter uncontrollably, and she couldn't have said whether it was from fear or shock or pain any more. It was all the same to her. All she wanted was for Gabe to come and for this agony to end.

'Oh Marnie, you were the clever one,' she sobbed through

271

her gritted teeth. 'Telling me what a fool I was to get into this mess. I'd change places with you now . . .'

Her sister had come into her mind as if she'd conjured her up out of nowhere, and the image stayed in front of her as if she was real. She stood there watching, with that tight-lipped look of shock on her face, just as she'd had when Jenny blurted out about the child. And she looked accusingly now, without pity, saying hadn't Da always said there was no good at all in those Irish navvies? Jenny should have listened to Da, his clever one, his pretty one. The picture changed, and the Marnie in front of her was younger, her dyke-straight hair gleaming down her back and a rose-pink satiny ribbon trailing along its length, and a younger Gabe was stretching out a hand to stroke it, with hot, eager eyes . . .

Jenny gave an agonised gasp as the pictures faded and the pain took a new shape. From being pulled apart in two directions there was suddenly a feeling of urgency; a frantic desire to push against heaven and earth; a grinding of her teeth and blowing out of her cheeks until the screams became a low-pitched animal growl that never seemed to end; a gripping and twisting of the towel as she spread-eagled on the rag rug and prayed to die.

'God damn you, you bastard Gabe O'Brien,' she screamed over and over. 'Damn you for leaving me like this . . .' her face contorted as the need to push drove her on again, as if she had to expel all the demons in hell out of her body. She was splitting in two; she was tearing; there was something hot and wet and sticky between her legs and she desperately needed help.

The screams dwindled to a whimper. The next pain gathered her up and kept her high on a mountain top. She had no strength to push any more. There was nothing left. She was suddenly numb, floating somewhere above the ground, looking down at the crumpled figure on the rag rug that was reddening with an ever-spreading stain . . .

Gabe eased his aching shoulders and blinked his eyes. Jesus, he'd have to go. The saloon had closed its doors hours ago and only the back room with poker players showed any sign of life. He'd made a killing tonight, but he'd be no good to anybody in the morning if he didn't get home and get some sleep. Morning–it was morning now. The sun was streaking pink and gold across a pearly sky, but there was money jingling in his pockets that was going to put the smile back on Jenny's face. Maybe he'd even buy her something, a warm shawl she could snuggle into when she fed the babby at night. A cheerful whistle came to his lips at the thought, for the idea of pretty Jenny with a babby fastened to her breast was suddenly a pleasurable one. For the first time he thought of the child as a separate person and not as an encumbrance.

He let himself into the shack quietly, noting that Jenny had left the oil-lamp still burning for him. It was a considerate thought. He stopped suddenly as the smell of stale burnt broth met his nostrils, and something more . . . and within seconds the full horror of the little room hit with the force of lightning, so that he could hardly breathe for the shock of it.

'Jesus Christ,' he said hoarsely, and crossed himself swiftly as he pulled back the curtain to let the daylight in and reveal the bloody mangled mess on the floor. For an instant he averted his head, unable to look. But he *had* to look . . . there was blood everywhere, congealing thick as mud. Jenny . . . Jenny lay on her stomach, her head turned sideways on the rag rug, her face still contorted in agony, her lips pulled back in a hideous grimace. She'd been dead a long time. Her legs were still buckled ludicrously in an undignified frog-like position, as if she'd been straddling something and then just keeled over. They were caked in blood, and between them . . . between them . . .

'Sweet Mother of God,' the words were wrenched out of him past the racking sobs welling in his eyes and his throat. A tiny waxen body with thin wisps of hair the colour of autumn leaves plastered to its damp head lay silently, its limbs still curled in the foetal position, and the

273

purply-coloured cord twisted round its neck. It was a perfect replica of Jenny, of Marnie . . . no, Jenny. Gabe tried to gather it up in his arms but it was cold and rigid, and near to it was a huge spongy lump of liver . . .

He suddenly convulsed and dropped it on to its horrendous cradle, and stumbled, retching and spewing to the sink. Hot scalding tears poured down his face as he gasped out his vomit, for the child he hadn't wanted, and for pretty Jenny who'd ended up like this because of him.

And all the while she'd been struggling towards death, he'd been drinking and playing poker. He suddenly flung the coins out of his pockets in a fury of self-condemnation. *Bastard*, he wept from the depths of his soul. The worst bastard that ever lived . . .

How long he leaned over the sink he didn't know, but eventually he splashed cold water over his face and swilled out his mouth. He couldn't turn and look at them again, but he couldn't leave them like this. He had to find somebody . . . a doctor . . . it was too late for that. A priest then! Oh God, if he'd ever needed a priest, he needed one now. There were things to be done, things he couldn't see to himself. He'd pay. He had money. All the money he'd won at poker last night to buy her a present, never thinking that it would be a burying sheet.

He covered her legs with a towel, smothering an idiotic urge not to cover the baby's face in case it should miraculously begin breathing again. He was half demented with grief as he staggered to the door, a grief that surprised him, because it was as if he mourned all of the past as well as the two still bodies he'd just left. He moved like a man running through a nightmare, to hammer on the priest's door and try to communicate some sense from his incoherent babblings.

'Martha!' Father Rourke roared at once to his house-keeper as soon as he'd grasped the gist of it. 'Go for the doctor and Mrs Biles and tell them I've need of their services immediately at the old shack off Main Street. And bring this lad a stiff drink for medicinal purposes.'

274

'I don't need a drink,' Gabe said harshly.

'Yes you do,' the priest answered. 'Don't argue and do as you're told. And sit down on the sofa before you fall down. You need every bit of outside help you can get, as well as inner strength and I assume you're aware of that to come to me at this time.'

'Christ, I don't want a sermon,' Gabe shouted. 'I want . . . I need someone . . .'

Suddenly he found himself in the throes of a spasm of weeping again, with the priest's arms holding him and his gut turning to water. Jesus, he felt as if he was in danger of losing control of his bladder. A fine thing it would be if he peed all over Father Rourke's best quality sofa. The incongruous thought allowed him to drag himself together with a stupendous effort, managing not to slop the glass of whisky that was thrust into his hands and swallowing it at a gulp. It steadied him enough to get to his feet when the priest asked if he was ready.

'I don't want to go back in there,' he stuttered like a gibbering idiot.

'It's the last thing you can do for your wife,' the priest said gravely. 'And the child must be baptised, my son.'

Gabe's head was spinning like a top. He didn't even know if he had a son or a daughter. What did it matter? It had been an inanimate doll that wouldn't move or cry and would never know how much he'd have loved it.

'Will you see to it all?' he gasped. 'I–I can't . . .'

'Naturally. But we must go now or the doctor and Mrs Biles will be there before us.'

'Who is this Mrs Biles?' Gabe couldn't care less, but it was something to say as they walked quickly through the dawn-pink streets towards the shack.

'Just the lady we call on to help with things,' the priest said carefully.

He wished he hadn't asked then. The layer-out, with her grisly bag of tricks. Gabe shuddered, telling himself it was a job that had to be done. But once he opened the door of the shack the stench of blood almost curdled his stomach.

Surely it hadn't been so strong before? But the first time he hadn't been expecting it, when now he'd known only too well what lay on the rag rug.

'I'm sorry,' he mumbled as he leaned over the sink again. There'd be nothing left to bring up soon, he thought dispassionately. He could hear Father Rourke intoning over the bodies as he knelt on the floor, disregarding the mess and the smell, and suddenly he heard himself being called.

'The name,' the priest was saying. 'It's a little girl child. Had you and your wife chosen a name for her?'

Gabe had been determined not to look at the baby again, but his eyes were drawn to her like a moth to a flame. The rigor had begun to soften by now, and though she lay motionless in the priest's arms it was almost possible to believe she was only sleeping, that she'd open her eyes at any moment and turn to look back at him.

He felt light-headed. What colour were her eyes? Would they be clear and brown with an unblinking stare that would tie men's hearts in knots as she grew to glorious womanhood? He swallowed hard. He'd never know, of course, and it would never happen. And because she'd been born so prematurely the eyelashes were sparse and pale, the finger-nails and toe-nails unformed. Gabe knew the sight of her would be imprinted on his brain for ever. She was beautiful. He swallowed again the enormous lump that kept filling his throat. She was a perfect tiny replica of . . .

'The name, please, for the baptism,' the priest urged. 'You'd not offer your daughter nameless to God?'

'Marnie,' Gabe heard himself choke out the word. 'She's to be called Marnie.'

Then he rushed out of the shack into the cool morning air, to lean against the outside wall with the tears still blurring his vision. He couldn't bear to stay inside and hear the meaningless ritual or to hear *her* name on the priest's lips. He felt that in some way what he'd just done was blasphemy, even though it was what Jenny had wanted.

276

He'd had to do it for her, knowing that she'd loved her sister so much.

But not as much as he did . . . the thought swept into his mind like a chill little wind stirring the leaves on the trees, shivering and pulsating along his nerve-ends, and right now it seemed the most blasphemous thought of all.

PART THREE

CHAPTER EIGHTEEN

There had been a time when Gabe had thought mornings his favourite time of day. If he ever thought back to those days now, when he and Mick had breakfasted on hunks of bread and honey and swilled them down with a strong brew of tea before starting out on another day's dyke-digging across the dew-fresh fields of the English fens, with the peculiar yellow-green dawn sky gleaming on the cool ribbony dykes, it was as if he saw them through a shadowy grey mist. They were part of another world, in which a girl with inviting brown eyes and dewy lips and a fall of glossy brown hair had unwittingly started off a chain of events in his life that had ended here in this miserable shack in a small town some miles North of Washington, where Jenny and the baby had died.

Gabe didn't welcome mornings any longer. Evenings were a mite easier, because once his work at the stables was done for the day, he'd make his way to one of the town saloons where he spent most of his time with his drinking companions. And when the haze of the drink was on him he could manage to blur the edges for a little while of the scene that had met his horror-stricken eyes when he'd gone home to Jenny that night when he was supposed to be visiting the white house on the hill. After that night, he'd had no further wish to seek out other work, nor to better himself. Why should he, when there was nobody to answer to but himself from now on?

He'd leaned heavily on Father Rourke at that time, searching for the man beneath the priest's pomposity, yet resisting every effort on the priest's part to draw him back into the church. He was in no mood for being urged to confess his sins, or listening to mumbo-jumbo or the hollow promises of forgiveness. You confess and He'll forgive ... tit-for-tat, no thank you ...

'You'd not turn your back on the Mother church just now, Gabe?' Father Rourke would say sorrowfully. 'When you've such need of her strength?'

'What has she ever done for me? Can you tell me one thing?'

The priest would cross himself quickly at his brash words, and Gabe thought irreverently that he'd like a dollar for every time he'd seen a man do that. It was just a ritual, meaningless and flamboyant. It meant nothing. Half the time the folk were unaware they'd even done it at all.

He knew full well the priest still grieved over the fact that he hadn't followed Jenny and the baby for the burying. He knew folk would think it unmanly to stay away at the last mortal sight of a wife and child, but Jenny wasn't his wife and never had been, and to have listened to pious platitudes at such a time would have been little more than farcical. Better that the priest should think he was so overcome with his grief that he'd had to shut himself away in the shack on the day of the burying, alone with his guilt and a bottle of whisky.

He'd thought perhaps the feeling of guilt would lessen with time. He'd tried to involve himself with other people, even attempting to work up a semblance of interest in the rumblings of civil war threats that were on every man's lips, from those who believed implicitly that it was heading towards them like a darkening cloud, to those who still lived in their own rose-coloured cloud of disbelief.

Gabe cared little which side won the arguments as the discussions got ever more heated. It wasn't his country and it wasn't his war, if and when it came, and Abe Lincoln was a hero or a devil, depending on the mood of the hecklers when they began putting the world to rights in bars and saloons.

But no amount of throwing himself into whatever caught his temporary interest could stop the guilt flooding back in unguarded moments. The knowledge of his neglect of Jenny on the ship and here in America, and his neglect of things he should have done since and hadn't, weighed heavily on him and gnawed away at his conscience.

He knew he should inform Jenny's family of her death, but somehow he couldn't put the words to paper, and if he did there was always the fear of recriminations on his brother Mick. He knew only too well how the Bray brothers would react if they knew the truth of Jenny's disappearance. He could write to Mick, but the thought of doing that filled him with shame, knowing what Mick thought of him for getting a Bray girl in this mess. And besides, to admit to Mick what a dismal failure he'd made of it all, his fine dream of life in America, and squandering all Mammy's money as well as the tragedy that had befallen Jenny and the baby, was more than he could ever do.

There was only one other person . . . but how could he write unemotionally to the one who still held all of his heart? How could he pour out all his guilt and contrition without becoming maudlin and begging her forgiveness? How to tell her he'd killed pretty Jenny–because that was what it amounted to? It twisted his gut every time he even considered it. And how could he tell her that he'd named the baby after her, picturing for an instant the still, waxy form of his tiny daughter, with such a look of his Marnie about her it had stunned him.

And even if his conscience told him sternly that he was shirking his duty, it was more than his spirit could endure to try to put the words down on paper, knowing it could only alienate Marnie still further, if that were possible. So he did nothing, but he was constantly tortured by the fact that her family had a right to know what had become of Jenny, and it eased his mind not one whit to tell himself that at least he was sparing them the sorrow of it all. And the nightmares went on . . .

Gabe woke up to find himself shouting, and the bedclothes wringing wet with his own sweat. It was dawn. He crawled out of bed and down the stairs in the eerie half-light to

283

sluice his face under the cold tap to try and clear his mind from remembering. The nightmares came with sickening regularity, and always with a procession of death-mask images looming up in front of him to shock him into wakefulness. But not until he'd registered every one of them in his mind, drying his mouth with terror, yet dousing him in sweat.

Little Davey Bray, golden and fresh-faced; Mammy, ghoulishly shrouded in black; Farmer Lester, a gaunt shadow of his old robust self; Jenny and his tiny, beautiful Marnie, hideously contorted in the clasp of death.

It was at that point he always awoke in a fever of anguish, because the two of them were always pictured in the horrific blood-bath in which he'd found them. In six months, the picture hadn't faded, and he was still obsessed with thoughts of death. He'd got rid of the rag rug and scrubbed at the wooden floor until his hands were raw, and he'd burned every bit of Jenny's clothing, but he still imagined he could see her there, huddled on the floor, and every time the nightmare ended, he felt the compulsion to creep down the stairs, just to check once more that there was nothing there . . .

He shuddered and reached into the cupboard for the remains of a bottle of whisky, swilling the last drops straight down. It stung his throat, but it was what he needed to stop him shaking. It was the only thing that gave him a brief forgetfulness, that and the gambling that could still stimulate his brain for a while. And his small group of companions who'd rallied round when they'd known Jenny had died in childbed.

He'd been grateful, even touched by their rough and ready concern, but he was certain in his own mind that no-one could help him over this, and it was something he had to come to terms with in his own way and his own time. The hell of it was, he hadn't expected it to take so long, but his companions had got used to his plunging moods of depression, and either tried to lift him out of it or totally ignored it.

284

'Christ man, you can't blame yourself for the rest of your life,' Brad said time and again. He was a huge, swarthy man with Indian blood in his veins and a coldness in his character that went back to his ancestors. But he had a cold logic that got through to Gabe, and he tried to listen and believe in Brad's words.

'He can't just forget she existed neither,' Deeker would argue. ' 'Twouldn't be right to forget a wife like she was so much deer meat, would it?' Older than the rest of the little group, Deeker was the cutest of all when it came to a hand of poker, and he had a canny eye for the women. But he was shrewd enough never to get entangled with one permanently. For all that, he had a healthy respect for marriage, as long as it was other people's. 'What you need, Gabe, is a bit of whoring to take your mind off things. You'll soon find there's no difference once you get them under the sheets in the dark. That'll be what's ailing you, after gettin' it reg'lar, but a virile young bucko like you shouldn't have any trouble finding consolation.'

'I ain't looking for consolation,' he'd say harshly. 'I just want . . .'

What did he want? Not Jenny, if he was brutally honest, not as a person, and knowing it only made his guilt more acute. Not the babby . . . not any more, if it was going to grow up looking so much like the real Marnie it would cut his heart to little pieces every time he held her. Sweet Jesus, if that had happened, he'd probably have had incest on his conscience as well as everything else in ten years or so.

'Come on, Gabe,' his third crony said persuasively on the previous night. 'There's some new skirt just arrived in town, and I'm told they've headed for the new whorehouse. Came over on the boat from France, and some very fancy pieces, I'm informed. They probably don't even speak the lingo yet, but I'll wager they all know how to say yes to a silver dollar.'

Cal was nearer Gabe's own age, and more of his temperament than Deeker and Brad. And the four of them had been swinging along the sidewalk when Cal had

285

decided he'd been without a woman long enough and had stopped opposite the new whore-house and suggested they give it a quick work-out.

'You're a randy little bugger, aren't you, Calvin?' Brad grinned, his teeth glinting yellow in the gas light near the whore-house with its red plush curtains and air of opulence and welcome. 'I never knew you to be quick with a woman ever since I known you.'

'Okay, squaw-man, you do what you want and me and Gabe'll do what we want. Coming, Deeker?'

'I ain't said I'm going yet,' Gabe snorted.

Jesus, he'd never thought he'd see the day when he was off women, and he hoped to God his instincts weren't leading him in the other direction, but the only feeling inside him at the thought of going inside that whore-house was one of apprehension. There was no fire in his belly for it any more.

And right soon after Jenny's death he'd almost drunk himself silly one night, picked up a girl from the streets and taken her back to the shack. He'd fumbled and fondled and sweated as he lay on her trying to make himself rise, and in the end he'd felt her heaving with laughter beneath him before she pushed him off her on to the floor, and told him laughingly to get his ass in order before he tried doing a man's job again.

The humiliation still burned inside him whenever he remembered how he'd cursed her and yelled abuse after her as she'd clattered out of the shack, her laughter still ringing in his ears, leaving him alone in the dark. Remembering to his shame how he'd felt as if he was dissolving into a useless heap of jelly, crying in the dark like a baby.

'Well, Gabe? Are you coming in or not?' Deeker said impatiently. 'The rest of us are anxious to see if any of these French tarts know a trick or two.'

'All right.' He gave in. What else was there to do? The night was still young, and he didn't want to go home. Maybe he'd even find some girl who'd want to talk--or listen--though he doubted it. A whore was a whore. They

286

didn't earn their money talking.

An overpowering mixture of perfumes met their nostrils as soon as they entered the establishment.

'Jesus wept!' Brad exclaimed. 'Good job none of us have got wives to go home to after this. The smell's going to stick with us for days, from just walking into the place!'

Gabe pushed Jenny's sorrowing brown eyes out of his mind as a sleek middleaged woman dressed in swishing black silk came smilingly towards them, assessing them quickly.

'Good evening, gents,' she said smoothly. 'If you'd like to come through into the salon, I'm sure we can accommodate you all, and it's mighty nice to make your acquaintances.'

She spoke with a heavy Southern drawl and informed them her name was Mrs Lacey and that she was the owner of the establishment.

'A very responsible position, as I'm sure you'll appreciate,' she said delicately, 'with so many charming young ladies waiting to give discerning clients pleasure. And because a lady can't be too careful, I do ask my gentlemen to leave a little something on account before they sample the delights that await them.'

They'd entered the salon by then and Gabe's eyes widened. He'd been in whore houses before, but never anything like Mrs Lacey's. The whole room was sumptuously furnished, with thick, cream-coloured carpets on the floor and silk coverings on the settees. Several girls lounged on them, and they too were covered in silk, in glowing jewel colours. Silk seemed to be the order of the day, and Gabe felt a stirring of interest as the muted lights gleamed seductively on the rounded silken curves of the waiting girls and everything else in that shimmering room. He could hear Cal's quickened breathing behind him, and see the way Brad and Deeker were giving each girl their practised eye.

'We understand there may be some French girls here,'

Deeker said without preamble. Mrs Lacey smiled, her eyes brightening.

'Ah, I see you are gentlemen of taste. Some new young ladies from France have arrived here only this week, and as luck would have it they are joining us for the first time this very evening.'

The four men glanced at each other, a derisive expression on each face, knowing it was a tale the old bag would repeat to every new client for the next few months until she couldn't get away with it any longer. They also knew what was coming next.

'For such special services, we do charge a little extra, of course, but I'm sure such discerning gents as yourselves will think it worth every nickel.'

'Pay up, buckos, and let's see what these French tarts have got up their skirts that's so special before we have to start paying for the air we're breathing,' Deeker said crudely.

He threw some money on to the small table where the 'house charge' was displayed prominently, and to which Mrs Lacey had pointed delicately. Her smile was more frigid than before, but it still remained firmly fixed to her lips. She spoke to one of the silk-clad girls.

'Will you ask the young French mademoiselles to present themselves, please, honey?'

She turned to the four men as she slipped the proffered money from each one into a black bag hanging from the waist of her gown, and her Southern drawl became even more pronounced.

'Now, you just make yourselves right at home and stay just as long as you want. The girls will be here in a moment and will introduce themselves, and I shall hope to see you all at the end of your entertainments.'

She simpered at Brad and glided out of the salon. To go and count up her pennies, Gabe thought cynically. He had no doubt she'd been one of the girls herself until she took on as Madam, and wondered if there'd ever been a Mr Lacey . . .

The second girl in the room slid off the settee and smiled at the four men as the first one came back with four other girls. As far as their shapes went, they were like peas in a pod, from their red smiling mouths and large breasts and tiny waists to the rustling, sensuous movements and unpinned hair that hung over their shoulders in a way that made a man immediately want to stroke it. Only in their colouring did they differ, and the fact that one of them was black-skinned.

'Would you all like a drink?' the first girl who'd fetched them said softly in an accent just like Mrs Lacey's. There was a distinct resemblance too. Her daughter, perhaps. Some inheritance, running a whore house, Gabe thought, but it was no concern of his.

He accepted the large drink she put in his hand, knowing it would be put on his bill. He took a great swallow of it as he saw his three companions were already making hay with three of the French girls. Well, he'd known Deeker's fancy right off. He always went for a touch of the tarbrush, and that little black Frenchy was quite something in a skin-tight gown of white silk split of the thighs. Jeez, Deeker was going to be all right there.

'Why don't you come and sit down, *cheri*, or would you prefer somewhere more comfortable?' a soft, husky voice with a strong French accent was speaking directly to him. Gabe wrenched his eyes away from Deeker's amorous advances towards the black girl on the settee and turned to look at the girl smiling up into his eyes. Her eyes were as blue as his own, her cheeks pink as a rose in full bloom, her mouth wide and shiny red. Her hair was the colour of ripening corn, and her body was encased in a blue-green gown that reminded him of the sea at Drory. She was a beautiful china doll. She put small, red-tipped fingers on his arm.

'Come,' she went on in her husky voice. 'I think it gets too noisy for us in here. We shall go somewhere where we can relax together, *non*?'

He was vaguely aware of Deeker's raucous laughter, and

some remark that Cal or Brad shouted after him about being the darkest horse of them all, and couldn't he even wait to get his pants off? He followed the girl's undulating movements out of the salon as if he was in a dream, with the neat whisky flooding his senses and relaxing him. Through soft-carpeted corridors and stairs to a room on the second floor that was as ornate as the salon, and lit with subtle gas lighting and fragrant with perfume. The girl turned as she closed the door, smiled into Gabe's eyes and took the glass from his hand and placed it on the bedside table.

'For afterwards, *oui*? I think it is not wise to drink too much before we join.'

He felt a sudden wild urge to laugh. Was that what he was about to do then? Join with her. He'd always thought of it in much cruder terms. And why in God's name should he feel so bloody reluctant, when here she was, turning her slender back towards him and asking him to unfasten the blue-green gown, and he could feel his fingers fumbling awkwardly against the silkiness of the material and the smooth softness of her hair and her skin as if he was some idiotic greenhorn?

A sudden sharp sensation in his groin reminded him that he was still a man after all. The feeling was almost exquisite, because it was so long since he'd felt it. He pushed the blue-green silk from her shoulders and it slid to a shimmering heap on the carpet. He caught his breath. She was naked beneath the gown, her breasts firm and full, as if they'd been fashioned just the way he liked them, accentuated by the tiny waist curving below them towards the well-rounded hips. He let his eyes travel slowly and lingeringly downwards, and drew in his breath again. She was a beautiful girl, and she was his for as long as he wanted her. And suddenly he wanted her . . .

'You like?' she smiled, her voice soft and sensuous, and he realised she was deftly unbuttoning his shirt and moving her small palms gently against the black hairs on his chest. 'I am called Sylvie, *cheri*. What do I call you?'

'Gabe,' he mumbled. He still felt ridiculously gauche, like

290

a child on its first lesson in seduction, and he couldn't think why she made him feel that way. She paused in her sensual movements to smile her liquid smile straight into his eyes.

'Ah, like the angel.'

He stared at her.

'The angel,' she repeated huskily. 'Gabriel! Are you an angel, *cheri*?'

His mouth curved into a broad smile, and then it was her turn to catch her breath. She broke into a string of husky French words that he couldn't understand, and then laughed at his expression.

'Forgive me, Monsieur Gabe! I sometimes forget to speak the English when I am much excited. But do you realise it is the first time I have seen you smile! And such a smile! You have many broken hearts behind you, I think?'

He shrugged. He was beginning to feel more like his old self, and aggressively male as he heard her say so frankly that he excited her. He fondled her breasts, hardly realising that he did so until he felt the nipples respond, and then felt the hardening of himself.

'Never mind what's left behind,' his voice was suddenly thick with desire. 'But I'm no angel, Sylvie.' He smiled again, flicking one finger against her nipple teasingly. 'Do you have a fancy for joining with the devil instead?'

She looked startled and crossed herself immediately, until she realised he was teasing, and then she laughed and moved back a few steps towards the bed. She threw back the silken coverlet invitingly.

'*Mon Dieu*, but I thought you meant it, *cheri*! But if you are the devil, I think even that might be very enjoyable . . .'

He was across the room in seconds, discarding the rest of his clothes as he went. His body was still firm and very masculine, despite the copious quantities of drink he poured into it, and the sight of her eyes feasting on him filled him with a sudden savage need of a woman. He would have mounted her right away, but Sylvie had other ideas.

'*Mais non*, *cheri*,' she whispered seductively as her hands caressed him. 'Have you no desire to make this a joining to

291

remember? There is no need for hurry, and we have the whole night to make the loving before we join.'

'Just for a minute,' he begged her, his need becoming an almost excruciating pain.

'And then we stop and enjoy each other in other ways?' she ran a small pink tongue around his lips.

'Yes, *yes*,' only let me feel the heat of that lovely golden place giving me blessed relief . . .

He slipped inside her with the ease of a ship gliding into the ocean. Her body was warm beneath him, her arms backwards on the pillow in sweet abandonment as she arched to meet him. Those glorious pointed breasts teased his lips, and sweet holy Jesus, he couldn't wait . . . he couldn't wait.

'I'm sorry, Sylvie,' he heard himself mumble against her throat. 'I never meant it to be so quick. It's been six months since I had a woman, and I wanted you badly. It was a bloody failure, wasn't it?'

To his amazement he heard her laugh softly, somewhere deep in her throat. Not scathingly, the way that other tart had when he'd failed completely at the shack, but gently, her hands caressing the hair on the back of his neck and running down his back in little tantalising movements.

'Ah no, Gabe! Never think of it as a failure. More as an *aperitif* before the main course. We still have all the night, don't we? Now we can pleasure each other without the joining until you get the rise again, and next time it will last much longer.'

She had that blue liquid smile in her eyes again, and she pulled his head down to her, pushing her small pink tongue inside his mouth and exploring it sensuously, easing herself away from his body so that they lay side by side, and moving his hand slowly over the curves of her breasts and down over her rounded belly until it reached the soft fleshy growth of corn-coloured hair.

'Please Gabe,' she whispered against his mouth. 'My angel. My oh so wicked angel . . .'

He'd been with whores before, but never one like Sylvie. He learned more at her fingertips that night than he'd

292

known in the whole of his life before. And when the time eventually came for another joining, he exulted in her panting beneath him, and the words that were torn from her lips in a language he didn't understand. But the language written on her face was clear enough, and it was hours later when he finally moved reluctantly from her bed, completely sated.

'You see?' Her husky voice reached out to him from the silken sheets. 'Didn't I tell you it would be worth it, *mon cheri*? Even if Mrs Lacey gets all the payment while I do all the work, but it was a lovely joining? She'll be waiting for you downstairs, Gabe, and adding up the hours we've spent together. You will recommend me, *non*?'

Her red mouth was still smiling, and he'd just spent exquisite hours between her thighs, but her words jarred on his senses. While he'd been with her everything had been dulled for him except for the intense pleasure between them. He'd murmured words of love, and even obscenities that seemed to delight her. He'd heard her soft little cries of pleasure as he responded to her gentle instructions or thought up new tricks of his own.

Led like a lamb to the bloody slaughter, he thought harshly, and he saw that his first clumsy copulation was no good at all for her purposes, for the price would be small for such a short amount of time spent in her bed. And that was why she'd gone through all those other delights with him that had led to the last lengthy joining that had had her body glistening and throbbing beneath him. Oh, she'd enjoyed that all right. She was made for it . . . but it had all been merely *work* to her. She was a whore, and he'd been fool enough to forget it for a little while.

He tossed some money on to her naked body.

'Buy yourself something,' he said harshly. 'That was what you wanted, wasn't it?'

She scrabbled towards it and stuffed it quickly in a small drawer in the bedside table, no doubt out of Mrs Lacey's sight. It sickened him. He gulped down the rest of his whisky and moved towards the door as she still lay there, cocooned in silk.

'Thank you, *cheri*,' her husky voice came after him and she blew him a kiss. 'You will come again, yes? We make good love together.'

'Perhaps,' he said. He turned on his heel and left her there, knowing he'd never come here again. He found his way back to the salon where his three companions were sprawled out on the settees. Brad snored noisily and Cal was curled up sleeping like a baby. But Deeker let out a great cheer the minute he saw him appear that woke the others, and grinned at Mrs Lacey's black figure as she stood like a vulture at the table waiting to collect payment.

'How the hell d'you do it, Gabe?' he roared. 'We took bets on who'd last out longest, and you weren't even in the running. Thought you'd have gone out like a damp squib for all the enthusiasm you had about it when we came in. Must have been a hot piece you had!'

Mrs Lacey frowned at him and told him coldly to be quiet because her girls needed their rest. Deeker cackled loudly.

'Why? They spend most of their time on their backs!' He prodded the other two again. 'Come on, you buggers. Gabe here's just got to pay for his skirt and then let's get the hell out of here. I need a drink. That bloody scent's got right down in my windpipe.'

Mrs Lacey smiled warmly at Gabe as he handed over the money.

'Come again, honey. Preferably without your friends.'

'Yeah,' he muttered. He was too weary to make any snap remarks. Jeez, he was buggered. He was wrung out like a wet bedsheet, and he stumbled out into the night air with his companions. All he wanted was to fall into bed and sleep the clock round. Thank God tomorrow–today–was Sunday, and there'd be no sweating horses to be fed and groomed and exercised. Not by him anyway. But Deeker wasn't letting him go so easily.

'Ain't you going to tell us how you made out?' he

hollered. 'Aw, come on, Gabe. Tell you what. We'll get you home before you get run in by the law from staggering about, and have a shot of your whisky before I'm parched . . .'

'I'm not in any mood for drinking . . .'

The others stopped in their tracks, and as they were holding him up he had to stop too.

'Christ, now I've heard everything,' Brad said. 'Well, we are, me Irish bucko, and all the saloons are shut and you're the only one with any drink available, so that's it!'

They frogmarched him out of town and through the silent streets to the shack. He was the champ, they kept telling him, the randiest buck in town, and he had to celebrate in style. They told him he'd better make the most of Mrs Lacey's whore house while it lasted, because with a Southern accent as thick as treacle she'd be high-tailed out of the place as soon as the first welcome Yankee shot was fired on those Southern bastards when the war came. They downed his whisky and ate his food, and by the time they left they'd tipped him out of his clothes and left him lying inert on his bed with the coverlet thrown roughly on top of him.

When he awoke, with a mouth like the inside of a bear's skin, the church bells were ending their insistent calling for all good catholic folk to early morning mass, and Gabe was crawling wearily down the stairs towards the sink to be sick, after yet another nightmare that last night's debauchery had done nothing to expunge. Leaving him shaking and parchment-faced and reaching for the near-empty whisky bottle.

And now it was really empty and he flung it away from him. He shivered, and yet the shack was stifling him. Closing in on him and making it difficult for him to breathe. As if she was still there, accusing him . . .

He had to get out of there. He threw on some clothes and left the shack and its memories behind. It was a cold sharp morning, but Gabe felt nothing of it. It was as if he wore an invisible shield around him through which no outside influence could penetrate. The nightmare was still vivid in his mind, and what could hurt him more than the pain already eating away at him constantly?

He strode through the streets, where few but the early Godfearing Catholics were about. Past the saloons and the whore houses, where Mrs Lacey's establishment suddenly looked as tawdry as the rest, despite the red plush drapes still pulled across the windows while the occupants lay sleeping after their night's exertions. Through the small green wood on the edge of town, and along the banks of the winding stream that was still and glassy in the first shimmer of sunlight of the morning.

Gabe's footsteps slowed as if some other force than himself commanded them. He stood on the bank of the stream, his feet sinking a little in the soft peaty soil. The sunlight dappled through the trees, blurring his own image in the water as it rippled in a small breeze. Or was it his eyes that were suddenly blurred with salty stinging tears?

Because the stream was suddenly transformed in his mind from the cool waters of a small American town, to the once-familiar gleaming dykes of the English fens. And he was thirteen again, and on his way to the old disused mill near Kettle's farm, with a full moon high-sailing the evening sky, and Marnie Bray was waiting for him.

A small animal scuttled out from the bank, scattering earth into the stream and the illusion was broken. But for a few heart-rending moments it had been so real . . . *she* had been real, his beautiful, treacherous Marnie, who'd gone running to her brothers with the tale of his seducing, when he'd believed she was as enchanted by the secret between them as he'd been . . . all those years ago, and yet more real to him at that moment than anything that had happened since. He suddenly plunged his head into the crystal clear water, to come out gasping and spluttering, the water running out of his eyes and ears, and tightening his hair into glistening black corkscrews.

Again and again he dived his head under the water, until the shock of it cleared his thinking and sobered him completely. And still he crouched there with the water dripping from him, until the time for mass was over and the churchgoers would be gone home. And only then did he get to his feet and make his way purposefully to Father Rourke's church, mindless of the state he was in.

The priest turned quickly as the footsteps shuffled into the church as he was extinguishing the last of the candles. His outraged eyes took in Gabe O'Brien's unkempt appearance, the wild eyes that were haggard and heavy from lack of sleep, the water and dirt that clung to him and was dripping all over his clean church floor. He straightened his back and moved quickly towards this unwelcome intruder into his holy of holies. His voice managed to be hushed and yet scandalised at the same time.

'What on earth do you mean by entering here in this condition?'

Gabe let out his breath in a mighty roar and threw his head back as he stared defiantly back at the priest.

'Is God going to mind that one of his sinners drops a bit of mud on the floor, Father? Is He really so unforgiving that he can't even take a little *mud*? Or is it the blessed virgin you're worried about? Has she never seen a mortal man in a state of distress before? A *very* mortal man, who needs help and understanding, not the pompous preachings of a man in frocks when he's in dire trouble.'

'Will you please control yourself?' the priest put his hand on Gabe's arm. 'I can see now that you're very troubled indeed, my son. And of course Our Lady will forgive. But unless you want the whole of this town to know that you've come here shouting and railing in this holy place and have them up in arms against you, I beg you to be calm, and I suggest you come with me to the confessional.'

'I want no confessional box!' Gabe shouted. 'God damn your eyes, why won't you listen? I need your help, both as a priest and a man, but I'll not make confession this day! I need you to do something for me that I'm unable to do myself, yet it needs to be done. It *must* be done, but I'm thinking you'll need to hear the whole tale before I can get to the real point, and I still don't know how I'm to do the telling.'

He ran his shaking hands through the sodden hair on his head. He shook with the effort of saying that much, but he'd made a vow to himself back there by the stream. It was just as if Marnie had stretched out her hand and touched him from across the vast ocean, gazing up at him with bewildered eyes, and beseeched him to let her know what had become of her sister.

'Shall we sit here?' Father Rourke said gravely. He led the way, and Gabe sat heavily beside him on the hard pew.

'You'll doubtless need to write it down, for I'll be so confused in the telling, it'll come out in haphazard order.'

'I have a retentive memory, my son. Just tell it as it comes into your head and let me know what you would have me do for you when you've finished. I know you've not been able to come to terms with life since the tragic happenings six months ago, but we will pray together after our talk that your mind and soul will be eased in the telling of whatever troubles you so. And give thanks that you sought to come here, and that you are aware that Christ has not abandoned you, Gabe. And that you remembered that one of the glories of God's house is the charge of His servants to lighten a sufferer's load.'

Gabe stared ahead as the old fool prattled on, but dear God, the complacency was going to be wiped from his face any minute now. When he heard the truth of why Gabe O'Brien had arrived in America, and the events leading up to it all. He swallowed, still finding it hard to begin, now the moment was here . . .

'Why don't you tell me, my son?' Father Rourke said gently. 'It'll be something to do with your sweet wife, of course.'

'That will be the place to begin all right,' Gabe's voice was thickened with emotion, and he still didn't look to right or left, but stared stonily ahead into the body of the church,

298

seeing nothing but the memories relived, 'because she was never my wife, and neither was she the one I truly loved. Her name was Jennifer Bray. She had a sister . . . called Marnie . . .'

CHAPTER NINETEEN

'So we are to go to France for the wedding,' Geraldine had announced caustically. 'My future sister-in-law's parents are evidently so delighted to be getting rid of their ugly duckling, they are to make a grand affair of it. And they have written to offer Darryl's family the hospitality of their house for two weeks while the bridal pair are touring the mountains of the South. What do you say to that, Marnie?'

The very idea of it was still frightening, though she'd had two months to get used to it now. The farthest she'd been from home was King's Lynn, and here was Miss Geraldine talking calmly about journeying across the English Channel. She had a momentary respect for her sister Jenny for even agreeing to Gabe O'Brien's suggestion to go to America. But there was a chance she might not be included in the wedding party—she was not a member of the family after all.

'Not be included?' Geraldine exclaimed when Marnie mentioned it. 'And would you have my new French relatives think that Darryl's sister was too much a provincial not to have a maid attend her at all times? Of course you will come, you ninny. It will be an experience not many of your class can expect. You'll be doing better than your sister Jenny, heh?'

Marnie was immediately on her guard. It was nearly a year now since Jenny and Gabe had run off together, leaving behind the shattered remnants of her dreams, and in all that time Geraldine had never let the matter drop for many days at a time, convinced that Marnie held the key to the mystery, and intrigued beyond measure to know what had really happened to her.

It had been a strain at times to keep to the story she'd invented for Jenny's sake, but at least the necessity to keep up the play-acting about Jenny's 'new position' to her parents had been removed when they had both succumbed to the influenza. She'd heard from kitchen talk at Larksby that Farmer Dan too had died of it, and that Effie Pinnock had gone South to live out her days with her sister.

'Have you been to Paris before, Miss Geraldine?' Marnie refused to be drawn into a conversation about Jenny. She bent her head over the gown on which she was stitching fresh ruched trimming for her mistress.

'I have not, so it will be an experience for us both.' She looked at Marnie thoughtfully. 'Did I hear tell that one of your brothers had married recently?'

'Yes, Kenneth. It was a very small affair, and only my two other brothers and myself were present, besides the bride's parents.'

'Shotgun, was it?'

Marnie shook her head. 'They preferred it that way.' She could have added that there was no money in Peggy's family to pay for fancy weddings like Darryl Larksby's. Nor in her own, come to that.

'And how do you like your new sister-in-law?' Geraldine asked idly, not really interested in her maid's family. But she was bored, bored, bored, and it was something to keep her mind from stagnating until she could begin organising which clothes she would be taking to Paris. She suddenly realised Marnie was stabbing the needle into her gown, and rebuked her sharply, her mind instantly alert.

'Well?' she demanded. 'Kenneth's wife. Is she agreeable?'

'Not to me! She resents me going back to my own home! And she's no housekeeper. The place is like a hovel, and Ma must be turning in her grave to know it, but Kenneth's so thick in love he cares little about that as long as Peggy falls over herself to whisper sweet nothings to him all the time. He's like a lovesick calf, and the boys snigger about it behind their backs. She knows it and it makes her more sharp-tempered with everybody but Kenneth. She thinks I look down my nose at her because she's fat and blowsy and looks just what she is—a barmaid at the Duck and Drake Inn!'

Geraldine listened with interest to this impassioned tirade about the habits of the lower classes. She smiled mischievously at Marnie.

'Well, I must admit that for a servant you do have a very haughty look about you, and sometimes that nose of yours looks as if it has a bad smell beneath it. Perhaps this Peggy feels guilty about not keeping the place spick and span when she sees the way you look at her.'

'Are you defending her? She's a trollop, and why on earth Kenneth married her I can't think. She can only be good at one thing!'

'Men have married for less,' Geraldine commented. 'And if she makes him happy in bed he has a lot more than most.'

She tired of hearing about Marnie's family as quickly as her interest had been caught. She tired quickly of everything lately. She gazed gloomily at Marnie.

'You and I are in the same trap, my girl, both without a man. We're two frustrated females tied to each other by Victorian conventions when what we both want more than anything in this world is to have a man of our own, and a ring on our fingers. You envy Peggy her Kenneth and that's the truth of it, just because she has a man, and that's why *you* resent *her*!'

'Perhaps I do.' Marnie bent further over her stitching, her eyes suddenly bright. 'I don't like her, but I see the way he looks at her sometimes, and yes, I wish a man would look at me like that.'

'I thought you hated men?'

'I do—mostly. But commonsense tells me they can't all be bad—at least, not all of the time.' She bit the cotton between her teeth and held the gown out for inspection. She wanted no more probing questions from Geraldine, and she took the gown away to press and goffer it, for Geraldine would trust no-one but her to do it properly. In the laundry room, where she tested the irons carefully against her skin before touching them to the soft fabric, she thought about Mick

O'Brien, because she'd been doing this very same job in the laundry room when he'd come personally to Larksby a week ago to inform Mrs Caine that he was now the owner of the Pinnock farm, and that he still hoped for the Larksby custom for eggs and dairy produce, that he had a good stockman who was living in, and a young lad to help with the deliveries.

'Bless my soul! Come up in the world, haven't you, bor? But I must say a boss's hat sits well on that curly black head of yours. You'll be needing a wife next to help run things smoothly.'

Marnie heard Mick laugh. The sound of it made her heart give a sudden leap, for it was more like Gabe's laugh than she realised before. With the thickness of the half-open door between them, she could almost imagine it was Gabe's laugh as she heard him ask Mrs Caine teasingly if she was applying for the post of farmer's wife.

'We manage well enough with a homely body from the village who comes in to cook and clean and see to washing the clothes at present.'

Mrs Caine tutted. 'She can't give you everything a fine young bor like you would be needing, though, can she?' she dug him in the ribs. 'Sit you down there, Mick, and take a glass of parsnip wine. There's one that's brewing to perfection, and I'd have your opinion on it, being something of an expert, I hear.'

'And a piece of blackberry pie to finish off,' Cook put in her half-penn'orth. 'And tell me if your homely body from the village can do better than that!'

'I never pretended there was ever a better cook than you, Cookie,' Mick laughed.

At that moment Marnie stepped out of the laundry room into the kitchen, Geraldine's gown draped over her arm. She caught her breath quickly as she looked right into Mick O'Brien's laughing blue eyes as he flirted outrageously with Cook, and for a few crazy seconds in her mind it was Gabe, Gabe. The laughter on his face faded, to be replaced by a look of acute embarrassment. In all the time since Jenny and Gabe's disappearance, the two of them had never come face to face. In fact, Mick had wondered sometimes if he ought to make some contact with her, if only to find out how the absconders had fared. But she was a Bray girl and best left alone, and the momentary thought had stayed where it was, in his mind.

'Don't stand there gawping, Marnie,' Mrs Caine said, with a grin on her face. 'Didn't you recognise our new gentleman farmer?'

'How are you, Marnie?' Mick said gravely.

His blue eyes assessed the way her figure had matured and rounded, and that the fine-boned face had grown even lovelier, even though the expressive brown eyes had a strange haunted look about them. But her hair was as glorious as ever, still with the soft sheen on it that had so taken his breath away the first time he'd seen it.

'I'm well, thank you,' she replied evenly. 'Do I congratulate you on your good fortune?'

'He made his own luck by solid hard work,' Cook defended her new favourite at once. 'If ever a man was at one with the land, it was Mick O'Brien, and he deserves to prosper on it. I'll wager Effie Pinnock was proud to leave her land in such caring hands!'

'Stop it, Cookie, or you'll be seeing a grown man blush for the first time in your life at such praise,' Mick laughed again, but his eyes were still on Marnie.

She excused herself quickly, saying that her mistress was needing her to go on an errand, but the image she took away with her was of Mick O'Brien sitting in the Larksby kitchen as if he was squire of all he surveyed, with the two women twittering round him like middle-aged lovebirds.

The sight of him had startled her. Not only because of his resemblance to Gabe, which she'd never fully realised until now, but because of the change in Mick himself. Over the years she'd heard Da and the boys refer time and again to the two Irish navvies in nothing but the most derogatory terms. She'd known only too well the opinion they had of the O'Briens. Her own most vivid memory of Mick was when she'd seen him in the fen cottage after bringing Jenny home with her splintered foot. She'd barely noticed him then, for he was a man grown to her eyes, and she'd been too busy feasting on Gabe's dimpled smiles, but if she stopped to recall Mick's appearance at that time, it was muddy and filthy, with the smell of the dykes on him; a shapeless dyke-digger's slop covering the top half of him, and a squashed chummy on his head.

He cut a very different figure now, she thought. He was clean and handsome–probably he'd always been as handsome beneath all the dirt–and with a tidy green waistcoat and jacket in which to come calling, heavy brown corduroy country trousers like all the gentlemen farmers wore, and gleaming brown boots and gaiters. Every inch a gentleman farmer, as Mrs Caine had said, even if it was most likely that he'd dressed in his Sunday best to go paying his respects as a man of property in order to make a good impression on neighbouring folks. It was still quite a shock to see him like that.

Geraldine was waiting impatiently to send her on her errand when she took the gown back upstairs, and Marnie tied her bonnet under her chin and hurried out of the house to go to the village. Mick O'Brien hovered outside the gates in a pony and trap. His bare head inclined towards her as he let the reins slacken, and then jumped down as she approached. She felt her heartbeats quicken.

'I lingered deliberately in the hope that I might see you,' he said quickly.

'Why should you do that? I have nothing to say to you . . .'

He stopped her attempt at a spirited reply by placing one hand on her shoulder. She could feel the warmth of it through her shawl and her dress.

'Don't pretend that you and I don't share a secret known to no-one else, Marnie! Does that not make us . . . '

'Conspirators?'

'I was about to say too close to act as enemies. I feel no enmity towards you, though God knows I've reason,' he muttered beneath his breath, but the fight at the farm was too many years ago to rake up now, 'I hope you have no bad feelings towards me either. This–conspiracy, if you like, was none of our choosing, but it was thrust on both of us and has forged a bond between us that you cannot deny. And surely it has been so long now since they fled the country that we can find it in our hearts to forgive them? I know I have, and have tried to understand why Gabe did what he felt he had to do. Gabe and meself–we were as close as two brothers could be. Sometimes our thinking was so alike it was as if we shared the same skin, so I'm bound to understand a little of his reasoning. You don't forget easily someone who meant that much to you.'

'No.' She met his blue gaze at last, seeing the sadness there. 'I–miss Jenny too.' Despite everything.

But he would know none of her true feelings, of course. He wouldn't know how she'd raged and wept and wanted to die because her little sister had got the man she'd wanted so desperately. Mick would think her merely distressed at Jenny's foolishness, and furious with Gabe for putting her sister in such a compromising position and then running away with her.

'Have you heard anything of them?' Mick said urgently. 'That was what I really wanted to ask you. I'd give a great deal to know that all goes well with them and that Gabe found what he was looking for.'

Marnie felt a thickening in her throat as she shook her head.

'Not a word. It's as if they vanished off the face of the earth. I suppose it's what they intended to do . . .'

'They should have known we'd be worried to death about them,' Mick said angrily, and then his face broke into a boyish smile. 'You and I will be aunt and uncle by now, Marnie. How does it make you feel?'

'Old!' She didn't want to think about the baby, a mixture of Gabe and Jenny. She tried to be flippant. 'I'm not ready to be a maiden aunt yet!'

'Nor should you be, a beautiful young woman like

yourself. I'll bet you've half a dozen lads begging for your favours and you're keeping them all dangling on a string.'

Despite the tension she felt in his presence, she felt the smile on her lips, and her brown eyes were teasing.

'Not a one! What do you say to that, Mick O'Brien?'

'I say it's high time you were courting, and it's me that's asking you out on your next free evening, if you've a mind to come visiting the Pinnock farm and take a bite of supper with me. It'll all be conducted quite properly, and I'll see that Mrs Yard stays on and serves it up so's you won't be compromised!'

Afterwards, neither could have said who was the more surprised–Mick for asking her so spontaneously, or Marnie for accepting. One minute they were still wary of each other, still over-conscious of all that had gone before, and the next they were making plans for a meal together at the farm.

And now the evening was here, and if she didn't hurry up with the goffering of Geraldine's gown and do it to her entire satisfaction, she'd be sent back to do it again and probably lose her free evening as well.

Marnie had been in a fever of confusion ever since she'd accepted Mick O'Brien's invitation. Why on earth had she agreed to it? she asked herself time and again. It was only going to rake up old memories, and wasn't it best to let the past stay dead? She was never in her life going to see Gabe again, and surely it would be best to have nothing to do with Mick and the reminders he'd inevitably bring her. The love for Gabe had to stay locked up inside her, burning and unfulfilled. There was no point in trying to revive it. She admitted in her private moments that time had dulled the fierce hatred in her, and now there was only a smouldering sorrow for the wrong he'd done her. But love had been stronger than hate after all, and deep inside her she knew she still loved him and would do so until the end of time.

But there had been something about Mick when he'd asked her that had taken her by surprise. A male aggressiveness that had stirred a chord inside her . . . anyway, it was done now. She'd said she was going, and so she was. And she was curious to see how a man on his own coped with a farm . . . forgetting for a minute that of course he had adequate help. A stockman for the animals and a young lad for the deliveries, and Mrs Yard from the village who cooked and cleaned and was paid for her services, Oh yes, Mick O'Brien was a somebody now, she admitted.

He came to fetch her in his pony and trap. It felt strange to be leaving Larksby all dressed up in one of her few better outfits, in the company of a young man. Mick, too, was in his Sunday best again, dressed for courting, the word jolted into her mind. This was how everybody would see it, of course, and hadn't Mick mentioned the word himself?

But she'd never really thought of it so seriously, her and Mick O'Brien courting . . . marrying Mick O'Brien. Her thoughts shied away from the idea, but it played about in her subconscious all evening as she ate the sizzling duck and green peas Mrs Yard had prepared, and helped herself to a dish of fresh fruit and then some of Mick's own dairy cheese and pronounced it all wonderful. He was very nicely set up, and a girl could do far worse than marrying him. He was a handsome man, striking even, tall and broad-shouldered, with Gabe's blue eyes.

'Well, Marnie?' he said softly, as he drew on a pipe of tobacco near the fire and watched the changing expressions on her face. 'Would it be fitting to bring a wife to the O'Brien farm?'

The use of his own name for the farm and the pride with which he said it didn't escape her. But she would not be rushed.

'I'm sure any woman would be happy here,' she said evasively. 'It must have been a wrench for Mrs Pinnock to move out.'

'Aye,' he agreed. 'But her heart was no longer in the farm without Farmer, and she did the right thing, in my opinion. And some might say she was lucky in having such a ready buyer who was willing to pay handsomely for the farm and the land.'

A kind man too, Marnie added, glad the talk had veered away from dangerous personal channels. She didn't want him getting any serious ideas about their future–not yet, if ever. The idea of it was still too new–too preposterous–she'd need to know him a lot better, and besides . . .

'We all go to France at the end of next week,' she said quickly. 'For Mr Darryl's wedding.'

She stopped suddenly, wondering if Mick knew about Darryl and herself. Wondering if Gabe had told him, but there was nothing in his face to alarm her, and she breathed more easily.

'So I heard from Mrs Caine. Someone has tamed him at last then,' he smiled. 'How long is the visit?'

'Two weeks. I don't look forward to it. I shan't be able to speak with any of the French servants, and I'll be glad to be back.'

'And when you come back, you and I must meet again. Is it agreed, Marnie?'

She nodded slowly, after a momentary hesitation. Was it right? But then, was it wrong? She hadn't been married to Gabe, even though it had felt like it in her heart, and she knew she still belonged to him body and soul. But what harm could it do to see Mick and talk to him? She'd enjoyed talking to him, she realised. And they'd mentioned Gabe very little that evening, yet he'd been as real in her mind as if he sat beside her. Being with Mick brought Gabe close in a strange way. She hadn't seen until now how alike they were, nor how much Mick was a link with Gabe. She smiled more warmly into his eyes without analysing her reasons.

'I think I should like that,' she said.

There were no more evenings off before the Larksbys left for France. There was too much to be done, and both Geraldine and her father were in a bad humour at having to travel so far, and took it out on their servants. As always Marnie took the brunt of it from her mistress, but consoled herself with knowing that this journey ended with seeing

Darryl Larksby safely married, to her intense relief, and the surprisingly pleasurable feeling that she'd see Mick again when she came home.

On the day of the wedding, she couldn't resist a secret smirk at the bridegroom from the back of the church where she sat with the quietly gabbling French servants as they waited for the bride to arrive on her father's arm. Remembering the last time she'd seen him, clutching himself in agony on her bed where she'd bitten him. It was to be hoped for Mademoiselle Dupont's sake that he had recovered completely and bore no scars. The thought of her own little teeth-marks in him brought a twitch to her mouth, but the look he shot her in the church was coldly vindictive, and she turned her eyes away from him at once and gazed instead at the fine stained glass in the tall windows of the building.

Marnie didn't like France and neither did Geraldine. The sights of Paris were impressive and magnificent, and Monsieur and Madame Dupont went to endless trouble after the wedding celebrations to escort Colonel Larksby, his daughter and her English maid around the splendours of their city. They visited Notre Dame and the Palace of Versailles, and the more picturesque quarters of the city, but their heads ached from the effort to understand and communicate even the simplest sentences, for apart from their daughter, who had had an English tutor, the Duponts spoke only the sketchiest English, and the Larksbys very little French.

As well as the language difficulty, the food did not agree with their English stomachs, being too rich and oily, and the wine was too copiously drunk for them to be able to enjoy it properly without being fuddleheaded at night and queasy by day. All in all it was not a good trip, and each side of the marital party heaved a silent sigh of relief when it was all over and the Larksbys were ready to return to England.

'Let's hope they don't expect us to return the hospitality too soon,' Geraldine said, as she waved a silk kerchief and smiled with false heartiness as the boat slid away from Calais harbour.

'I hope you will make Darryl and his wife welcome, my dear,' Colonel Larksby's voice was suddenly irritable. 'When I die I shall expect him to come home and look after the estate, though God knows I'd wish for a more worthy successor. But I think it might be unwise to let your antagonism towards him show too keenly, or you may find yourself looking for a new home.'

'Don't talk of dying, Father! You've years ahead of you yet!' Geraldine chose to ignore the rest of his words, even though it had been a warning and she knew it. Once Darryl was Master of Larksby, her position wouldn't be worth a brass farthing unless she watched her step, and it was something she knew she must keep in mind, for it was true her father was far from active any more. The time would come when Darryl brought his pale bride home for good. She shivered at the thought, and guessed rightly that she wasn't the only one to feel uneasy.

As the onlookers on the Calais shore receded from their sight, Marnie's smile froze on her lips. She'd never really considered that one day Darryl Larksby would be back for good. She'd assumed he'd be happy to stay in France, but when he did he'd still be looking for sport, because she knew instinctively that his kind never changed. A shudder ran through her. When the time came, she'd be gone, she vowed. Anywhere, as long as it was out of reach of his odious attentions.

They arrived back in England wearied and nauseous from the sea journey, for the Channel had been like a boiling cauldron on that day, and the Colonel had sworn noisily never to visit that Godforsaken country again. They put up at an Inn for the night, and then began the long ride back to Larksby in a hired carriage that jarred their bones. Never had any of them been so glad to see a place as the sight of the square grey building looming towards them out of an evening mist.

Even then there was no rest for Marnie until Miss

Geraldine had been waited on, her clothes unpacked and hung, and a cool cloth laid over her tired eyes as she finally lay between the sheets in her own welcoming bed. Only then could Marnie slip away to the kitchen to ask Cook if there was a cup of tea brewing for she was parched.

'I daresay I can soon brew you one, my girl,' Cook peered into her face. 'You don't look as though the holiday's done you a power of good, though. You look tuckered out.'

'It was no holiday for me!'

'Aye, well, that's a servant's lot,' Cook said. She reached her hand up to a shelf. 'Anyway, here's something that may put the sparkle back in your eyes. A thick letter come all the way from America and addressed to you! Now who do you know in America that would be writing to you, well, I'm blessed! The manners of young people!'

Marnie had snatched it out of her hand and held it close to her thudding heart, unable to speak. It was from Gabe . . . it had to be Gabe. She could think of nothing else and no turbulent ocean or spiralling hatred or sense of betrayal could diminish the flooding joy inside her. It was Gabe's letter to her, explaining, begging her forgiveness. Gabe, oh Gabe . . .

'Never mind about the tea,' she choked out, and rushed out of the kitchen and back upstairs to her own room, all tiredness forgotten.

She stared at the letter for several minutes before she tore it open, loving the curve of the letters that formed her name and the address at Larksby. Never having seen his handwriting before, they were moments to savour before she unfolded the pages inside.

And then she started reading Father Rourke's letter.

'I have been asked to contact you on behalf of Mr Gabe O'Brien, as he feels too distressed to write to you himself.'

Dear God, what was this? The thudding of her heart became a savage pain as she read the words Gabe had stutteringly asked the priest to write. Read and re-read, because they wouldn't sink in the first time, nor the second, but when they did, they struck her with the sharpness of knives.

> 'I understand that Jennifer–Jenny–was your sister, my dear young lady, and so it grieves me to be the one to write to you with such bad news. It will cause you great pain–but I will be brutal and not prolong the most important fact of all, and that is that your sister is dead.'

Marnie sucked in her breath, realising that the taste of blood was on her lips as she chewed them to try and stop them trembling. Jenny . . . Jenny was dead. Sweet, pretty, silly Jenny. Oh God, she'd never wanted that. The sobs tore at her throat, and she brushed the tears from her eyes as she read on, anxious to know what was happening to Gabe–and the baby too. A man alone with a baby, and in a strange country.

> 'Your sister died six months ago.'

The shock of Father Rourke's statement made her sit heavily on the bed. She held the pages tightly together, trying to stop the words blurring through her tears and shaking hands. Six months ago? Six *months*? But that meant–she counted rapidly on her fingers, gave up trying to work things out and read on.

> 'Mr O'Brien does not excuse himself for his neglect in not informing you until now. He begs you to understand his feelings when he returned to their home to find your sister had died giving birth to their child. I am deeply sorry to tell you the child was also dead. It was a little girl, and she was baptised before burial. It may give you some small comfort to know Mr O'Brien named her after you.'

Marnie crunched the letter tightly in her hand, letting the tears run down her face and into her mouth, as she'd done when she'd read the letter Jenny had left her, full of hope, full of certainty that Marnie would forgive, that Marnie would see to everything, cover their tracks.

'Oh Gabe, how could you? Naming her for me, when it should have been *my* child, not *hers*,' she whispered in anguish.

It seemed the ultimate slap-down, as if her name and her love meant nothing to him. As if he could quite happily have spoken it to his daughter every day of his life and never connected it with her. And yet, and yet, might it not have been his way of keeping her with him, the way she had suddenly discovered his nearness when talking with Mick? She slowly unfolded the crumpled letter and read on.

'I have been instructed to say that Mr O'Brien is very conscious of the wrong he has done to you and your family, and that your forgiveness is now his dearest wish. He begs too that you will inform his brother of these events, tell him he is well and wishes him luck.

'There seems little more to add, except to send you my own condolences, and to say that I will continue to pray for you as I am doing now, and for Mr O'Brien's brother, knowing the shock that this must be to you both. Mr O'Brien thinks it best that you both try to forget him now, while he tries to build a new life here in America, which he now considers home.

'God bless you, dear young lady, and may He help you over this trying time.'

It was signed, 'Father James Rourke.'

For a long time Marnie sat without moving a muscle, her eyes pained and unseeing. It was the end. She'd thought the end had been when Gabe had taken Jenny away, but she'd accepted in these last weeks that she'd always clung to a futile hope that one day in the hazy future he'd be back. That somehow they'd be together again. Now all hope was gone.

In Father Rourke's stilted words she read what she took to be the truth of it. Gabe and Jenny had married, and he'd been away from the house when her labour had begun, resulting in the death of both Jenny and the baby. And Gabe, Gabe had loved her so much he couldn't even bear to speak of it or write the words to tell anyone. He was still distraught at losing her and his child, so much so that he'd had to get a priest to do it for him. In six months he wasn't reconciled to losing her. The breath was ragged in her throat, recognising it as a love that was as deep as her own. And no, she thought despairingly, she could no longer condemn him, because she understood just how much it hurt. Even in suffering they were united.

But there was something she had to do. Mick had to be told, and now, tonight. The pain was too much for her to bear alone, and he had as much right to know as she did. Her brothers . . . she dismissed the thought of telling them before it was even formed in her mind. There was no need for them ever to know. She rarely went to the fen cottage now, and no-one seemed interested in Jenny now that Ma and Da were gone. The tears smarted in her eyes again, thinking of Da and how he'd loved his pretty Jenny.

She wiped her face quickly and threw a shawl over her shoulders. The only thing she had to do was to tell Mick. She must keep her mind free of all else. She went through the house, uncaring of her duties, and out to the stables. She told a sleepy stable-lad she needed the trap for an urgent errand for her mistress, and sped along the country lanes, white with moonlight and a glistening hoar-frost, until she reached the farm. She slid from the trap without bothering to tie the pony, and rushed to hammer on the door.

'My dear Marnie, what's all this! Couldn't you wait until tomorrow to see me?' Mick threw the door open wider, letting a stream of light illumine her features.

His expression changed at once as he saw the tears on her cheeks, and drew her inside the warm farmhouse. He removed her shawl and chafed her cold hands as he pulled her nearer the fire blazing in the hearth.

'What's happened, my lovely?' he said gently.

The small endearment blurred her eyes again, and she handed the letter to him mutely. His jaw tightened as he read Father Rourke's words, and every few minutes he let out a smothered oath as the tragedy revealed itself to him. Listening to him, watching him, realising she didn't have

315

to bear the burden of knowing all by herself any more, numbed the first sharp pain inside her.

She stood motionless while he absorbed all the priest had told them, stretching her frozen fingers to the fire's warmth. And at last he put the letter on the table and held out his arms.

She went into them as if in a dream, wanting only the comfort of another human being at that moment. And Mick was touched by the fragile, brittle beauty of her, so near to breaking at learning her sister and the baby had died, and by the strange ethereal immobility that had come over her since her frenzied arrival. He wanted to calm her, and yet she was already too calm. He found his hands were stroking the silkiness of her hair. He heard his voice murmuring endearments to her, loving her, glad to his soul that she'd turned to him, because who better than someone who loved her?

He looked down into her wild, drowned eyes, and slowly, very slowly, he bent his head towards her and touched his lips to her mouth in a kiss that lengthened and deepened and seemed as if it would be never-ending.

CHAPTER TWENTY

The war rumblings in America were no longer fantasy, but fact.

The Confederate army fired the first shots on Fort Sumter on April 14th, 1861, and the following day President Lincoln called a Cabinet meeting and issued a proclamation appealing for all loyal citizens to rally to the support of their country. Recruitment posters appeared as if by magic on every available surface, whipping up a frenzy of patriotism among the unlikeliest groups of Union supporters. Even if it was not always for the noblest of reasons.

The largest of the four figures lurching along late one night, arms linked, drink-hazed, down Main Street, suddenly stopped dead, nearly pulling his companions off their feet.

'Jesus, you nearly had us down on our knees, Brad,' Gabe swore loudly. 'Can't you give us warning if you're in need of a piss?'

'Shut your grumbling, you Irish bastard,' Brad's voice was amiably slurred. 'It's not a piss-house I'm looking for, though I reckon I could hit a tin can at fifty paces with all the beer swilling inside me tonight.' He yelled at the rest of them to shut their noises as well, at the raucous shouts of 'prove it', and 'down with his pants', and he lashed out at the grovelling hands pulling at his breeches.

'Cut it out, you bums. Ain't you got no respect for the flag? Over there, look, in the drapery store window.' He pointed an unsteady hand to his right, and the four of them sidled as one body towards the huge, ornate poster in the drapery store window, inexpertly draped with the Union flag, flanked on either side with bolts of Spring materials and reels of cotton, to catch customers of both sexes and inclinations.

'A hundred dollar bounty to all inexperienced recruits,' Deeker read out. 'Four hundred dollars to veterans.'

'Well, none of us are veterans, unless you count yourself as ancient, Deek.'

'Shut up, Cal. It means if you've served in the army previous to this, and I ain't. I'd be as raw as the rest of you if I put my name to one of their enlistment forms, which I ain't!'

'Why not?' Cal said belligerently. 'We'd whip the day-lights out of them rebs in a month. You turning yellow all of a sudden, Deek?'

His fist in Cal's mouth was answer enough.

'Any man who calls me yellow can have a taste of the same,' Deek growled as Cal spat blood on to the ground. The four of them stared intently at the recruitment poster, concentrating hard to focus clearly on all the words.

'Enlist now to avoid the draft,' Gabe read. 'So if we don't volunteer it sounds as if they'll get us anyway!'

'By the short and curlies,' Brad agreed. 'Anyway, this is a cavalry poster. Probably the bounty wouldn't be so good for foot-soldiers which is all we'd be good for.'

'Why shouldn't it be?' Cal was in an argumentative mood. 'Ain't we as good as horseriders?'

'Who'd want to walk to South Carolina anyway?' Deek grunted.

'D'you think the whole war's going to be fought round Fort Sumter, you silly bugger?' Brad snapped. No, Washington's the place they'll aim for, up through Richmond and Virginia, and *POW*!'

He slammed one huge hand against the other, the sound ringing out in the dimness and silence of the street.

'We ain't letting no rebs take Washington,' Cal snorted. 'What do you say, Gabe? Do we join the infantry?'

Gabe shrugged. 'What's it to me? I won't get drafted anyway. I'm Irish . . .'

The other three hooted with laughter.

'Who's going to worry about that when half of New York

318

speaks with an Irish accent, you cluck? Deek here's Italian if you go back a generation, and Cal's old man was as German as the Rhine. So what's so special about you? You're as American as the rest of us now, and as long as you can aim a rifle, boy, you're eligible! How's about it then?' Brad was warming to his role as patriot now. 'Do we get ourselves rigged up in some fancy uniforms and show these rebs who're the bosses? Tell you what, Gabe,' he gave him a dig in the ribs that made him wince, 'the broads go for guys in uniforms, and there ain't that many of 'em about round here yet. We'll be able to have the best pickings in town, four handsome yankees like ourselves!'

'Let's find us a recruiting office and sign on the dotted line then,' Deeker grinned.

'OK, Gabe? A hundred dollar bounty buys a lot of booze,' Cal said persuasively. 'There ain't much else livening up this town now Mrs Lacey's closed down. She'll be down South by now, giving those reb buggers a treat with her perfumed floosies. That's summat else they owe us for, ain't it? Seeing as your Sylvie will have gone with her?'

'OK, OK,' Gabe gave in as another group of late drinkers jostled behind them on the sidewalk, straining to see the poster that was causing so much interest.

They'd all gone mad, the bloody lot of them, he thought, as he listened to the aggressive brawling and arguing. All flag-waving lunatics, just because some guy in Washington with a face like a funeral director, by all accounts, decreed it so. Still. Gabe shrugged again. Why not? Nothing seemed to be happening in this bloody war anyway, except a lot of talk. And it would at least give his life some kind of purpose, even if it wasn't his battle. Like Cal said, there was nothing else to liven up this town any more. It still had bad memories for him, and maybe the best thing he could do would be to rid himself of it for good. He nodded, trying not to let his head swim nauseatingly as he did so, and the rest of them whooped and cheered and swung him around in the direction of the recruitment office listed at the foot of the poster, the other group following close behind, all swept along in an expansive wave of patriotism, accelerated by booze.

The office was on Third Street, unmistakeable with the Union flag fluttering out of the window above. The office was closed and in darkness, but here was a group of ten determined men, all eager to fight for their country, and small considerations like closed doors and unlighted premises were no deterrent to them. After ten minutes hollering and hammering, a light went on inside the office, to be met with loud cheering as an irascible man in a dressing-gown poked his head out the door, told them the office was closed and to come back in the morning.

'Jeez, is this the way Abe Lincoln expects his loyal recruits to be treated?' Brad roared. He pushed the door open with one huge hand, sending the poor guy staggering, and the lamp rocking in his hand. The rest of the group poured in behind him, filling the tiny room with determined voices and menacing eyes. Brad, the spokesman, slammed his hand flat on the desk, making the little pile of papers on it jump. 'We come here enlist, and we want do it now. You savvy, white man?'

There was a flicker of apprehension in the recruiting officer's eyes as Brad reverted to the Indian parly he kept for awkward cusses. And as always, it worked. Within minutes the papers were brought out, names and other details filled in, and ten drunken signatures scrawled on dotted lines.

'All right, soldiers,' the old guy had a sudden steely glint in his eyes. 'Now clear off home and tell your families what you've done, and report back here in daylight for orders. On the double!'

He commanded a salute from each one as the ten of them shuffled outside. The second group disappeared into the night as Gabe and his companions stood swaying outside on the sidewalk, and then the light in the office went out. There was silence between them for a few seconds, then Deek slapped each of the others on the back.

'That's it then, boys. We're in the army now, and we're

gonna whip these Southern bastards. Right?'

'Right up their Southern asses,' Brad hollered.

A window shot upwards above their heads.

'Go home,' the recruitment officer roared. 'Or so help me you'll be sorry you ever enlisted!'

The window slammed down again, rattling in its frame.

'You old shit,' Brad swore, but softly this time. 'Let's get away from here and find us a drink and some women to celebrate.'

They were all too fuddled to argue. It sounded like a good idea . . . Gabe's head felt ten sizes too big for his skin, and it wasn't until the next morning, when he woke up on the floor at Deek's place, his arm thrown carelessly over a half-clad street-woman and peered round the room to see his companions similarly disposed, that his head cleared enough to realise what he'd done. And sure, the women they'd picked up last night had been proud of them for enlisting . . . sure, they'd been delighted to help them celebrate. He dug his hands in his pockets and groaned as he realised how much money he'd parted with–and on top of all that he couldn't even remember whether he'd enjoyed himself or not.

There was only one thing chillingly clear in his mind, and that was the fact that he'd enlisted. Jesus, he was now in the Federal Union army of the United States, and he'd be expected to fight and kill, when it was against everything in his nature. For some peculiar reason, the far-off memory spun into his mind of the way he'd puked at the sight of the Pinnock ferrets clawing and scratching at their spoils, and of himself forced to slit and gut the rabbits' bellies, and the hot smell of blood on his hands. Here he was, signed up to do the same to his fellow-men. Jesus, he was sick to his stomach at the thought. The woman shifted under the sudden convulsive movements of his fingers on her breast.

'You want more, honey?' she drawled at once.

'No. No more,' he muttered. 'Get out of here, will you?'

He rolled over on to his stomach away from her, his eyes tightly shut. He could hear her muttering, and the clink of her cheap, trashy jewellery as she dressed, and then there were other voices, other movements and cloying smells until the street-women finally left, and Gabe opened his eyes to find Deeker handing him a mug of coffee.

'Come on, soldier,' he said thickly. 'We've got us some reporting to do.'

'And some uniforms to collect, to say nothing of the bounty money,' Cal added, his voice brash and a mite too loud.

Gabe suddenly realised they were all avoiding each other's eyes, even Brad, who could usually outstare the horniest card-sharp with those unwavering black Indian eyes of his. But Brad was hunched over his coffee the same as the rest, and it dawned on Gabe that he wasn't the only one having second thoughts. They were as shit-scared as he was, excepting Brad, no doubt, but it was too bloody late for that. The Union army had their signatures and it was as binding as marriage vows. It wasn't going to let them go just because the four of them had had time to think and turned up like naughty schoolboys, tails between their legs, and said they'd changed their minds! Anyway, they weren't schoolboys, nor cowards, but grown men. Gabe drained his coffee and banged his mug on the table, suddenly the calmest of the four of them.

'I reckon we got ourselves a job last night, me bors,' unconsciously he used the old familiar fen-name, 'and it's up to us to see it through.'

Deek cleared his throat.

'Gabe's right. This ole country ain't done so bad for none of us, so let's show her whether we care or not.' He gave the flicker of a smile. 'And let's show that old fruit at the recruiting office that we meant business last night. Don't let him see . . .' he stopped.

'There ain't nothing for him to see but four yankee soldiers ready to fight, is there?' Brad growled. They all looked at Cal. He smiled crookedly.

'Let's shake on it,' he said solemnly. 'You know, I used to play at soldiers when I was a kid. We was always against

322

the Indians then, Brad. But I'm proud to be shaking your hand, and glad you're on our side. Never thought I'd ever get to be playing at real soldiers!'

Gabe drew in his breath. The Duck and Drake Inn, with its thick warm smells of ale and close-cramped bodies . . . Fred Jackson and himself, warm and snug in the cellar, and the ale dripping from half-empty barrels into eager young mouths . . . the games of soldiers and wooden battles, and lurid tales of Mick and Peggy, and the first sweet stirrings of his loins . . . a girl with gleaming hair who'd waited for him at the old mill by Kettle's farm, who'd welcomed him lovingly with her body in his room at the Pinnock place and let him glimpse heaven for a second time . . . who'd wound her way into his heart and his life so long ago, with loving tendrils as strong as steel. And a sharp sweet longing to redress all the wrong between them stabbed at his soul, Marnie, sweet, sweet Marnie . . .

'Shake then, Gabe! We'll pledge our lives to stick together as far as possible,' Cal's solemn voice penetrated, and he felt the clasp of hands as he dragged his mind back to today. To now, to the late Spring of '61, when the army was mustering, and victory was certain under Abe Lincoln's enthusiastic leadership. And he was going to do battle for what was right, just as he and Fred Jackson had manipulated those little wooden soldiers all those years ago in another lifetime.

Two months later, the fear had settled into complacency. Gabe and his mates wore fine belted uniforms of dark blue, with high-buttoned tunics and jaunty caps on their heads. They had greatcoats for when it was cold, capes for when it rained. For Gabe it seemed sometimes nothing more than a real-life continuation of the game at the Duck and Drake. As yet there had been no battles for them. He and the rest of them obeyed orders, drew their pay, paraded in their uniforms to reassure the local citizens of wherever they happened to be, played at practising manoeuvres, company drill, marching and counter-marching to the cheerful accompaniment of the company band. It didn't feel like a real war. It wasn't a real war. In a way it was a paid tour of the countryside South of New York and North of Washington. Until the day finally arrived when they got their real marching orders, and Brigadier-General Irvin McDowell decided the time was ripe to move his troops towards the railroad town of Manassas, by way of Centreville to the West of Washington. It was mid-July.

'So we're on the move at last, boys,' Deek said with satisfaction. 'I'm cheesed off with all this play-acting. Let's get in and get the bastards, and then it'll all be over.'

'We ain't gonna surprise them with all the troops McDowell's sending,' Cal said uneasily. 'They'll see us coming miles off.'

'We've got 'em beat with sheer weight of numbers, boy. We'll outnumber them easily, and we'll soon get 'em on the run and screaming,' Deek was confident, brushing all argument aside.

It took most of four days to assemble the mass of troops at Centreville. It dawned on Gabe that there must be thousands. He'd had no idea there were so many dark blue uniforms in the world, and he began to think Deek's optimism could be right, though most of them were as raw as Gabe and Cal and Deeker and Brad.

But once massed at Centreville, the feel of the war turned it into reality. The scent of it was in the air; the sudden feeling of expectancy, of urgency, of tension and quick-flaring tempers. The minor skirmishes that broke out from time to time added constant fuel to the flame that was still burning low, ready to erupt into the holocaust, and the knowledge that the Confederate army was very near sent ripples of unbearable excitement through the Union ranks. They'd come to fight, and they were ready to fight.

Gabe and his companions were in the main body of troops sent from Centreville to Bull Run, to cross the river upstream at Sudley Springs ford, the idea being to sweep down on the rebel army and crush them swiftly. It was a Sunday, July 21st, and the battle suddenly exploded into being around 9 am. From their position on the hill the

Union troops could see clear across the valley where the rebs were spread out, a light grey cloud of moving uniforms. And from early morning the batteries of artillery blasted away across the valley between the two armies until the air was thick and choking, yellow-grey with gun-smoke and the acrid smell of gunpowder. The footsoldiers took advantage of the cover the smoke provided and pressed ever-forward, sensing victory. They had the weight of numbers on their side, the valley would soon be theirs, the enemy crushed and pushed back.

'Christ, what's happening?' Deek said hoarsely, wiping one grimy hand across his sweat-lined face. It was mid-afternoon by now and blisteringly hot. The sweat trickled uncomfortably down his chest, tangling the thick matted hair. 'Where in God's name are they all coming from?'

'The railroad! Manassas Junction!' Gabe's voice was just as hoarse. The smoke and the stench was drying his throat, and so was something else too, as the sight of new hordes of Confederate troops appeared from the direction of the railroad trains. Fresh and young and thirsty for blood.

The battle scene changed. The Union soldiers were suddenly too exposed and too vulnerable in the valley in this new onslaught from the rebs, and sitting targets for the eagle-eyed newcomers. There were suddenly too many of these counter-attackers, seemingly too few of McDowell's men by comparison. The Union flags continued to flutter, but the spirit was suddenly gone. This was no longer surging forward in a blaze of glory, but hand-to-hand fighting for survival; crawling behind the cover of dead companions; or dying ones with half their guts spewing out and staining the grass crimson; trying to keep closed ears to the screams and moans till the roar of cannon that muffled them was almost welcome even while it stunned the senses . . . gut-scared at the whistle of shells overhead; the trundle of wagons and ambulances; the sight of orderlies who were only yesterday white-faced musicians in the company band, doing double duty in trying to stem impossible wounds and avoid throwing up; dreading the gleam of steel as a bayonet seared through the air and struck its target; praying you weren't the next target.

'Cal! My God, look out, Cal!' Gabe heard himself scream as the Confederate soldier seemed to loom out of nowhere in the blue haze and lunged towards Cal, to stick his bayonet clean through the jugular vein in Cal's neck, where the rich blood bubbled and gushed out immediately. Cal dropped like a stone, the bayonet still part of him as the reb stumbled to pull it out for the next attack.

'Get the bastard, Gabe!' Deek's voice right behind him screamed in his ear, but Jesus, he couldn't, he couldn't, not right close up with the reb's ragged breathing panting so near to him, and the acid smell of him in his nostrils as sudden fear dilated his eyes at the sight of three Union soldiers advancing at a run to avenge their comrade. Gabe hesitated just a fraction too long, and Brad leapt past him with all the coldness of his Indian blood in his stance as he stabbed his rifle within an inch of the reb's eyes, fired, and blew the top of his head clean off, spattering blood and brains everywhere.

'Jesus, what have you done?' Gabe screamed as the vomit surged up inside him. Brad ignored the bloody mess on his uniform and lashed out with his rifle at the next reb soldier within range, his eyes wild and murderous.

'What you should have done, you shit,' Brad roared. 'What are you—a woman or a half-wit? Start moving back. There's too many of them. They're on all sides of us. We'll have to get back to the hill, if you can get your tacky legs to move!'

Gabe was only too thankful to do as he said. There was nobody else around giving orders. There was only the overpowering noise and the smell and the fear. And he was suddenly running and stumbling and sobbing, with fear tightening his throat and turning his guts to water. And it seemed as if half the Union army was doing the same. He could no longer see Brad or Deek, and he'd never see Cal again, except in his mind, with the blood gushing out of his neck . . . he'd been a good bor, his buddy . . . he dashed the angry tears from his face with a filthy hand, uncaring who saw them.

Who'd notice anyway? Every man was intent on doing the same as himself. Getting back across Bull Run, a raging mob of once-proud dark-blue uniforms, now tattered and dusty and stinking, until they reached the Washington road and headed for Centreville. Back to safety and away from the horror of the battlefield. Impossible to believe that in the dawn-morning of that same day the meadows would still have been green, the farmhouses peaceful and the river cool and not awash with blood . . . now there was nothing but an agony of confusion and noise, with Gabe doing as many of them, and throwing away his rifle in his need for haste, and managing to ignore the shame of it.

He fought to get a foothold on the hot, dusty road that was swollen with people. Had the whole of America converged on this one small corner of the country on that hot Sunday afternoon? he thought hysterically. It surely felt like it. Jesus, it was hot. The heavy uniform was sticking to his body. He longed to be rid of it and to dip his head under the cool water of the river, but the river ran with blood, and even if it didn't, there was no time to stop for such pleasures. No space either. As he hustled his way alongside other foot-weary, battle-stained young soldiers as stunned by the day as himself, his shocked, dazed eyes took in the wide slopes to the East of Bull Run, littered with hundreds of Washington citizens out for a Sunday afternoon with their carriages and their picnic baskets to watch the battle as if it was a play put on for their amusement, and many farmers and their wives in spring wagons swelled the numbers of sightseers.

Something of the army's urgency had clearly spread to the sightseers, for as the army began to retreat so did the onlookers. And the highway leading from the stone bridge back to Centreville gradually became jammed with jostling footsoldiers completely disconnected from their units, ambulances, army wagons and carriages all stirring up a great choking dust, with the noise of isolated Confederate shells suddenly bursting out nearby to add to the sudden panic on all sides.

A bridge over a little brook collapsed with the weight of the struggling crowds, talking a farm cart with it, and a hamper of provisions drifted ludicrously downstream. It *was* a play, Gabe thought with fast-mounting hysteria. It was all a grotesque pantomime. It wasn't real. It wasn't happening. He'd dreamed he saw Cal stuck with a Confederate bayonet, and Brad blowing off a reb soldier's head. It was the stuff of nightmares . . . his mind refused to accept it.

'Please–can you help me?' a scared little voice spoke beside him, and he felt a hand tugging at his. 'I seem to have lost my folks, and I live at one of the farms across the valley. Have you time to escort me there, please?'

It was Act Two in the pantomime. The gallant Union soldier helping the fresh-faced country girl in the flower-sprigged muslin dress back to her folks. A girl of about fourteen with pink and white complexion and an apple-pie freshness about her, and a polite all-American smile on her lips. What was this–be-kind-to-the-gallant-soldiers week, he asked himself with sudden savagery? Why hadn't she asked Cal thirty minutes ago? Maybe Cal would have been the one to see her home, then he wouldn't have been lying bleeding all over the valley right now.

Gabe's mind twisted and revolted with the remembered horror of the moment. Suddenly, in his mind, she was to blame, this girl. She should have asked *Cal*, not him. His mind blotted out the fact that she couldn't possibly have been anywhere near the battlefield. He saw only what he wanted to see, and that was the blame for Cal's bloody murder attaching to her. Even if she hadn't wielded the bayonet, she'd had it in her power to stop the terrible thing that had happened. He grabbed her small cool hand.

'Over there, you say? Come on, we'll have to run to get away from all this dust. We should make it all right. Everybody's going in the other direction.'

He was surprised that his voice sounded so normal when

328

he felt so evil towards her. She had no fear of him, no warning. He couldn't see any farmhouses ahead as they struck out at right angles to the rest of the dense stream of people heading for Centreville. But they must be there beyond the drifts of yellow smoke obliterating the skyline, and the dark clumps of trees and hills between him and his purpose. His jaw was granite hard as he ran, pulling her with him. Maybe when he got there he wouldn't be able to make it, maybe her folks would be back . . . he wouldn't let himself think of failure. Cal had to be avenged somehow, and he'd failed miserably once.

'Oh please, I can't run so fast,' the girl gasped. 'Can't we go more slowly? There's no danger out here, is there?'

Only from him. Gabe slowed, and glanced around him. He'd thought to get her back to the farmhouse, still pretending help. He'd thought to get her between soft clean sheets and bloody them as Cal had been bloodied. But here would do as well as anywhere, here between the trees where the grass was still green and sweet and unstained. He looked round quickly once more, but they seemed to have got away from everyone quite successfully, and he pushed her roughly to the ground and pinned her there.

'What do you think you're doing?' she gasped, and then the gasp changed to a scream of terror as he pushed her dress above her waist and ran his hot filthy hands over her smooth warm pink skin. 'Please, no! Oh, please, no . . .'

Gabe spread her legs with his own and forced himself into her, although she fought like a tigress at first. It was an effort on his part, but the smell of her fear and her firm young flesh beneath him goaded him on, despite his tiredness and his nausea, and he thrust himself into her cruelly. One hand was across her mouth to stop her screaming out, the other over her eyes so that he wouldn't see them. The clawing of her hands against his chest fluttered to a stop, as his body reacted in fury rather than lust, and lay uselessly at her sides.

'This one's for Cal,' he snarled over and over. 'For all the good times he won't have any more. And this one's for *me*!'

He jerked himself inside her several times and shuddered to a stop before he withdrew. She lay inert, exactly where she was, and he could see the bright stain of her blood on the grass between her legs. He didn't want to see it. He pulled the dress down over her roughly and looked at her sharply. Her eyes were closed, and his fingers across her face had made great purple weals where they'd been pressed so tightly.

Jesus, he hadn't killed her, had he? His heart thundered in his chest as he stared at her, but she still breathed shallowly, though her eyes were tightly shut, the lashes spiked with tears.

He rolled away from her and was violently sick in the grass. Sweet Jesus, what had made him do it? He suddenly felt as if he was sobering up in speeded-up time after an all-night drinking session, and the shock of it was nauseating. He hadn't wanted to rape her because she stirred him physically. The only way she'd stirred him was with a blinding, unreasoning anger on Cal's behalf, until he'd got himself between her legs.

She gave a sudden small moan, deep in her throat, drawing her legs together involuntarily. She looked what she was—a child, and the shame of his action swept over him in a red mist of horror. But self-preservation sharpened his wits, and he knew he mustn't be caught here. Once she recovered her senses, she'd scream and yell and raise the alarm and they'd come hounding him. He'd heard tell of some of these farm folks. A law unto themselves, and they'd probably string him up as soon as look at him for raping a young, innocent child.

He fled back the way he'd come without giving her another glance. Trying to ignore the heavings of his stomach and the bitter shame he felt, until he reached the masses still surging towards Centreville. It was easy enough to merge in with them, and try to make sense of the gabbling accounts of other soldiers who all had their own tales of horror to tell to wide-eyed civilians thirsting for second-hand thrills.

It seemed McDowell still wanted the troops to make a stand at Centreville for a further attack on the rebs. But there was no way these troops were stopping until they reached Washington. Time and again Gabe heard the same story. No-one was going voluntarily into another blood-bath. Washington meant safety, and Washington was where they were heading. Gabe too. There was no way of finding out what had happened to Deek and Brad, and he saw no-one he recognised from his own unit. He was on his own, in a heaving mass of humanity all frantic with panic and fear and the need to survive. And he just kept on walking with the rest of them, knowing that every mile put him farther away from the wrath of that girl's family, and every mile filled him with searing shame and guilt, so that by the time he limped towards the banks of the Potomac river and the Union camp, he was ready to collapse into its soothing waters and let himself drift unresistingly down-stream.

'Gabe, for God's sake, old buddy, where'd you get to? You look bloody terrible, and you stink worse than a skunk's ass!' Deeker was shaking his arm as he slumped by the water's edge. The wild relief flooded into his soul as he looked beyond Deek and saw Brad working his way towards him through the weary bodies sprawled on the grass, with two plates of hash in his hands.

'I thought I was never going to see either of your two ugly faces again,' his voice was choked, and he had to force down a violent urge to blubber like a baby. Deek gave his arm an embarrassed squeeze and squatted down beside him.

'You can't kill old Brad and me. We're tough as old boots. It was a shame about young Cal though,' he added gruffly.

Gabe nodded, not wanting to look at Brad. Not wanting to see the derision in the Indian's eyes, knowing he'd seen him for a coward. But a plate of hash was shoved in his hands, and he was forced to meet Brad's steady black eyes. They were as expressionless as ever, with that cold, impenetrable Indian stare.

'Eat this, and I'll fetch some more. You look as if you could use it, so no arguments. And Gabe–it had to be done. If not me, then it would have been somebody else. Believe it, boy.'

But not that way! To blow a man's head right off, savagely and swiftly. Gabe thought briefly of that farm girl, the girl he'd raped for Cal. She was still living, and yet she'd died a hundred deaths back there in the woods while he raped her. Not swiftly like the reb soldier had died, but slowly and painfully and humiliatingly, with every vicious thrust of his body. He was no better than Brad after all. Worse, if anything, because she'd trusted him, thought him her friend, and not one of the recognised enemy. He was a bastard, like he'd always been.

'Eat, Gabe!' Brad's huge frame focussed in front of his glazed eyes. And not until he'd seen Gabe force a forkful of the hash into his mouth, and go through the mechanics of chewing and swallowing and tasting nothing, did Brad move off, shouldering his way back through the milling soldiers for another plate of food. A giant of a man, indestructible as his race, a survivor.

In the same instant, Gabe saw himself as one of the world's losers. Right back as far as he could remember, he'd been a loser. He'd lost Marnie, and even when he thought he'd found her again, it was only fate tantalising him before she was lost to him all over again. He'd lost Jenny and the baby . . . his mind veered away from them, because the memory was still too painful. He'd lost Mick, who'd been brother and father all rolled up in one and now thought him a fool. He'd lost Cal, his friend.

He'd lost any real home he ever had, and now he was rootless, belonging nowhere. He was doomed, and he wasn't going to get out of this alive. It had been fate that had sent him lurching drunkenly down Main Street three months back and directed his footsteps to the recruitment poster in the drapery store window. His time was running out, and he saw it as clearly as he'd see little Davey Bray's golden face if he stared long enough into the waters of the Potomac.

'Sweet Jesus, won't you ever let me forget?' he whispered,

and suddenly hurled his half-empty plate into the glittering water, shattering the surface into a thousand ripples.

'Christ, what's got up your nose, Gabe?' Deek started to laugh until he saw the anguished look on Gabe's face, and then his face softened. 'Come on, boy,' he said gently. 'It's the first battle, and maybe that's always the worst, but we'll see plenty more before we're done. Sure, it was a bad one for us, losing Cal the way we did, but we got to live through it, don't we? Try to think of it as one day out of our lives, that's all. Tomorrow's another, Gabe, and we'll all be a little saner for a good night's sleep.'

But sleep brought nightmares, and it was too hot beneath the canvas to rest. Gabe tossed and turned, and always inside him was the gnawing conviction that he wasn't going to survive this war, and the need to put things to rights with Marnie. Oh, he'd sent her a letter through Father Rourke, but that didn't spill out the heart of him like he wanted–needed to. That only told the surface of it, not the soul of him that ached for her and loved her as God had intended a woman to be loved by a man.

In the early hours of the morning, while half the camp slept from sheer exhaustion, and the other half moaned and bled and pleaded with the medical orderlies for something to put them out of their pain, Gabe crawled out of the tent and made his way to a lighted tent where an orderly crossed out yet another name from the list on the paper in front of him at the table. He eyed Gabe sharply.

'What d'you want, soldier?'

'Do you have some writing paper and a pencil–and an envelope?'

The orderly stared at him in disbelief.

'There are men dying here, and you ask me for writing paper! What are you–some kind of amateur newspaper reporter or something? Get back to bed and leave me to my work.'

'Please.' Gabe put his hand on the orderly's arm. 'It's important–you could say it's a matter of life or death.'

'Yeah, you could say it, but I wouldn't,' the orderly shrugged. He jerked his head. 'Over in the cupboard. Don't

333

take more'n you need. And I hope you ain't got a string of girls you want to write to. The army ain't got an endless supply of writing materials!' His face broke into a thin smile. 'Some girl, is she?'

'That's right.' Gabe took what he wanted and strode out of the tent towards the river. Some girl. Some girl . . .

It was as bright as day by the river. Bright enough for him to write by the light of the moon that shone silver on the water. It was difficult to begin at first, but once he started the words poured out of him. She was his life, his love, the other half of him, and she wouldn't read the words he wrote until he was dead, so he let himself go in a way he'd never dreamed he could. Holding back nothing of his feelings, his emotions, his deep, unending love for her, and the desolation he carried with him to the grave because he'd never have one more sweet taste of her, never in his life again.

He wrote passionately, unforgiving towards himself and the wrong he'd done her in running off with Jenny, sparing her nothing of the agony of the night he'd found Jenny and the baby locked in death, nor the shock he'd felt at seeing *her* face mocking him from the face of his dead child.

He ended with the memory of that sweet afternoon at the Pinnock farm heady in his mind, and his writing became tender and loving, and everything he'd long wanted to say to her became easy, until at last he raised his head, knowing that once she received this letter there'd be no more secrets between them. He read it through once and sealed it, writing her name and the address of Larksby on the envelope. He crawled back inside his tent and shook Brad awake.

'What in hell's goin' on?' Brad snarled, still half-asleep.

'I want you to keep this in the safest place you know, and when I'm dead I want you to post it for me. *When I'm dead*, and not before. You savvy, friend?'

He stared steadily at Brad, who looked at the envelope Gabe thrust into his hands. His eyes were as inscrutable as ever, but the handclasp he gave was affirmation enough.

And finally, as the moon paled to an insignificant white blur in a dawn sky, Gabe O'Brien crawled over to his own bedroll and slept.

CHAPTER TWENTY-ONE

Mick fastened the last of his waistcoat buttons and surveyed the fine fellow looking back at him from the mirror in his bedroom. Oh yes, a fine fellow and no mistake. His hair was still thick and black and curly, and there was a new air of authority on the handsome thirty-year-old face now that replaced the brashness so hated by the fenmen. Mick O'Brien was no Irish tinker, and God help anybody who said he was. He was a somebody in the community now. Owner of the old Pinnock farm that thrived and prospered under his hands and those of his right-hand man, his stockman, Tom Baker. Mick was respected and well-liked, and it was time he took himself a wife and thought about the next generation now that he had something to leave behind.

His blue eyes softened as he thought of Marnie. She was never very far from his thoughts these days. It was six months now since she'd come running into his arms with her face all damp and tear-stained, with the sad news of her sister and the babby. Six months . . . and in that time Mick O'Brien had discovered there was more to loving than the swift urges Peggy at the Duck and Drake once stirred in him so regularly, and it still amazed him to acknowledge it.

If anyone had told him that lusty Mick O'Brien would ever be content with a girl who held him off whenever he wanted desperately to lay with her, who'd permit him only the mildest of liberties, who could look at him with those sensuous tawny brown eyes of hers and that soft trembling mouth and evoke every bit of protectiveness of which he was capable, he'd have said they were mad. But then, nobody had ever affected him quite like Marnie before.

He realised he'd never really known her, even while it

seemed as if he'd always known her. She'd drifted in and out of his life for eleven years, from the time he'd first seen her in the fen cottage and caught his breath at the sight of her, gauche and knowing and beautiful, until now, when she was soft and ripe for loving and the darling of his life. Mick had never been as articulate with words as his brother Gabe, but something about Marnie brought out the poet in him. Something undefinable that he couldn't explain that was accentuated by the strange untouchable, almost ethereal quality about her that yet managed to touch his soul.

He laughed ruefully at himself in the mirror as he drew on his jacket. Was this really himself talking? Lusty Mick who'd never thought fine respect for a girl would be of such prime importance in his thinking? It hadn't been uppermost that night when she'd come to his arms for comfort, when the melting of her body against his had roused him instantly as her arms wound around his neck. And she'd finally become aware of the urgency in his body as the pressure of his mouth on hers became more demanding.

'No, Mick,' she'd mumbled then as she stiffened in his embrace. 'This isn't what I came for. It's not right.'

His voice was thick in his throat.

'No, it's probably not right at such a time, with the news you've brought me, Marnie. But I'm still thinking there could be nothing more right in this world than a man needing a woman and a woman needing a man. It's what life is all about, my lovely girl, and I'm humbled and touched at knowing you felt the need of me this night.'

Oh, she needed *someone*, anyone . . . she needed human comfort, and he'd been the one closest to Gabe, whom she needed most of all, so it had seemed natural to run to him. For a few blissful minutes in Mick's arms she'd even been able to blot out the tumultuous past and pretend it was Gabe's arms holding her. Oh, that was the wicked thing . . . wicked, wicked, to be using Mick like that, but the pretending had been exquisitely sweet, and perhaps it could be construed as slightly less wicked as long as the secret remained locked in her own heart. But the moments had

336

passed, and here was Mick looking down at her with more than tenderness in his eyes and a different kind of need calling to her from every part of him . . .

'Mick–I can't–' she said tremblingly. 'It's been a terrible shock, hearing about Jenny. I can't think of anything else . . .'

'Forgive me, sweetheart,' he said at once, his voice still husky, but subdued now. 'I was forgetting everything but my own selfish desires in the delight of having you in my arms. And I can't deny that it is a delight, Marnie, unexpected and exciting, and one I've been dreaming about for weeks now. You can't expect to grow into a beautiful young woman and not have men wanting you.'

Her eyes were suddenly tear-bright and watchful as she looked at him.

'Lusting after me, you mean? Is that how you feel for me, Mick O'Brien?'

His arms still imprisoned her, but they held her less urgently now. She could have moved out of them if she'd chosen to, but she remained where she was.

'A man who loves a woman lusts for her too,' he said evenly. 'It's the way of things, and it's in a man's nature. Would you have me be less of a man by telling you that my love for you is not enhanced by lust? If I'm truthful then I must tell you that I want you in my arms every day and in my bed every night. That I've hardly stopped thinking of you for a second since the day I went to Larksby and saw you again. I had no intention of pouring it out to you like this, especially now, when you're vulnerable and upset, but it turns a knife in my heart to see you like this, and it's more than I can do to stand by and mutter the kind of platitudes of a casual friend.'

As she stayed motionless in his arms he pulled her closer to him. Her head was against his chest and she could hear the uneven thudding of his heart and knew he was deeply affected by her nearness. She could hear it too in the vibrating of his voice as he spoke to her. She could feel the stroke of his strong gentle hands on her hair, and she was

337

unable to throw such emotions back in his face.

'Marnie, I'll not deny that I want you more than I've ever wanted a woman before, but I love you too, and one feeling is worthless without the other, I'm learning. But if you'll let me come courting fine and proper and say we can be wed in due course, I'll give you my love and respect for as long as you say that's all there can be between us. Mind you, I'll not say I won't be praying for the day you'll let me lie with you, whether it's before or after the wedding!'

A smile teased his mouth and brought an answering one from her trembling lips, and almost without realising it she found herself nodding slowly in agreement. And then his mouth was on hers again, firmly, possessively, this time a promise, and a strange thrill ran through her knowing how difficult it was going to be for him to hold himself in check. Knowing instinctively it wouldn't be in his nature, and that he must have known many women before. But he loved her so much he was content to wait if she said it had to be so. He loved her that much . . . it brought a lump to her throat to know it, and she tried to tell herself he was worth a hundred of his brother, Gabe, who'd thought nothing of taking all she had to give and then discarding her in favour of her sister. And Marnie badly wanted to belong to someone, and to have somebody of her own.

'Now we've decided, don't let's wait too long for the wedding,' she said breathlessly. 'Then neither of us will feel the strain too much, Mick.'

She heard the indrawing of his breath and realised he'd taken her words as meaning she'd be just as impatient for the day she'd belong to him, body and soul. It hadn't quite been what she'd intended to convey, rather that if it was to happen, the sooner it was an accomplished fact the better, and the final ghosts of the past could be laid for ever. But his kisses grew more passionate, and when she felt the gentle circling pressure of his hand on her breast she was unresisting, telling herself that this was Mick, her future husband, for whom she had a deep regard, if not an

338

earth-shaking love, and he had every right to expect a certain response from her.

And the gentle caressing of his hand was hypnotic, soothing, not stirring her into answering passion, but filling her with a warmth she hadn't known in a very long time. To Mick she was like a fragile young fawn beneath his hands, so nearly poised for flight and yet drawn to him almost irresistibly, and everything that was in him wanted to keep her there. Even though it became increasingly more frustrating to him as the weeks passed into months, and he was no nearer to knowing the full sweetness of her than at the beginning.

'It can't always be like this, Marnie,' he'd groan against the soft whiteness of her throat, when he longed to let his lips stray further. 'When we're wed I shall want a woman who warms my bed in every way. You know that, don't you?'

'I know it, Mick,' she'd reply, 'and you have my promise that you won't be disappointed. It's just that I–I can't–not yet. There are–reasons. I can't explain, but please, please be patient.'

And patient he'd been, he thought now, as he closed the travelling bag that contained all he'd need for a week's stay at Drory. Patient beyond his limitations, and if he hadn't had the utmost regard for her, he'd have smashed his way through that preposterous modesty of hers long ago. He loved her, and he lusted for her. He echoed his own words to her and the lust for her was the reminder that Gabe had used her ill on at least one occasion in her childhood. How many times he didn't know and wouldn't ask, and she'd never dream that he knew anything about it, of course. But he appreciated that scars like that cut deep. No, he would never ask or pry where the truth wasn't readily offered. Besides, Mick's own past wasn't exactly unsullied.

Even since asking Marnie to marry him, he'd had occasion to visit certain ladies of a dubious reputation to relieve the ache inside him, and there was always the memory of his long-lived affair with Peggy, who'd eventually tired of waiting for him and upped and married Kenneth Bray after all.

No, he wasn't blameless by a long chalk, but he'd no more want Marnie to know the truth of it than probe too deeply into why she sometimes acted so frigidly towards him when it came to his basic urges, when the faraway longing in her brown eyes spoke just the opposite. But at least he was assured that it would all be resolved when he had the ring safely on her finger in four weeks' time, and today he was taking her home to Drory for a week to meet his family, leaving the farm in the capable hands of Tom Baker. It wasn't often a farmer felt able to take time off, but Tom was a good bor and the most reliable stockman a man could wish for, and he'd see to everything in his absence. And after the wedding, neither had wanted a honeymoon, because all of life ahead would be a honeymoon.

He collected her from Larksby in the pony and trap and arranged for it to be taken back to the farm. Not for Mick O'Brien and his fiancée the inconvenience of trundling across country in a jolting cart. Now they waited at the village Inn for the regular coach to pick up its passengers for Bristol. They were the only two travellers for a good part of the journey, and Mick held her hand loosely in his own, his heart swelling with pride at the sight of her, and knowing she was so soon to be his bride.

'You don't need to be nervous, my lovely,' he said softly, seeing how pale she was. 'Maureen will love you on sight, and I've already written and told her and Jack all about you.'

'And who I am?' the words were out before she could stop them. Mick looked puzzled.

'You're my future wife. What else is there to tell?'

'They know about Gabe going to America, of course,' she rushed on, knowing she had to continue now. 'So I presume they know about Jenny too, and the—the baby.'

He nodded, still not sure what she was getting at.

'Well then. Will they think I'm a suitable wife for

you–the sister of a girl who behaved so wantonly?'

'Will they think I'm a suitable husband for *you*, the brother of a man who behaved so shamefully?' Mick said quietly. His hand tightened on hers. 'You think too much on the past, Marnie. Why can't you let it go and forget them? It does you credit to grieve for them so much, but they belong to the past, and it's the future–our future–we should be thinking about now. Maureen won't look at the two of us and see a man who failed in his duty to his young brother, nor a young woman who once suffered at that young brother's hands. She'll see two people who love each other very much and give us her blessing. She *will* see that, won't she, darling?'

'Yes of course.' She leaned across and touched his lips with her own as the sudden anxious frown creased his brow. The coach stopped for more travellers to get in, and the opportunity for intimacies was past, to her relief. Maybe Mick hadn't been referring to herself and Gabe at all, but in an oblique way suggesting he knew how Gabe had hurt her by his treatment of her sister, maybe that was all it was, but it had been an uncomfortable moment to wonder if he really did know–or guess–that she and Gabe had once been everything to each other.

She didn't want Mick to guess. She cared too much for him to want to hurt him. But he was right about one thing. She was nervous about meeting Maureen and Jack and the four Haggerty children. And she'd never considered before that it was going to be a little like stepping back into Gabe's own childhood, being surrounded by people who'd known him, seeing the places he knew, being with the people who'd loved him and had as many memories of him as she did.

It was a poignant journey for her, for the most private of reasons. Given another chance, if life's twists and turns had taken a different direction, she might have expected to see Drory with Gabe by her side, in the glory of sweet young love when everything would have looked green and beautiful. As it was, she alighted from the boat on the other side of the Irish Sea with Mick's arm guiding her along the slippery surface of the quayside, shivering a little in the cool wind whipping into their faces, in a fine drizzle of rain.

'There they are!' Mick pointed a little way along the road to where a rotund, snub-nosed man with thinning hair stood outside a waiting carriage. A dark-haired, rosy-faced woman leaned out of the door of the carriage, her face lighting up at the sight of Mick. Two young children appeared at the window and were told to move over and make room as Mick and Marnie arrived at the carriage and had their baggage stowed away.

'Ah, but it's so good to see you, Mick,' Maureen's voice was warm with welcome, her eyes affectionate and moist. 'And the day's come at last that we've all been waiting for! It's delighted we are to welcome Mick's future bride, Marnie!'

She leaned forward and kissed her, and Marnie felt a surge of gratitude at being made part of the family so quickly. It was a bit different from the way she'd informed Geraldine Larksby of her impending marriage and the request for some holiday before the day arrived. She had been met with the most caustic of replies and a grudging agreement since Marnie had had little holiday all the years she had been in Geraldine's service.

'She's only green with envy, the dried-up old crabapple, because you'll be having a man to warm you nights, and she can't find one of her own,' Mick had laughed when she'd told him, her feathers ruffled. 'And as well as losing a butt for her sharp tongue, she's going to have to look for a new maid as well. 'Tis not only a time of change for you and me, my lovely, but we know who's getting the better bargain, don't we? Forget the old minch and come here, where you belong.'

Marnie remembered his words now as Jack Haggerty rejoined them in the crowded carriage and shouted for the driver to get moving out of this damned rain. He beamed delightedly at the visitors.

'So we're to have a Mrs O'Brien at last,' he said jovially.

'And not before time too. And maybe some little O'Briens soon to carry on the family name, eh, Mick?'

'Jack, the children,' Maureen said severely. 'Marnie, these are Kathleen and Nora, named after our two little sisters who died in infancy. The boys have been taken out for the afternoon, but you'll be meeting them soon. They argued fine who was to come and meet you, but Jack said the boys were to behave like young gentlemen and let their sisters come.'

'Besides, we said we'd hit them if they didn't,' Kathleen said candidly. 'We're bigger than them!'

Jack tried to shush her as Maureen burst out laughing, but even his eyes were twinkling, and Marnie found her heart warming to this big, friendly family that was part of Mick's and soon to be part of hers. She compared them briefly with the angry arguing and rivalry that had gone on in her own childhood in the fen cottage, and found it very wanting.

'What news of Gabe, Mick?' Maureen's words suddenly caused her heart to leap wildly. She hadn't expected his name to remain unmentioned, but neither had she expected to hear it so soon.

'None, save what I've already told you by letter,' he replied. 'It's my feeling we'll hear no more of him. The letter he got the American priest to write to Marnie was very final, in my view. I feel he'll not try to make contact again, and perhaps 'tis better so.'

'I can't accept that,' Maureen said passionately. 'He's part of us, and we love him, no matter what he's done, and I can't believe he'd turn his back on us for ever.'

'Maureen!' It was Jack who spoke warningly now, glancing at Marnie and the children, who sat with wide eyes, listening, and to whom clearly Gabe's name was no mystery. And it was clear to Marnie that this O'Brien/Haggerty girl had all the passion and fire in her nature of her brothers, and she felt a wave of sympathy towards her, knowing instinctively how much more she'd be missing Gabe, knowing he was so many miles apart from his family.

'I brought the letter with me,' she said hesitantly to

Maureen. 'I've wanted to tear it up so many times, but somehow I couldn't do it. If you'd like to read it sometime, you'd be most welcome, since it concerns us both.'

Maureen nodded. She said no more then, but from that little exchange a bond of friendship and understanding was forged between them.

It wasn't a long ride from the quayside to the fine house at Drory where the Haggertys lived. It wasn't so grand as Larksby, of course, but grander than anywhere else Marnie was accustomed to visiting. Maureen had help in the kitchen and someone to help with the children. It was an idyllic place for children to live, and she wondered suddenly how Mick could have wanted to leave it.

'It wasn't always like this,' he told her later, as they strolled in the garden, arms entwined, in the reddening glow of the setting sun. 'There was a time when the fields were black and stinking, and the potato crops shrivelled and died, and things were very bleak. We were very poor, and none of us was used to grand living such as Jack and Maureen have now. Gabe and I were two less mouths to feed when we went to England, but if we hadn't gone, I'd never have met you, would I?'

His hand squeezed her waist, but she was hardly listening. Suddenly she wanted to see all of it; the church where they'd sat as children; the fields where they'd played; the old tumbledown cottage where they'd lived, where the ghost of Gabe still played among the ruins . . . she wanted to picture him there, so that the memory of it was imprinted on her mind for all time.

'Marnie. Come back,' Mick said softly.

She forced a small laugh to her lips, but she shivered all the same. It shouldn't be like this, she told herself. She shouldn't try to relive the past, to conjure up the scenes Gabe knew and try to bring him into her subconscious this way. It wasn't fair to Mick . . .

'It's getting chilly. Can we go in–and I'm anxious to meet those nephews of yours,' she said quickly. 'Kathleen and Nora are very sweet, aren't they? It must be lovely to have

344

such a close, loving family life. Mine was never like that.'

'Our children's will be the same,' he promised. 'And the sight of you so relaxed in Maureen's house makes me the more eager for it. Only four more weeks, Marnie, and you'll really belong to me for always.'

He ran his finger round the softness of her mouth before he kissed it, and she closed her eyes weakly. He was a good man and she loved him, oh she did, but it wasn't love like she'd given Gabe, and she prayed that it would be enough . . .

'Uncle Mick! Uncle Mick!' Two hurtling little figures appeared in front of them as if by magic. They'd been taken safely away for the afternoon while the visitors arrived, but now they were ecstatic at seeing again the tall, tanned uncle from over the sea in England, and Marnie stood smiling while he scooped them up in his arms and let them plant their slobbering kisses on his cheeks.

'Come on now, boys, where are your manners? Will you not say hello to your new auntie who's come all the way from England to see you? This is Auntie Marnie, and this little plump pudding is Ben, who's all of four years old. Isn't that right, Ben?'

'Four and a quarter,' Ben said solemnly. He clung to Mick's neck while he eyed Marnie up and down. He was very sweet, with his father's snub-nose and round face, and straight brown hair. The other boy, Patrick, slid out of Mick's arms and turned round curiously to look at this new auntie. He studied her for a long moment as Mick introduced him, then his face broke into a smile as he yelled hello, grabbed Ben and said they were to go inside and wash their hands because they were to be allowed to stay up for supper tonight as there were visitors in the house.

And Marnie stared after him, stunned into silence at the sight of him. Six years old, and already Patrick was the living image of Gabe, from the black curly hair and vivid laughing blue eyes, to the dimples that dented his cheeks.

'You see it too,' Mick said softly. 'Maureen will never lose Gabe while that one bears such a strong resemblance. I wonder sometimes if it's a blessing or a curse, for sometimes she dotes on him too much, as if to keep Gabe's memory alive through the boy.'

'He's uncannily like him,' Marnie tried to speak steadily. 'It was quite a shock to me for a minute.'

She shivered involuntarily as they followed the two little boys indoors, seeing the likeness to Gabe as something different. Almost as an omen, she thought uneasily. As if something bad were going to happen–or had already happened–to Gabe, and this little Patrick had been sent to replace him, as a kind of–of reincarnation. She shook herself. She didn't like to think that way, but it was a thought that she couldn't rid herself of, no matter how hard she tried.

There was no doubt that the visit to Drory was a big success. Marnie had never felt so at peace anywhere. She and Mick took the children everywhere with them, and they quickly became attached to their new auntie. She sat with Maureen while she read Father Rourke's letter and wept over it with her, and neither asked any questions, nor seemingly needed to. She was as much at home at the Haggerty house and at Drory as anywhere she'd been in her life, and at first she was reluctant for the week to come to an end. She'd been to the church with Mick and received Father Flynn's blessing on their forthcoming marriage, and taken a sprig from the young tree flourishing in Mick's name at his Mammy's request, to plant in the garden at the farm when they returned home.

But everywhere she looked there was Gabe. She pictured him running in the fields and coming home to the house if she happened to look out of a window. She dreamed of him constantly, and suddenly it was beginning to unnerve her. She realised it was because she was hearing constant talk of him, more naturally than she ever had before. His name had been a secret in her heart all these years. Her family had hated him, and Jenny had never guessed how she loved him.

Here in Drory, it seemed almost like a conspiracy to keep

346

his name and his image alive. The priest spoke of him every time they met; old friends stopped Mick in the streets to be introduced and to ask for news of Gabe; and to wonder and surmise over his doings in America, since Mick gave only the barest details. Maureen couldn't let a day go by without mentioning his name, it seemed to Marnie, and the four children, who only had a hazy remembered picture of him, nevertheless knew him as well as anyone by their mother's continual references to him. It was as if he'd walk in the door at any moment, Marnie thought, and if he did not one of them would be remotely surprised.

She realised all the talk of Gabe was making her unsure of herself, for she too was beginning to long for Gabe with a new wave of impatience. And that mustn't happen, since she was to marry his brother in four—no, less than four weeks' time. It was wrong to be so obsessed with thoughts of Gabe, and by the last night they were at Drory, she knew it was time she left, before she gave up pretending and implored Mick to release her from their engagement, because she didn't love him enough and never could.

'Are you feeling unwell, Marnie?' Maureen asked sympathetically after supper on that last evening. 'You look very pale.'

'I do have rather a headache. If I can get to sleep tonight, I hope it will have passed off by morning before we make the journey home.'

'I have some marvellous powders that will help both problems,' Maureen said at once. 'You must take one half an hour before bedtime, and I guarantee your head will be pleasantly muzzy before you fall asleep, and you'll sleep in the lap of the gods.'

'I'd rather it was in my lap,' Mick grinned.

'Have you no patience, you wicked man!' Maureen's eyes sparkled at him. 'I'm sure the last thing Marnie will be wanting this night is to fight off your amorous advances.'

It was on the tip of his tongue to say she didn't welcome them any night, but she did look pale, and he sat with his arm round her shoulder on the sofa after supper, his fingers smoothing her forehead, and she took the headache powder at once, saying she'd go upstairs in half an hour or so anyway.

Somehow, the sight of her, pale and small and pliant in his arms, stirred him as he hadn't been stirred for days. And he wanted her. Jesus, how he wanted her. Thank heaven he didn't have to wait much longer or he'd be a raving madman because of the wanting inside him. 'I'll go up now, Mick,' she said eventually. 'We've a long journey ahead of us tomorrow, and I'll be glad of a good night's sleep.'

She made her escape, suddenly needing to be alone. And yet not alone, because Gabe was as real in the room with her as if she could hear him breathing. She could feel his presence, his love reaching out to her. She closed her eyes and breathed the essence of him. Oh Gabe, Gabe, don't stop loving me, her spirit wept. Remember me . . . the powder Maureen had given her was having its effect, and her head was muzzy and thick, her thoughts blurring so much she was unsure where dreaming began and reality ended.

And closing her eyes with her hands held tight-clenched by her sides was making her head spin. She felt the pressure of the bed behind her knees and sank down on it without undressing, lying in the darkness with her eyes still shut to keep the image of Gabe strong in her mind, unwilling to push him out any longer. Unable to lose the feeling that if she dared to open them the present would come rushing back to her, and she didn't want it. She wanted to stay in her half-floating dream-world with Gabe. As the drugging effect of the powder gradually overcame her she relaxed, but the little soft moans that escaped her lips echoed his name, over and over . . .

Mick came upstairs an hour later, after a companionable sit by the fireside with his sister and brother-in-law. It had been a pleasant interlude at Drory, but now he was anxious to get back home and make the final plans for the marriage. The sooner it was all settled and Marnie was his wife the

348

better. He felt an odd sense of urgency tonight, a need to have things settled and in order, and if he'd thought she'd agree, he'd have whisked her off to the church in the morning and got Father Flynn to officiate there and then. But he knew she'd not agree to anything so hasty, and he was too afraid of losing her to risk upsetting the applecart at this late stage.

There was a rueful smile on his lips as he passed Marnie's bedroom door on the way to his, and then he paused, listening. He could hear sounds coming from inside. At first he'd thought she was crying, and his heart had lurched, because why should any woman cry so near to her wedding-day? But it wasn't crying, it was little moaning sounds . . . and the sounds suddenly excited him, even while they mystified him, for he'd heard soft moanings in a woman's bedroom before. He pushed the door open gently and peered inside.

She hadn't pulled her bedroom curtains, and from the light of the full moon through the window he could see her lying across the bed still fully clothed. He hesitated a minute, then he closed the door quietly behind him and moved towards the bed, looking down at her.

She was soundly asleep, yet still making those little whimpering noises. But she couldn't stay like this all night! Mick moved beside her, lifting her in his arms and undid the fastenings at the back of her dress, removing it carefully. She didn't stir, and as he laid her back on the bed again in her white cotton chemise, he heard his own ragged breathing.

She was so beautiful. He pulled the unresisting pins from her hair and it fell on to her creamy shoulders in a glowing cascade. He caressed it softly. He'd always loved her hair. And then he found himself slowly removing the rest of her clothes until she lay naked beneath his hot gaze. His eyes roamed freely over the lush mounds of her breasts, the curves and hollows of her body, the thick dark triangle of hair at her groin between the white thighs. He smothered an oath deep in his throat, knowing he should never have taken her clothes off, never risked seeing her like this, so exquisitely inviting, because it was more than any mortal man could do to resist the temptation.

He was tugging at his own clothes then, and covering her with his body, warming her as he wanted to do for so long. His eyes unconsciously misted, because he knew this was tantamount to rape, even though she lay, lovely and unresisting, under his mounting passion. And then his heart nearly stopped beating, for her arms suddenly wound themselves round his neck, and he felt her legs part to give him entry, and he was suddenly surging inside her, his passion aflame, and the strange little mutterings were still gasping from her lips as he thrust home again and again . . .

'Love me, oh love me, love me, love me . . .'

'For always, my lovely girl,' Mick whispered into her shoulder as he shuddered out his climax, and then he slid away from her, his body glistening with sweat, and covered her with the bedclothes. He looked down at her with infinite tenderness for a long moment before stepping back into his clothes and stealing quietly back along the corridor to his own room. She hadn't stirred, had made no movement or sound after he'd left her, but his spirit was jubilant, and now he could wait patiently for the next three weeks or so until she was truly his, for she'd never belong to him more than she had this night.

Marnie stirred restlessly as the drug began to wear off, and realised she was shivering. She stared down at her naked body where the bedclothes had slipped off, and got quickly into her nightgown. She must have been more muzzy than she realised to climb into bed like that! And she needed still more sleep, though she felt unutterably relaxed. The moonlight stabbed into her eyes and she turned her back on it and curled up into a ball. And as she did so, the fine-drawn fragments of memory spun tantalisingly into her mind, just out of reach, but piquant enough to make her roll over on to her back after a minute or so, to gaze up at the shifting patterns of moonlight on the ceiling.

Maybe it was because of the moonlight, she thought dazedly, because of the fullness that shone directly on to her face like a benevolent father, and it was a very long time since she'd thought of herself as Moon Child with anything but derision, maybe she really had been dreaming so deeply, or maybe something stranger than she knew had conjured him up across the miles of ocean that separated them. Whatever it was, she'd dreamed or imagined, or believed, that Gabe had come to her that night, had lain with her and held her, and filled her with the sweetness of his love as she remembered, and the sweetness still lingered to tease her, and make her want him even more.

Her head was clear by morning, though she was still pale, and Mick was very gentle towards her, just as if he knew she was as fragile as glass. In the long sleepless hours since she'd woken in a fever of longing for Gabe, she'd told herself this situation had to end. Either she broke with Mick right away, or she married him and tried to forget Gabe ever existed. But her instincts told her that was impossible, and neither could she face a life of loneliness now. Oh, she was weakening, and she knew it . . .

She imagined the alternative to marrying Mick. Telling Geraldine Larksby the wedding was off, and knowing her life with that vitriolic madam after such an admission would be intolerable. And hadn't she always affirmed that she did love him, even if it was a luke-warm affection compared with that other? But life with Mick would be very sweet all the same, and she wasn't exactly averse to his caresses.

She put away any thought of decision-making, letting things remain as they were, and suffered the hot sticky kisses of the Haggerty children as they made their tearful goodbyes at the quayside.

'You come back just as often as you can, Marnie,' Maureen hugged her warmly. 'I'm just beginning to realise what I missed in not having a sister all these years. Any time you and Mick can spare the time from the farm, we'll love to see you, and I don't need to tell you how the children feel about that!'

Even Jack echoed her sentiments, and as the boat left the Irish shore, Marnie had very mixed feelings. It was almost like saying goodbye to Gabe, in a way she'd never had the chance to before. And that was what it must be, she told herself. Goodbye to Gabe and all there had been between them, because now she was going home, and she was going to marry Mick and be a good farmer's wife.

She smiled into his eyes, and her heart leapt at the sudden warmth she saw in his blue eyes, and felt the tightening of his hand on hers.

'Not long now, my lovely girl,' he said softly, and she caught her breath. No one but Mick ever called her that, and yet she'd heard it last night, she was certain, last night when she thought she was living out the dream of Gabe's loving; but she couldn't ask . . . she could only wish desperately she could see through the blur of last night and know if it had really been a dream, or incredibly, gloriously real?

CHAPTER TWENTY-TWO

Perhaps it was because she was still lulled by the feeling of well-being within the Haggerty household and the sudden longing for her own family unit to be as complete, or the thought that it would be comforting to have someone of her own sitting in the dimness of the church while she and Mick made their vows, and it may just be that Peggy and her brothers would agree to turn up on the day if she asked them . . . perhaps it was just the restlessness that had stayed with her ever since she'd discovered that Gabe's presence was as inescapable as her own shadow, and that having her family around her would make the marriage ritual more solid, more real.

Whatever the reason, Marnie said nothing of her intentions to Mick, meaning to surprise him, hopefully, with the knowledge that she still had three brothers who cared enough for her to see her properly wed. And she set off from Larksby across the fields in the direction of the fen cottage on her next evening off, completely unaware of the consequences of such a simple action.

It was one of the rare occasions when they were all there, for Joey and Ted were idle for the present, with work being slack on the river, and Kenneth just back from the farm where he was presently labouring. Peggy looked up from the depths of Ma's kitchen, her hair steamy and lank from cooking, her once-pretty face coarsened and fat. Her heavy breasts strained against the tight bodice of her dress as always, but she gave a semblance of a smile as she saw Marnie arrive.

'Just in time to help me dish up the stew if you've a mind to take a bite,' she said in a surly tone.

She resented everything about Marnie, from her gleaming hair to her neat, well-rounded shape, and most of all the way she always looked at Peggy in a vaguely disapproving way that unnerved her. She heaved the stewpan on to the table, uncaring about the splashes on her clothes and hair as it slopped about.

'I didn't come here to skivvy,' Marnie retorted. 'I'm supposed to be a guest here now, in case you hadn't noticed.'

Peggy glared at her. 'And I ain't here to wait on you neither!'

'Oh, shut it, the pair of you,' Kenneth said irritably. 'You're worse than Marnie and Jenny used to be when they were babbies. There's some excuse for babbies squabbling, but not grown women. I think that's what you both are, ain't it?' He was on his way in from the privvy, and he gave Peggy's fat backside a friendly squeeze as he passed her. 'Well, this one is all right. But it'd take a good man to fight his way through the icy bad-smell look of that one's, I reckon,' he grunted towards his sister.

Marnie lifted her chin defiantly. No matter with what good intentions she came to the cottage, within five minutes it seemed as if there was wrangling, and she was put on the defensive.

'That's just what I came to see you about,' she snapped. 'Only you always manage to spoil things before I get the chance to tell you anything, don't you?'

'Tell us what?' Joey grunted from his seat near the fire.

She took a deep breath.

'That I'm getting married in just over two weeks, and I'd like it very much if you'd all come to the church, if you can spare the time.'

Peggy stared at her in amazement. 'Getting wed? You? Some man's actually risked asking you then!'

'Will you come, Kenneth?' she ignored Peggy and appealed to her eldest brother. 'It would mean a lot to Mick and me.'

It was suddenly as if she'd mentioned the devil himself. One minute the room had been pleasantly hazy with the reminiscent smell of Da's pipe as Kenneth drew deeply on a blackened clay; Peggy doling out five dishes of stew; Joey and Ted dozing by the fire. The next minute Kenneth had slammed his fists on the table, making the dishes hop, and stood there breathing noisily, and the two other brothers leapt to their feet and glared at her aggressively.

'Who?' Kenneth roared. 'Did you say Mick? His name's *Mick*?'

Marnie involuntarily backed a few inches towards the door, but Joey was behind her, barring flight. She licked her suddenly dry lips. Anyway, it was *her* life, wasn't it? And time this ridiculous old feud between the O'Briens and the Brays was ended. She couldn't think why her brothers had borne a grudge for so long, except that it was in their nature to fight.

'Mick O'Brien,' she said angrily. 'You remember . . .'

'Oh aye! We remember Mick O'Brien, don't we, bors?' Kenneth's voice vibrated all round the cottage. 'Even *Peggy* remembers Mick O'Brien, don't you, wife? And I'll tell you summat for nothing! No sister of mine marries an O'Brien, so you can get back and tell him that for a wedding present, girl!'

Marnie's face filled with a furious, burning colour.

'What right have you got to tell me who I'll marry?' she shouted. 'You and your fat trollop . . .'

Kenneth's hand lashed across her face, taking her so much by surprise she lost her balance and fell against the table. The blow split her lip until she tasted blood. Kenneth hauled her to her feet, his face purple with rage. And then she was spun round to face her brother Joey, maddened to the point of screaming what seemed like gibberish.

'You see my wooden shoulder that's no good to man nor beast, and keeps me from sleeping nights and working properly days, even now? And you know who did that, my beauty? Your bloody precious Mick did that with a rabbiting spade. Out in the Pinnock fields, one fine morning, and I ain't never forgotten or forgiven, and nor am I likely to.'

'They're not the Pinnock fields any more! They're Mick's fields now and his farm, and it'll soon be mine as well, and we'll make sure no river scum come dirtying it . . .' she screamed as Joey's good arm shot out and punched her full in the face.

'You can talk about dirt, you whore! When it's on account of you I'm crippled for life!'

She trembled with shock, staring at him uncomprehendingly, her breathing hoarse and stifled where she tried not to cry out at the bruises they were inflicting on her. She wouldn't give them the satisfaction of seeing her cry, but what in God's name was Joey going on about?

'You're talking in riddles,' she snapped. 'I don't know anything about your battered shoulder . . .'

'Then it's time you did,' Kenneth shouted. 'Do you mean to say you're ignorant of the fight at the Pinnock farm all those years ago when we got wind of that little Irish shit-bag poking you when you were little more'n a babby?'

The shock of it stunned her. Her eyes misted and blurred.

'*Gabe*?' his name was a whisper of pain on her lips. A sudden sharp memory of the long scar on his arm came to her mind, the scar he wouldn't explain to her when she'd seen it for the first time in his room at the farm. Was that something to do with this fight her brothers referred to? Was it?

'Aye, that's right–Gabe,' Joey taunted. 'Your pretty little blue-eyed boy. He wasn't quite so pretty when we'd finished with him, and neither was that bloody nancy mate of his, Fred Jackson, for letting on about it to us. Didn't know your blue-eyed boy couldn't keep his trap shut about his fancy piece, did you? He had to go rushing off to his nancy bor and tell him all the gory details. And now you come here and tell us you're going to marry the other one. Not bloody likely you ain't!'

His words jumbled and whirled and seared through her mind. And all she could think of was that Gabe hadn't got wind of her and Darryl Larksby after all, when he'd called her by all those hateful names and shocked her so badly.

The fact that he'd apparently confided in Fred Jackson about their time together in the mill was nothing to her. If she'd had a close friend at the time she'd have dearly liked to confide how spectacular it had all been, but Gabe hadn't called her a kitchen whore because of Darryl's visits to her attic room, but because he thought she'd gone blabbing to her brothers and got them to go gunning for him.

And now at last she saw the meaning of Fred Jackson's garbled, red-faced mutterings when she'd come face to face with him at King's Lynn. She closed her eyes for a brief moment. If only Gabe had hurled what he thought to be the truth at her all those years ago, instead of letting the hurt fester between them until it was an impossible wound to heal, all those wasted years.

She licked her swollen lips, and now the tears were blinding her eyes. It made no difference now, she thought dully, and Gabe was too far out of her reach ever to put things right, and anyway, it changed nothing of the present situation. She'd come here full of elation about her future, and in a few minutes her brothers had managed to ruin everything again, she thought bitterly. Well, she wouldn't let them. She held her head high, though her legs were shaking and her heart pounded.

'You can't stop me marrying whom I choose!' Her voice was shrill. 'I should have known better than to come here expecting any kind of family feelings from you three. You don't know the meaning of the words. If Ma and Da were alive they'd give me their blessing and be glad for me.'

'You can marry the devil himself as long as his name ain't O'Brien!' Kenneth thundered, smashing his fist on to the table again. 'No sister of mine's going to shack up with an Irish tinker. . . .'

'It's a bit late to be talking like that!' Marnie was screaming now, uncaring what she said. What did it matter anyway? 'Because your precious Jenny was married to one of them. You didn't know that, did you? All the time you thought she was set up in some fancy big house as a lady's

357

maid, she was on the boat to America with Gabe O'Brien, and she was having his baby.'

She was suddenly being shaken so violently her teeth rattled in her head, and Kenneth's piercing eyes bored deep into hers, willing the truth out of her.

'What are you saying, you lying bitch?' he snarled. 'You were always jealous of Jenny, even as a child. Jealous of her pretty face and curly hair and the way Da preferred her to you with your pouting looks and flouncing ways ... Don't come here with your made-up lies about Jenny, because we had her letters to prove where she was, even if we ain't had any recently.'

'You fools!' Marnie was still screaming. '*I* wrote the letters, every one of them, so's Da wouldn't get wind of what had happened to his precious Jenny. And all the time ...' she heard the hysterical laughter bubbling from her throat ... 'all the time she was gone off with Gabe O'Brien with a child in her belly, so how do you like knowing I wasn't the only one he ...'

Joey's hand against the back of her head almost knocked her senseless.

'You're a bloody wicked liar,' he shouted. 'Our Jenny wouldn't do such a thing, not with the likes of an Irish tinker!'

'What makes you think she was so perfect? Why don't you try looking for the big house where she's supposed to work, and find the people she talked about in her letters, you fools? You'll never find them, because they don't exist. I made them all up, every one of them, and I'm *glad* she got away from you, do you hear? I can just imagine what would have happened if she'd tried to get help from her family. Her *family*! Look at you! You're filthy and stinking and you shame me ...'

'All right, so you helped her,' Ted suddenly spoke up, his eyes wild and furious. 'It must have been the first time ever. But if what you say is true, then she's still got an Irishman's babby, and that's summat else we ain't likely to forgive.'

Marnie swallowed with difficulty. Her throat was so raw

358

and swollen she thought she must be near to dying.

'You're wrong again, brother,' she ground out. 'There's no baby and no Jenny any more. They're both *dead*. Some American priest wrote me a letter on Gabe's behalf a long while ago to say Jenny had died in childbed.'

She heard Peggy gasp, and saw a glimmer of compassion in her sister-in-law's eyes, but she didn't want a trollop's sympathy.

'He killed her!' Kenneth roared, after a moment's stunned silence while this new piece of news sank into his brain. 'The Irish shit-bag killed her!'

'Why won't you let things be?' Marnie sobbed, all the fight suddenly gone out of her. 'It all happened a long time ago, and nobody was to blame. These things happen . . .'

She realised Peggy had moved round the table and had her arm round her shoulders. She smelled of stale body sweat and stew, but it was the first time since coming to the fen cottage that anyone had shown the slightest bit of humanity towards her, and momentarily she stayed where she was without flinching away.

'Let her alone, Kenneth,' Peggy muttered. 'She's had enough.'

'Oh, that's rich, that is,' Kenneth's voice was suddenly taunting and vindictive. 'And aren't you going to put your spoke in on Mick O'Brien's behalf, my lovely whore-wife? Aren't you going to vouch for his performance in bed and in the hay and in the cellars of the Duck and Drake and anywhere else where he could get his cock in you? Go on, whore, tell us all what it's like, so we'll all know, and our Marnie will know what to expect when he lays her. Why not? The young 'un had a good poke at both my sisters, and now it looks as if my wife's lover is going to have his fill of this one. Are they devil-touched or something, wanting to keep it all in the family? Go on, *tell* her,' he goaded, 'are you struck dumb all of a sudden? You never tired of telling *me* what a fine . . .'

'Shut up!' Peggy screamed at him as Marnie leapt away from her as if she'd been stung. The colour drained from her face and her eyes dilated in horrified disbelief as Peggy sprang at Kenneth, pummelling against his chest, while the other brothers laughed coarsely, clearly used to such a performance.

'Why should I?' Kenneth suddenly twisted Peggy round so she had her back to him and was pinned there. Her scarlet face contorted with rage as his hands suddenly pushed down between the tight bodice and her flesh and began fondling her breasts. 'Go on, whore, tell my gawping sister how often her Mick's been down here, and how many time he's pleasured you, if you can count that much . . .'

Peggy suddenly bent her head and sank her teeth into one of his wrists. He hauled his hands out of her bodice with a howl of pain and slapped her face. Her nipples stood out like spikes, but she stood her ground and screamed at him.

'You bastard! There was no need for her to know! It's not true, Marnie, not for a long while anyway. I knew Mick once, and this one was always jealous of it, but it's been over a long time . . .'

Marnie's teeth were chattering again with the shock of discovery. She'd never thought Mick was innocent of women, but to learn that he'd been this slut's lover and that Kenneth knew of it and gloated on it, sickened her to her stomach.

Mick . . . since coming back from Drory she'd had a lot of time for thinking about those soft whispered words she'd heard against the nakedness of her skin on that night. She'd dreamed that Gabe had come to her in spirit, but the truth had gradually crystallised in her mind, and hadn't been as unwelcome as she'd expected. Because there had been a delight between them, even if she'd been only half-conscious at the time. She'd heard the words since . . . 'my lovely girl', and known them for Mick's words. Mick's voice, but now, the fragile love for him that had been growing slowly inside her all the months of knowing him, shattered and splintered into irretrievable fragments in a single moment. And she hated her brothers more than she'd known it was possible to hate, for making it so.

'Let me get out of here.' The words came slowly from her lips as if she was a child, labouring to learn them. 'I never want to see any of you again as long as I live.'

She twisted on her heels and pushed Ted out of the way, tore out of the cottage and into the moon-whitened fields with their strange, incandescent glow about them. She couldn't think coherently; couldn't breathe properly; couldn't see clearly through the blur of her eyes. She ran, heedless of where she was going, the sobs gathering in her throat, alone again. They were the only words that stabbed time and again into her brain. Alone again. Alone . . .

For she could never marry Mick now. There was too great a distance between them with the knowledge that he had been Peggy's lover. It humiliated her beyond anything she could have imagined, even Gabe's betrayal with her own sister, for in her saner moments she truly believed that she and Gabe shared a love that would remain untarnished no matter who came between them.

It was a strange kind of logic she could never attempt to explain, even to herself. It made no sense, even to her, nor why the knowledge of Mick's lusting with Peggy was so utterly degrading to her mind. Or was it simply a way out that her mind seized upon so readily?

Her footsteps gradually slowed, and the thudding of her heart lessened a little. She looked round her uncertainly, not realising how far she had run, and then she saw the ghostly grey shape of the old mill looming up alongside her, and her throat thickened. You can never go back, the thought whispered along her nerve-ends, but suddenly she *had* to go back, wanting to be where it all began, where an eager young girl with knowing eyes had laughed into Gabe O'Brien's searching blue ones as he discovered she had no drawers on.

As if it was part of a dream, she moved inside the old mill and up the rickety wooden ladder to the top platform, its top open to the weather, the hexagonal patch of velvet sky above. Her breath caught in her throat as the musty smells of earth and straw and decay sharpened her senses, tantalising them with bitter-sweet memories.

'Gabe,' she breathed his name in a long sigh. 'We should have waited until we were old enough to know what we were doing. We shouldn't have grabbed at the idea of making love as if it was a toy to play with. It's something too precious to waste on children, too beautiful to throw away as we did. If the chance to love ever came for us again . . .'

Her legs gave way beneath her and she sank down on the musty floor, the tears running unchecked down her bruised and swollen face. There'd be no other chance for them. They'd almost found it, one beautiful afternoon at the Pinnock farm, when he'd held her and loved her, and she'd begun to believe that dreams did come true. But it had only been fate playing with her, because so quickly afterwards she had lost him for ever, and Jenny had won.

Marnie curled up into a ball in the dankness of the mill, wanting the memories and the darkness to surround her, too weary to move any farther. She ached all over from her brothers' ill-treatment of her, and she had no wish to meet Geraldine Larksby's prying eyes that night. She'd be in trouble in the morning, but tomorrow was another day. She shut her eyes tightly with the tears still wet on her cheeks, and slept from sheer exhaustion.

She had no way of knowing how long she slept or what had woken her, but she was cramped and cold and shivering. She had to drag her senses together to remember she was in the old mill, and that the sky above was considerably lighter, though still not daylight. The thought that she was here alone didn't scare her, for there was nothing on the fens to make her afraid. But something prickled her skin all the same. Some sixth sense of danger, of disaster, of panic. Marnie scrambled to her feet, swaying dizzily with the sudden movement, and clattered back down the ladder.

Even before she reached the bottom, and the gap that

had once been a doorway, the stench of smoke was in her nostrils. There was a crackling like firecrackers sizzling on the early morning air, the sound carried across the flat plain of the fields. There was a weird red glow in the sky that was spasmodically brightened by great showering sparks leaping high towards the dawn-streaked heavens. And a great pall of grey smoke hanging above it all, as if it was a fire that had been going on a long time, consuming and devouring all that it touched. It was . . . it was . . .

'Oh God, *Mick*!' Marnie suddenly screamed out his name, all else forgotten, as the location of the blaze was imprinted in her brain. The Pinnock farm, Mick's farm; she gathered up her skirt and raced as fast as she could across the dew-fresh fields, her breath tortured and sobbing in her throat, her whole being suffused with a great fear, knowing instinctively who had been responsible for this terrible thing.

The pain in her side and her chest stabbed at her as she neared the Pinnock fields and the farmhouse, or what was left of it. Even from several fields away the heat was intense. She could see it shimmering on the grass and shrivelling the vegetation in its path. She could see the chain of men with buckets and pails and anything that would hold water, silhouetted like gaunt black shadows against the blaze. The barn was burning so furiously with its stacks of hay inside it hurt her eyes to look at it. The dairy was already a blackened hulk, steaming with water from the futile attempts that had been made to save it. The roof of the farmhouse was well ablaze, throwing down great burning sheaves of thatch every few minutes that sent the bucket brigade scattering, and shouting a warning to each other. And there was little left of the interior.

Marnie rushed towards the scene like a madwoman, searching for Mick. How could she have *slept* while all this was happening? While her brothers came here with murderous intent and fired the farmhouse, destroying all that Mick had worked for. The smoke was choking her, the black stinging smuts blinding her even as her furious tears washed them out, but where was Mick? She couldn't find him, and a new and terrible fear was clutching her.

'Come away, girl,' a smoke-grimed farmer she didn't know shouted out to her. 'You'll be hit with one of they burning torches from the roof if you get too near!'

'Clear off,' another one shouted angrily. 'This is no place for ghouls. There's sickening enough work to be done here while we search for the bodies.'

The scream was suddenly stifled in her throat as a broad country hand was clamped round her mouth, and her eyes swivelled in her head as the voice of Mrs Yard from the village shouted back angrily.

'Shut your noise, Jed, this here's the poor lad's intended, and she's every right to see what's left of her man if she's the stomach for it.'

'What do you mean, what's left of him?' the faintness sent her giddy for a minute as she took in Mrs Yard's meaning. She twisted away from the hand across her mouth, tasting the smoke that was left behind on her face.

'Where's Mick?' she sobbed hysterically. 'In God's name, Mrs Yard, tell me!'

'There, there, my lamb, he's feeling no more pain where he's gone,' the woman tried clumsily to soothe her. 'He and poor Tom Baker must have been sleeping in their beds when the fire started, and the flames spread so rapidly, they had no chance. The smoke would have choked them even before the fire charred them to cinders.'

Marnie shook convulsively. The woman had a vivid turn of phrase that whipped the scene instantly into her mind, the blackened, shrivelled bodies, the bones sticking through, the flesh burned away, oh God, no, no. She was screaming again and then she felt the sharp sting of a broad hand against her cheek. Was everyone in the world going to hit her until she was a senseless lump of jelly, she whimpered dazedly?

'Where is he?' Was that her voice, that hoarse thread of sound?

'You don't want to look at him, my lamb,' Mrs Yard said

364

sorrowfully. 'What good would it do? And he wouldn't want your last memory of him to be as he is now. Remember him for the strong handsome bor he was, I beg you. Come away with me, lovey, back to my cottage and take some brandy, for you're sore in need of something.'

'I should stay,' Marnie mumbled. 'I should be the one to order what's to be done. But I can't, I can't . . .'

'It's men's work, lovey. They'll see to it all, and there's nothing to be saved, however hard they work. My Jed will be back when they've stopped the last of the flames spreading, and he'll be able to tell us what's what.'

Marnie allowed herself to be led away, because there was nothing else she could do. She'd never felt so helpless. She was numb as Mrs Yard walked her woodenly towards the village and into a small cottage huddling against its neighbours in a cobbled street. She took the large glass of brandy that was offered in her shaking hands and forced the liquid down until it burned her throat.

'What a state you're in, my lamb,' Mrs Yard exclaimed once she took a good look at her. 'Your dress is all dirtied and your face all cut and bruised. But you'll mend, and what you need now is a bed and some sleep. Come you upstairs with me for what's left of the night, and try to blot out the things you've seen until you're rested and more able to think clearly.'

Still in the dreamlike state, Marnie was led to the one bedroom, where Mrs Yard told her to get right in the double bed and never mind a bit of dirt on the sheets, while she tucked her in, fussing over her like a mother hen. Like she'd always wanted Ma to fuss over her, Marnie thought, with a stinging in her throat.

She must have slept after the brandy, because she was suddenly awake and aware of the sound of low voices from below, Mrs Yard's and her husband's, the man called Jed.

'Nothing left of 'em, Missus. A real bad burning, and both of 'em likeable bors, for all that the boss was an Irishman. When we tried to lift 'em to take 'em for layin' out, they fell apart. Fair made your stomach turn, it did, and it'll take a deal of scrubbing before I get the smell of 'em off me hands.'

Oh Mick, Mick, have I brought you to this? A heap of blackened flesh and bone that crumbled without even the dignity of burial?

'Hush, Jed. The maid will be waking soon. Poor lamb, and her so soon to be wed. 'Tis her I'm sorry for now.'

'Aye,' Jed said heavily. ' 'Tis the living that bear the longest pain, when all's said and done.'

Marnie sat up in the double bed, and it creaked sufficiently for the voices to stop and for Mrs Yard to appear at the bedroom door to ask if she could eat some breakfast.

'I couldn't eat anything at all,' she mumbled, 'Just a drink of tea, for my throat's so parched. Thank you, Mrs Yard–for everything.'

'Away with you. It's no more than Mr O'Brien would want me to do, lovey.' For the first time the tough old face crumpled a little, and she turned away quickly and went back down the stairs.

An hour later Marnie was on her way back to Larksby, finding that the cottage and its embarrassed occupants were suddenly stifling her. In the village she could hear folk whispering as she passed, and first one and then another farm yokel tapped his forelock to her. It touched her so that she could barely keep from crying as she walked.

She didn't want to look at the farm again, but some compulsion drove her footsteps there, one last time. It was a blackened, smoking shell, silent as a tomb now all the helpers had gone wearily home. That was what it was, she thought bitterly. Mick's tomb, and Tom Baker's as well. Poor Tom. A fresh wave of hatred filled her mind as she thought of her brothers. Whatever their twisted minds had thought of the O'Briens, they had killed an innocent man as well.

She had no doubt that it was their hands that had set this fire, though Jed had made it plain it was being generally accepted as an accident. She could tell differently if she chose. She could point an accusing finger at the Bray brothers and stir up a hornet's nest and have a lynching mob out to the fen cottage in no time, but there was no proof, only the certainty inside her, and such vengeance would blacken her as much as them.

She had no stomach for any more vengeance. Someone had to call a halt to it all, and anyway, now Mick as well as Gabe was out of their reach for ever. Old Jed was right. It was the living that bore the longest pain, she thought, as she turned away from the remains of the farm. And hers was only just beginning, for she had never felt so alone in the whole of her life.

CHAPTER TWENTY-THREE

The news of the fire had reached Larksby long before Marnie arrived there, and she was obliged to listen to the sympathetic chatter of the kitchen staff before she could escape to her room to wash and change her 'stained and crumpled clothes, and try to compose herself. She stared at her wild, haunted eyes in the mirror and winced as she touched the bruises on her face with the face-cloth, feeling low enough to wish momentarily that she'd perished with Mick.

She was still applying the face-cloth very tenderly to her swollen cheeks when Geraldine appeared in her room without warning, and sat down heavily on her bed.

'Well now, this is a dreadful thing that's happened, Marnie,' she said awkwardly. 'And you look ghastly. I'll not say anything about your failing to return at the proper time last night in the circumstances, since I suppose you were with your young man, and neither of you could have foreseen that it would be for the last time.'

Marnie lowered her eyes. Let her think what she liked. Let anybody think the worst of her. It didn't matter. Nothing mattered any more. Mick was dead and she was still too stunned to believe it.

'Of course, you may stay on here now, Marnie. I don't mean to be so blunt at such a time, but it may ease your mind a little to know right away that I should prefer things to continue as before, now you won't be getting married.' She went pink with embarrassment. 'I'm not making a good job of saying all this, but I think we've got on tolerably well together all these years, and there's no question of my looking for someone else if you wish to stay. I'm very sorry about your fiancé, and if you feel you need a day or two at home with your family, I shall quite understand.'

'No!' Her voice was so sharp, Geraldine looked startled for a minute. 'My brothers and I don't get on–it's best that I keep away from them. I shall need a little time to see the priest and to attend the–the funeral–but apart from that, I'd rather be working. It'll stop me from thinking too much if my hands are kept busy.'

Her composure cracked a little and her mouth shook, and she knew it would take more than the daily round of Miss Geraldine's frivolous activities to take the horror of last night from her mind. But Geraldine nodded, obviously seeing herself in a new role as the saviour of her little maid's sanity.

'Then once that's all over, we shall go to King's Lynn again for a few days. I shall ask Papa to arrange it, and the change of air will do us both good before the Winter sets in.'

She moved towards the door, clearly pleased that she had thought of it, and told Marnie she could go to see the priest that afternoon if she wished, as she would be going visiting with her father and would have no need of her once she was dressed after lunch. She swished out of the room and left Marnie alone.

There had been a lot of compassion in her voice, Marnie acknowledged, and she'd sounded more like the old Geraldine, before she'd become so vinegary. But Marnie herself was becoming more cynical, and she'd recognised the tinge of relief in Geraldine as well, because she wasn't losing her maid after all, and things would carry on as they had done before. At least, they would for *her* . . .

Marnie's face crumpled, knowing she was going to miss Mick. Even if there had been no earth-shaking love between them, at least not on her part, there had been a deep, growing affection, and oh yes, she was going to miss him. He'd been hers and he'd wanted her, and now there was no-one in the whole world who did. It was a desolate thought, and hardly knowing how she got there, she found herself prostrate on the bed in an agony of weeping. For Mick; for herself; for

Jenny and for Gabe; for all the twists of fate that had shaped their lives and left her the lonely one.

Finally she washed her face all over again and swallowed resolutely. There were things to be done . . . her senses balked at the idea of telling Maureen and Jack, but the letter had to be written, and as calmly and unemotionally as possible. She had to be the strong one, calling on reserves of strength she didn't know she had. And Gabe, should she try to contact Gabe?

Her strength didn't go as far as that. It would be impossible to try to put the right words on paper to Gabe, without becoming unbearably maudlin. In the end she wrote a restrained little note to the American priest who'd informed her about Jenny's death, asking him to relay the information about Mick. She could do no more.

It took all her time and mental energy to compose the letters, but before she could go to the village to see the local priest, he'd arrived at Larksby to see her. And she found herself in the unusual position of receiving a visitor in the Larksby drawing-room, at Geraldine's insistence, and having to listen to platitudes and the long-drawn-out sentences such people seemed to find so essential at times of bereavement, as if such intoning helped to lessen the sharpness of loss. Perhaps it did if one was a devout believer.

'I've spoken to Mrs Yard and learned all the details of this dreadful thing, my dear, so there's no need to distress yourself by telling me more,' he said. 'If you wish to leave everything in my hands, I'll see to everything for you.'

'Thank you,' Marnie said. 'I would be very grateful . . .'

'There'll be other matters beside the immediate mournful ones to attend to,' the priest went on delicately. 'Mr O'Brien's financial situation—a bank in King's Lynn, I believe? Most of the farmers in the district have their business dealings there. If you wish me to ascertain with them any arrangements he may have made . . .'

Marnie felt hot with embarrassment. Was he enquiring about payment for his services? She knew nothing of such things, and the thought of discussing fees at such a time was making her slightly hysterical.

'Please do whatever needs to be done,' she said quickly.

The priest nodded, and she was glad when he finally left the house. She sat quite still, hands clenched in her lap, eyes closed, hoping the tension in her body was eventually going to relax. She'd had a horrible choking feeling at seeing the priest.

The next time she'd expected to see him had been as a bride. Now, she wasn't even a widow. She was nothing, exactly as she'd been before, and yet completely different. Bereft without the dignity of widowhood, but mourning Mick as deeply as if she'd actually been his wife. In some strange way, she felt closer to him now than she ever had while he'd lived, and a shuddering surge of guilt ran through her, remembering how she'd clutched at Kenneth's revelations last night as being a last-straw way out from marrying Mick at all–but she wasn't going to think about that. None of it mattered any more, and she still had a job to do that afternoon. She had to walk to the village and post the letters she'd written so painstakingly.

The day was soft and warm, as if to compensate for the horror of last night. There was no smell of burning to sour the air, no breeze to waft the bitterness of it into mouth and eyes and lungs.

She would never forget completely . . . deep down she would always hate her brothers for what they'd done, but she was so weary of hatred and the knowledge of what it could do. There was no way Mick could ever return and in some strange way the softness of this balmy afternoon had tempered her grief a little and sent a trace of warmth into her soul, reminding her that there was still something good to be found beneath the sun.

The brief death-wish she'd felt when she'd faced the stark fact of a future alone, was ebbing away from her. She was young and she was alive, and even if she didn't fully understand her reasons for feeling as she did, Marnie was aware of the strength returning to her limbs with every step she took towards the village. So that she was able to knock at Mrs Yard's cottage door and inform her quite steadily that the funeral for Mick and Tom Baker would be in three days' time, and she hoped Mrs Yard and Jed would sit with her in the front pew.

'We'll be proud to, my lamb,' the countrywoman's face was ruddier than usual, and Marnie guessed that she'd been crying. 'Will you come in and take some tea and cake and sit awhile? There's an old friend of yours inside who's been visiting with me today, and we've been talking about you and your poor man, so it's a wonder your ears haven't been burning all afternoon.'

An old friend of hers? Marnie frowned. She had no friends, unless it was Sal, her old kitchen ally. She went inside the tiny cottage with Mrs Yard and stopped short at the sight of the bent old woman supping tea by the fireside.

'Mrs Kettle! It's a long time since I've seen you!'

The farmer's wife's eyes were as watery as Mrs Yard's, her face as apple-cheeked.

'Aye, it's a long time since you came a-visiting, Marnie,' she agreed. 'And now to see you on such a sad occasion, it fair tears my heart in two. Such lovely girls, you little Bray lassies were, and for one of you to know such grief as this!'

Marnie bit her lip to keep it steady. What would Mrs Kettle say if she knew the truth of it–about Jenny and the baby, and of Marnie's own hand in unknowingly shaping the destiny of her sister and the two Irish brothers?

Mrs Yard was urging her to sit down and pushing a plate of seed cake towards her while she poured some tea. And the chatter between them flowed back and forth until the words droned and merged into a hazy background noise in Marnie's head, and the only clear thing was the memory of a conversation she and Mrs Kettle had once had. The echoes of it were so strong in her mind, and the voice she remembered as Mrs Kettle's was stronger and more mysterious and deliciously shivery to a gullible little twelve-year-old on the brink of discovery . . .

'. . . You're sometimes pulled in two directions and have

372

to decide for yourself which way you want to go in life : . . . part of you wants one thing and the rest of you wants another . . . I'd have laid odds you were born at the time of the full moon . . .'

Marnie took a sudden gulp of tea as the two old women clucked and sympathised over Mick and the unfortunate Tom Baker, but Marnie's thoughts were away in another dimension, another time.

'. . . you mark my words, lovey,' Mrs Kettle's voice had lowered and thickened and enthralled her, 'because all the important things in your life will occur at such times. You're a real moon child and no mistake, headstrong and wayward, and sometimes as cold and remote as that great big ball in the night sky, but always with the capacity to bring light and joy into somebody's life . . .'

The words were as sharp and clear as if Mrs Kettle was saying them now. Marnie glanced to where she was taking another piece of cake and telling Mrs Yard how good it was and she must have the recipe before she went home and the two of them were somehow blurred at the edges, their voices muffled, as if this was the dream-world, and she was in reality an eager bright-eyed twelve-year-old with a way about her that was far beyond her years.

Moon child. Moon child. In the fantasy world of her own imagining she had managed to overlook the one essential word in Mrs Kettle's monologue. The full impact of it was only just seeping into her mind. She'd gazed at the moon riding high in the heavens and seen it as a benevolent father figure, smiling down at her, looking after her, she'd expected everything to be marvellous when the moon was full, but Mrs Kettle had said all the *important* things in her life would occur at such times. Not that they'd all be *good*.

And there had certainly been bad times, such as the night she'd opened up Jenny's letter and learned the truth about the father of her baby, and all her worst nightmares had begun. She'd been too much of a romantic at twelve years old to listen properly to all Mrs Kettle had told her, only picking out the pretty bits that appealed to her, like plucking petals from a daisy and discarding the stem.

'Are you all right, my lamb?' Mrs Yard's face loomed in front of her. 'You're very pale and quiet.'

'Oh yes,' she said quickly. 'Just listening, that's all.'

And planning on bringing that special characteristic she was supposed to have into being–to be cold and remote and detached when she did the things she still had to do for Mick, because it suddenly seemed the only way she could bear it. There'd been a time for passion in her life, once it had been all she lived for, wanting Gabe so badly and loving him so much . . . there'd been a time when love had begun to grow inside her again, for Mick, but now there was nothing left in her to give, and it would be easier if she put the brittle shell around her that shielded her from hurt, and forgot all about the Marnie who could be warm and loving and passionate. She said goodbye to that girl right there and then in Mrs Yard's tiny cottage, and knew she'd be better able to face the ordeal of the funeral with head held high and eyes undimmed by tears. She'd done all her crying for the O'Brien brothers.

Her resolve faltered a little when the priest came to see her again a week after the funeral. Again, Geraldine allowed him to sit with Marnie in the drawing-room, and it felt as uncomfortable for her as the first time. They were to leave for King's Lynn the following day, and Geraldine left the two of them together while she continued sorting out her clothes for Marnie to pack.

'I've been to the bank in King's Lynn, Miss Bray,' the priest told her. 'It seems Mr O'Brien had already made over a sum of money into an account in your name which was intended as a wedding gift, so you are at liberty to draw on it whenever you wish. I understand there was no will, so the residue of his estate will go to his next of kin in due course. Do you know if he has any living relatives?'

'He has a sister,' Marnie found it difficult to speak. She was overwhelmed at the news that Mick had done this for her. 'I have her address if you want it.'

'It would be best if you called at the bank yourself if you

can face it, my dear. They'll want to know full details, and you will naturally want to know what funds are available to you. Sad though the circumstances are, the Lord has strange ways of providing for His flock.'

By burning Mick to a frazzle? God surely couldn't have wanted that to happen just so she would have a few pounds!

'I will call at the bank while I am in King's Lynn with Miss Larksby,' she murmured. 'I have already informed Mr O'Brien's sister about the–the accident, of course, and I am only sorry they were unable to attend the funeral. She has a husband, and four little children . . .'

She swallowed, because the answering letter she'd had from Maureen had been an hysterical outpouring of grief. Marnie had been able to read it only once and then thrust it to the back of a drawer. It had almost been like listening to both Gabe and Mick talking in one of their own impassioned outbursts to read Maureen's letter.

But it was right that whatever money Mick had to leave should be going to his sister, and she was touched that he'd been so considerate on her own behalf. It had been intended as a wedding gift, but now it would give her a small feeling of independence. She discovered at the bank in King's Lynn that it was a modest sum, but even so it was more money than she'd owned before, and somehow that fact alone enabled her to hold her head up high.

Geraldine too was treating her more carefully than of late, as if fully aware of the brittle facade that was likely to shatter at any moment. And the two of them got on tolerably well for the ten days they were at King's Lynn, which did much to restore the delicate balance of their relationship, decidedly shaky at times.

Marnie tried to assure herself this was all she wanted now–a calm, orderly existence, with no men in her life to quicken her blood or stir her senses. And if there was a feeling of guilt inside her at knowing she didn't after all grieve as deeply for Mick as people assumed, she chose to ignore it and to tell herself she'd given him as much love as she'd been able while he lived, and he'd had no cause for complaint, or suspicion that her love wasn't the utmost of which she was capable.

'I think we must take this kind of little holiday more often,' Geraldine told her as they strolled along the promenade on their last morning. 'The sea air suits us both and we are both more relaxed than when we came. I was quite worried about you after your terrible shock, you know, but it's good to see the colour back in your cheeks again. One can't go on mourning for ever.'

Marnie was tempted to say that as it was less than a month since Mick had died, surely she was entitled to a short period of mourning? But the guilty feelings inside her reminded her that she'd mourned the loss of Gabe far longer, and there seemed something so badly wrong about that, it was best not to try to analyse it too much.

But she knew she wasn't mourning Mick the way people would expect a prospective bride to mourn. It shocked her to know it, but she had always been scrupulously honest with herself, and she was more certain than she had ever been of anything that it would have been wrong to marry Mick. No, the grief, if anything, was for the utter waste of a good man, and the knowledge that she had been instrumental in procuring his death through her brothers' violence.

They arrived back at Larksby to a great to-do. The Colonel had been taken ill and the doctor was in attendance. And late that afternoon Geraldine rang the bell furiously for Marnie to come to her room at once. She was ashen, and Marnie felt a surge of alarm.

'My father is very ill,' Geraldine said at once. 'The doctor has been quite blunt with me and tells me he does not expect him to last more than a month. I have written to my brother to inform him and his wife, and you are to take the letter to the village at once.'

Her voice was agitated, and it was obvious that the doctor had been brutally honest. Marnie licked her suddenly dry lips.

'Will your brother get to England in time to see his father?'

'He *will* come,' Geraldine snapped. 'It's always been understood that when my father dies, Darryl will come home to run the estate. He'll come to stay this time, he and Suzanne. Larksby will be under her control then, so we'll all have to mind our p's and q's while she gets used to playing the gracious lady.'

And Geraldine wasn't going to like that at all, Marnie knew instantly. But that was the least of her concerns. The most enormous one was the fact that Darryl Larksby would be coming back to stay, and it was enough to set her stomach churning, remembering the last time he'd visited her room and she'd outraged his dignity so painfully.

'Well, go on, you ninny. If you don't hurry and get the letter in the post, Papa will be dead and buried before they get to hear he's ill!'

Oh, but it was a temptation! If she didn't post the letter . . . or the next one, or the next . . . maybe he'd never come home. But she was too well-trained in a servant's duties to think seriously of destroying her mistress' letter, and too frightened of the consequences if such an action were ever found out.

But it seemed as if she was sealing her own fate as she hurried to the village, for to be at the mercy of Darryl Larksby again was worse than death as far as Marnie was concerned. Once he was the Master here he'd take no notice of her threats to tell his wife of his perversions, for every one of them would be dependent on his generosity to exist. He'd control them all.

The Colonel had always commanded and got every loyalty from his servants, she thought. How many would feel the same towards Darryl? How many would even stay on when he was Master and ruled roughshod over the house? There'd be those who sought other employment, she guessed. Her footsteps slowed. Well, why shouldn't she do the same? She didn't have to stay, and if Mick hadn't died she'd have left anyway, and been mistress of the Pinnock Farm by now.

She owed it to Miss Geraldine to stay at least until the

worst happened, she reminded herself: She'd need supporting, but afterwards . . . when Darryl took charge, she'd think of her own future. She walked more resolutely, knowing she'd come to some kind of decision, however hazy, but the idea of just where to go and what to do eluded her completely and she didn't even attempt to think of it.

Geraldine seemed totally shaken by the news about her father, as if she'd expected him to live for ever. It surprised Marnie to see the extent of her anxiety, though she knew illness in general upset the other girl. And as the days went on, Geraldine's distress became more evident every time she came out of her father's room to seek out her maid.

'It's the smell!' She spoke through pinched white lips and tried not to gag. 'They call it the death smell, I'm told. I try not to breathe when I go in the room, but he pulls me down to him when he tries to talk, and it all but stifles me.'

'Can you not put some perfume on a handkerchief and hold it to your nose?'

'I'll try it next time. Or some smelling-salts. Anything! If it gets much worse I shall faint as soon as I go into the room. The doctor has forbidden us to open the windows for fear of the cold getting to his chest. Be glad you're not obliged to wait on him, Marnie.'

But she didn't need to go in to know what Geraldine meant. The smell exuded from the vicinity of the sickroom like an evil pall. It clung to Geraldine's clothes and permeated the air they breathed. It was impossible to be unaware of it, and when the Colonel had been near to death for close on three weeks, his son came striding into the house cursing and shouting at the appalling stench everywhere.

'Be quiet!' Geraldine ran to shake his arm, while his wife stood in silent embarrassment at such an exhibition as soon as they arrived. 'The doctor insists on the windows being kept shut. I know it's dreadful, but don't let Papa hear you. He is quite unaware of it himself, and the end can't be long now.'

'A good thing too, if we have to live in this stink,' Darryl

378

grunted. 'Suzanne can't stand much of it in her condition. I thought women were supposed to blossom in pregnancy, but this one's wilting by the hour.'

His voice was scathing, and impending fatherhood had clearly not improved his manners. Nor the news about his father, with whom there had never been much rapport.

Marnie averted her eyes from Darryl's sweeping glance over her figure as she went to offer his wife some assistance at Geraldine's bidding. The poor thing looked horribly sickly, and Marnie guessed that any marital contact between them had long since stopped. She shivered at the thought, knowing Darryl would be seeking his pleasures elsewhere if it was denied him at home, and the fact that his father was dying would not deter him one bit. She was thankful when he left the little group to see his father right away. He was gone ten minutes, and was visibly shaken when he returned.

'My God, the man's raving!' He helped himself to a large drink of whisky, his hands unsteady. 'How long has he been like this?'

'Only two days,' Geraldine told him. 'The doctor warned me it would happen. It's a pattern the illness follows. He says he'll gradually quieten until he slips into unconsciousness, and then the end will follow.'

'Is he some bloody clairvoyant then?' Darryl snapped. His hands jerked on the glass and some of the contents slopped.

'Darryl, may I please go to bed? The journey has exhausted me.' Suzanne's thin voice was apologetic, and Darryl looked at her with indifference as he nodded. Geraldine spoke quickly to cover her brother's ill manners.

'Marnie, will you attend Mrs Larksby, please? You know which room hàs been made ready for her and my brother.'

Suzanne rose gratefully and leaned on Marnie's arm as she escorted her slowly up the long staircase to the room put at their disposal. As she helped Suzanne out of her clothes and tried not to notice her gently swelling body, Marnie was irresistibly curious as to how these two unlikely partners behaved in bed. She guessed that Suzanne would have been terrifed at first, and then completely subservient no matter what his demands. And a completely subservient wife would soon bore him.

Suzanne gave a small sigh as she lay, limp and colourless beneath the bedcovers.

'Thank you, Marnie. I shall sleep the clock round now.' Her eyes were already drooping as Marnie left the room.

Darryl was outside in the corridor. She tried to sidestep him, but his hand shot out and caught her by the wrist.

'Not so fast, my beauty,' he muttered. 'Can a man not ask after his wife?'

'She's quite well,' Marnie kept her voice distant. 'She needs sleep, that's all.'

'Good.' His mouth leered at her. 'Then let's hope she sleeps soundly every night, for you and I have some unfinished business to attend to, don't we?'

She was suddenly enraged. 'Have you forgotten that your father is dying?' she hissed.

His free hand reached out and slid over her breast. He laughed softly as he felt the instinctive response.

'I haven't forgotten, and don't you forget who'll be Master here when he's gone. I've nothing to thank him for but that, but by God, I'll enjoy my inheritance when it's finally mine!'

He squeezed her soft flesh under the fabric of her dress and she twisted away, wrenching her wrist free of his clamped hand. She could hear the breath ragged in her throat. It was exactly as she had feared, and it would be impossible for her to stay. She had to get away from here. Not when the Colonel died, or when Geraldine had found someone to replace her, but now, tonight, for the fear was bubbling up inside her like a cauldron, and she wouldn't stay under the same roof as Darryl Larksby for one more night.

She sped to her own room, knowing Geraldine would have no more need of her now until bedtime. And by then she'd be gone. Marnie clenched her hands at her sides and

380

felt the stinging tears in her eyes. Where would she go? There was no-one and nowhere in the world where she could flee to. Gabe was on the other side of the world and didn't want her anyway; Mick was dead; her family–her jaw tightened at the thought of her family–there was nowhere. Unless, a small feeling of warmth seeped through the coldness of her limbs, and she set about pushing everything she owned into her travelling bag.

Then she drew out some writing paper and wrote a carefully worded letter to Geraldine, explaining as delicately as possible why it was so necessary for her to leave. Why she *couldn't* stay any longer, partly because of the new regime that would exist when Darryl became Master, partly because there were too many memories around the fen country and she'd decided it was more than she could do to try to live with them.

She begged Geraldine not to think too badly of her for taking this way out, and at such a time, but it seemed the only way. And should there be any reason for contacting her in the future, she referred Geraldine to the bank in King's Lynn. It was highly unlikely, of course, unless one of her brothers died, and even then no-one would be interested enough to want to inform her. She sealed the letter slowly, slipping it on to Geraldine's pillow beneath the bedcover where she couldn't fail to see it.

She waited until everyone was at dinner and then left her room for the last time, feeling strange and unreal as she did so, for Larksby had been her home for a very long time. Her heart thumped sickly in her chest as she held her travelling bag tightly and moved quietly out of the grounds under cover of the trees and the darkness, and made her way towards the village. Towards Mrs Yard's cottage and sanctuary, knowing she'd get a welcome for the night with no questions asked. And in the morning . . .

Marnie stumbled slightly over a rut in the road and stepped out into the clear grey path lit by moonlight. Her eyes were drawn involuntarily towards the great yellow ball above, and her jaw ached with the effort of being determined not to cry.

'Is this one of the important times of my life?' she mouthed at it silently. 'It feels more like running away . . .'

Or running *towards*. She was suddenly too weary to analyse her actions. She just knew there was only one place on earth she had to be. Tonight she would sleep on a hard chair at Mrs Yard's, and tomorrow she would go to King's Lynn and remove all the money Mick had left her. And then she would seek out a coach to take her to a boat bound for Ireland. And soon, very soon, she would be in Drory.

CHAPTER TWENTY-FOUR

Two years as a soldier had toughened Gabe considerably, though he'd long since decided there must be an odd quirk in his nature that made him more squeamish about the wounded horses that bloodied the battlefields than about his fellow-men. It could be, of course, that since Cal's murder nothing was ever going to touch him so deeply again. He'd got used to the sight of men crawling out of the line of Confederate fire with half their legs torn away or their guts falling out. And used to the sounds of screaming and moaning from the hospital tents that carried so ghoulishly on the night air. He'd grown used to sights and sounds that would once have had him retching . . .

'Come on, boy, we're on the move,' Deeker hauled himself to his feet from the dusty ground, coughing and spitting into the dryness. It invaded eyes and lungs and turned their voices into hoarse rasps. 'Goddamned country's gettin' hotter by the minute.'

'You want to tell 'em next time to fix their battles for some time other than mid-summer,' Gabe grunted in agreement. 'I wonder how Brad's liking it? Heat never seemed to bother him.'

Deeker grimaced. 'Got it made, that one. Away from all these stinking bodies and discipline and off on his own.'

'Would you change places with him then? I wouldn't be a scout if they paid me ten times as much.'

'Brad'll survive. He's part Indian, ain't he? What he don't know about stalking and hunting ain't worth knowing. That's why they picked him for the job. They'll turn their noses up as soon as they get the sniff of an Indian, but when he's going to be useful, he's the greatest thing that ever lived,' Deeker said derisively.

They plodded along the dusty road together, jostled and sweating by the troopers moving alongside them, all of them clanking and cussing as they tried to move their artillery and personal belongings into a less uncomfortable position. The road to Gettysburg was hot and dry and heat-hazed, and they longed for the comparative coolness of the woods ahead towards which their unit was making steady progress. One day's battle was behind the Union troops, and victory had gone to the South, but they weren't finished yet, and Gabe's unit had been ordered to Cemetery Ridge. He'd hoped it wasn't a prophetic place in which to await the next attack from Lee's rebs.

But once positioned, it seemed to be another day of waiting, and the morning dragged by interminably while their throats became more parched and their eyes were gritty and strained from the effort of trying to ascertain the slightest movement in the enemy flank.

Looking down from their vantage position, Gabe could see farm buildings dotted among ploughed fields and meadows, once rich with grass and grain, but already flattened. It reminded him depressingly of the way the potato famine had swept through the crops in Ireland with devastating suddenness.

'There are too many of them.' Deeker eased his aching joints and peered through the screen of chestnut- oaks, his voice scratchy. 'They're circling us, ready for the kill . . .'

'How can you know that? You can't see any better than me,' Gabe strained his eyes across the plain below, searching for the movement of grey reb uniforms that merged all too easily into the heat-haze.

'I don't need to see 'em. I can feel 'em and I can smell 'em,' Deeker grunted. 'They'll be coming in on the trains, and we're gonna need everything we got to hold 'em, boy.'

Gabe ran his tongue round his cracked lips. The acceptance of death at a reb soldier's hands had left him way back, and he had no wish to end his days spiked on the end of a Southern bayonet like Cal. And by the time the battle burst into being late that afternoon he was in as murderous a mood as the rest of them. It was a case of kill or be killed, and he was no longer the raw recruit who'd signed on the dotted line in a rush of drunken patriotism with his buddies. He was a professional killer, and it was with all the know-how of previous battles that he and Deeker surged down Cemetery Ridge with their comrades.

By the time the air was acrid and yellow with gunpowder and their senses rocked with the blast of cannon and the whistle of shot zinging past their ears, they were caught up in the blaze of battle. Noise all around them was a tangible thing, pulsating and living, and the fields were soon running red as Union and rebel soldiers mingled in desperate eyeball to eyeball combat. Somehow the two of them managed to stay close. They were a team. They supported each other.

'Get the bastards,' Deeker yelled as three rebs hurtled towards them, and this time there was no holding back on Gabe's part as there had been at Bull Run. He wore a dark blue uniform and he marched behind the Union flag, and he did whatever was asked of him. He no longer saw the faces of the rebs, only the grey uniforms that were the enemy. But by the time they crawled away towards the Ridge when the fighting cooled, the smell of blood wafting all around them was beginning to sicken the strongest stomachs, and the only way to avoid it was to bury your nose in any damp clump of foliage to be found. It was a stinking war and at dawn on the following day, July 3rd, it flared up again.

'Bloody hell!' Deeker roared, as the crack of gunfire shattered the fragile early morning peace. 'Are we to get no rest from the devils? Let's get at 'em, boys, and finish the bastards off once and for all, before we're just picked off like a lot of flies.'

His mood was echoed by the rest of the Union troops, and the orders were given to attack. The battle raged on all day in sweltering heat, with a concentrated artillery attack from the rebs when the day was at its hottest, around 1 am. Retaliating as fast as guns could be swabbed and loaded, the Union soldiers fought on, but the rebs slowly gained control, and it was obvious they smelled victory—and then came new tactics from the Union commanding officers.

'Orders from Hunt,' the ripple ran through the ranks where Gabe and Deeker knelt shoulder to shoulder in the dust. 'Hold your fire for an onslaught. We're out to get the buggers, so let 'em think we're out of ammunition and draw them out into the open.'

'Will it work?' Gabe grunted.

'It'll work.' Deeker nodded towards the cover of the woods behind which the enemy lay. 'They'll think they've got us, and once out in the open, they'll be ours. Hunt knows his business.'

It was eerily quiet after the noise of battle, but the onslaught, when it came, was so overpowering it stunned the senses. The first rebel wave surged towards the Emmitsburg Road, clearly jubilant behind their flag and assuming the battle was won. When they were just five hundred yards from the Union lines, they were suddenly blasted with solid-shot and shells, and were thrown into complete confusion at being within short range as the Union troops poured down the hill to the attack, unprepared for such opposition, fighting for their lives with bayonet and clubbed musket, with hands and fists and boots.

And now the Union soldiers were soaring to victory . . . they had them. Gabe felt suddenly as if he and Deeker held the whole of the Ridge between the two of them. They couldn't lose. The smell of victory was now theirs and it was very sweet. The rebs were falling back, they followed relentlessly, stumbling over bloated bodies several days dead and stinking in the heat, and not noticing; ignoring the wounded, groaning, hands clutching the air in a futile need, for there was no time to stop or look or help. The battle was the only thing that mattered and victory the only stopping-place. The field was crimson with blood and it would take days of rain to wash it into the parched earth and to get rid of the stench, but they smelled nothing of it,

386

only the scent of victory.

Gabe and Deeker surged on with a small group from their unit, yelling and firing and stabbing at anything that came within range, into the smoke-hung dip of a small gulley, and there they were brought up short as a pocket of reb soldiers reared up in front of them with guns blazing.

'Get them!' Gabe screamed. 'Before they get us!'

He threw himself at the nearest reb and heard the crack of his jaw as his gun crashed up under his chin. The reb dropped like a stone. But sweet Jesus, there were too many of them . . . and there were several loose horses appearing from nowhere in the gulley, frightened and whinnying, their eyes rolling, coats glistening with sweat, froth dropping from their mouths. They were all in danger of being trampled to death on top of everything else . . . the horses were pushing together, hooves lashing out in terror at the noise enveloping them. And Deeker was suddenly on the ground between them . . .

'Move out, Deek,' Gabe bellowed. He lunged forward and kicked him so that he rolled farther down the gulley out of the way of the flailing hooves. The rebs had begun to close in again, but there were enough Union men to hold them and, anyway, Gabe was too concerned with the loose horses at that moment to worry about anything else. They were in danger of becoming maddened, and if they ran amok they'd easily stampede all the other animals in the vicinity and there'd be even more bloodshed. He hauled at the two bridles, attempting to keep them under control, talking as soothingly as he could against the background noise. The terror in the horses' eyes was transmitting itself to him, and his tongue felt twice its normal size and stuck to the roof of his mouth. Deeker could see what he was about and yelled at him to stay with it as they nearly had the reb bastards now, and they didn't need to be pulverised by a pair of rogue stallions in the process.

But there was no hope of completely stilling the animals. He could only grip their bridles and talk as calmly as possible, and see the foam gradually stop dripping from their mouths, the blowing of their cheeks lessen, the rolling of their eyes slow up, and know that at least he'd stopped a few of his buddies being killed by enemy horses if not by the enemy.

The incongruous thought swept through his head that his brother Mick had always said he had a way with horses. Even as he thought it there was a sudden deafening burst of shellfire in the gulley, and a bright yellow flash right in front of his eyes that blinded him and had the horses instantly panic-stricken again. So much so that they surged together with Gabe between them until he felt the sudden crushing of his bones and the vomit spewing out of him, and the sickening sensation of being squeezed into an ever-diminishing space.

The first thing he was conscious of when he awoke was the utter silence. His ears had got so used to being assaulted by noise his nerves jumped from the very strangeness of it. That and the darkness.

He seemed to be cocooned in a world of blackness that was occasionally stabbed by a bright flash of light that hurt his eyes and his whole nervous system and sent great tingling sensations searing through him. He discovered he was cocooned in more than darkness, after what seemed an interminably long attempt to move any part of himself. He appeared to be bound from head to foot and he could neither see nor hear any human sound.

Sheer panic engulfed him. Was he lying shroud-wrapped ready for burying, while nobody realised he still lived and breathed, if that was what this hell was? Or was he already dead? Was this the transition period between this world and the next when you were supposed to see all your past life passing before your eyes and repent all your sins?

He saw nothing but the jazzing blackness in front of him, but if he couldn't see, he could feel. And what he felt was every little splintering part of him, a throbbing mass of pain so that he couldn't tell where one pain ended and the next began. He felt as if he was disintegrating, bit by

388

agonising bit. He tried to force the gagging panic down. And to try and analyse things more clearly.

Was he blind? And mute? The sounds he tried to make got no farther than his throat, even though he felt as if he was shouting. Jesus, he was going to die, and he didn't want to die! God knew how low he'd sunk in his lifetime, and surely God wouldn't want such a low bastard? Not without giving him the chance to make some amends, but amends for what? The evil in him was merely a jumble in his mind, and the pictures of his past wouldn't appear. Had there been a girl who'd needed him and clung to him as he tried to do what was right by her?

And had it all turned sour on him? The girl–he couldn't even remember her name, but somehow he remembered the way she'd clung to him, suffocating him with her need. And he remembered a tiny, innocent child who'd almost opened her eyes and looked at him and he'd wanted so desperately to will some life into her frozen little body.

'Marnie,' the croaking sound escaped his lips. 'Marnie, forgive me . . .'

The stabbing lights were hurting his eyes now, and suddenly he was aware that he was no longer alone and floating somewhere in space. There were other sounds, human voices, the pad of footsteps on a floor, the smell of human bodies, the touch of another hand on his. He could have wept if there had been room between the bandages and his eyes.

'All right soldier, keep quite still and don't try to talk,' a male voice spoke calmly right beside his ear. 'You're in bad shape, but we're going to patch you up as long as you co-operate. That was quite some trick you did back there in the gulley, holding off those horses before they trampled the lot of you to death. I reckon you'll be getting a citation for bravery before you're done, and that'll be something to show the folks back home, won't it?'

Folks? He had no folks. He had no-one. But he couldn't get the words out to tell the orderly so, even though he discovered that the bandages on his head only covered his eyes and skull after all, when a feeding cup was inserted gently into his mouth and he felt the cool trickle of water dribbling down his parched throat. Only to gasp with shock when it reached his belly in a red-hot, searing pain.

'Hold on, soldier. Not too fast,' the voice was close to his ear again, and he realised he was threshing on the bed. But at least he could move! He wasn't paralysed and he could still feel his fingers and toes . . . or was that an illusion? He'd heard enough tales of men who'd lost limbs and still felt the phantom pains of wounds long since removed for ever.

Jesus, what was there left of him? Would he open his eyes when the bandages were removed and see a mere carcass of a man? A trunk without branches, a vegetable without feeling? Ah, but there *was* feeling. Sweet Jesus, there was pain, so much pain, and the sharp sting of a needle somewhere on his body that he was too confused to distinguish.

He so wanted to ask about his injuries, but he was too afraid. And anyway, the chance was slipping away from him, and his senses were swimming again. The images he'd tried to conjure up were blurring, and the voice at his side was becoming a thick buzz of sound, the words no longer distinct. He felt as if he was suddenly receding from everything that was real, spinning backwards into an endless vortex of nightmare proportions, assaulted on every side by the shattered remnants of men who'd gone before him so that he was still threshing in his mind, fighting off the horrors of dismembered bodies, and eyes that searched hopelessly for a face and clawing hands that were tipped with blood and groped at him for assistance.

Jesus, let me die, the need of it implored and screamed inside him through the nightmare. Death surely couldn't be worse than this. It was a horrendous experience from which there was no awakening until the effects of the drug wore off, and with each stabbing of the needle into his body it began all over again.

But there were lucid moments in the confusion of his

390

mind. Moments when he was aware of being lifted from the bed on which he lay and transported to some other place on a moving trolley. He was vaguely aware of murmuring voices and more needles and the sweet sickly smell of chloroform permeating the air and dulling his senses. Of returning to consciousness to more pain, differently distributed, to feeling more needles, to the reassurance of more voices, to becoming used to the smells that were all around him including the nauseating smell of burned flesh that frequently met his nostrils, the horror of hearing a grown man suddenly scream in agony, the humiliation of knowing the sound came from his own throat. And always the darkness.

How long he stayed in his half-world he could not judge. He became attached to the faceless voice that he heard most frequently, that spoke encouragingly in his ear from time to time. He grew to know the feel of the man's hand gripping his own, and holding the spoon for him to eat until it was as familiar as his Mammy's had been. It had the same effect on him. He was a child again, trying to learn the things that had once been so simple, and were now like trying to scale a mountain. And he felt he was in danger of becoming a gibbering idiot on the day the bandages over his eyes were finally removed, and the clamouring fear that was in him became a reality as he saw only blurred grey shapes swirling in front of him.

'Don't expect miracles all at once, soldier,' the voice was urgent, deliberate, knowing his panic. 'It'll come. Just give it time, and you've got plenty of that.'

His mouth suddenly worked convulsively, though it seemed a hundred years since he'd used it for anything other than babbling nonsense.

'Gabe,' it was a mere whisper of sound in his throat. 'I'm–called–Gabe.'

'I know you are, buddy. We've got your papers and we know all about you. But it was important that you should remember it yourself. And now you have. That's real progress, that is.'

Gabe tried to focus through the swirling grey mass in front of him as he heard the cheerful note in the orderly's voice. Progress? To remember his own name? It was about the one sensible thought in the maze of his mind and he clung on to it as if it was a lifeline. Gabe. Gabe. Gabe. Gabe O'Brien. He was a genius! He knew his own name!

The sudden hot tears gushed down his face and he couldn't even wipe them away. The orderly did it for him with gentle hands. Gabe could feel the warmth of his breath on his cheeks and smell the faint scent of tobacco on his clothes. He swallowed back his acute shame at weeping and blinked hard, and the swirling slowed and steadied until he was aware of a round shape in front of him that moved and smiled and was flesh-coloured, and he realised he was seeing a face. A real living human face that wasn't the stuff of nightmares. His arms lifted painfully as if in slow motion, and his hands gripped the white-clad body that was gradually assuming human shape in front of him.

'I–see–you–' he croaked. His head slumped back on the pillows, exhausted, but before he slipped into another drug-filled sleep, his spirits soared in exultation, and he thanked God with an ingrained instinctive fervour, for he was going to live. He was going to live.

It was a long, painful road to recovery. His memory played constant tricks with him, so that just when he thought he grasped it in the palm of his hand, it slid tantalisingly away from him. It angered and frustrated him, and he was far from the easiest of patients. The orderly, his friend, whom he now knew as Willis, impressed on him the need to take things slowly, that he'd suffered massive physical injuries, complicated with the shell-shock that had contributed to his temporary blindness and his mental condition, but that he would recover, given time and patience. Gabe brushed him aside.

'Physical injuries,' he said bitterly, 'and what will I say when they ask what I did in the war? Do I confess that I was crushed near to death by two runaway horses? A fine

war record that will look! As for my mental condition . . . '
he spread his hands helplessly.

There was no persuading him when he sank into one of
his black moods, and Willis was wise enough to leave him
to stew in his own juice, as he called it. Gabe stared after
him broodingly as he marched away, telling him shortly
that he was after looking out for patients who were more
grateful for his services and didn't try to get his back up
every five minutes. And Gabe knew as well as Willis that
he'd be back to check that he was all right before very long.

They both knew that Gabe was more uncertain of
himself than he'd ever been in his life before. Gone was the
brash young man who'd incensed the fenmen years before,
and in its place a shell of a man who couldn't even
remember their existence. There was no purpose in him
any more and the future was a shadowy place in which he
had no part to play. In his worst moments he sometimes
thought it would have been better if he'd died honourably
on the battlefield than had to live this half-life. His physical
injuries would mend, but it was the mental ones that scarred
him.

If only he could remember everything . . . he was
obsessed with the need to know, convinced it would help
him readjust. But there were great blanks in his past, like
yawning chasms he couldn't cross. Willis had been able to
fill in the details of all that had happened since Gettysburg,
and he knew the Union army had won a great victory
there. He knew the war was now over for himself, and that
he had spent the last few months in a military hospital
outside Washington while the doctors tried to put his
crushed and battered body back together again.

He vaguely remembered hearing Deeker's voice telling
him not to pull out now, old buddy, and that he and Brad
would be back to see him one of these fine days and they'd
take up where they left off on their poker-playing circuit.
Even more hazy was the recollection of a gaunt-faced man
leaning towards him over the hospital bed and speaking to
him in a solemn voice. Telling him his President and his

country were proud of him, and of himself clutching at the hands that held his and babbling about his country being not here, not here, nor even the fens, but anywhere where there was Marnie.

'Poor fellow,' the President had slipped his hands from Gabe's clawing fingers. 'He has a long way to go yet.'

He'd leaned forward again and spoken compassionately into Gabe's unreceptive ears, trying to ignore the haunted, vacant blue eyes that had seen more than most men wanted to see in a lifetime.

'The battle's won for you, soldier. You've acquitted yourself well, and now it's time to go home. Go home to Marnie as soon as you're able.'

The blue eyes continued to stare at the ceiling as Lincoln turned away to the next patient on his tour of the hospital. God knew where Marnie was, he was thinking. Some place in Ireland, perhaps, but that was obviously where the poor devil should be.

The hospital was home to Gabe as far as he was concerned. The refusal of his mind to accept anything but the more recent past put an effective shutter over all that had gone on before the war. The memories of the comradeship he'd shared with Brad and Deeker and Cal were sharp and clear, and he knew that in his heyday he'd been as lusty an Irishman as the best of them, but it was just as if it had happened to someone else and not to Gabe O'Brien at all.

The hospital staff had seen plenty of cases like his, and knew it took more than the skill of healing to put a shattered mind together. And even the special rapport that existed between him and Willis, that had grown out of the weeks of darkness and dependence, were put sorely to the test when Gabe's aggressive frustration got the better of him.

'I'll come back when you're ready for talking, soldier,' Willis told him calmly one afternoon in mid-December. He knew from past experience that Gabe could be on the brink of remembering everything, and that as the tantalising shadows took shape in his mind, he was torn between the desire to know and the fear of possible re-established pain.

'Looking at that one, he's probably got a bevy of beauties lined up at every port,' one of his fellow orderlies joked, when Willis remarked on Gabe's sullenness. 'That should put the smile back on his face.'

'Yeah–maybe,' Willis said. 'Listen, buddy, I heard wind that that Indian scout he was so friendly with copped it a while back. Best not to let him know it, or it'll put him back another couple of weeks, and we need the beds!'

And a while back, another orderly in another hospital had gone through Brad's personal effects and found a crumpled envelope with an English address on it all ready for posting. If he hadn't been so pushed for time with all the new admissions from the battlefield, he'd have handed it over to his superior to go through the proper channels. As it was, it was one more job he didn't have time for, and he slipped it into the mailing-box and forgot about it.

Gabe sat brooding by the hospital window looking out at the soft rolling farmland that stretched as far as the eyes could see. Farming should mean something to him. He felt it as surely as he felt the strength returning to his wasted limbs now he was being pressed into taking exercise every goddamned morning. He hated it, but Willis said it was necessary, and Willis had the last word in the ward. It was worse than being hog-tied in marriage . . . his heart gave a sudden twist. Was he married? Was there someone waiting with agonised suspense for his return? He frowned, for once not pushing the questions away from him, closing his eyes, trying to imagine who'd be waiting for him.

For the first time in months he tried to imagine the softness of a woman's skin, warm against his, melting against his. He imagined his fingers running through the sheen of dyke-straight hair that was the colour of leaves in Autumn. He pictured luminous brown eyes and a mouth that was parted and ready for kissing. He knew the feel of her in his arms. He wanted her. He needed her with a desperation that was suddenly exquisitely painful. Marnie, Marnie, his beautiful Marnie . . .

'You ready for the visitors, Gabe?' Willis appeared beside him, and the images faded before he could properly grasp them.

'Visitors?' he dragged his whirling thoughts together and glared at Willis for making him do so.

'You remember me telling you, don't you? The Washington ladies make a tour of the hospitals just before Christmas, bringing their own home-made preserves and little gifts they've sewn or knitted. You may strike lucky and get a pen-holder!'

'Who would I be writing to?' he tried to grin back at Willis, but the grin changed to a puzzled frown. Who *would* he write to? Somebody must want to hear how he fared, somebody in the world out there beyond the hospital walls.

He allowed himself to be escorted back to the ward and into bed along with the other patients so that everything would be in decorous order when the Washington ladies arrived. He didn't care who came. It would make a change in the routine boredom of the days, and one was beginning to merge into the next as far as he was concerned. Willis could have told him that fact alone meant he was becoming restless of inactivity, and therefore on the road to recovery.

The ladies made their appearance, well-dressed matrons with rounded bosoms covered with high-buttoned capes and bonnets adorning well-sculptured curls. Some were accompanied by equally well-dressed children, after being assured that in this ward there was nothing to offend or upset. Gabe watched their stately progress round the ward and accepted his pot of quince preserve in its knitted cover. The small girl standing with the donor at his bedside smiled toothily at him.

'I knitted the cover,' she lisped. Her hand reached out and traced round the ribbon that was tied in a careful bow at the waist of the pot, exploring slowly its glossy pink surface.

'Come along, Emily dear,' the lady whisked her away and moved on down the ward with a gracious smile.

Gabe found that his eyes were suddenly fixed on the jar of preserve, so that he hardly saw the visitors leave or heard the general explosive sighs of relief and raucous comments among the rest of the patients. For all his concentration was riveted on the smooth shiny ribbon and the memory of the involuntary movement the small girl had made to stroke it.

And the memories that had been so long denied him rushed back at him so vividly they almost made him reel with the shock of remembering. Little Jenny Bray and her longing to be called Jennifer . . . and a splinter he'd removed from her heel that had made her his adoring slave, a rose-pink satin ribbon her sister had snatched from her hand and smoothed so lovingly, so sensuously, as if it was a man's skin . . . brown knowing eyes and a warmth of welcome that had taken a young boy's breath away, the old mill by Kettle's farm where he'd taken both of them, where he'd loved one so completely, and pretended with the other. The Bray brothers circling him in the Pinnock fields with murder on their minds, and Mick defending him as always, Jenny and the baby, sweet Jesus, the baby . . . and Marnie, his own, his precious Marnie. And it wasn't the corpse of a child he saw when he breathed her name, but his love, his woman . . .

'Well, Gabe?' Willis was suddenly beside his bed, an intent look on his face. 'Your eyes have lost their blankness for the first time since coming here. Is it all coming back to you at last?'

He nodded, unable and unwilling to speak. He just wanted to lie back and let the flood of memory fill his mind in case it should try to escape him again. And he couldn't bear to lose it now, not even when so much of it made painful remembering. But it was his life, the essence of him, and he needed to know himself all over again. It was like being reborn in a strange unreal way. And his world was suddenly peopled again with familiar faces and remembered voices, and a deep longing to be among them burned inside him like a flame.

'Willis?' he spoke huskily. 'How long before I can go home?'

The orderly's face broke into a broad smile.

'Well, that's the best thing I've heard you say yet, soldier! You hear that, boys? Old Gabe here wants to go home. Where is home, anyway? New York way, wasn't it?'

Gabe shook his head slowly. He hadn't really formed any clear idea of it himself before he'd put the question to Willis. But there was only one place in his mind. Only one place where he'd find the peace he sought, and if by any chance Father Flynn was still lording it over the community, he might even make the confession the old priest was always grieving over. He'd always kicked hard against it, but maybe it wouldn't be a bad thing to do after all. Whether it did any good, Gabe didn't know, and didn't really care, but that was the cynical Gabe talking, and there was still enough of the gentle Gabe somewhere inside that still had a voice, and told him to go, and go now, back to his roots.

'You'd never have heard of it anyway,' he told Willis. 'It's just a sleepy little village in the South of Ireland, but the grass grows greener and sweeter than anywhere else on God's earth, and it's home. There comes a time in every man's life when the only place to be is home, Willis, and that's what Drory is to me.'

CHAPTER TWENTY-FIVE

'Will you take us to the sea today, Auntie Marnie?'

'Oh yes, *please*!'

The children's voices clamoured to be heard, and Marnie told them to be patient while she helped their mother with the bedmaking, or they'd be going nowhere. And to go downstairs and wait quietly while she thought about it.

'They take more notice of you than they do of me!' Maureen laughed at her across the bedsheets, with no malice in her voice. ' 'Twas a good day for all of us when you decided to make your home here, Marnie, even though poor Mick had to leave this world to bring you here.'

But that was long ago now and they were able to talk about it without flinching, even though at the time Marnie had arrived, unannounced and distraught, it seemed as if the two of them would pull each other down with grief rather than help each other out of it. And it had done credit to Jack's prosaic nature to keep them both on an even keel at that difficult time. But it had gradually eased, and they were constantly warmed now by the knowledge that they had grown closer than sisters.

It had stood them in good stead some time later when the letter had arrived for Marnie. She had stared at it for a long time before opening it in the privacy of her room, her stomach tightening, her hands clammy, just as if some sixth sense warned her, even before she ripped open the King's Lynn bank envelope to find the enclosed letter inside bearing the strange American stamp that had been readdressed to the bank from Larksby . . . and then it had been just as if Gabe had been sitting beside her and holding her hand as she sat in the window seat in her room, and speaking the words he'd written to her more than two years before.

'I have no way of knowing when you'll read this, my darling,' she read, and her eyes were instantly damp at the unexpected endearment. 'But when you do read it, I shall be dead.'

She'd caught her breath then, and her fingers had pressed tight against her mouth to stop herself from crying out. Oh God, no, please, no . . . she blinked away the hot tears and read on.

'So as this is the last chance I shall ever have to tell you what's in my heart, it's only right that you should know everything about Jenny and me, and what I feel for you.'

He'd written in great detail about his life with Jenny, and even what had led up to their clandestine meetings in the old mill. How he'd felt so drawn to her because of Marnie, how he'd held her in his arms, knowing it was Marnie he wanted and despising himself for his weakness, sparing her nothing of his shame for not marrying Jenny after all, and for letting her go on believing she'd been Mrs O'Brien and married by a ship's captain. When he'd written his letter by the banks of the Potomac, Gabe had known it to be the most honest thing he'd done in his life, and the sincerity of it came through every word Marnie wept over.

And then she'd come to the final part of the letter, when he'd opened up his heart and called her his soul's darling, and told her that for him no wide expanse of time or continent had the power to destroy his love for her. That while he lived she would always be his woman, the one he loved for all time, as he had always done.

She had felt near to choking when she'd finished reading it, from the effort of trying not to weep. But the tears had to come, and now she didn't try to stop them, and all she could think of was the utter waste of so much love that had existed between them. And now she knew just how deeply Gabe's feelings went, and it was all too late, because he was dead, somewhere on an American battlefield, presumably, and she'd never have the chance to tell him how exactly, how perfectly, their feelings matched, as if they were two halves of the same heart.

It had been a deeply despairing time for Marnie after the letter arrived, and there was the knowledge too that she must tell Maureen and Jack that Gabe was dead. It had taken her days and all her courage before she'd been able to face it, but they had taken it more calmly than she'd expected, with none of the wailing grief Maureen had shown over Mick. She'd kissed Marnie sadly, clearly assuming she'd been the one to be informed because of her sister's connection with Gabe.

'My love, Gabe has been dead to us for so long now that while it saddens my heart, it's almost a relief to know the truth of what's happened to him. It's so much worse not knowing, and I shall light a candle and pray for him on Sunday.'

She'd gone out of the room abruptly, and for all her composure, Marnie guessed she'd shed her tears in private. For Gabe had always been her darling, her baby brother, and of course, it hadn't been the whole truth she'd told them that night. She'd told it with dignity, as a dear sister-in-law might be expected to do, without ever offering to show Maureen the letter.

It was for no-one's eyes but her own. It was intensely private, and she'd read it so many times she knew it by heart, and in one thing she would always differ with Maureen. For Gabe would never be truly dead in her heart, and she made a vow to herself that she would marry no-one else. Fate had intervened for both of them. No matter what his motives, Gabe had been unable to wed her sister, and her brothers had set the torch to her plan of marrying Mick. It was a wicked thing they did, but it had saved her from doing something just as wicked in the eyes of God—marrying a man for whom she had only a luke-warm love, while the whole of her heart was given to someone else.

It was the only thought that gave her peace while the weeping inside her continued.

Living in the Haggerty house had been her salvation.

Even though the two handsome uncles who'd gone over the sea to England had become romantic, almost legendary figures to the four children by now, and they never tired of asking questions about them, and were especially enthralled to know their Uncle Gabe had become a soldier in a land even farther away than England. Maureen had looked at her oddly one night when she'd heard Marnie telling them the tale yet again, and once the children were in bed she'd spoken softly in the firelight.

'Marnie, forgive me for prying, and tell me to mind my own business if you must, but there was something in your voice just now when you spoke of Gabe, and a very private, very special look on your face.' She stopped in embarrassment, and the next moment Marnie was beside her on the curled rug by the hearth, her head pressed against Maureen's knees. There was a time to be silent and a time to speak.

'I loved him so much,' her voice was breathy and tight. '*So* much, Maureen. And we could have had all the joys that you and Jack have known all these years, if we hadn't thrown it all away like the foolish children we were.'

Maureen's hand went automatically to the soft-coiled hair that shone like burnished silk in the firelight, smoothing it as she would one of her daughter's.

'I always felt there was something missing between you and Mick,' she said gently. 'Oh, I'm sure you'd have been happy together, but now I've heard the way you speak about Gabe, I'm glad you didn't marry the wrong man, for there must be nothing worse.'

'Then you don't hate me for it?' Marnie said in a muffled voice.

'I love you as a sister, you know that. And I thank you for trusting me enough to tell me about you and Gabe.'

Marnie drew back and clasped her hands round her knees, gazing with bleak eyes into the leaping flames in the fireplace.

'It doesn't help, for nothing will bring him back, and the greatest sorrow of my life is that he never knew how much

I loved him. But perhaps you'll understand now if I sometimes go a little quiet, if I'm moody and a bit temperamental . . .'

'You're never that, my love!'

But she was, and she knew it, even though the children did much to allay it. And there was no being sad when they climbed all over her as exuberantly as they did on that fine Spring morning when she went downstairs after the bedmaking with Maureen, demanding to know when they were going to see the sea.

'All right,' Marnie laughed. 'If it's agreeable with your mother, we'll take a picnic lunch.'

'That would be such a help,' Maureen said gratefully. 'I've promised to do some sick-visiting in the village this morning, lunch was going to be a scrappy affair, and as you know, Jack and I have to prepare ourselves for this evening, so it'll be an early dinner, Marnie. Help yourselves to all you need from the pantry for the picnic, and enjoy yourselves.'

The children were only too happy to carry the food and drinks, and raced down the hill ahead of Marnie from the Haggerty house as soon as they were all ready. Through the winding streets of Drory and down to the coast, where a mellow breeze blew in from the sea. They turned away from the harbour, along the stretch of new road that ended in a mossy track and down the rough-hewn steps leading to the small bay. It was uninhabited save for a few locals like themselves, and the gulls that wheeled and screamed overhead.

'Can we paddle, Auntie Marnie?' Patrick shouted in her ear.

'I'm not deaf!' She laughed into his eager, dimpled face. 'As long as you stay close to the shore then, and mind and look after Ben!'

Kathleen and Nora were content to take off their shoes and stockings and wiggle their toes in the early sunshine, and search for crabs and molluscs among the rock pools that circled the bay.

'Did the uncles go on a boat like that one?' Kathleen squinted her eyes against the brightness of the day as a ship inched carefully towards the harbour, her deck a mass of activity as the sailors prepared to bring her in.

'Oh, the boat for England is smaller than that one . . .'

'Would that one have come from America then, where Uncle Gabe went?' Nora said eagerly.

'I shouldn't think so. They don't put in at little harbours like Drory, love.'

And if they did, they'd not bring Gabe O'Brien back home . . . but the girls were persistent as ever.

'What did he look like in his uniform, Auntie Marnie? Was he very handsome?'

'Oh, I'm sure he was. The most handsome soldier in the whole American army!' Marnie smiled brightly. 'Now then, are you going to help me with this picnic? The boys will be shouting for food any minute now.'

She was suddenly reminded of another picnic lunch as Patrick and Ben came running out of the water squealing with laughter. A picnic that had ended in tears and tragedy when her little brother Davey had emerged limp and lifeless in Gabe O'Brien's arms. She pushed the thought away from her, wondering what on earth had made her think of it today. Unless it was the similar situation, and the memory of Gabe that these children kept alive so innocently. She smiled wryly as she handed round hunks of bread and Maureen's orange peel marmalade, knowing she kept his image alive all by herself without any help from anyone.

It was mid-afternoon when they climbed back up the rough steps and paused to take a breather before making their way back to Drory. The sun was warm and the children were tired, and there'd be no trouble getting them to bed that night, which was just as well, since Maureen and Jack would be out to the small hours at a smart concert in a distant town with some of their important friends, and she'd be left in charge.

As soon as they got back to the house she sent them to their rooms to wash their sticky faces and hands and to

404

change their clothes, reminding them that dinner would be ready early. She stood smilingly, listening to their tired grumbles from the foot of the stairs, when Maureen came out of the sitting-room and called her name. She was very flushed, her eyes over-bright as if she'd been crying, yet her mouth had an upward tilt to it.

'Will you come in here, Marnie? There's someone ... we have a–well, hardly a visitor ... oh, come quickly, Marnie, please!'

There was something in her voice, in her eyes, in her clenched hands, that had Marnie's heart frantically pounding. It couldn't be, and she knew it couldn't be, but she hardly remembered crossing the distance between the stairs and the sitting-room, or knew she'd entered it. She moved as if she was gliding in a dream, afraid to blink her eyes in case she awoke before the searing hope within her became reality or was dashed for ever. She was hardly able to breathe as the man standing by the fireplace with his back to her slowly turned, as if he too was afraid.

The image of him that was stamped indelibly in her mind was of a young Gabe, with black curly hair and blue blue eyes, and a dimpled smile that could send her nerve-ends tingling in seconds ... this new Gabe had a slightly stooping posture and a dusting of silver in the black of his hair. There were deep-etched lines and shadows moulding his face, but the sudden glow in his eyes as he saw her, and the smile on his lips that dented his cheeks was the same, was the same, was the same ... he said not a word, but merely held out his arms, and she was running, stumbling, the gladness inside her sharp as a physical pain as she met his embrace with her own. And it was such a little distance after all to be back in his arms, after the miles of ocean and continent and the years of longing that had separated them.

'I thought you were dead,' she sobbed against his chest.

'I know. I know. Maureen told me ... '

The craziest thoughts were swimming round in her head. So much to be said between them, and so impossible to know where to begin ... as if it could all be said in a moment ...

'Has she told you about Mick?'

'She told me ...'

And about how she'd been all set to marry him? Marnie's heart jolted, and she was finding it hard to breathe steadily. What would have been his reaction to that? But hadn't he gone off with her own sister, tit for tat? And what did it *matter*—what did anything matter but the sheer joy of holding him and loving him when she'd thought he was lost to her for ever? There was a thickening in her throat as she looked into his blue eyes that were somehow remote and unfathomable, even though he was so close to her. So close, yet somehow he was a stranger to her with that haunted look in his eyes, as if he'd seen things of which she could have no comprehension, and the memory wouldn't leave him yet ...

'Was it very bad, your war, Gabe?' she said softly.

He nodded slowly. 'You could say that.'

'But you came through it ...'

'Some of my best bors didn't,' unconsciously he used the old fen term. Brad and Cal and a legion of others; he'd heard about Brad and wept over him. Brad, the survivor, but *he'd* been the one to survive after all. And Deek, as far as he knew. Marnie felt the brief closeness between them slipping away from them as his mind grappled with his war years.

'I–got your letter, Gabe.'

He made an embarrassed noise in his throat.

'I can't remember much about that night. I was shot to pieces–not literally, but mentally. My buddy had been bayonetted and I–' his eyes focussed on her properly. He'd been about to tell her he'd just raped a fourteen-year-old child in the sweet green meadows, but the sudden recollection of Marnie at twelve-years-old in the old mill had spun into his mind, and he didn't want to reveal the self-disgust that tortured him after the flight from Bull Run. 'I wasn't fully in control of myself that night. I just wanted to make retribution as far as I could, and try to make you believe how desolate I was for the way I'd spoiled your life. I never expected to be standing here explaining it!'

His words were clumsy, his voice embarrassed, and it was as if he'd thrown cold water into her face. Hadn't he meant it then, about loving her, needing her, the way she needed him? He'd sounded almost angry . . . but if she could have looked into his mind she'd have seen the anxiety that was gnawing away at him, because he wanted her so badly and it was so long since he'd held her—or any woman. So long since he'd made the kind of sweet talk that had once come so glibly to his lips, and he felt every bit of confidence in his masculinity draining away from him.

It was a sickening, humiliating feeling, and one that Gabe couldn't tolerate. Better for her to think he was still unfit than to realise he was so unsure of his ability to be a man again. And anyway, wasn't he presuming one hell of a lot, he argued with himself? They'd just met after God knew how many years, and he couldn't expect her to be eager and willing for his embraces, especially after the way he'd behaved in the past . . . but there'd been a moment, and she'd felt so soft and pliant in his arms, the way he remembered, and it had made him momentarily dizzy, as if he was drunk with too much wine.

The children were suddenly at the door of the sitting-room, chattering like magpies in their excitement.

'I couldn't keep them away any longer,' Maureen said over their heads. 'They're so anxious to see you, Gabe. They don't quite believe you're real!'

Patrick pushed forward. 'Are you staying for always now, Uncle Gabe?'

Seeing them together was like seeing an echo of the young Gabe who'd started on the great adventure with Mick that had taken them to the English fens. Even he must see the ghost of himself in Patrick. He laughed shortly.

'Always is a long time, Pat, but I can't think of anywhere else I'd rather be.'

'And will you tell us about the war?'

'I don't want to hear about shooting,' Kathleen pulled a face.

'Well, I do,' piped up Ben. 'Girls are silly . . .'

The talk flowed on between them, and Gabe was clearly a hero in their eyes. He told them superficial things about the war while they listened enraptured, betraying none of the horrors to their young ears. His eyes constantly lingered on Marnie's face as he spoke, as if he couldn't get his fill of seeing her, and a small feeling of warmth began to seep back inside her. When Jack Haggerty joined his family in the late afternoon he hushed the clamouring children.

'You'll have plenty of time to talk to your uncle,' he admonished them. 'And he'll be tired of your noise already after just arriving home.' He turned to Gabe apologetically. 'I'm only sorry Maureen and myself have to go out this evening, Gabe, but it's something that's been long planned, and would be difficult to get out of at short notice.'

'I'm quite sure Gabe and Marnie will have plenty to talk about without needing the two of us around!' Maureen said smartly. 'And if I don't get the dinner started we'll never get the children to bed and be on our way.'

'I'll help you,' Marnie followed her to the kitchen. Her face was as flushed as Maureen's as she stood inside the door unmoving. Not knowing whether to laugh or cry as Maureen handed her a cooking pot and some potatoes to peel. She didn't move for a few minutes.

'Oh Maureen, he's so changed,' she said in a rush.

'What did you expect? A man can't go through a war and come out of it unchanged,' she was matter-of-fact.

But it was more than the war, of course. More than the physical effects of injury, it was life that had changed him, as it changed everyone. It had changed her too.

It was a relief when dinner was over and the children finally put to bed, protesting all the way, but nearly dropping with sleep after their day by the sea and all the excitement since. Was that only today when they picnicked by the sea? To Marnie it had already slipped into the realms of fantasy, and the only reality was that Maureen and Jack were leaving the house for the evening, and she and Gabe were alone together in the sitting-room at Drory, with the dancing firelight throwing flickering shadows about the unlighted room. It was intimately warm and cosy with the curtains drawn against the cool evening air, yet suddenly there was nothing to say between them, despite all the words that needed to be said, and the silence stretched as vast as the ocean that had separated them.

Marnie shifted from her position on the sofa, sliding down to her favourite spot on the curled rug by the fire, not looking at Gabe's slumped figure in the arm-chair. Not needing to, because every bit of him was imprinted in her mind. She'd never thought to see him in her life again, and yet here he was, a hand's reach away from her and as remote as the stars, and the shock of it stunned her.

If she'd been able to read inside his head, she'd have known that Gabe was suddenly stricken with the most appalling attack of impotence. Not merely the physical impotence of his loins, but an impotence of the mind. He'd wanted her and loved her and ached for her through all the years of his life, through lust and pain and war. And now to have come limping home to recover himself, to suddenly find her in his sister's house, to hear from Maureen that Mick had perished so shortly before Marnie had been going to be his wife . . . his confidence was shattered as completely as his joy had surged at seeing the welcome for him blazing in her eyes, he was horribly afraid of himself, of her, of life . . .

She leaned forward to put another log on the fire, and the lines of her body were etched against the flames, taut and full and rounded. She'd pulled the pins out of the coiled hair at the nape of her neck, and it fell in a golden gleam over her shoulders, kinking into glowing waves where it had once been dyke-straight. He watched the firelight through its parted golden strands, and his breath sharpened involuntarily.

Marnie turned to look at him, seeing the unsureness laced with the longing in his blue eyes. Seeing the fine lines

409

of tension around the mouth she loved, the tightening of his jaw-line, seeing suddenly all there was to see, and knowing with a deep certainty that she had to be the one. She knelt at his feet and put her head in his lap, feeling his hands go at once to the sheen of her hair. She spoke softly and slowly, as if to a child.

'We have a choice, you and I, Gabe. To talk about the past or to leave it behind us for ever. It's very tempting to leave it and pretend we can forget it, but I don't think we're the kind of people who can do that, are we?'

'No,' he said in a low voice. He cupped her chin in his hands so that she was looking up into his face. 'So tell me, Marnie, how much did you love Mick?'

'Not enough to marry him,' she had to be honest, as she'd always been honest with him. 'I needed someone, and he wanted me, but it would have been wrong. I knew it then, even though I tried to ignore it, and oh, I know it now . . .'

'But you'd have gone through with it?'

'Are you blaming me for that? When you . . .' she bit her lip, but he finished it for her.

'When I'd already been with Jenny and acted about as badly as I could have done as far as the two of you were concerned. Do you think I haven't blamed myself a thousand times for that, knowing it was wicked, when she wasn't the one I wanted?' his voice was tight with anger. 'I thought I was doing the right thing by her, and I suppose she thought it too, but look how she ended up, the poor little devil!'

'And look how Mick ended up!' Marnie swallowed dryly. 'Gabe, I have to tell you this. I'm certain in my own mind it was my brothers who set the farm alight that night, because I'd told them I was going to marry Mick and they hated him–and you. I haven't told another living soul. There seemed no point, when I had no proof, but there are some things you know instinctively.'

She stopped speaking, seeing how his face had whitened, and his hands had clenched on her shoulders without realising it.

410

'Those bastards! If I could get my hands round their throats, I'd throttle them one by one and enjoy doing it!' He glanced at her. 'I'm sorry if I shock you . . .'

'You can't think any worse of them than I do already. I've wondered times beyond counting whether I did the right thing in not speaking up, but I decided finally that it was time the feud between the Brays and the O'Briens was ended, so I said nothing.'

She could have told him then that it had been his friend, Fred Jackson, who had inadvertently started it all, but this didn't seem the time and place, and that could wait. She realised his hands were stroking her hair again in an agitated way. He frightened her a little. It was as if he wasn't really here with her at all, but away in a world of his own imagining. She still hadn't reached him, and she wanted him so badly . . .

'So now there's only you and me, Gabe,' her voice was husky, caught on a surge of emotion. 'The way it was, right back in the beginning when you came to our cottage on the fens and I looked at you and thought you were so beautiful.'

'Did you?' he gave a harsh laugh. 'And now you see the wreck of a man come home to lick his wounds.'

She shook her head, her eyes glowing tawny in the firelight.

'That's not what I see, Gabe.' She reached up and traced her fingers round his face, his beloved face. 'I see my soul's darling, for whom no expanse of time or continent can have the power to destroy my love. And while I live, you'll be the one I'll love for all time. I've always known it, and it's the way I've always loved you, totally and for ever . . .'

She quoted and misquoted his own letter, but before she had finished saying the words he had pulled her roughly into his arms, and he was kissing her eyes and her mouth and the smooth white hollow of her throat, and murmuring all the endearments she had ever wanted to hear from his

411

lips. And she exalted in the undeniable fact of his rising passion that had lain so dormant in him until now, so that she had been afraid of just what the war had really done to him, not for herself, but for Gabe himself . . . but all misgivings were forgotten as he slid to the curled rug beside her and held her close in his arms and told her everything she needed to know.

His hands moulded her breasts and slid over the curves and hollows of her body, and she felt the sweet tingling surge of desire deep within her. He removed her clothes one by one, until she lay naked in the glow of firelight, unflinching under his gaze, wanting him to look at her, to touch, to hold, with a wantonness that took her by surprise. His fingers caressed her contours as if he was a blind man needing to imprint their image on his mind for ever, and then the urgency of his own desire sent him shedding his own clothes until he was as naked as she.

Marnie saw none of the battlescars that scissored his body, nor how thin and gaunt he was compared with the Gabe she'd known. She saw only his love for her shining out of his eyes and in every taut part of his body as he lay against her, gently at first until the first tremulous moment of union brought a breathless gasping from her throat in the joy of knowing such completeness again. All their pent-up emotions were finally released as the loving between them was enacted with infinite tenderness and sweetness, and then gathered momentum as her arms pulled him closer and his own pressed her tightly to him. It was the first time, the best time, the only time . . .

The feel of his lips on her mouth, murmuring her name over and over, was the sweetest sound she had ever heard, and nor had she thought to hear it ever again, save in her dreams. But this was no dream, and when he finally went rigid against her so that she moaned with the exquisiteness of the moment, and then relaxed in her arms, she still held him very tenderly, and his mouth was still soft against hers even when all passion was spent, as if he was reluctant to move away from her. They lay as one person, bathed in the

412

fireglow and the aftermath of loving.

'If you won't marry me, I might as well have perished on the battlefield,' he murmured raggedly against her lips. 'For it was only the thought of you that kept me sane . . .'

She answered tremblingly. 'If you hadn't asked me, I'd have died all over again, for I hadn't known how alive I could feel until now.'

His hands were caressing her anew, as if he couldn't have enough of her, nor she of him, and she knew the hungry passion between them was soon to be revived again. He was a starving man, and she exalted in the knowledge, knowing too that Gabe now knew himself for a man again, in every sense of the word.

'I should be proposing to you in the moonlight, my sweet darling, with flowers and gifts, and all the things your romantic heart deserves,' he told her unsteadily, and a deep throaty laugh that was near to being a sob caught on Marnie's voice as she told him breathlessly that none of that mattered.

Perhaps one day she'd tell him what someone had once called her, all those years ago when such things had seemed important. Moon child. And that all important things in her life were supposed to happen at the time of the full moon. But tonight fate had proved stronger than an old woman's prophecies, and the moon was new and young, and as tender as their love.

One day she'd tell him that nothing had ever been so important as now, as this day when he'd come back to her so miraculously. And as Gabe's arms drew her towards him with a new and demanding urgency, Marnie knew at last that she had no need of such artifices as Mrs Kettle's mysterious folklore. She only had need of him, and these precious moments they shared that told her he was truly hers, irrevocably, and for all time.